THE GIRLS ARE ALL SO NICE HERE

LAURIE ELIZABETH FLYNN

Published by Simon & Schuster

New York   London   Toronto   Sydney   New Delhi

Simon & Schuster Canada
A Division of Simon & Schuster, Inc.
166 King Street East, Suite 300
Toronto, Ontario M5A 1J3

This Simon & Schuster Canada edition March 2021

SIMON & SCHUSTER CANADA and colophon are trademarks of Simon & Schuster, Inc.

For information about special discounts for bulk purchases, please contact Simon & Schuster Special Sales at 1-800-268-3216 or CustomerService@simonandschuster.ca.

Interior design by Erika R. Genova

Manufactured in the United States of America

10 9 8 7 6 5 4 3 2 1

Library and Archives Canada Cataloguing in Publication

Title: The girls are all so nice here / Laurie Elizabeth Flynn.
Names: Flynn, Laurie Elizabeth, author.
Description: Simon & Schuster Canada edition.
Identifiers: Canadiana (print) 20200248154 | Canadiana (ebook) 20200248197
    | ISBN 9781982145026 (softcover) | ISBN 9781982145033 (ebook)
Classification: LCC PS8611.L945 G57 2021 | DDC C813/.6—dc23

ISBN 978-1-9821-4502-6
ISBN 978-1-9821-4503-3 (ebook)

For every girl who got what she wanted
at a cost she couldn't afford

THE
GIRLS
ARE
ALL
SO
NICE
HERE

THEN

Together we ruled. Our realm unfurled, grassy campus and its tangle of parties. We marked the territory as our own, matchstick legs capped in sharp heels striking the ground, mouths witchy with lipstick and upturned with laughter. There were boys whose names I forgot, boys I might have passed by and not known were ever inside me. When I did pick out a king, the crown was too heavy for his head.

Then a fist closed around our world and knuckled out the light. We stood in front of the dorm with everyone else, taking in the same scene, a carnage that had started within us. Our ability to create waned in our instinct to ruin.

Her voice in my ear, never scared enough. *We have to stick to the same story.*

I wanted to run, but she wasn't done moving her pawns.

Our reign was short and bloody.

What came after it was worse.

NOW

To: "Ambrosia Wellington" *a.wellington@wesleyan.edu*
From: "Wesleyan Alumni Committee" *reunion.classof2007@gmail.com*
Subject: Class of 2007 Reunion

Dear Ambrosia Wellington,

Mark Your Calendar!

The Wesleyan University Ten-Year Reunion for the Class of 2007 will take place May 25–28, 2017. Join us for a weekend of catching up with former classmates and attending exciting events, including the All-Campus Party and formal class dinners.

Online registration is available through May 1.

If you're planning to attend, a full list of area hotels can be found on Wesleyan's local <u>accommodations page</u>. A limited amount of on-campus housing in our dorms is available. Most rooms are doubles—perfect for reaching out to your old roommate to relive some memories!

Sincerely,
Your Alumni Committee

I delete it instantly, just like I do the sale emails from Sephora and Michael Kors and the reminders from Fertility Friend that ovulation is right around the corner. Then I empty my recycling bin, because I know better than to think anything is ever really gone.

Two weeks later, a second email arrives. *We haven't received your RSVP! We really hope you're joining us.* It's the written equivalent of a wagging finger. I delete that one, too, but not before scrolling down far enough to see her name, bolded, right under the list of Alumni Committee members. Flora Banning.

I forget about the two emails, because out of sight really is out of mind. It's easy when each day is a variation of the same—taking the N from Astoria to Midtown; stopping at Key Food for groceries, reusable cloth bags cutting into my forearms. Happy hour shouldered in with hipsters at the Ditty, a second glass of wine, despite Adrian's half-teasing *Maybe you shouldn't.* But then I come home from work on Friday, shoulders sagging from the weight of the week, and there's an envelope on the counter addressed to me.

"Hey, babe," Adrian shouts from his position on the couch, tablet in hand, where he's undoubtedly working on his fantasy football league instead of the perpetually unfinished novel he likes to talk about. "How was your day?"

"You left the door open again. Can you please start locking it like I asked?" One of the myriad things I nag Adrian about on a regular basis. *Lock the door. Close the cereal bag. Pick up your dirty laundry.* Sometimes I feel more like a parent than his wife.

"Relax. It's a safe building. Hey, something came for you. I think we got invited to a wedding. Except somebody doesn't know you got married and changed your name." My new last name, a point of male pride that Adrian pretended wasn't important to him. *I don't care, but do you really want the kids to have two last names? And yours is so long,* he said during wedding planning, the first puncture in my newly engaged bliss. *The kids,* a brightening certainty on his horizon, my concessions for them expected and inevitable.

The envelope on the counter is addressed to Ambrosia Wellington, in neat calligraphy. Not Ambrosia Turner, the woman I became three years ago when I walked down a tree-shaded aisle at the Mountain Lakes House toward Adrian, his eyes already tear filled. I let him think

Turner was for us, for *the kids*. He has no idea why I was so eager to get rid of *Wellington*.

Adrian turns around to watch me open it, expectant. He loves weddings, or rather, he loves the receptions, where he can get drunk and pose for pictures with people he's just met, instant best friends, and invite them to dinners and barbecues we all know will never happen.

"Well, who is it?" he says. "Let me guess. Bethany from work. Is she still dating that really tall guy? Mark. The lacrosse player."

Adrian and his friends, five and six years younger than me, still post engagement photos on Facebook and Instagram: girls with long hair and Chanel espadrilles, gel manicures to show off pear-shaped rocks, posing next to boys in plaid shirts. The PR girls who work under me at Brighton Dame are the same.

So basic, we used to call them, back when there was no way we would turn into them.

"Bethany's twenty-two," I murmur when I pull the card out. I ignore Adrian's response, because I'm fixated on what's inside. It's not a wedding invitation. Nobody is requesting my presence at Gramercy Park or telling me the dress code is black tie or mandating an *adults-only reception*.

It's more calligraphy, red and black against cream card stock. Wesleyan colors. The letters tilt slightly to the right, as if whoever wrote them was in a rush to get them out.

You need to come. We need to talk about what we did that night.

There's no signature, but there doesn't need to be. It can only be from one person. My face is hot and I can tell my neck is marbling red and white, the same way it always does when my anxiety flares up. I grip the countertop. She knows I deleted the emails. I shouldn't be surprised; she had a way of knowing everything.

Adrian's voice interrupts my spiraling thoughts. "The suspense is killing me. It better be an open bar."

"It's not a wedding." I stuff the card back into its envelope, then shove it in my purse. Later, I'll put it in the place I hide everything Adrian can never see.

He puts down his tablet and stands up. Of course he chooses now to grow an attention span. "You okay? You look like you're going to puke."

I could shred the card, but I know what would happen. Another one will come in its place. She was insistent then. She's probably even more so now.

"It's nothing. Why don't we go up to the roof and have a drink?" The rooftop patio with its slices of Manhattan skyline, a feature of our building we thought we would use but rarely ever do.

He nods, curiosity temporarily assuaged, and arches across the counter to kiss my cheek.

I smile at my husband in relief, taking in his mop of curly hair, his dimples, and his pretty green eyes. *So freaking sexy*, my best friend, Billie, said when I showed her his photo. He looked exactly like his online dating profile, which is probably why I went home with him after our first date, the two of us reduced to sloppy mouths and hands in the back of a cab barreling down Broadway. I later learned that while his picture didn't lie—not like a dozen other men before him, all of whom were at least twenty pounds heavier than advertised—his life story did. Yes, he went to Florida State, but he never graduated, instead dropping out in his third year to work on the same novel he has yet to complete a chapter of. Nowhere in his bio did it say he was a bartender, the only consistent job he has ever had.

But I overlooked that because he treats me well, because people are drawn to him, because *I* was drawn to him, to his steady warmth and self-assuredness. He didn't know the person I was in college but loved the new embodiment of me so simply that I figured I couldn't be as horrible as everyone thought. I never imagined I would end up with someone five years younger, but being older has had its benefits. Our age gap is small enough that we look good together but big enough that his instincts are softer, more malleable. When I pushed the idea of a proposal because I was creeping into my late twenties, he took the hint and picked out a ring. Not the one I wanted, but it was close enough.

Adrian tries to make conversation as we head up to the roof, but the voice in my head is louder. Hers. *We need to talk about what we did that night.*

There were two different nights, and I'm not sure which one she means. The one that started everything or the one that ended it. She never wanted to talk about either. Then again, she was the best at breaking her own rules.

2

THEN

would be spending freshman year in the Butterfields, living in a double room on the first floor. Butterfield C was shaped almost like a question mark, hugging a courtyard where I pictured myself sitting with a book, wind lifting my hair. I had emailed with my future roommate a few times, but we'd never actually met. Her parents were helping her break a mini-fridge out of its cardboard jail when I first saw her, along with a younger girl who must have been her sister. I had just seen my own parents off—my mom would probably weep all the way back to Pennington, my dad placating her with promises that I'd be back. My older sister, Toni, had left for college at Rutgers two years before, but she was close enough that she still came home most weekends, bulging laundry bag in tow.

"This is your time, sweetie," Mom had said before she closed the car door, her lips on my cheek. "Enjoy it. But stay out of trouble." As if trouble were labeled with a Do Not Disturb sign. As if a sign would have kept me out.

I wished my best friend, Billie, were with me, but Billie hadn't gotten into Wesleyan. She was spending the next four years at Miami University in Ohio, which was known more for partying than anything else. Our friendship was comfortable—a bond forged in our awkwardness when we started ninth grade and our shared willingness to do something about it. Billie knew who I was and who I wanted to be, and she loved both versions. I had already texted her since arriving on campus. *I hope people like me.* Her buoyant *they will!!!* brought some comfort.

My new roommate's hair was white blond and her dress was gingham, like something I had been forced to wear as a kid to the Memorial Day parade. She didn't look like the girls I had gone to high school with, all of us in the same uniform of miniskirts and Uggs buttressing legs slathered in self-tanner. But she was exceptionally pretty—freshly scrubbed, wholesome. Billie probably would have given her a nickname. It was our meager defense against the mean girls at Hopewell Valley Central High. We studied them, then peeled them like overripe fruit in marathon gossip sessions to lessen the sting of not being invited to their parties. *My roomie is Heidi*, I'd text Billie.

Her real name was just as bad.

"I guess you already know from our emails, but I'm Flora." She gripped me in a hug. "It's nice to finally meet in person. You look just how I pictured. These are my parents, and this is my sister, Poppy." Poppy gave me a shy wave, all bangs and big blue eyes.

"Ambrosia," I said, more to them than her. "Just call me Amb." Flora didn't look how I'd pictured—she was a lot prettier. I knew from our emails that she was involved with student council at her Connecticut private school. She didn't smoke or drink and wanted to become a child psychologist. She wore her niceness so openly. She was exactly the kind of friend my parents wanted me to make. What Billie would call a *try-hard*.

"Amb," Flora's mom said, fixing me with a frosty stare. "Where are you from?"

"Pennington," I said. "New Jersey."

"That's nice," she said, but I could tell by her pinched mouth that it wasn't, that I had already committed some kind of wrong. "You take care of Flora. She tends to trust everyone too easily."

"Mom," Flora said, her cheeks turning petal pink. "Stop."

Flora's mom looked like she wanted to say more but pressed her mouth into a line. I rolled her words around. I didn't know if I had been folded into her confidence or warned not to be a person her daughter couldn't trust.

"We're going to have such a fun year," Flora said when her family was gone—she had squeezed her sister the hardest, whispered something in her ear I couldn't hear. "My mom is actually still best friends with her roommate from freshman year."

I felt a blip of excitement. It *was* going to be a fun year. I had worked hard to get here, to make things happen. To chisel out a Technicolor future, panoramic in scope, with me as its star.

"Your accent is so cute," Flora said as she tacked photos to her corkboard.

"Thanks," I managed, but I wasn't thankful. She didn't mean it as an insult—*probably*—but she had made me self-conscious about something I hadn't considered noticeable before. What I said was as important as how I said it. I couldn't be an actress—and I'd come to Wesleyan for the theater program—if I couldn't escape Jersey.

As we unpacked, our door stayed open, and people from our floor lingered there, making introductions. I smiled, returned hugs, nodded forcefully to future invitations to parties. But inside, I trembled. Some of the girls seemed to be friends already, with easy laughter and inside jokes from Upper East Side private schools. Two model-thin blondes were from Los Angeles, thumbing their phones, laughing about some prom after-party at a club where a classmate screwed two guys in the bathroom.

These weren't the girls I had gone to Central with, ones with Starbucks cups attached to their hands, who punctuated their vocabularies with *like* and *whatever* and one-upped each other with discussions about who'd made out with who at some shitty party in someone's basement, boys sitting around in sweatpants holding video game controllers. I had copied their hip-hugging jeans, parted my hair like them, saved a year of paychecks from my part-time job at the Stop & Shop to buy a small Louis Vuitton bag—the same multicolor monogrammed one that lived on the bony shoulders of celebrity it-girls.

At Wesleyan, I was ready to slip effortlessly into the person I imagined I could be. But I realized that first day that *effortless* might not be in the cards. The girls here seemed casually beautiful in a way that felt unachievable, dewy and shiny without being overtly flashy.

There weren't just girls. Our floor was coed, something I had been happy about. The boys were a blur of darting eyes and white smiles. They probably weren't going to pick me, not when there was a better selection to choose from, a veritable buffet, girls served up all-you-can-eat, with long limbs and understated clothes. And boys were always hungry. I briefly pictured my high school boyfriend Matt, before willing the image away. I didn't want to taint my first day with the memory of what he'd done.

"You should come with us to get lunch," Flora said. "I'm heading over with some of the other girls. I hope there's something I can eat—did I tell you I'm vegan? I saw this documentary when I was twelve about how animals in slaughterhouses are treated, and I cut out all meat and dairy right away. It's really not that hard, if you're willing to learn."

She didn't sound self-righteous, just matter-of-fact. I already knew she was a vegan from our emails. But I didn't care about Flora's diet. I was fixated on her knowledge that lunch was happening, the reality that a plan had been made without me. I had been here less than a day and was already failing.

We all ended up in Summerfields, the dining hall that topped Butterfield C like a blocky hat, a big group of us pushing tables together. Pathetically, I wanted to call my mom and tell her I'd made a mistake. I texted Billie instead. *Help. The people here are so different.*

She wrote back immediately, like she always did. *Isn't that the point?*

A girl sat down beside me with a greasy grilled cheese sandwich, bringing with her a whiff of too-sweet perfume. Her hair looked like a Posh Spice imitation gone wrong. "I'm Ella Walden," she said. "I'm just down the hall from you guys. How cool is this place?"

Somehow the shape of Ella next to me brought instant relief. She was pasty and chubby and unfashionable, the proof I needed that not everybody at Wesleyan was innately cool. I watched her eat the sandwich, both jealous of it and judgmental that she would eat something so calorie laden in public when she obviously had a few pounds to lose. I hated eating in front of anyone.

A loud *fuck* made my attention jerk up—it came from a girl at the head of our table, with wide eyes inside a tunnel of black eyeliner, a blond ponytail, and an oversized button-down that showed her lace bra. Her eyebrows, thick and dark, moved up and down animatedly as she talked, a stark contrast to the maniacally tweezed arches that marked the girls from my senior class. I tuned out Ella and studied those eyebrows, how they guarded her whole face, a face that instantly held everybody's attention.

"Then Buddy was like, 'Please don't leave, I'll do anything for you,'" she said, her voice throaty and deep. "And I said, 'That's the problem,' and left." Everybody laughed. I wondered if they all knew who Buddy was.

"You're pretty," she said to the stylish Asian girl next to her—Clara, I vaguely recalled, my memory already riddled with too many names. "You should definitely be single here." Her fingers trailed down Clara's arm. I wanted it to be my turn, for her to land on me.

And then, like she could read my mind, it was. "Who are you? Where are you from?" she said, spotlighting me with an intense green gaze.

"I'm Ambrosia. From Pennington. In New Jersey."

She opened her mouth to say something, but Ella spoke first. "Pennington! No way. I'm from Morristown. We're practically neighbors. We should look at yearbooks later. I bet we have friends in common."

I bit my lip hard, wishing I hadn't said *Pennington* and wishing Ella didn't exist. The girl at the head of the table wasn't even looking at me anymore. She had moved on to a boy beside her, sweeping an arm over his shoulder.

"That's my roommate. She has zero attention span," said the girl on my other side, a freckled brunette named Lauren whose room was next to ours. "We went to Spence together. She's insane."

I wanted to know what she meant by *insane*. "What's her name?" I asked, but my question went unanswered. Lauren was already talking to someone else about where to get decent weed on campus. The only person who wanted to talk to me was Ella. Between mouthfuls of food, she told me about her senior prom and her cat named Freddy as I feigned interest. It would have been easy to fall into a groove with her, to flesh out our similar backgrounds. But I didn't want to go back to where I came from.

When Lauren's *insane* roommate got up and left, followed by Clara and a couple of the guys, I swallowed my disappointment. I wanted to be part of that group. I stared at the can of Diet Coke in front of me as Gemma from Saint Ann's whined to Flora about her boyfriend at Yale and how much she missed him.

"I know it's hard," Flora said. "But he misses you too. Look at you. How could he not?"

It wasn't even what she said but how she said it. So genuinely *nice*. My spine prickled. Flora, in her babyish Mary Janes and high collar, was fitting in better than I did. She knew how to be herself—it seemed like everyone did. I only knew how to imitate other people.

Lauren surveyed Flora with interest. I was sure she would tear into her later with her roommate. But when the group broke apart, Flora gave her a hug. At first, Lauren stiffened, but Flora said something I couldn't hear—something that made Lauren's bored expression curve into a smile.

Later, when we were back in our room, I hung up dresses I realized were tacky and cheap as Flora unpacked photos of high school friends and her boyfriend, cheeks obscured by acne, even in grainy black and white.

"This is Kevin," she said, holding a photo close enough to kiss it. "He goes to Dartmouth. Second year."

"He's cute," I said, even though it was a horrible picture and he really wasn't.

"He's the best. I'm sure you'll meet him. He said he'd come to visit me all the time, when he can get away from school. It's not all that far. Less than three hours."

I imagined he had already cheated on her and she just didn't know it yet. Boys made us idiots. My mom seemed certain that I would find "someone special" at college, the same way Toni had met her boyfriend at Rutgers: Scott, with his impeccable manners, *such a good guy*. But the idea of a storybook college romance just seemed unattainable.

"What about you?" Flora continued. "You have a boyfriend, right?"

I stared at the photos I had deemed good enough to occupy the space on my corkboard. There was one of me and Matt, his easy smile and the slug of his arm across my shoulders. I resented the fact that Flora assumed I had a boyfriend as some kind of certainty. I almost wanted to tell her the whole ugly story but decided against it.

"No," I settled on. "There was a guy, but it's complicated."

"Complicated," she echoed, as if she didn't understand the word.

I had lost my virginity to Matt the summer before senior year. Billie had already given hers up and I wanted it gone, my stupid hymen, the arbitrary line drawn between girls who'd had a penis inside them and girls who hadn't. But the decision to have sex was about more than that. At the time, I honestly thought Matt would be not only my first but my last. *It's always going to be us*, he had said, his arms wrapped tightly around my waist at a school dance, my face hidden in his neck.

"You're so lucky," Billie used to whine. "He's, like, too good to be real."

But he was real, and he was mine. He was in my junior-year drama class and later claimed that he took the class just to ask me out—*I've seen all of your plays. You're so talented.* I let myself thaw and trust him when he picked me up for our first date, brandishing flowers for me and a handshake for my dad. His fingers, when they veered under my clothes, were gentle, his voice questioning. The boys Billie and I had previously orbited around didn't know we existed unless they were drunk and wanted something. I wasn't used to being treated well because I didn't even know what it felt like to be noticed.

I knew other girls wanted Matt, but he never even looked at them. He only saw me. After his basketball games, which Billie and I diligently attended in our Central colors, it was me he swept into a sweaty hug, me he kissed at parties in front of everyone. *Forever*, he liked to say when we were in his bed after school, fan whirring lazily overhead. *You're my forever.*

I had no reason not to believe him.

"I ended things," I told Flora, savoring the surge of power that accompanied the lie.

"Well, I'm sure there's somebody better for you here." She grabbed my hands. "Can I paint your nails like mine? Then we can match for the party tonight." Hers were cardinal red and black, Wesleyan pride already.

I was embarrassed by my nails. They were never the same length, rarely ever painted, and when I did take the time to do them, I always picked the polish off. But Flora was reaching for a pink nail file, so I let her knead my fingers between hers and watched her work. When she was done, she helped me choose an outfit—a low-cut blue dress from Forever 21, wedge heels handed down from Toni.

"Are you sure I look okay?" I asked. I felt cheap and greasy, my hair too brassy, my skin fake-baked. Worst of all, I felt average.

"You're beautiful," Flora reassured me. "That dress makes your eyes pop." Her words provided the smallest bit of warmth.

The party that night was in Butterfield A, in a double belonging to girls with fake IDs, which I soon learned most people already had. I spent most of the night with my back against a wall drinking vodka Sprite from a paper cup, watching girls take their turns retreating to a corner to dip their heads over a locker mirror, where I glimpsed neat lines of cocaine. I was too afraid to try it, and nobody offered anyway. The only drug I had tried in high school was weed, and all it did was calcify my paranoia that people were talking about me into a too-tight exoskeleton.

I saw Gemma from lunch flitting around the room in jeans and a white T-shirt that offset her peachy tan, simple but stunning. I suddenly felt ridiculous, sausaged into my dress, my makeup heavy-handed. Gemma's eyes met mine just for a second before landing on my colorful little LV. Eyebrows raised, she turned away from me toward Clara and her nondescript brown bag. My purse was a misstep. The girls here didn't flaunt their labels like status symbols. What had reigned at Central was all wrong now.

Flora left early after sipping from the same water bottle all night. "Kevin is calling me at ten. Want me to come back and get you after?"

"I'll be fine, but thanks," I said. I didn't want to be the drunk girl she cleaned up after.

Lauren and her roommate showed up when Flora left—fashionably late, except only Lauren was fashionable. Her roommate, the *insane* one, was wearing boxers and a ribbed tank top, no bra, as if she had just woken up. I downed another drink as she beelined for the cocaine, then started dancing in the middle of the room, grabbing a boy by his shirt. I saw the way she pulled back just a bit when he tried to kiss her, and noticed how she tilted her head, pushing her hair back to show her neck, grinding her hips into his crotch. His face grew more pained as hers got more playful, and the shriek of her hyena laugh was the loudest sound in the room.

I watched him go from wanting her to *needing* her. It was a transaction, her sucking power from him like a vampire. It was performance art. She had done this before, owned boys. When she finally let him kiss her, it was because she had already drained from him whatever she needed.

She pulled away from his urgent mouth long enough to look directly at me and wink. I smiled, then immediately hated myself for it. She had noticed me staring and would tell everyone how creepy I was.

I fixed my eyes on the ground just in time for someone to spill a drink on my purse. "Sorry," the guy said without even looking up at me. I felt myself deflate.

I unzipped the dripping purse and slipped my phone out. Then I left the purse on the floor, slumped beside the wall. I wouldn't need it anymore. Billie would be horrified, but Billie wasn't here and wouldn't understand.

When I stood back up, I realized how drunk I was. I shuffled over to Lauren and Gemma, hoping to gain entry to their conversation, but they either didn't notice me or didn't want to. I bobbed to an invisible beat and pretended not to care.

"She already fucked his friend," Lauren said. "It's some kind of game."

A shiver ran up my arms. I didn't know the rules, but I wanted to play too. A scan of the room told me what I already knew. Lauren's roommate was gone.

Whoever was in charge of housing assignments had gotten it all wrong, because that girl should have been my roommate. Whoever had matched me with Flora instead would be to blame when Butterfield C became Dorm Doom.

3

NOW

To: "Ambrosia Wellington" *a.wellington@wesleyan.edu*
From: "Wesleyan Alumni Committee" *reunion.classof2007@gmail.com*
Subject: Class of 2007 Reunion

Dear Ambrosia Wellington,

Your ten-year reunion is less than a month away! There's probably somebody you've been meaning to connect with—now is the perfect time to reach out. If you haven't joined our Class of 2007 Facebook group, we encourage you to hop online and log in. You might be surprised by who you find.

Sincerely,
Your Alumni Committee

I don't tell anybody about the reunion. Not my mom when she calls to ask if Adrian and I are coming up for Pennington Day, or Toni when she texts me photos of Layla, my two-year-old niece. Not even Billie, whom I message about everything—Billie, who knows more about me than anyone else in my life. She would encourage me to go. But she doesn't understand. Her past hasn't yielded casualties.

Hadley and Heather, the only girls from Wesleyan I keep in touch with, ask me in our group chat if I'm going, and I tell them I have something else planned for that weekend. *Boo*, Hadley says. *Justin will be sad without Adrian to talk to*. I check the mail in our building every day to snatch any potential notes before Adrian has a chance to see them. Adrian doesn't ask many questions, but when he gets curious, his need for answers rivals that of a six-year-old. *Why. Why. Why.* It's not even the insistence that I hate most. It's his simplicity, the very quality that I was once drawn to. His belief that there's a solution to every problem.

No more notes arrive, and I honestly think I got away with it. Then the past finds me in the last place I expect it. At the Skylark, where Adrian occasionally meets me after I'm done with work, making his rare pilgrimage away from the soft shell of Astoria and its craft beer. The Skylark is my favorite Midtown bar, my own glittering nest on top of New York. We're sipping our drinks—a martini for me, *just one*, Adrian likes to say, *just in case*—when Tara Rollins appears at our table. Tara from Wesleyan, who was assistant editor for the *Argus* and now works in book publishing.

"Ambrosia!" she squeals. I haven't seen her since Heather's bachelorette party—a boozy weekend on the beach in Sag Harbor where Tara tearfully admitted to cheating on her husband with a fellow editor—but here she is, and already, Adrian is standing up and pumping her hand with embarrassing vigor.

"Look at you. You look great! Please tell me you're going. It wouldn't be the same without you." As if we were ever anything beyond party acquaintances.

"Going where?" Adrian says.

Tara laughs. "The reunion, of course. You're coming too, aren't you? My husband wouldn't miss it."

I gulp my drink, smile intact as vodka burns my throat. *Your husband misses a lot.*

"Reunion?" Adrian makes the word an open wound. I stare at his tanned forearms, the brush of dark hair creeping up to the sleeves of his plaid shirt. "I didn't know—"

"I just haven't had a chance to talk to you yet," I say, sparing him the humiliation. "It doesn't matter anyway. I don't actually want to go."

Tara knows why but plays dumb. "Of course you want to go. *Everyone* will be there."

"It's our anniversary weekend," I explain. "We'll be doing something special to celebrate. Three years." Now is one of those times I wish I had a bigger ring to flash.

"No way," Adrian says. "We can't miss your reunion. We can do our anniversary anytime. It's just pizza on the patio anyway." He smiles up at Tara, all little-boy charm, as if she's going to be impressed with our low-key date night.

"Exactly," Tara says. They start talking like I'm not even there. It takes less than a minute for Adrian to mention his novel and less than two for Tara to mention Butterfield C. Anger surges through me. I want to protect Adrian, not just from the truth but from Tara's inevitable judgment of him, of us.

"I got pretty wild back then," she says with a laugh. My eyes search the room for a waiter who can bring me a second martini. "But of course, not as wild as Amb."

"You must have the wrong girl," he says, reaching for my wrist. "This one kept her head down and studied."

I can't look at Tara because I know what I'll see there. *She kept her head down, all right.* She's a time bomb, and I need to get rid of her before she detonates.

"Fine," I say, fingers closing so tightly around my glass that I picture it shattering. "We'll go."

It's only once I say those words out loud that the truth hits me.

I do need to go. Not for Tara, not for anyone else, but for *her.* Because maybe she knows something that will absolve us. I keep picturing her wherever she is, taking the time to write such careful calligraphy—so unlike her; she was always in a rush. But she summoned me for a reason, and I need to know what it is.

I said *We'll go,* but I didn't mean *we.* I rack my brain, scour the Internet for reasons to leave Adrian behind. Maybe this will help our marriage. I can face the past, shed my dead skin, and come back with some of the gratitude I used to feel for my husband instead.

I find a weekend writing workshop offered at NYU, excitedly presenting it to him as a great opportunity to take his *craft* seriously. "Consider it my anniversary gift. Just imagine how much writing you'll get done," I gush. He's almost ready to enroll when he notices the date.

"Not this time," he says. "There'll be another one. Hey, should I get a suit for your reunion?"

A message comes in from Hadley. *Are you guys signing up to stay in the dorms?*

I imagine it. Adrian beside me, holding hands on Foss Hill. Maybe it wouldn't be that bad. We see Hadley and Heather and their husbands every couple months for dinner and drinks, and the boys retreat so deep into their conversations about sports and action movies that they forget we're even there. Hadley and Heather know that I haven't told Adrian about Dorm Doom—at my engagement party, I said I didn't want to taint what Adrian and I had with all those awful rumors, and they gave me sympathetic hugs and promises of *It's not our business, we'd never say anything*. I could get through a weekend at Wesleyan. *We* could.

I let the idea marinate, cautiously. Adrian brings it up again when we're out for dinner with Billie and her husband, Ryan, in Brooklyn. We've been making that hour-long commute from Astoria with decreasing frequency, and they never come to us because of *the kids*. He grabs my hand when we sit down, a small gesture that makes us a team, the way married people are supposed to be.

"Amb's reunion is going to be sweet," he says through a mouthful of steak after our main courses arrive. "Ten years. Makes me wish I had graduated."

"Reunion?" Billie says. I take a swig of wine, the second glass Adrian didn't want me to order. I can feel her eyes on me, the hurt there that I didn't tell her myself. "Wait. For Wesleyan? And you're going?"

"Yes," I say quickly. "I thought I told you about it."

"You didn't," Billie says. "You must have forgotten."

She knows I didn't forget. I picture the blue glow of Billie's face at the Hamilton Manor when we were drunk at Central's senior prom, her cold hand wiping tears from my cheeks. *Matt's here. With her. Don't look. Fuck them, it will always be us.*

I grapple for something else to talk about. "Your last post was so cute. The girls are starting to look so much like you."

Her pinched expression relaxes, but I'm not off the hook. She'll message me later tonight, wanting me to *spill*, like I'm a drink teetering on the edge. "Oh, yeah. I had to bribe Sawyer with cookie dough to get her to sit still. I'm mother of the year, didn't you know?"

Billie hasn't technically worked since Ryan got promoted to some kind of private banking job in the Financial District and she had Beckett. But she calls herself an "influencer." Her online persona—a blog called GurlMom that turned into an Instagram account with a following of nearly thirty thousand—is nothing like her real self. She's a paragon of the #2under2 contingent, moms who wear their babies like clingy purses over skintight yoga pants. They worship Billie and the state of blush-pink staged flawlessness she embodies.

I don't have Instagram for that reason. Because I don't want to cultivate a #nofilter life, a pastiche of fake smiles. I learned at Wesleyan that people don't envy the girls who are the smartest and prettiest. They envy the ones who are smart and pretty without trying. Unlike Billie's, my attempt at effortlessness played out live. There was no delete button, no way to undo.

"I remember my five-year reunion," says Ryan. I hate him for bringing the conversation back around. "We stayed in the dorms and got shitfaced. I was planning to hook up with this girl I used to be obsessed with, except I barely recognized her under the bad plastic surgery."

"My dorm room was awesome," Adrian says. "It used to feel like a palace to me."

The palace of pussy and weed. Adrian fully copped to being a slut in college. He even told me his wake-up call was when chlamydia sent him running to the campus nurse, fearful his dick would fall off from overuse. It's one of his many anecdotes, which never failed to entertain me when we were dating, even when I suspected some weren't entirely true. Adrian is a bartender. He's used to listening to other people's stories. It's only natural that he tries to pass some of them off as his own.

"The dorms were full when I called," I say. "I already booked us a hotel." Not one of the ones recommended in the email, but one farther away from the school, outside of Middletown, a more expensive Uber ride.

"Bummer," Adrian says at the same time Billie says, defensively, "Can you blame her for not wanting to stay there?"

"What do you mean?" Adrian asks after a silence that lasts too long.

"Amb's roommate—" Billie starts.

I cut her off. "My old roommates are going, too. Hadley and Heather. It'll be great. Is anyone getting dessert?"

Billie purses her lips. She is very aware that I haven't told Adrian about my other roommate, so I don't know where she's trying to take the conversation. Her forehead would be furrowed if it weren't for her recent Botox injections.

I'm afraid of what Billie will bring up next, but then her cell phone chirps and her attention is diverted. "Fuck. It's my mom. She says Beckett's refusing to sleep." She drains the last of her wine. "I guess that's our cue to leave." Ryan waves the waiter over, scribbling in the air with his index finger and thumb pressed together.

The waiter is mercifully fast. Billie's on the phone with Beckett, telling her, "Mommy and Daddy will be home soon, go to bed for Nana, sweetie." I chug the rest of my drink, and that's when I see her. It's not actually her, though. It never is. Deep down, I know this, and yet I keep seeing her, in different places.

In a summer dress with tights, a slick of lipstick when she wants to feel fancy. She watches me on my commute to work, fish-belly-white hands pressed against smudged train windows, getting off with me at Bryant Park. She's holding an iced coffee in the lobby of my office building, watching me take the elevator to the twenty-fourth floor, where the hive of Brighton Dame buzzes, where I complete my transformation to basic PR bitch. Her glare, the moment our eyes meet, splits my skull. The question she wants to ask. *Why?*

The therapist my parents made me see the summer after freshman year told me something I never forgot. "You went through a trauma," she said, a string of words she was paid generously to dole out. "You wish there was more you could have done. But maybe you're scared to let things go because you aren't sure what to hold on to otherwise."

Secretly I was impressed that she had dug all that insight out of my silences and nods. The truth wasn't that I held on to things. It was that I clutched them in a death grip.

I wish I had done a lot more, I told her. It was what she expected to hear. The reality is that I wish I had done so much less.

"Amb," Billie says, smoothing the lace skirt puckering around her thighs. "Call me later. We should talk."

When we hug goodbye, the girl is coming out of the ladies' room, still staring at me, silently judgmental. She hates my lipstick. She doesn't think red is my color. And she's right. It's forever hers.

4

THEN

My first week at Wesleyan was a twisted treasure hunt, different spots on campus marking the spoils. The girls were my new language to study, the campus my personal geography project. Stoli and Sprite in various rooms in the Butterfields, which I soon started calling "the Butts" like I heard others do. Olin Library, all pillars and light, where my body buzzed like a live wire when I tried to concentrate on my first assignments, too acutely aware of the people around me. MoCon, affectionately dubbed the Mothership, hulking over campus like a watchful sentinel atop Foss Hill, where we ate most of our meals, lining up for a perpetually wilting salad bar, my hands hot as I scanned the tables for Flora or even Ella, because at least I didn't have to impress her.

And my home base—our room, Flora's half impeccably neat. She had every color of nail polish lined up in a rainbow. "Don't even ask," she said. "Just take whatever you want." I did, but not right away.

I had tacked up pictures of me and Billie and, pathetically, left up the one of me and Matt—the only one that had survived becoming origami in the aftermath of our breakup. We wouldn't be together again—

not until a drunken mistake the next summer, although I didn't know it at the time—but I needed to look desired, because being wanted was the local currency.

I hated seeing his face on my wall, but it was a necessary reminder not to give out my trust so easily. I wouldn't be blindsided again. I wouldn't be the girl who believed her boyfriend when he canceled plans to go to a party because he was sick. I wouldn't be the girl who went to the party with Billie instead. The most humiliating moment of my life, when I drunkenly staggered into the basement and found Matt's head between Jessica French's legs.

The worst part wasn't even that carnal image, burned indefinitely into my brain. It was that I stood there, shell-shocked, unable to find my voice. *That's not Matt*, I tried telling myself, except of course it was. Instead of hurling at him the wrath he deserved, I slunk away unseen, cannibalizing myself for my flaws, the ones that drove him to pastel-perfect Jessica French. *Of course he cheated*, I told myself. *I'm not special.* Every compliment he had doled out detonated in my brain. He had never meant any of them.

When Billie found me, I was a waterlogged mess on the front porch. She hugged me tightly and unleashed hell. "Fuck him, Amb. Seriously. Break up with him, and be really fucking savage about it."

We went back to Billie's house and planned the epic breakup speech I would use, all the ways I'd hurt him. I turned off my phone and barely slept all weekend. Matt acted like nothing had happened when I saw him at school on Monday, putting his hand on the small of my back and kissing my cheek. I couldn't muster the right words, so I pathetically repeated his *I love you*, hating myself more with each syllable.

"Are you feeling better?" I finally managed, blinking back tears.

"Yeah, way more like myself," he said. "I figured you were sick too, since you never called me back."

Now was the time to unfurl my prepared speech, but it was stuck in my throat.

"I wasn't sick," I said just as the bell rang.

I told myself I'd call him and end things that night, justifying the delay to Billie by saying it would be easier over the phone, but I didn't get a chance to before his text arrived. *I think we should stop seeing each other. I'm really sorry, but I need to focus on school.* It was a fresh stab wound.

I finally retaliated. *You're a pathetic excuse for a boyfriend if you can't even break up with me in person. I know what you did.* But it was too late. My words had lost their impact. From that moment, I decided to use boys the same way they'd been willing to use me. If none of them mattered, I couldn't get hurt.

At Wesleyan, I cleaved to whatever invitations came my way, not wanting to be chained down to Flora, who barely went to any parties, even though girls fluttered into our room to invite her. Every night before she went to bed, her phone would swell with Aerosmith's "I Don't Want to Miss a Thing"—Kevin's ringtone—and they would proceed to talk for almost an hour, hushed tones punctuated by the occasional soft laugh.

When I was in our room during the calls, I put my headphones on and pretended not to listen, but I couldn't help but overhear. They were the most banal conversations, peppered with anecdotes about every single thing that had happened to Flora on that given day. MoCon's lasagna, lacy noodles hard around the edges, *gasp,* not vegan friendly. The vegan hot chocolate her sister sent her in a care package. Something one of her professors said. Something I said. My name came up a lot. *Just wait till you meet Amb. She's so nice!*

I tried to reciprocate her enthusiasm, but it felt like an inconsistent performance. To me, being nice was as naïve as being trustworthy, which had gotten me nowhere. Flora must have known the power she was giving people to hurt her. There was a danger in being too soft in a world that required a protective coating.

I wasn't going to be soft again. Not when girls like Jessica French existed, smiling to my face and betraying me behind my back. As much as I hated Matt, I might have hated them even more. I was a joke they were all in on.

So I worked on my coating instead. I copied the styles of the girls from our dorm, girls prettier and more fashionable than me: Gemma with her ripped jeans and oversized flannels, and Clara with her miniskirts over tights, and even our RA, Dawn, whose curly auburn hair rippled down her back in a twisted current, miraculously shiny and frizz-free.

Before classes started each day, I fastidiously flat-ironed my hair and painted my face with tools from my Bobbi Brown arsenal. I resented how my clothes fit, everything so intentionally tight. My flaws were magnified in every mirror.

But I could overcome them. I was an actress, and I had come to Wesleyan to learn. I was pretty enough with the right makeup and thin enough with the right diet, but I wasn't *enough* to run off to Hollywood and live in my car, blow-drying my hair under hand dryers in fast-food restaurants between casting calls. I needed to truly learn the craft.

I had feigned shock when my acceptance to Wesleyan came in the mail. I wasn't surprised, but I felt the need to pretend I was, and I didn't understand why. It would be years before I realized that girls weren't supposed to own their ambition, just lease it from time to time when it didn't offend anyone else.

I was confident that I'd act in college, until I got to Wesleyan and met Dora from one of the other Butts, who'd already performed on Broadway, and Sienna from down the hall, who had shot a TV show pilot over the summer, and realized exactly what I was up against. I had planned to get a role in one of the Theater Department's fall plays. But fear of rejection, suddenly a white-hot certainty, made me skip the auditions. I told myself I'd try out next semester. By then, I would have studied the competition and found a way to stand out.

I didn't know how right I was.

Flora wanted to be a psychologist and to work with troubled kids. She had already become a guru for the other girls on our floor, doling out tampons and boyfriend advice, leaving colorful Post-its on our doors with scribbled affirmations. *You can do anything! You're amazing!*

She paid special attention to me, wearing her syrup smile as she braided my hair, wanting to know my high school stories, maybe as an excuse to bring up hers. She talked a lot about Kevin, whom she'd met at the Fairfield country club where their dads golfed.

"Long-distance is hard," she told me. "But we're both patient. We make it work."

"Why didn't you apply to Dartmouth too?" I asked one day while we ate dinner at MoCon. "It's just, you must miss him a lot."

What I really meant: Long-distance relationships don't work. Or else, they only work if neither person is jealous. And Flora, as much as she claimed to trust Kevin, was jealous. There was no other way to explain the nightly calls, more frequent than bowel movements, and the ringtone itself. She didn't want to *miss a thing* he was doing.

"I didn't get in," Flora said. It was the first time I'd heard resentment in her voice. "I got rejected. I could have gone to the University of New Hampshire to be closer, but Kevin thought Wesleyan would be a better fit for me."

"He obviously wants what's best for you."

"Yeah. He didn't try to talk me into moving there."

I could tell she wished he would have.

Years later, I pictured high school Flora, sprawled on her king bed in her Fairfield mansion, private school uniform adhered to her perfect body, pamphlets for colleges spread out in front of her like a fan. The world, literally at her fingertips. She looked at the Wesleyan brochure and cast it aside. I considered how her life would look today if she had.

I formally met Lauren's *insane* roommate, the other girl living next door, during an icebreaker at the start of the semester. She was in two of my classes, Acting I and Introduction to Playwriting. She probably had the same acting dreams as I did, and she was a girl I could absolutely never compete with—a graduate of the Spence School in New York City who had dabbled in modeling and spent part of her childhood in France.

Her name was Sloane Sullivan, but she told everyone to call her Sully. Her parents had obviously taken one look at their wailing pink bundle and known she would grow into a certain kind of girl. I had been saddled with ten syllables in total, Ambrosia Francesca Wellington. It didn't even have the decency to abbreviate well, so I was Amb, a pathetic amputation that most people assumed stood for Amber. I rarely corrected them.

Sully had her pick of friends. She could have been one of the preppy Butterfield bitches as easily as a WestCo hipster, because something about her defied categorization. She skulked down the Butts hallways in fishnets and Docs one day, wore sweatpants and a men's button-down to class the next, smoked joints with flagrant disregard, and was never not surrounded by people, girls and boys trailing her like a cape.

She had no reason to talk to me, because her charisma had already pulled in enough followers. But her boredom and my need for attention intersected at a party at Nicolson Hall, known as the Nics, a couple weeks into the semester.

"This party sucks," she said, migrating over to where I stood with Lauren and Flora, who had actually taken a night off from Kevin to join us. "I get bored easily. I think we should liven things up."

"Oh god." Lauren shook her head. "Please don't."

"I wasn't talking to you," Sully said. "I was talking to Ambrosia from Pennington. And you guys." She pulled Gemma and Clara over. "See that guy over there? The one wearing those god-awful khakis? That's Long-Distance Dave. He's the most pretentious asshole in this room, and that's saying something."

"You mean Dave Holman," Clara said. "He's in my stats class."

"He won't shut up about his girlfriend at UCLA," Sully said. "It's annoying. Let's do something about it."

Nobody took her bait. Except me, because I was hungry to set myself apart. Besides, I did know Long-Distance Dave. He lived in Butts

A and whined constantly about *Leslie*. The way he said her name, so cotton soft, made my blood curdle.

"He's a dick," I said. "What do you want to do?"

Sully fixed her gaze on me. It was like being anointed. The other girls were silent, waiting for Sully to give me her orders. But it was like they no longer existed, and I did.

The music got louder. Sully leaned in and her mouth buzzed against my ear. "I want you to get him to cheat. Tonight. Prove that he's the same animal as the rest of them."

I don't know why she didn't just do it herself. If anyone was capable, it was Sully. I was keenly aware that my reaction would somehow define the rest of my semester, but I didn't realize just how much.

It didn't feel like a decision at all.

"Fine," I said.

Her fingers brushed my cheek. "*Showtime*," she whispered, almost too soft to hear.

"Amb," Flora said. "I'm heading back in a few. Do you want to come with me?"

I knew she was trying to give me an out, but I didn't want it. "I'm going to stay," I said.

I caught the judgmental flicker, the pinch between her eyebrows. Somehow, her disapproval emboldened me.

When she was gone, I knocked back a shot of tequila and advanced on Long-Distance Dave. Sully and the other girls watched. It was a performance, same as being onstage at Central, except with a much more critical audience. I knew that flashy displays of skin would be lost on Dave. The slaughter had to be more subtle. My tears, when they came, looked real.

"Are you okay?" he asked, concern in his chocolate-brown eyes. "You look so upset."

"It's my boyfriend," I said, burying my face in my hands. "He just told me he can't do long-distance anymore. He said we never should have tried."

Dave's hand was reassuring on my back. He offered me a tissue. I leaned into his salmon-pink shirt instead and felt him stiffen against my closeness. "That sucks, Amb. But you're better off without him. He doesn't respect you."

"The fucked-up thing is, he was always trying to convince me I was doing things wrong. Like, every guy I talked to, he asked me about. He was paranoid." I stretched the word into something grotesque. The same way I knew, from snatches of Dave's conversations, that Leslie did. Leslie, who in my head became pink-lipped Jessica French.

"I'm sorry," he said. An apology on behalf of all men that meant nothing.

I dug in. "Do you have any idea what that's like? When somebody doesn't want to believe you, even when you're not doing anything wrong?"

"Yeah, sometimes I do," was what he offered up, and it was enough.

It took another half hour and one more cascade of fake tears for Dave to ask if I wanted to go somewhere quiet to talk. We ended up back in his room, which smelled like Axe body spray. He wrapped a blanket around my shoulders. I shrugged it off.

I don't know how long I sat there before Dave started hinting about Leslie's flaws. I don't know what time it was when both of our heads hit his pillow, exhausted from our heart-to-heart, but not too tired for me to tuck myself under his chin. And not too tired for his dick to be hard in his jeans. He moaned when I touched it through the fabric, his lips finding mine in the dark. Even though I wasn't the least bit attracted to Dave, with his bad skin and weak chin, I was strangely turned on by the time I climbed on top of him, bulletproof with power.

Dave came in his pants, which was both a disappointment and a relief. I slipped out as he snored beside me, sneaking through serpentine hallways until I was back in Butts C, splashing water on my face in the bathroom. Sully was barefoot in the hall when I emerged, wearing shorts and a hoodie, probably fresh from leaving a different boy.

"Showtime," I said, returning the wink from that first party, the one I was suddenly sure was meant for me. I couldn't stop smiling as I entered my room, with its neon-green Post-it gleaming on the door—*You can do anything!*

Fucking right, I thought. I had never felt more alive.

5

NOW

To: "Ambrosia Wellington" *a.wellington@wesleyan.edu*
From: "Wesleyan Alumni Committee" *reunion.classof2007@gmail.com*
Subject: Class of 2007 Reunion

Dear Ambrosia Wellington,

The ultimate blast from your past is just around the corner! Don't forget to bring a camera, scrapbooks, photo albums, yearbooks, and Wesleyan memorabilia to reflect on the old memories—and make new ones. And remember your red-and-black best for your class dinner!

Sincerely,
Your Alumni Committee

Her name is on every reminder email, nestled underneath the Alumni Committee, bold in a way she never was. Flora Banning, forever a joiner, protestor of non-vegan cafeteria food and organizer of movie nights. I'll inevitably have to see her face when Adrian and I arrive on campus, her white smile and complete lack of wrinkles—her moisturizing rituals were a masterwork of skin-care dedication. Of all the people I'm going to see, I'm the most terrified of her.

But that's only because someone else—someone who suspects the very worst about me—won't be at the reunion.

I google Detective Tom Felty—now Captain Felty—on my work computer while I finish the leftovers of an overpriced salad I got for lunch. I look him up periodically because it makes me feel safer to know he's in Middletown, far away from me. His blue eyes spear me through the screen, as if he knows where I am. I still hear his barrage of questions in the police station. *Did you notice? Were you aware?* He wanted me to self-immolate. I never did.

I'm too wired to go right home, so I head to the gym in our building after work, sneaking in the back entrance, where old Mrs. Lowe always wedges the door open with a piece of wood to carry her groceries inside. I don't want to risk running into Adrian in the lobby. When he and I signed our lease, we thought we'd work out every night instead of sinking into the couch and turning on the TV.

I put in effort when we started dating. I'd shave my legs and hack away at any hint of pubic hair that strayed from the anemic landing strip I maintained like my personal secret garden, and we met up to jog in Astoria Park every weekend. We moved in together quickly, and that was when things deteriorated. When Adrian started leaving the door ajar when he took a shit and gained a bit of weight, a soft paunch over the front of his jeans. "Dad bod," he joked, except there were no kids, and he wanted there to be.

And I stopped trying so hard, too. Adrian didn't care if I didn't put makeup on. He didn't notice when I did. For once in my life, something was easy. But it wasn't natural. I didn't know who I was when I wasn't trying to be someone else.

I step onto the treadmill, stretching out my arms. Adrian once offered to get us a treadmill of our own. "Then you can run and I can write," he said. When I asked where it would go, he wasn't able to answer. Our apartment is seven hundred square feet, with just an arched doorway separating the kitchen from everything else, our bedroom attached like a tiny tumor. Twenty-three hundred dollars a month to have no space of my own, to brush my teeth over a pedestal sink furred with my husband's beard hair.

I start running, jerking up the incline to burn more calories. The TV mounted on the wall across from me plays a local news channel, the latest crime stories. It makes me think of the footage from Dorm Doom, all of us girls huddled outside Butterfield C, straw-pale legs quaking in the grass, a young cop telling us to *stay back* from the fluttering yellow tape. I had no idea I'd soon be facing Felty's artillery fire of questioning. It was my role of a lifetime.

My feet pound and I increase the speed to seven, heat radiating from inside my body. For the hundredth time, I fantasize about bailing on the reunion. Hadley and Heather won't stop asking me what I'm wearing to the dinner, and they're already making plans for us to have photos taken outside the wood-frame house on Fountain Avenue that we shared senior year. And then there's the note, already fused to my brain. *We need to talk.*

Why now? Why the reunion? Why hasn't she tried to contact me once, and why wasn't she around the times I tried to find her? No Facebook, no Instagram, no social media presence at all.

My sweaty finger increases my speed to eight. Her words chase me. *We need to talk about what we did that night.* They morph into other things she should be saying. *We need to talk about what we became that night.*

I have no idea what she's like now. But then again, I never really did. She was barely more than a stranger the entire time. A friendship that lasted just a few months, one that was built on the idea of us more than the reality. But my skin is still raw where she grafted herself to me, and I can so easily conjure an alternate dimension where we're those girls, the inseparable ones.

Sometimes I let myself live in that alternate dimension, just for a minute, the two of us in Hollywood, reading scripts, sun-streaked and starry-eyed. And sometimes I like it better than this one.

Despite my constant pleas for Adrian to lock up, the apartment door is open. Adrian is on the couch in his sweatpants when I return. Our faux-suede couch from the Furniture Market, the first piece of furniture that was ours. The day we bought it, I didn't care that it was cheap, because we were happy.

I take in the detritus around me—a pizza box and beer bottles on the counter; white-handled Wüsthof knives cast carelessly into the sink; socks and papers strewn on the floor. "Didn't you have the day off? You could have cleaned up."

I expect his typical refrain of *Chill, babe*, which I hate, because whenever I get like this—uptight and irritable—it's a reaction to his being the opposite. But he doesn't tell me to chill. Instead, he turns around and holds up a photo. "Who's this, Amb?"

I squint at the image he's waving around and tighten my ponytail with trembling hands. "Where did you get this?" I march over, plucking the photo from his fingers.

"I was looking for that screenwriting book you bought me last Christmas. The one about saving a cat. Some book was on top of it and I picked them both up, and this fell out."

He's lying. He was snooping, but I can't exactly call him out. I chew on my bottom lip.

"John Donne." I force myself to laugh.

"Who's John Donne? An ex?"

"He's one of the most prominent metaphysical poets," I say. "The book is full of his poetry."

"Oh," Adrian says. "But you know I'm asking about the guy in the picture. Why do you have it?"

"He was just a guy. Someone from a long time ago."

"A boyfriend, then," Adrian says, almost jealous, which would be a welcome respite from his perpetual state of man-child chill if not for the deadly quagmire he has wandered into. "From college?"

"Not exactly," I say quickly. He narrows his eyes. "I mean, I guess so. The book was from a class we had together."

"Will he be at the reunion?" Adrian puts his beer on the coffee table. "This isn't a big deal. We're married. You think I care that you had boyfriends before me? I had girlfriends before you."

Which he told me about in detail. The crazy one who tried moving her stuff into his dresser drawers after dating for a week. The one who was obsessed with meeting celebrities. The one who still slept with a stuffed rabbit, which remained on the bed during sex. The one who only ever wanted to watch Leonardo DiCaprio movies. It was like he wanted me to know it was always their fault, never his, and see how normal he was? See how lucky I was that he got out of that thicket of girls unscathed?

"We were together," I say. I need to hear how it sounds out loud, my sick little fiction. "He won't be there, though. He's actually—well, he's dead."

"Oh, fuck." Adrian claps a hand over his mouth. "What happened to him?"

I shake my head. "I don't want to talk about it right now."

He nods. "I mean, sucks that the guy is dead, but you freaked me out with this photo. I thought there was some meaning behind it. Especially since I found this tucked in the same book." He pulls out the envelope, my name in her calligraphy.

"Did you open it?"

"I'm sorry. I was curious. But what did you do that night? What night?"

I shouldn't get angry. Adrian thinks he has seen me angry, but he has only seen the diluted version.

"It's just an inside joke," I say. "Something one of my friends gave me."

He studies me for a beat too long, then picks up his beer. "Was it serious? You and him?"

The photo cartwheels between my fingers, corners poking into my palm. I don't look at *him* and I can't bring myself to look at Adrian. "Serious enough. But I moved on. I forgot I even still had that book. I haven't looked at it in years."

Adrian's eyes crinkle up. "I bet you were such an adorable poetry nerd. I hope you didn't get made fun of. Even if you did, wait till we show up. All the mean girls are gonna be jealous."

Oh, sweetie. We were the mean girls.

I take a sip of his beer. He pictures me trudging across a leaf-starred campus, backpack turtled on my back, always studious, never late for class. He has no idea.

I can't change what we did. What *I* did. I turned into a monster, but the world knows exactly how to make monsters out of girls who want what they can't have.

The boy in the picture—he won't be at the reunion. I made sure of that. Just like I made sure that his girlfriend won't show up, and that I'll never see either of them again.

6

THEN

Long-Distance Dave was my gateway drug. I was certain that my boldness with him would link me to Sully, imbue me with a mystique that she would recognize as the counterpoint to her own. But for days, nothing changed. A few times in class, she would hold my gaze, but she didn't talk to me again until a party at Beta that weekend.

I wanted male attention, so I drank a lot, wore very little, and danced, letting my hands rove across my body. Lily from Butts C was with me, having been ditched by her own friends, her pale cheeks rosy from vodka consumption. I sensed people watching us and hiked up my skirt even higher. Then a voice that didn't belong to Lily entered my ear and a cold set of hands clamped down on my collarbones.

"You don't have to do it, you know," Sully said.

"Do what?" I tried to turn around, but she held me in place, her fingers pinching my skin.

"Bleed for their entertainment."

This time, she spun me into her. "You think they like you. Or want to be with you. But they're just looking for something to keep them entertained."

"The boys, you mean." They surrounded us, in packs, former sports kings with predatory eyes.

Sully barked out a laugh. "No, not them. The girls, you idiot." She said *idiot* softly. "They pretend they're so edgy and up for anything, but it's all a performance. Or even worse, they act sweet, then talk behind your back. Kind of like your roommate."

Flora, with her Post-its. The one on our door today had said, *Kindness costs nothing*. She had been quieter than usual since the night of Long-Distance Dave. I knew she was judging me.

"Fuck them," I said.

Sully pressed her thumb into my chin and didn't break eye contact. "You're not nice, are you?"

I didn't know if it was a question or a statement, but I had the same answer. "No."

"Good. I hate nice girls."

We hovered like that, me trying to capture the source of her magnetism like trapping a butterfly between my hands. Her pupils were massive—she was obviously high—her lips red, hair swishing. But all of that could have been imitated by other girls, even by me—and in the coming weeks, I would do my best. What made Sully impossible to say no to wasn't about how she looked. It was how she made you look at yourself. Her kamikaze attitude, the life it pulsed into everyone around her. You didn't know what she was going to do, or what you would do when you were with her.

"I know what you need," she said, sweeping her hand across my collarbone. "You need to get fucked."

I nodded. She didn't know—nobody here knew—that Matt was the only boy I'd ever slept with. The idea of sex with someone new was simultaneously exciting and terrifying. It could be the emotional bloodletting I needed, a ritual necessary to purge the memory of Matt's betrayal.

"Yeah. I was just thinking that." I wouldn't shrivel under her stare. Maintaining Sully's attention would require constant upkeep.

"I have just the guy," she said, pointing with a long finger. "Him. With the Stones T-shirt. He needs to get laid too. Go forth and conquer."

It wasn't an order—it was more like a challenge. I took it.

"He" was Murray, a stoner with tufty blond facial hair, Wesleyan's low-hanging fruit. Two drinks later, we were back in his room, kissing, which would quickly lead to more. I was suddenly overwhelmed by the idea of allowing a stranger inside me. *He hasn't taken me on a date*, I thought frantically. *He doesn't even know anything about me.* They were supposed to know us—it was the price of admission. But Sully was right. I was done being anybody's entertainment.

"I don't do this kind of thing often," I said, trying not to shake as his fingers pushed into me. It was a line I hoped was the perfect mix of adventurous and apologetic. I understood that I had to somehow be both.

"Yeah," he snorted. "I can tell." I couldn't tell what I had already done wrong.

I would have gone through with it, the sex, but Murray's dick had other plans. He blamed the cocaine. Just like with Dave, I felt a gush of relief. I had never attached any particularly special meaning to sex, but I knew that having it at Wesleyan would assign some kind of meaning to me. It was a line in the sand, what I would or wouldn't do. Maybe it meant something that my first two attempts at a conquest ended in apologies. But I wasn't in the mood to look for signs from the universe. The embers of my post-Matt humiliation still burned hot.

"How was it?" Sully asked me the next morning in class.

"He couldn't get it up," I said, a hangover assaulting my skull. At first, she just stared, and I immediately regretted my admission. Then she cupped a laugh in her hand and slid her coffee cup my way.

"Same thing as when I tried fucking him. He actually tried to put it in me soft. At least he's good with his tongue, right?"

I nodded, unsure if it was some kind of test, and even less sure if I had passed or failed.

I wasn't a person who gave up. I decided that sex without emotion was exactly what I needed. And a week after Murray, I finally found it with Drew Tennant, a guitarist I flirted with after watching his band perform at Eclectic. Sex with Drew was a lot like sex with Matt— sweaty and perfunctory, a crescendo of grunts and tangled sheets. I still brought him back to our room another day when Flora was in class, pretended to come when he did, as if it were that easy.

Pathetically, what I liked best about Drew was the moment after sex when he lay with his arm around me, spent from his efforts. The heat of his skin against mine was satisfying in a way that sex with him never was. *You need to leave*, I willed myself to say, but he beat me to it. "Gotta go," he said, buttoning his jeans over the rich brown expanse of his ab muscles. "Study time."

I never even found out what he was studying. The last time we hooked up, I stood on my tiptoes and kissed him at the door, and when he pulled away, he looked at me like he had no idea who I was.

Sully kept inviting me to parties, where I would only ever see her briefly, across a crowded room, long hair swishing like a pennant, her vanguard of followers constantly regenerating. She was always doing something in excess—drinking, dancing, drugs, her lips on someone new—and that's why everyone luxuriated in her. She did what they wanted to but wouldn't. Whenever her eyes flicked to me—and they did, without fail—I knew I was still being tested somehow.

Flora existed in her own quarantine, separate from Sully's gravitational pull. "Sloane goes out every night. I wonder how she gets any work done," she said one evening, obviously waiting for me to fill the silence with my own judgment. I shrugged. Flora was trying to pull me in her direction—the note on our door that morning had said, *Be yourself! Everyone else is taken!*

The gap was closing. I wasn't a city girl or an old-money golf-club princess, but I also wasn't a suburban nobody like Ella Walden, with her too-tight jeans and frosted makeup and braying laugh. I fit in with the cool girls. Until the last Monday in September, when I found out that Lauren had a power I didn't. A social pull so gossamer-fine I didn't know it was there until my strand had been snipped.

"I meant to ask, are you going to Lauren's thing this weekend?" Flora said, folding her shirts into perfect pastel squares. "It was nice of her to invite everyone, but I have a huge paper due. Too bad, because I love the Hamptons."

My chest was a sinkhole. I struggled to breathe.

"I don't know," I choked out. "I'm not sure what I'm doing yet." I wasn't going to tell Flora that Lauren had excluded me on purpose, for reasons I didn't fully understand. We'd sit together at lunch every once in a while, occasionally swapping party stories. I had just seen her the day before, and she hadn't mentioned the Hamptons.

My confusion reached a boil when I ran into Ella in the bathroom that afternoon, her face flushed with excitement. "Can you believe we're going to the Hamptons? I've never been there before, have you? Lauren's family has an actual beach house. I have no idea what to wear. We should help each other pack."

"I've been. They're kind of overrated." It was a lie. I couldn't believe that even Ella was invited to *Lauren's thing*. My bottom lip wobbled. I stormed out, leaving a bewildered Ella behind, before I started to cry.

I went out that night with Lily and Clara, seeking validation that I was wanted. I found Hunter from Butts A, with his waxy, pimple-studded forehead, and let him grope me on the dance floor at DKE. It translated to actual sex two days later, an unsatisfying encounter that warranted another fake orgasm. He got dressed and went to leave just as Flora returned from class.

"Oh, hey," I said to Flora. "We were just studying." I noticed Sully across the hall. She paused outside the bathroom and didn't even try to hide her laugh.

"See you around, Amber," Hunter said. My cheeks flamed. He was a jock—the perfect kind of guy to have sex with and never see again. But I couldn't be the powerful one if he didn't even remember my name.

"Bye, Hudson," Sully called after him, sticking out her tongue.

"It's Hunter," he said, annoyed, then he looked back and saw her. "Sully. Hey."

I couldn't face Flora, who I knew would disapprove, so I grabbed my bag and decided to walk to Olin, where I could hide among people busy studying. Sully darted after me, putting a decisive hand on my shoulder.

"He has, like, one brain cell," she said. "And his dick is crooked. Did you notice?"

I spun around. "You slept with him too?"

That made her laugh. "There are only so many toys to play with, right? I guess we have to learn to share." Her fingers went to my

necklace—a gift from Billie for my sweet sixteen—moving the flow-
er pendant back to center. "I would never forget your name. It's too
important."

"It's fine," I said. "He was a lousy fuck anyway." Truthfully, I hadn't
slept with enough guys to know the difference between good and bad
sex. It was more or less the same, a collision of parts, jabbing and
grunting in the dark.

"This place is crawling with lousy fucks. The trick is to have some
fun with them anyway. Come on, I'll show you."

At a table in Olin, her fingers tangled in her ripped tights, making
the holes bigger. She was striking, her eyebrows slanting majestically
over big green eyes. She reached into her hoodie pocket and pushed
something across the table to me. A silver Nokia. "I went to this party
at the Nics with Gem last night. Everyone was all coked out, and I met
this guy. Buddy."

That chill came back, the abrupt certainty that parties were happening all around me, *people* were happening all around me, and I
wasn't worthy of an invitation.

"I was going to ask you," Sully said. "But your roommate said you
guys had plans to watch *America's Next Top Model*."

Flora, holding me back, just like she controlled her poor boyfriend,
forcing him into those inane phone calls. I bristled with fresh irritation.

"Anyway. Buddy was kind of an asshole. Trying to push my head
down, that whole thing. You know. When I didn't want to blow him,
he called me a bitch. So I took something of his. Just check out all the
girls he has in there. I bet he treats them all like shit."

I picked up the phone. It was new, a nicer model than mine. I went
into his text messages, an encyclopedia of girls. Sarah. Nicole. Steph.
Anna. Bridget. Ethics chick. Molly. Jazz.

"Let's fuck with him," she said, fingertips digging into the table like
a cat using a scratching post. "Pick a girl. Send a message. Get him in
trouble."

I didn't hesitate. The impulse to *outdo* was too great. "Okay, I pick
Anna." The last message she had sent was three weeks ago, at four
in the morning. Anna reminded me of somebody. Myself, my skinned

pride as I texted Matt after we were already over. I pictured Jessica French's overplucked eyebrows. This felt, somehow, like a warped version of revenge. This boy hadn't even answered Anna's last text, a pathetic *I thought u were coming?*

I thumbed out a message. "How's this. 'Hey baby, I miss hanging out. Let's hook up again sometime.'"

A snort and a shake of her head, sending unruly blond hair all over. "Come on. I know you can do better. Let's get them to actually meet up."

I deleted what I had written and replaced it with something else. When I read it out loud, Sully slapped the bony knee that poked out from her mangled tights. "That's perfect. I knew you'd be the best at this."

I let her compliment warm me. I stared at the words on the screen before hitting send. *Hey baby, come over later. I've been thinking about you and I need to see you again. Wear that thing you wore last time that I liked. I'll be waiting.*

"Showtime," I said, which prompted a smile.

Briefly, I imagined Flora's reaction, her features pinching in distaste. I didn't care. Flora had never had to figure out that to keep moving up in the hierarchy, you couldn't be content to hover in the same foothold.

The phone went off in my hand almost instantly. Sully grabbed it, then laughed at the response. "This girl is so desperate. She actually just said, *On my way.* Buddy is in for a real surprise."

I only worried for a minute about what would happen to Anna, what Buddy's reaction would be. I learned later that Buddy wasn't even his name—it was the name Sully gave to everybody she hooked up with, a generic placeholder.

"Have you heard of Sex Party at Eclectic?" she said.

"No, what is it?"

"I hear everyone is basically naked and things get crazy. It's this weekend. You're coming with me."

"You're not going to the Hamptons?"

She shook her head. "Fuck the Hamptons. We'll have way more fun here."

It was a better offer than anything Lauren could give me, better than spending a shitty weekend in her beach house lobbing her backhanded compliments.

Sully smirked. "I bet we can find some boys to play with."

She talked about guys like they were toys.

But her favorite playthings were the girls.

7

NOW

To: "Ambrosia Wellington" *a.wellington@wesleyan.edu*
From: "Wesleyan Alumni Committee" *reunion.classof2007@gmail.com*
Subject: Class of 2007 Reunion

Dear Ambrosia Wellington,

From meals at MoCon (RIP) to rituals only Wesleyan grads would understand (like studying in your undies in Olin), you bled red and black. We're counting down the days until we get to catch up in person with you—our alumni—to relive all the old traditions. We can hear your Primal Scream already!

Sincerely,
Your Alumni Committee

The weeks leading up to the reunion are short and tense, excited texts flying between Hadley and Heather. I respond with obligatory *yays* but all I can think about is the note.

I snap at Adrian for almost everything. Not knowing if he should wear a suit to the dinner or if jeans would be okay. Asking if he should pack an umbrella. Asking if we should see a fertility specialist, because it has been six months and I'm still not pregnant. He always brings it up casually, as though he's not expecting anything, but I know he's expecting everything. Like every man, he wants to create a likeness of himself.

"I'm getting worried, that's all," he says. "You're thirty-one. I read somewhere that your egg supply gets cut in half when you turn thirty."

I picture Adrian googling it in bed after I've fallen asleep. My annoyance coils up, a familiar snake. "Don't worry about my eggs. I'm sure I have lots. Maybe the problem is with you."

He doesn't react, just sits on the bed beside his half-packed suitcase—even though he isn't getting the annoying reunion emails, he somehow manages to follow their instructions like an obedient boy. "Maybe it is. But I'm willing to get my guys tested. I told you that months ago. I just want us to have a house full of kids. Little Ambians."

The first time he used that term was at our wedding, in his semidrunk speech at the reception, where he promised both sets of parents that grandkids would be on the way. I stood beside him, face sore from smiling, willing myself to want the one thing that would make him happiest. Adrian was so confident, so sure of us, so certain about our life together. *He's a great guy*, Billie had told me before I walked down the aisle, and I knew she was right. After everything I'd done, I got to be loved by a guy who really was great.

"I want that too." I don't point out the obvious, the lack of a house to fill with kids. We had big plans, once, fevered conversations that lasted all night. *We can travel. We can do anything we want.* But then reality set in. We had an apartment and bills to pay. And after the reality came the resentment, flaring under my skin like a sunburn. Adrian didn't need to go anywhere. He was content with the status quo. His romantic gestures and declarations of love did nothing to quell the anger gestating inside me, its own hard fetus.

I tried to picture what Adrian saw in his head, two toddlers crawling around my parents' backyard in Pennington while we sat on the deck, wineglasses in hand, cooing over how adorable they were. I could taste the wine, smell the steaks on the barbecue, but I just couldn't picture the part he actually cared about—the kids.

"Maybe we need to have more sex." Adrian's hand goes to my thigh. "We aren't exactly regular. You know, Justin told me last time we had beers that he and Hadley are gonna start trying. They want to put down roots."

"Good for them," I say, secretly pissed off that she didn't tell me herself. *Put down roots.* Everyone else feels safe when women are hooked into the ground like trees.

"Yeah," he says. "But when's the last time we did it?"

We used to have sex daily, always spontaneous, all over the apartment. I judged Billie when she told me she and Ryan had a standing Friday-night sex date. Now Adrian and I rarely do it weekly, and sometimes I actively avoid it by pretending I'm asleep.

"Well, let's do it later," I say. "I need to go. I'm heading out to meet Billie."

"It's my night off." His lips bow into a pout. "I thought we could hang out."

"I already made plans." I slip out of my pajama pants and step into a pair of jeans. "I barely ever see Billie."

Adrian sits up on his elbows, hair falling over his eyes. "You text her nonstop. It's like she's in the room with us. You barely ever see me."

"I see you all the time." I suck in and pull up my jeans. "It's not like we could get away from each other in a place this tiny."

"It's not so bad," he says. Then, more softly: "Do you hate our life?"

I meet his eyes as I button my blouse and resent the hurt that I see—the hurt I put there. "I don't hate our life. I just don't want this to be all our life is."

It might be the most honest thing I've said to him in a long time. He leans over and kisses me, hand in my hair, and something stirs inside me, the need to not just be touched but be felt and seen. His other hand migrates into my jeans and instead of making an excuse and telling him later, always some undefined *later*, I let him pull me on top of him.

"You know I love you, right?" His breath on my cheek, my own breathing getting faster.

"I love you too," I say, instead of my typical response. *I know.* Because I do love him. I love the way I'm reflected in his eyes. Marrying Adrian was like looking into a perpetually flattering mirror. He sees me as the person I want to be. I wish I could see that girl as clearly.

Billie and I meet at Broken Land, a Greenpoint bar that we consider the halfway point between us. She's already sitting at the bar when I arrive, glass of wine in her hand, her olive complexion flushed. I like drunk Billie best. She gets loud and flirty and forgets the world she left at home, the husband and kids and Instagram personality. Pictures of our nights out never surface in her online life, and that doesn't make me feel like a dirty secret as much as the only authentic, unfiltered pocket of her existence.

She kisses my cheek. "You're dieting, aren't you? For the reunion? You look skinny."

"No." I pull away. Back at Central, we would skip lunch when we felt bloated and weigh ourselves on my mom's scale, celebrating arbitrary numbers. "I'm just stressed."

"What's there to be stressed about? You didn't do anything wrong."

"I know," I say. "It's just weird. I'm not the same person anymore." Detective Felty would argue otherwise. In blips of panic, I let myself consider that he wrote the note. That he knows about the photo, tucked back inside John Donne where it belongs. That he knows the last words I ever spoke to that boy, and the ones he said to me.

When the bartender comes over, I order a glass of prosecco, then change my mind and get a bottle. If Adrian asks when I get home, I'll tell him I only had one, and it won't be a lie.

"You're going to sleep in that room again," Billie says. "In Dorm Doom. And you haven't told Adrian what happened. He's going to figure it out."

I roll my eyes. "You did not just call it that. It's only a building. Anyway, I booked a hotel, remember?" I ignore what she said about Adrian, because I still hope I won't have to tell him. He'll be distracted all weekend by Justin and Monty and open bars.

Billie grabs my hands. I notice her nail polish, Tiffany blue. I always notice people's nail polish. It's a good indicator of their mental health, as ridiculous as that sounds. Billie's nails are perfect. The day she shows up with red cuticles, angry skin gnawed down, I'll know something is wrong.

"Come on, Amb. I know you better than anyone. Something is up."

In my early days at Wesleyan, Billie wanted me to make friends. Just not best friends. I told her about Sully but not the details.

"I'm stressed out, that's all. Work's crazy busy lately." I squeeze her fingers, just hard enough to be painful, before letting them go.

She takes a sip of her drink, adding a second red-lipped stamp to the rim. When we both waitressed at Villa Francesco's when we were home in Pennington for summers during college, we made fun of women whose lipstick would cling to increasingly empty glasses.

"Are you going to see him?" she says, softer now. "The guy you were madly in love with and refuse to talk about?"

"Buddy," I say, more an exhalation of breath than an actual word. "Of course not."

"Relax," she says. "I'm not saying you're going to sleep with him. And I mean, you know what happened with Colton. We came *this close* the weekend of my bachelorette. And we would have, if it wasn't for his moral compass." She rubs her arms.

"Have you ever thought about messaging him?" I ask. Our bartender pops the cork on my prosecco. It feels like I should be celebrating something.

"To say what? 'Hey, I'm married with two kids now'? Sometimes I wonder about how things would have been different if he were a worse person." She pauses. "I tried to creep him on Instagram. It's private, but his profile picture is of him and a dog. Hopefully that means he isn't married."

"Hopefully? Why, so you have a chance?"

She shrugs. "He can't belong to me. I just don't want him to belong to anyone else, you know?"

I know all too well.

Every time Billie spills part of her soul, I ache to give a bit of mine, just like we did in our Central days, trading secrets in the dark at a thousand sleepovers. She knows I loved a boy called Buddy and that things went awry. I wanted to bring him home for winter break and introduce them.

"He won't be there. Buddy. He isn't going."

"Well, maybe he'll show up. Just keep an open mind, that's all." She swirls the last drops of wine around in her glass. "I'm not saying to cheat. You know I love Adrian. But maybe you need the closure."

I drain part of my glass to keep my mouth from forming the expression it wants to make. I drink more so I can't let myself know if it's a smile or a frown. The truth is gratefully confined to my brain.

He can't show up, thanks to what I did to him.

8

THEN

There was everyone else, and then there were Sully and Flora, the two extremes I bounced between like a rubber ball. Most of the other girls were outwardly nice enough, but I could never relax around them and be myself, even though I didn't know exactly who that was anyway. I worried constantly about what I'd said when I was drunk, how much of my Jersey accent slipped out, and how many dumb stories about Central I told. I cobbled myself together with traits absorbed from the other girls, my personality a mosaic. Maybe what I envied most about Sully was how well her skin fit, how everything about her was interesting or quirky or cool.

I was convinced that nothing about me was inherently interesting or quirky or cool, but I had a skill. I was a good actress, and I could mimic someone enough to tug them into my orbit. Who I was with Sully and who I was with Flora were two entirely different people. And for a while, I was both.

Flora would have been the easy choice. My parents would have approved of her manners and her charm, her perpetual *please* and *thank you*. She was homesick, something she confided to me, especially for her sister. Poppy was four years younger than us, a freshman in high school whom Flora called almost as often as Kevin.

"Poppy wants to come for a visit," Flora said. "I told her all about you. She's super artistic, and she wants to go to Wesleyan too. It's been tough for her since starting high school."

I talked to her briefly, when Flora passed her phone my way. "She's having a bad day. Tell her it gets better," Flora whispered.

"It gets better," I lied.

Flora was safe, a down comforter. She was always *there*. She held my hair back when I threw up violently the morning after drinking in Dora's room and even checked on me between classes. We walked around campus together on cool September evenings, talking about our dreams—I could tell her mine without fearing she would whisper them to the other girls with an eye roll. *Ambrosia actually thinks she can make it in Hollywood.* Her brand of nice wasn't an act, no matter how hard I tried to poke holes and deflate it.

But she worried about me, and her concern was more than just friendly. I chafed against the hints of disapproval that spiked through.

"Where are you going?" she asked me when she saw me getting ready for Sex Party, lacing up the corset top Sully had lent me.

"Just a party," I mumbled.

"Oh," she said, bunny slippers dangling off her bed. It was one syllable, but I unfolded it into a whole book. *Another party. With Sloane.*

"You could come," I said, knowing she wouldn't.

"I have to work on my paper. But call me if you need anything." She held up her phone, knowing I wouldn't.

Where Flora was feather soft, Sully was the black swan wing I was swept beneath. At Sex Party, I stumbled after Sully like a baby deer, halls bleeding with pounding music and porn, couples having sex right out in the open, a Dionysian orgy reincarnated. All of us reduced to animals. It was in a room at Eclectic that night where I first tried cocaine, watching Sully's neck, an elegant question mark bent over a neat line. Embarrassingly, my head was filled with overdose scenes from stupid TV shows Billie and I had watched. There was no room for fear in Sully's shadow. My nostril burned, but I was still alive, more alive than ever.

"So who are you going to hook up with?" Sully asked a few minutes later, as casually as if she wanted to know what I was ordering for lunch. "I'm going for that Buddy in the kitchen. After that, we'll see." She threw her head back.

"I'm not sure yet," I said, clenching my jaw to stop my teeth from chattering. I had to choose someone.

"You'd love my best friend from home," she said, sweeping her pinky finger across her gums. "Evie. She's up for absolutely everything. Fucking wild."

"Cool," was all I could manage. It wasn't *cool*. It was another competition, this time against someone I hadn't even met.

Later, when my nerves had burned off, I was alone with a boy upstairs, broad-shouldered with a California tan. Buddy, I called him, his real name unimportant. I let him reach inside my underwear and pull them down, then press me against a wall plastered with pictures of naked girls. I became one of them, arching my back, his grip on my hair something primal.

The next afternoon, Flora came back from Olin and found me and Sully in our room, my entire body still pulsing like a giant bruise. "I was worried about you guys," she said, immaculate as she perched on her desk chair. "Amb, you didn't tell me you were going to . . . that party."

I didn't know who had told her about Sex Party—almost everyone was at *Lauren's thing*. The night came back in jagged pieces, the boy from the wall, the one after him who snorted a line of coke off my hipbone. Sully, gyrating, her mouth on everyone.

"It was just a party," I said. "Nothing to worry about."

"It was okay." Sully rolled over. "I kind of expected more."

My head spun with how something that seemed like so much to me was nothing to her. We weren't on a level playing field. But just when I thought I should stick to softer terrain, she looped her arm around me. "But Amb made it fun."

A few days after Sex Party, when we were walking back from Mo-Con, Flora said what I knew she was already thinking. "Don't take this the wrong way." She adjusted the dainty gold heart above her breastbone. "But I think Sloane is a bit out of control. I'm afraid she's going to do something crazy. And that you might too, if you're with her."

"She's fine. We both are," I snapped. Flora recoiled like I had smacked her—she had a low tolerance for any sort of disagreement. I learned later that maybe her parents had something to do with it—she never talked about them, maybe because she didn't want me to realize her life wasn't an actual fairy tale.

"I didn't mean it that way," she said. "It's just, I've heard stories about what happens at parties with drunk guys. I don't want anything bad to happen to you."

"It won't," I said, softer. "I know how to handle myself." Her arm slipped under mine, her skin soft and cool.

"I want you to find your Kevin," she said. "I know he's out there. Just be patient." A part of me—the part hammered into all girls that says the right guy is out there—wanted to believe it, because expectations were hard to shake.

But I wasn't waiting for my Kevin. That week, I hooked up with Hunter of the crooked dick again, and snuck another boy into our room for a quickie, his hot breath wilting in my ear, him not giving me so much as a compliment, much less an orgasm. In brief snatches of conversation, I overlaid their names with *Buddy*, because they were as disposable as the used condoms I wrapped in toilet paper and threw in the wicker garbage basket beside my bed.

"See you around," became the line I recited at the end, monotone and bored. But I rarely did. Maybe it was me—at the door, my hand migrated too close to theirs, like it wanted to be held. My body betrayed me in myriad ways.

I made a point of not looking for anyone special, even as a few of the other girls paired off and found boyfriends. Sully made fun of them. "Boyfriends are the universe's way of keeping us tethered," she said. "We're too dangerous otherwise." I nodded in vehement agreement.

But then the universe decided to up the ante.

It was your classic meet-cute, the stuff that made up the cheesy romantic comedies Billie and I used to worship. I was rushing into Olin to meet some of the girls to study and dropped one of the books I was carrying. He picked it up.

Short hair, buttoned up, with a Superman jawline. He looked older, maybe a senior frat boy, hopefully DKE and not Beta. "I believe this is yours," he said.

"Sorry," I said. "I mean, thanks."

"No problem." White teeth. Up close, he looked vaguely familiar. Maybe I had seen him at a party. He could have been one of the two guys from Sex Party, one face blending into the other, and I was suddenly horrified with myself.

"I see you've got John Donne," he said. "John Donne, I know. Practically in the biblical sense. Actually, I'm studying him right now."

"Me too." The words fused together. "Obviously. But I don't know him all that well. Actually, I'm having a really hard time understanding him."

That was a lie. What was there to understand about a dead white guy? They all had one thing on the brain.

He smiled. Those teeth glistened. The moment felt backlit with possibility.

"Sounds like you need my expertise." A cursory glance at his watch, a big blue face on a leather strap. "I can give you my special crash course."

It was a dumb line—even condescending, the implication that I needed anything from him—but I found myself nodding, parched for a boy's undivided attention that wasn't purely sexual. Instead of finding somewhere to sit in Olin, I led him to Foss Hill, passing trees shuddering brown leaves.

"Cool view," he said when we got to the top and sat down.

He really was passionate about John Donne, which was both adorable and kind of sexy. Even though I personally hated John Donne, I liked any guy who could get that enthused about something other than beer and boobs. If he could get horny like that for John Donne, who knew what else he was capable of? He'd be the kind of lover who made you feel like an equal, not an ATM.

"You know more than you're giving yourself credit for," he said. The wind pushed my hair over my face, and he swept it back behind my ear.

"You're smarter than you think. You probably don't know how beautiful you are, either."

It was the *beautiful* I glommed on to, three trilling syllables, their own music. That was the moment I would look back on, and it was such a simple thing. The other boys I had been with weren't in the habit of praising.

"John Donne was a romantic," he said. "He lost everything for the woman he loved."

I held my breath. He was going to kiss me, and I was going to let him. Suddenly Foss Hill seemed like somewhere I could fall in love. Suddenly, ridiculously, I wanted to *be* in love. His thumb grazed my chin, briefly, before he pulled away and checked that stupid watch.

"Shit. I'm out of time. But if you have any other questions about Donne, just email me. I don't mind." He leaned over, scribbled in my notebook: *bigmac10@gmail.com.* I wasn't going to let a lame email address ruin him. It was the kind of thing that could be overlooked, maybe even considered cute later.

"Thanks. I will." My imagination careened away, barreling far into the future. He would let me pick the color scheme for our wedding. He would tell the wedding planner, *Give her whatever she wants.* I would insist on peonies, big white ones that hid in waiting, sweet fat orbs, until they were ready to unfurl their heads like pinwheels. I would insist that I already had everything I wanted.

I texted Billie right away. *I think I met someone?* My body was a live wire, running on *beautiful.* I stopped for lunch at MoCon, and even my shitty salad tasted better somehow. Billie hadn't replied by the time I got back to Butts C, and I needed a reaction. That was when I realized I didn't know his name. I had somehow never asked, and he hadn't asked for mine, either. I recovered quickly from that barb of disappointment. I had his email address—we had just forgotten to introduce ourselves.

I could hear Flora's laugh coming from our room in garish, overly girly bursts, and I decided I would tell her, because her energy was exactly what I needed.

She was on her bed in the fluffy pink bathrobe she wore when she was cold. But she wasn't alone. He was sitting with her, the mystery boy, *my* mystery boy, *beautiful* boy, and for a minute it didn't register, how he knew where I lived, why he was on Flora's bed and why she was okay with it.

"Amb." She waved me in. "There you are. I want you to meet Kevin. He showed up and completely surprised me, can you believe it?"

He turned to me and shock crossed his face, but just barely.

"Hi," I said. For half a beat, I considered saying something like, "We already met." But I didn't.

He didn't either.

"I'm Kevin." His voice was different from the boy on the hill's. More formal, like he was someone else. "Nice to meet you."

"You too," I managed.

Kevin. That was why he had looked familiar, even though he didn't resemble his picture. His hair was shorter, fair skin no longer ravaged by acne. He was a liar, the same as Matt. The same as every guy.

Sully chose that moment to materialize beside me—I had left the door ajar. "Who's this?" she said, strolling in. "You don't go here, or I'd know you already."

"This is my boyfriend, Kevin," Flora said, grabbing his hand. I hated *boyfriend* in her mouth, how it swelled like a bubble. She'd be the type to say *fiancé* and *husband* with too much vigor. "Kevin, this is Sloane."

"Sully, actually." She leaned in to kiss his cheek, her generic greeting, then faced me. "Come over and we'll get ready together." All I could do was nod.

"So this is Amb," Kevin said when she was gone. "I've heard a lot of good things about you." I searched his face until I saw it—the glinting eyes, pleading for my silence.

"Likewise," I said.

Flora wanted me to meet my Kevin, but I never did. I met hers.

9

NOW

To: "Ambrosia Wellington" *a.wellington@wesleyan.edu*
From: "Wesleyan Alumni Committee" *reunion.classof2007@gmail.com*
Subject: Class of 2007 Reunion

Dear Ambrosia Wellington,

Friday is registration day! Check out the official weekend schedule <u>here</u> so that you don't miss a thing. When you check in at Usdan, you'll be able to pick up your meal tickets, itinerary, and key cards to your dorm room.

We look forward to seeing you for the start of what will be an unforgettable weekend.

Sincerely,
Your Alumni Committee

I wanted to drop out of Wesleyan during my first year. I could have started fresh at a different school, or even joined Billie at Miami University. But it would have looked suspicious. So I stayed, and I let my grades plummet until my overall average was in danger of putting me on academic probation. By sophomore year, I refocused and committed to the original reason I applied to Wesleyan—theater, not boys—and felt idiotic for letting myself veer so far off course. It wasn't too late, I told myself. Except when it was time to declare my major, I didn't have the requirements I needed or the motivation to follow through.

"I realized acting isn't for me," I told Hadley and Heather instead of the truth. They knew about Dorm Doom but either didn't believe the rumors or were too ensconced in their student-athlete bubble to care.

And there was another reason I stayed. *He* wasn't coming back—I knew that—but maybe Sully could.

But now, arriving in Middletown, with Adrian easing our rental car into V Lot off Vine Street, I wish I had transferred anywhere else. I wouldn't have this rock in my stomach, this heavy thing pressing down on my insides. *Why now?* I keep wondering. *Why ten years?*

"Nice," Adrian says as we enter campus behind the Nics and walk toward the crest of Foss Hill. "This place has a good vibe. If I had gone here, I definitely would have been inspired to finish school."

I roll my eyes behind my sunglasses. Sometimes he wears his college-dropout status as a badge of honor. If his novel ever gets published—if he ever manages to start it, much less finish it—he'll tell everyone that he doesn't even have a college education, implying that he was too gifted to need one.

"Yeah," I say. "Everything is nice here."

Campus is teeming with people. Several class reunions are happening this weekend, along with commencement on Sunday. I watch the graduates with their parents, who snap photos of the Van Vleck Observatory and the campus panorama from Foss Hill like tourists. I stare at lazy sprawls of girls and wonder who did the worst thing and who struggled to keep up.

Foss Hill offers an unfettered view of Andrus Field, with the back side of Olin cast in shade. Olin was always my favorite building on campus, stately and proud. I've wondered so often what would have happened if I hadn't been there the day I met Kevin.

"Is that where you watched football games?" Adrian asks. It's a legitimate question, but I just laugh.

"Football wasn't a big thing," I say. *We played other games.*

"So where were your dorms?" Adrian says. "I'm still bummed we can't stay there. Justin said they all got rooms. I guess they can't assign roommates, but they try to put you near people you know."

"It's too bad it didn't work out," I say. "I'll give you the full tour later."

I lead Adrian into Usdan. People are milling everywhere, clustered in knots. I expect them to recognize who I am. Some of them turned on me after it happened, dog-piled on the AW thread on the ACB—the Anonymous Confession Board, where spores of gossip bred into battlefields. Some of them swore it was my fault, somehow, or even me who did it. Others just know I did something.

We wait in line to register. Tara Rollins is across the lobby, her hair twisted into a milkmaid braid she can't pull off. I grab my phone out of my purse and send a text to Hadley and Heather. *Are you guys here?*

"Ambrosia." I whip around. It's not Sully, of course—she would never call me by my full name. It's Lauren. In second semester of freshman year, she started a rumor about what I did at the Double Feature party. I never hung out with her again, but here she is, leaning in for a hug.

"Hey. Lauren. Good to see you." I'm surprised at how easily my voice slips into the fakeness I cultivated here.

She pulls away, her smile wider than it ever was back then. She's faking too. "I was literally just thinking about you and wondering what you've been up to. I thought I sent you an invite to the group I made on Facebook, but maybe you never got it."

Maybe you never sent it. I shrug, flashing back to the Hamptons weekend and my non-invite. Lauren's power was always exclusion, her tool a chisel used to shape the group and excise the fat. Speaking of which—she has put on a good deal of weight since I last saw her, a fact I let myself feel smug about.

"This is my husband, Adrian." He enthusiastically pumps her hand. Adrian is all about first impressions. He must have read somewhere that a strong handshake means everyone will like you.

"Hey," he says. "It's so cool to meet more of Amb's friends."

Thankfully, Lauren doesn't correct him.

"Nice to meet you, Adrian. I should go find my husband. I met him here, actually," she says, turning to me. "We were just friends, though. Do you remember Jonah Belford?"

"I don't think so. But that's great."

I do remember Jonah Belford, or more accurately, I remember the night we spent together sophomore year, both of us wasted at a WestCo naked party. I had expected to see Sully there—she never used to miss any event where the dress code was no clothes—but instead I found Jonah, or he found me, telling me I had a great body. We ended up in his room, where he asked me about Dorm Doom while he was still inside me. "Come on. Is it true?" he grunted. "You can tell me."

"Yeah, we're doing well," Lauren says. "How did you two meet?"

Adrian takes a deep breath, ready to thank the Internet, but I cut him off. "It's a long story. Maybe we can catch up later." I can't handle any more of Lauren's act—nice suits her as badly as it suited me. Mercifully, it's almost our turn to register and pick up our itinerary and the name tags I don't plan on wearing.

"Definitely," says Lauren. "I'm sure we'll see lots of each other. Oh, hang on, I have to show you the kids. We have three. And I never used to think I wanted any." She whips out her phone and swipes through pictures. Three blond heads, each one slightly smaller than the next. "Between these guys and my job, I swear, I solve other people's problems all day."

"What do you do for a living?" Adrian asks. He's playing into what she wants—an excuse to brag. I already know what Lauren does for a living because I creeped her on Facebook years ago. She's a psychologist in Brooklyn. There's a *Dr.* in front of her name. The thought of Lauren inside anybody's head is enough to serrate my skin.

"I'm a psychologist," Lauren says. "I work with kids, mostly."

The *kids* makes me snap to attention. That was Flora's dream. Lauren was always so drawn to Flora. Maybe because Flora made her feel special in a way that nobody else did.

"That's so cool," Adrian says. "I love kids. I can't wait to be a dad." I wish he would stop talking.

"Hopefully soon," Lauren says pointedly. As if the problem—of course, she sees a problem—lies with me. I want to defend myself, defend *us*, but she doesn't give me a chance. "I almost forgot. Guess who's here?"

Don't say her name, I want to demand, but I'm not even sure which *her* I'm referring to. "Who?"

"Ella. I mean, I knew she was coming, but wait till you see her. She looks incredible. And Gemma, apparently she was in an episode of *Grey's Anatomy*. Isn't that amazing?"

I nod. "Amazing." Lauren is pushing my buttons because she can. Because she knows Gemma graduated as a theater major, and I didn't.

I turn toward the lady at the folding table in front of us. "Ambrosia and Adrian Turner," I say.

"Ambrosia. What a lovely name. Oh, there you are. I have you in Nicolson Hall. Here's your key cards, welcome packet, meal tickets, and an updated schedule for the weekend. Don't forget to fill out your name tags."

"No, we're not in the Nics," I say. "We're staying at a hotel."

She peers at the paper on the table, creases forming near her hairline. "Not according to what's here, sweetie."

I rub my hands against my jeans. "There must be some kind of mistake."

The lady laughs. "With a name like yours, I doubt there are many mistakes."

Adrian is already reaching for the key cards. "Awesome. We can cancel the hotel, babe. You must have booked this and forgot about it." That's the thing about Adrian. He never considered I wasn't telling the truth when I told him the dorms were full. Just like he doesn't know I'm lying now.

"I don't—" I begin, but there's a line building behind us and Lauren is still lingering, amused. "Fine. Let's just go."

The Nics isn't Dorm Doom. I lived there sophomore year and appreciated the inner door between me and my roommate, a red-head named Veronica who wore only rock T-shirts, Jim Morrison's face stretched across her boobs, and called everyone "dude." Nothing especially memorable happened to me there, but suddenly it's all too much. I turn around, looking for an empty corner, an exit strategy, and that's when I lock eyes with the person I really didn't want to see.

Flora Banning doesn't say anything to me. Her mouth is curved upward, her face porcelain, her hair the same white blond, pushed off her forehead with a headband.

"You haven't changed a bit," I murmur, but quietly enough that even Adrian can't hear it.

"You okay, Amb?" he says. "We should go get our stuff and get unpacked."

My throat is dry. It's a staring contest between me and Flora and she won't look away first, so finally I do.

"I'm fine," I manage, reaching for his hand. "Let's get out of here."

When I turn around, Flora is watching us. Watching me.

10

THEN

I called Billie when Kevin went home the next day. I wanted to hear the story out loud the way it should have gone. Where I met a boy at the library and he called me beautiful. Billie would understand.

I didn't mention Kevin's name or what came after Foss Hill. I didn't mention what I found in my room, late the night before, after partying with Sully. The rustling sheets and muffled laughs, the moving lump that was Flora's and Kevin's interlocked bodies. I didn't mention how I couldn't stop picturing them, twined like a damp braid.

"So how are you going to find him now?" Billie asked. "You met him for a reason, and you need to see him again." Her optimism was jarring, the anti-Sully.

"I'm not sure," I said. "I have his email address. Or maybe I'll run into him."

When I looked up, Flora was standing in our doorway with two mugs. Actual mugs, not just the paper cups she usually brought back from the cafeteria to mix her vegan hot chocolate in. A white marshmallow peak jutted out from one like a little Mount Everest.

I didn't know how much she had heard. But she kept smiling—she was always *smiling*—and when I put my phone down she sat on my bed and handed me the mug with the marshmallow.

"What's this?" I said.

"Hot chocolate. I thought we could have matching mugs. Mine says *Best*, yours says *Friend*. Although if you want *Best*, you can have it instead. I just gave you *Friend* because it's the one with the marshmallow. I can't eat those because of the gelatin."

"That's really nice," I said. We weren't even that close. We talked about our sisters, she talked about her boyfriend, she asked me about Matt and I lied. We ate together sometimes and slept five feet away from each other and she painted my nails and braided my hair. But we didn't have what I had with Sully. The headiness, the excitement. The mug wasn't a gift. It was a way for Flora to keep me in her thrall, check *college best friend* off the list she had created in her busy head. I wondered, *Why me?*, whether it was sheer proximity or something else.

"Were you out late? I didn't hear you come in." Her flush was candy pink.

"I tried to be quiet." I took a sip that burned my mouth, wondering how she would react if I told her to stop keeping tabs on my nights out. "I didn't want to wake you." I watched her face for a sign of embarrassment—that I'd heard her and Kevin having sex.

"I miss him already." She leaned back on my pillow, her bun squished against the wall. "But I'm so relieved that he came. It's hard being away from each other, as much as I believe we'll make it through. Sometimes I worry about what he's doing without me."

"That's normal," I said. Maybe Flora's *nice* was a homing device, pressing into Kevin's conscience when she sensed him sniffing around. I watched my giant marshmallow bob in my hot chocolate and fought the sudden urge to drown it.

"I don't know. I can be paranoid." She took a sip from her mug. "But it was definitely like absence makes the heart grow fonder, you know?"

I nodded, but I didn't know. Nobody had ever grown fonder of me after being away. I had gotten dumped by my ninth-grade boyfriend, Wesley, when I went away to a summer performing arts camp in Newark. Wesley had kissed me fiercely and told me he would miss me like crazy, but when I got back and skipped the Kunkel Park After

Dark movie night to surprise him at his house, he stared blankly from the safety of his foyer and said he thought we'd decided to just be friends.

"He's coming back for Halloween," she said. "I want to do a couple's costume. Scarlett O'Hara and Rhett Butler."

I stored that fact away. I would get the chance to see him again.

"That's fun," I said. "I forgot about Halloween."

"It's my favorite," Flora said, sliding her feet into her slippers. "I love dressing up and being somebody besides myself."

It was that statement that sharpened my mood, made my back bristle like an animal's. Flora had everything, including the audacity to want to be someone else.

"Maybe you and Sloane can take us to a Halloween party," she said. "I want Kevin to get to know my friends. And you're my girl, you know?"

The hot chocolate was too sweet, and I wasn't Flora's girl. It was too much responsibility. I didn't need a friend like Flora, whom I would always feel slightly inferior beside, who would impose a standard I would forever fall short of meeting.

"Yeah," I said weakly. "I know."

I had no plans to actually email Kevin. It was satisfying, somehow, my private knowledge that he wasn't the saint Flora made him out to be. If he were, he wouldn't have given me his email address. He would have acknowledged to Flora that we had met. More likely, we never would have met at all, and he certainly wouldn't have spent time with me on Foss Hill, time that was becoming wispier in my memory with each passing hour.

As my slice of reality with Kevin faded, Flora's day with him was dissected in detail, over and over. "Oh, I forgot to tell you what Kevin said," she exclaimed in MoCon. She didn't even wait for me to ask before launching into a parade of plushy facts. "He said he keeps my picture on his nightstand so I'm the last thing he sees before he goes to sleep."

It was a barb, hooking into me, a reminder that I had nobody. I tried to ignore it. But she went on.

"Kevin looks at the stars at night and makes a wish for me. He said he feels connected to me that way."

I wanted to tell her to shut up about Kevin. I couldn't even bring myself to look at her ever-widening smile and flushed cheeks, the picture of happiness. I had once felt that way—I remembered Billie rolling her eyes and jokingly telling me I was *insufferable* when Matt and I were together.

Maybe that was why I found myself in front of my laptop three days after Kevin's visit, his *beautiful* only a faint echo in my head. I would poke at the connection Flora wouldn't shut up about until it predictably capsized. She had said something that I'd glommed on to. *Sometimes I worry about what he's doing without me.* She should have been worried. It was irresponsible to trust people like Flora did.

I used John Donne's Wikipedia page to craft a message that would make me sound effortlessly smart yet casual. *Hey, it's Amb! Thanks again for your help with my essay—I got an A!* I peppered the email with references to John Donne's work, clever lines Kevin would appreciate. Then I hit send.

It took him two days to reply. Two days during which I checked my email incessantly, morbidly curious to see if my laptop had anything to offer from bigmac10. After I came back from dinner at Summerfields with Sully and Gemma on Friday, it was there.

Hey Amb, it was great meeting u. JD is my specialty. I'm sure u rocked that essay—I can tell, ur smart as hell.

He didn't mention Flora. I was *smart as hell*, but the message wasn't flirty.

I could have chosen not to write back. But now I was invested. I wanted to see how far he would go, how much of himself he would reveal through a computer screen.

I emailed him back, but this time I didn't bring up our mutual friend John Donne. I bitched about my Introduction to Playwriting class and Professor Ogden, with his beady eyes. I told him I wanted to act. I was testing him, seeing what he would give me in return. I had watched Sully interact with enough boys to learn her methods. She treated them like transactions. Give a bit—lean in, laugh at a joke, let a bra strap slip down a bare shoulder. Get a lot back. With Sully, the returns never diminished.

He wrote back almost immediately. I pictured him hunched over his keyboard. His bed was almost too small for him, too full of boy.

Bad teachers suck. Yours sounds like a dick. What's it like being a theater major? Sounds pretty cool. I can see u as an actress—u have the look for it. I'm pre-law but I wish I was doing something cooler with my life. I don't think my parents would like that very much though and they're the ones paying for all this. lol

I ignored the *lol*. I hated cell phone lingo, the absence of actual sentences, the abbreviations. Under my bed at home in Pennington, I had a box of letters my grandpa Wellington wrote to my grandma while he was in the army. Life and death, urgency, all there in his stilted handwriting. *My beloved*, he called her. I ignored the *lol* because Kevin had confided in me. I doubted Flora was an outlet. She trapped him in her giant angel wings, denying his dark parts entry.

I got bolder. *I had to really fight mine to let me come here. But I figured, I have to go after things I want. Can't wait for them to come to me.*

It was too much, I decided right after I sent it. It was obvious I was baiting him, beckoning him toward a line he wouldn't cross.

But his response was fast. It was Friday night. Didn't he have somewhere to be? I was supposed to meet Sully later—there was a concert at Eclectic. Suddenly the idea of leaving my room was exhausting. Kevin was giving me more attention than anyone at Eclectic would. It had been so long since a boy actually listened.

Let me guess. U R a youngest child too. Youngest children are always willing to do whatever it takes (I'm no exception ;)

He was flirting with me—I was sure of it. I whipped out one of the spiral notebooks I used to take notes during class and jotted down, in bullet points, *Youngest child. Pre-law.*

My sister, Toni, is two years older than me. She got the good nose and the science brain.

It was risky, pointing out my own shortcomings. I wanted to pull the email back from the void. I would be another girl to him, insecure and obsessed with looks. I needed to be somebody else.

Don't be so hard on yourself. U have a great nose. Actually, ur whole face is great

I practically choked on the saliva building in my mouth. He was picturing me right now. Maybe his hand was detouring into his pants. I had the power.

Before I could think up a reply—the pressure was on to make it both witty and confident, self-aware but slightly self-deprecating—Flora barged in. She was on her cell phone and it was her Kevin laugh, sweet and girly.

"So you had lunch with Adam," she said into the phone, then looked at me with an apologetic smile. I wondered how long they had been on the phone, him carrying on conversations with both of us. She was policing who he ate with, making sure she knew where he was.

I typed out a response that was raw and real. I couldn't imagine Flora voicing her fears like this.

Sometimes it's like everyone expects me to be someone else. Nobody asks who I am. Nobody in my life ever puts in the effort like I do. Maybe it's like that for you, too. So tell me what you really want to do with your life.

If he wrote back while he was on the phone with Flora, it meant something. I needed this, the victory over a girl better designed than me. The longer I waited, the dumber I felt. I was constructing a fairy tale in my head, trying to build a whole palace where I didn't even have enough to work into a straw hut.

Then the reply came in, and it was worth the wait.

Typical story, dad wanted Thomas and me to become lawyers like him and make a bunch of money and buy big houses and have a couple kids each. Thomas was cool with it, because he wants to be rich. I just want someone to understand me. Can u keep a secret? I'm more into writing and poetry. Sometimes I think I should be a writer, but then I talk myself out of it.

My whole body thrummed, electrified. It was less a secret and more a gauntlet, gently lobbed to see how I would respond. I picked my words carefully.

You should totally do it. What's holding you back? Just start writing in your spare time. I bet you're super talented.

Lol. U R way too nice. The other problem is, I don't know what to write about. My life is like this wheel and I sometimes hate it and just wanna escape it but don't know how

He wanted to be understood, to be seen for who he was. I started to feel like Kevin somehow saw me. And there was no greater relief than knowing I wasn't invisible.

I totally get it. Maybe this is weird, but I feel like we understand each other. You can talk to me any time you feel like you need an escape.

When he didn't reply, I chewed my fingernails off. I was savage. I gnawed until it hurt, until the spongy surface under my nails was exposed in all its raw, red glory.

Flora's phone call continued. I sat there in the dark, on my bed, her occasional giggle puncturing the monotony of her continuous talking. Anger was a ball in my stomach, big and hot. She thought the world owed her a Kevin, which was why she didn't deserve him.

I refreshed my inbox at least ten times. When a new message finally came in, I almost dumped my laptop onto the floor in my scramble to get a firm hold on it. Kevin's reply was the validation I needed. *I was right when I met u. Your different. I think we can help each other but lets keep this between us for now ok? Other people wouldn't get it.*

Your different. I ignored his bad grammar. He was in a rush to type his truth, and it could be forgiven. I knew exactly what he meant by the last part. He didn't want Flora to know. I shivered. This was something solely ours.

When I realized what time it was, I put my laptop away and waved goodbye to Flora, who was still on the phone. Then I knocked on Sully's door. "Come in," she yelled over her music.

"You're late," she said from her stance on her bed, cross-legged in a tank top with no bra.

"Sorry. I was just trying to get some work done first." I closed the door behind me.

"Whatever." Sully eyed me critically. "What's up with your hair, did you just get fucked?"

I shook my head. "No. I just got too busy to straighten it." I couldn't tell by her expression if she was amused or disgusted.

"You're weird tonight," she shouted later, when we were thumping to a rock cover, bodies crashing around us. A group of boys alternately stared and pointed, as if we were a different species. They didn't *see* me, just the acreage of my sweat-slicked skin.

"I know," I said. "Sorry. I just have a lot on my mind."

"Tell me it's not a guy," she deadpanned, gripping my wrist. "Because they're not worth ruining everything."

"No." I wasn't ready to mention Kevin, and besides, I was stuck on her forceful *everything*, an unexpected dagger of vulnerability, and with it the knowledge that I had finally secured my foothold.

"Good," she said, leaning her cheek against my shoulder.

I didn't consider how dangerous it was that our existence was founded on her well-cloaked fear. That there wasn't anything to lose until she was afraid of losing me.

11

NOW

To: "Ambrosia Wellington" *a.wellington@wesleyan.edu*
From: "Wesleyan Alumni Committee" *reunion.classof2007@gmail.com*
Subject: Class of 2007 Reunion

Dear Ambrosia Wellington,

   Now that you're back, your old dorms are a great place to start the festivities. Remember the debauchery that went down? We all went a little crazy back then. Let's see who can still party like there are no consequences!

Sincerely,
Your Alumni Committee

We're staying on the first floor at the Nics, in a two-room double, the same setup I had with Veronica in sophomore year. I text Hadley and Heather to ask which dorm they're in, but they don't reply.

   As soon as we're in our room, Adrian presses me against the door. I kiss him back, but I don't close my eyes. And that's how I notice that the inner door leading into the second room is ajar.

   I rub Adrian's shoulders and slip past him, nudging the door open. I see the suitcase in front of the twin bed, a black-and-white checked pattern on wheels. Someone else has been here. Someone else is staying too.

Adrian pokes his head in after me. "Looks like we have a roommate."

"I thought Wesleyan didn't assign roommates," I murmur, but I should have seen it coming. I turn to face Adrian, my body hot and clammy at once. "I'm suddenly not feeling well. Maybe we should go."

Adrian fuses a kiss to the top of my head. "I think you're just nervous. But you shouldn't be. You look hot." His lips trail down my neck. "We can't go. It hasn't even started."

Exactly, I want to say.

The door to the hallway swings open with a click and there she is, exactly the same as I remember her. Sully.

Her hair is still long and she's teenage skinny in dark jeans and a tank top. Her eyebrows are her signature heavy slashes, lips curved in a perpetual smirk. She has the nerve to look shocked, her eyes wide, like she's as surprised as I am that we're in the same room. She leans against the doorframe, scuffing her ankle boots.

"So it was you who sent it." Hearing her speak is the most jarring part. I forgot how her voice sounded—its hypnotic pull, the spell its range cast on everyone.

Then I actually process what she said. "No. I didn't—" But I can't say more, because Adrian is standing beside me, expectant, bridging the gap with his predictable handshake.

"Sent what, babe? Hey. I'm Adrian, Amb's husband."

Sully's mouth forms a megawatt smile. "I'm Sully. Nice to meet you. And she didn't send anything. It's an inside joke."

"Wait. So you guys know each other?"

"You could say that," she says. "We both lived in the Butts, freshman year."

"Roommates?" Adrian says.

"We should have been," Sully answers before I can. "We did everything together."

"Cool," Adrian says. "I want to hear all about it."

Sully flicks a glance at me, and I know what she's thinking. *You naughty girl. You haven't told him anything.*

"You will," she says, lilting, flirtatious, so *Sully*. "You have all weekend to hear about the trouble we got into."

Adrian starts telling one of his own stories—one I've already heard about his freshman-year roommate, who made money by writing essays for other people—and I stare at Sully, at the contours of her face. I'm not scared as much as unbearably sad, lamenting the reality Sully and I were supposed to share. Getting photos in our graduation gowns, moving to LA and going to auditions, being each other's date to the Oscars. It's not just all gone—it never happened.

"Adrian," I say. "I think I left my charger in the car. Do you mind getting it? The parking lot is basically right behind us."

"Yeah, babe. No worries. I'll let you guys catch up a bit." He pulls on a baseball cap and heads out, car keys jingling in his hand. I almost don't want him to leave—I should be keeping him on a very tight leash—but it's more dangerous in this room right now than outside of it, my past blistering between us.

Sully pulls the door shut behind him and arches her back against it. She reaches inside her purse and fishes out a lipstick. "If I didn't know any better, I'd think you wanted to get me alone."

She's talking to me in the same tone she did back then. Amused, never serious, even when she should have been. Her eyes sear into me. The crazy thing is, I can feel myself being freshly drawn into the trance she creates, even though I know what she's capable of.

"I got this." I grab my purse and extract the note from its envelope. *"You need to come. We need to talk about what we did that night.* What is there to talk about? You made your feelings about it pretty goddamn clear."

She turns her back and strides into her room. I watch her unzip her luggage and rifle through it, emerging with an envelope. "Explain this." She presses it into my hands. I open the card, even though I know what it's going to say.

The same note, with the envelope addressed to her. Sloane Sullivan, in calligraphy. I catch a glimpse of her address—Manhattan. My heart skitters. She's nearby—we could have passed each other on the street so many times.

"I didn't write this," I say.

"Well, neither did I."

We stare at each other, each seeing who will uncoil and strike first. I finally relent. "Nobody else was there."

She laughs, sharp and humorless. "Everyone else was there. Are you kidding me? Half of those girls saw you go into the bathroom with him. The other half thought they saw me."

"But it's been so long. Who would send this now?"

She shrugs. Her jawline is sharp, her neck thin. "I guess whoever did wanted to get us in the same room together. And needed a good reason for it."

I shake my head. "How did they even know we'd show up this weekend?"

"Because they knew we'd come for each other," she says, as if she never sloughed me off like dead skin.

"What do they want from us?" I stare at my jeans, dizzy. Sully is right. Everyone else was there. We weren't careful.

Somebody knows. Somebody has known for a long time.

"It's pretty obvious," Sully says. "They want the truth."

12

THEN

My emails with Kevin continued over the weekend, details about our lives fired back and forth like a conversation. What had started as an experiment—or so I told myself— was quickly becoming addictive. Kevin was hundreds of miles away, but my interactions with him were more substantial than the ones I'd had with any boys on campus.

I learned that Kevin had struggled with his weight as a preteen until he tried out for football, the origin of his metamorphosis. I liked picturing young Kevin, soft-shelled, unaware of the power he was coming into. He told me he had woken up early that morning to write and asked if maybe one day I would read the story he was working on.

I know u will be honest with me. U have the best sense of humor. Whoever said girls cant be hot and funny and smart at the same time never met u ;)

Where my confidence had been stripped to marrow in the aftermath of Matt, Kevin was gently adding layers, building me back up. I told him about the acting roles I wanted. Not America's sweetheart, the endearingly clumsy girl who made men fall in love, but gritty, ugly parts. A shaved head, wasting away for one role, fattening up for another. A chameleon, they would call me.

U would be great at that, he wrote. *Just don't forget me when you become this huge movie star OK?* I ignored the *U*. He was holding up a mirror to me, but instead of pointing out my flaws, he was highlighting the good things.

I saved the emails in a KM folder in my inbox, which I revisited daily to read our entire exchange. It surprised me that what I thought must have been hundreds of messages was in reality only a handful.

The one subject that hadn't come up was Flora. I wanted to inject her into a message, just to see what Kevin's reaction would be. Maybe Flora was a floodgate. Once I brought her up, we would both start throwing her flaws into the void. I would tell Kevin about her thinly veiled judgments. He would admit that being away from her was freeing.

Two nights in a row, Kevin was on the phone with Flora and emailing me at the same time. Maybe I should have been insulted, but I was exactly the opposite. Girls compete against each other, like the sunflowers my mom tried to plant in her garden, the ones that never grew. She planted them too close together and they all vied for the same sun, choked green stems and sulking yellow faces. Flora was wilting, and I was about to be in bloom.

When a certain question came up, my body thrummed. *How are u single?*

My high school boyfriend cheated, I typed quickly. *I don't trust guys.* I almost stopped myself from sending it. I didn't want my value in his eyes to diminish—I needed the version of me that Kevin saw to actually exist.

His response made me tear up. *Hes an idiot Amb. Seriously u r so amazing and cool and if he didn't see that he doesnt deserve u. Don't settle for something less.*

On Monday, I told Billie about the emails but not who Kevin actually was. I called him Buddy, just like Sully called her revolving door of boys, the floppy-haired ones she hooked up with who kept coming by Butts C, waiting for her to acknowledge a connection that wasn't there. They craved her the same way they only needed one taste of me. But I didn't care anymore. I meant something to Kevin.

"You need to see him in person," Billie said. "I mean, great that you guys email, but don't you want to meet up? I can't believe you haven't run into him yet."

"It's a big school," I said. It really wasn't, but I didn't want to say that he went to Dartmouth. Part of me wanted to tell her everything. Billie would be wary that Kevin had a girlfriend, but she would be happy I'd found someone I felt good about. But I stayed quiet, because I was afraid she would think of Kevin as just another cheating Matt.

"Okay," Billie said. "But one day someone won't reply, and then what? Emails are too easy to ignore. If it were me, I'd do something to make sure he wasn't forgetting about me."

Suddenly it was like I had gotten in too deep, too fast. Nothing could actually happen with Kevin. He was Flora's boyfriend. But what I had with him felt so real, and the idea of giving it up made me sick. Maybe this was my love story, and it just wasn't going to be easy.

"I'll see," I told Billie. "Maybe you're right."

That night, Kevin sent an email that seemed like a sign. He wrote: *It's crazy how much u get me. If u were here we would hang out, too bad u aren't doing theater here.* It was a turning point. I could back away, or I could finish whatever it was I had started.

I rewrote and erased the same words several times before settling on something I liked. Something that demanded he answer. *We aren't all that far away—maybe I can visit sometime.*

I waited for his reply, but it never came. He was awake—Flora was still talking to him. I writhed with nerves and irritation. How did she have so much to say?

I convinced myself he was crafting the perfect response. When Flora finally hung up, I knew it was only a matter of time before his message came in. The more time passed, the more certain I was that he was writing something meaningful.

"Want to watch a movie?" Flora said, reaching for her slippers. "It's nice that you're staying in tonight."

I wanted to retaliate somehow, but it wasn't the time to strike a blow. I fixated on her nails, shrimp pink with white dots.

"I have a lot of work to do. Another time, though."

I must have refreshed my email a hundred times that night, clicking obsessively, my fingers stiff on my keyboard. I was pissed off more at myself than at Kevin—why was I so hung up on him, of all people?

When I woke up in the morning, my laptop was between my back and the wall like a neglected lover. Adrenaline surged through my body, making me shoot up like a human exclamation mark. His message would be waiting for me.

But nothing was there.

By the third day, the wait was driving me insane. He was still talking to Flora; her voice was the soundtrack to my nights as I attempted to study. In a recurring fantasy that played out in my head, Flora would be stunned silent by Kevin's sudden declaration that he wasn't in love with her anymore.

Sully dragged me to a party in Clara's room, all of us drinking Stoli and smoking pot, Sully twirling around, convincing me to go with her to a different party when she got bored. No matter how much she claimed to think the lacrosse boys at Beta were terrible, she kept going back to them. Maybe she craved validation just as much as the rest of us.

"Who are you going to hook up with tonight?" she said. "What about that Jordan guy? He said you had nice tits."

Jordan, who had indeed told me I had nice tits, passed out shortly after my bra came off. Another Wesleyan boy who didn't see me.

"I'm really tired," I said. "Maybe I should just go home." Suddenly I was exhausted. I had been at Wesleyan less than two months and it felt in that moment like years.

My excuse prompted a glare. Sully wasn't used to being told no.

"What? You can't leave me. We'll only stay another hour." Her nails dug into the skin on my arm.

"It's just—I don't know, I guess I don't want to party right now."

I wanted to tell her about Kevin, but I knew I couldn't. Boys were her accessories, something she swapped out as often as her underwear. She wouldn't understand.

"You're right," she said, nodding, and I let relief momentarily flood me. "This party sucks. Let's do something totally crazy. Have you had a threesome before?"

I gaped at her. "No. Have you?"

"Of course." She dragged her thumb across my lip. "With Evie and this guy. We took a bunch of ecstasy first. It wasn't a big deal." She stared at the ceiling and adjusted her choker. "I told her about you, you know. I think she's jealous."

It was the verbal equivalent of a whip on my skin, keeping me climbing, letting me know that the stakes would always get higher. I was sure Sully wished Evie were here instead of me.

"I can't tonight," I said. "I'm sorry."

She finally let go of my arm and pulled her hair over her shoulder. "I guess I'll find someone else who actually wants to hang out with me." The steel in her voice was unmistakable.

"You know I do," I said. "I think I'm stressed about midterms. We can do something tomorrow, okay?" I realized as I said it that I never spearheaded our plans.

"Maybe," she said quietly before turning away.

I left her at Beta, slinking back to Butts C by myself. It wasn't a fight, exactly, but I had done something wrong, smudged a line I hadn't even fully known was there. With each step, I fought the urge to turn around.

Flora was still awake when I got home, cross-legged on her bed in her fleece pajamas. "Amb. You'll never believe this." Her voice trembled.

This was it. Kevin had dumped her and she was in denial, because Flora wasn't capable of sadness or anger.

"What happened?" I said, suddenly breathless, desperate to check my email.

"Kevin wrote a short story about me."

It was less a punch in the gut and more a total disembowelment.

"Apparently he's always loved writing, but he never told anyone. So today he sends me this email explaining how his creativity is getting stifled, and he needed to not be afraid of what would happen and write what was in his heart. Isn't that the most romantic thing you've ever heard? Anyway, he attaches this story he's working on and asks if I'll read it, since it's about us. Well, he didn't say that, and the girl in the story is named Clarissa, but she's me. I swear, I actually died."

I wish you had. I would never get so lucky. It was a terrible thought. I willed my face into the appropriate degree of interest.

"And you know what? The story is actually really good. The way he described me? Like, the depths of his feelings are seriously infinite."

I wanted to wrap my hands around Flora's dainty neck and choke the *infinite* out of her.

"I can't believe he kept this from me, that he wants to be a writer. But nobody else knows. It means a lot that he told me first."

It took every cell in my body not to scream in her face that he didn't tell her first, he told *me* first.

"What made him start writing?" I asked, needing to say something.

Flora stared at her fingernails. Tiny pink hearts, painstakingly applied to each one. She had way too much patience. She even slept in manicure gloves—they sat next to her bed, in the prestige position most of us gave to our phones or boxes of condoms.

"He said he finally asked himself what was holding him back and couldn't come up with a good enough answer for not trying."

What's holding you back? He hadn't asked himself that question. I had asked him.

That was when I realized Clarissa might not have been Flora at all. She was *me*.

"That's amazing," I said. I was already putting it together. Kevin wasn't going to send me the story first—it was too much, too soon. So he'd sent it to Flora, her softness the ideal dress rehearsal for his creation.

"I can make us hot chocolate," she said. "I didn't expect you home yet. Is everything okay with you and Sloane?"

I didn't want vegan hot chocolate in my *Friend* mug or tiny hearts on my fingernails. I wanted to pick off her niceness like a scab, certain there was something bloody underneath it.

"Yeah. We're fine." I sat down on my bed and reached for my laptop. I had to see what my own email held. When there were no new messages, I wanted to hurl the computer at the wall. "I'd love to read it sometime," I said. "I'm a sucker for love stories." I twitched with the urgency to see his words.

But Flora surprised me. She crossed her arms, becoming a fleece shield. "I mean—I kind of want to be alone with it for a bit, you know? And I'm not sure Kevin would like it if I shared his work with anyone else."

"Of course." *I'm not anyone else. I'm fucking Clarissa.* I was right. Flora hadn't learned to share any better than the rest of us.

I hit refresh one last time, a Hail Mary tossed into the universe, and that was when I saw it. The message that would change my life.

Yeah it would be sweet if u came to visit sometime. ;)

The smile cracked my face. It wasn't just another email, another *good night Amb.*

It was an invitation.

13

NOW

To: "Ambrosia Wellington" *a.wellington@wesleyan.edu*
From: "Wesleyan Alumni Committee" *reunion.classof2007@gmail.com*
Subject: Class of 2007 Reunion

Dear Ambrosia Wellington,
    Join us at Russell House for a picnic lunch and games on the lawn. It's
the first official gathering to kick off the weekend, so come hungry—and
armed with your best campus stories. We all have them, so don't hold
back!

Sincerely,
Your Alumni Committee

Sully stands on our balcony, staring into the trees separating us from
Vine Street. "Did you see the girls?"

"Not yet. Just Lauren. She got fat." It's mean, but maybe I never
stopped being mean. Sully just draws it out of me like poison.

Sully laughs and lights a cigarette. "She was always fat. But no, I
mean the girls. The grads. They look so young. I can't believe it used
to be us."

But it wasn't us. By then, our friendship was long over.

"I was sure you sent the note," I say. "But if it wasn't you and wasn't me, there's someone else it could have been. Felty."

She taps her finger on her cigarette. "Felty. He had a hard-on for solving crimes. Do you think he's still a cop?"

"Yeah, he's still a cop in Middletown. He got promoted to captain a few years ago."

"He put on a tough front," Sully says. "But he's, like, a big teddy bear."

I shake my head, the breeze rippling my hair. There was nothing remotely cuddly about Felty. "He hated me. I could see him snapping."

I've had the same nightmare ever since I googled Felty, the one where he comes for me. I wake up rigid, arms at my sides like a corpse, not sweating or thrashing in my sheets, and it makes me wonder if that's how it would be if he did come for me. If I'd be all out of fight.

"I don't think he hated you," Sully says. "He wanted to fuck you."

"You thought every guy wanted to fuck me."

"Well, most of them did." She holds my gaze. "I forgot how much fun you used to be." I need to look away—I should look away—but I'm transfixed by the version of myself I see in her glass-green eyes.

There's a knock at the door and even though it's Adrian, I jump, and so does Sully. Just for a second, her hand grazes mine, and we're eighteen again.

"I couldn't find the charger. It must be in your bag," Adrian says when I let him in. "I got a text from Monty. They're going to the picnic now, so we should head over too."

Suddenly I want to get out of this room, away from Sully and her magnetic pull and this looming threat, this black cloud. Hadley and Heather are safe. They knew the girl I became after Sully. They know who I am now.

"I'll walk over with you," Sully says, putting a hand on my back. "I'm starving. And this way we can catch up some more."

"Sure," I say, even though there's no catching up to do. The notes are all we have in common. Two pieces of card stock tying us back together.

"Sounds great," Adrian says. "I bet you guys have some good stories. I'm dying to know what Amb was like."

Adrian carries the conversation on our walk to Russell House, keeping us from plummeting into dead silence. He wants to know everything about teenage me, and even though there's so much Sully could say, she doesn't give my truth away. "Amb was the only girl who could keep up with me," she tells him. "The best kind of friend."

I would have given anything to hear her say that back then. Sully didn't show affection like most people. There were no mugs, no *Best* or *Friend*, no declarations.

To get to Russell House from the Nics, we have to walk past Jackson Field through the Center for the Arts, a series of haphazard concrete trolls punctuated by green space where we would sometimes sit at night, drunk or high, and stare at the sky. Tour guides loved to tell prospective students that the buildings were constructed in their strange configurations to avoid cutting down the trees that were there first. That was Wesleyan, always wanting to save the world but filled with girls who couldn't save themselves from it.

We see Flora, behind a bunch of grads in front of the CFA Theater. She stares at us over the sea of heads. Sully doesn't look. Part of me wants to stop and say something to her, but I don't have the words. In an alternate reality, where Flora wasn't so *nice*, I might believe the notes were her doing, a modern-day take on the Post-its—the ones I always assumed were passive-aggressive—that colored our doors. But I know she isn't capable of something like that.

Russell House is beautiful, all pillars and class. Big white tents are set up on the green space. People are sitting on the lawn in knots, talking and laughing, relaxed and happy. I don't fit in here, and I never did.

"Do you want to eat with us?" Adrian asks Sully. "We're meeting some other friends. You're welcome to join."

"Thanks," Sully says. "But I'm supposed to meet some of the theater crew. I haven't seen them since the last time I was in LA. I'll see you guys back at the room later, okay?" She's wearing sunglasses so I can't see her eyes, but I wonder if she said that to hurt me, because she still knows how to cut. *The theater crew.* I'm not one of them.

But I don't have time to analyze it, because Hadley and Justin are suddenly in front of us holding paper plates bearing cheeseburgers. "You guys made it!" Hads says, her freckled snub nose crinkling up. "No surprise, but the food is just as bad as it always was. Nice to know MoCon lives on."

I'm relieved to see Hads. She's easy to breathe around, with her go-with-the-flow attitude, her presence a welcome relaxation. That's what drew me to her, after Dorm Doom, and she came with Heather, so I managed to make two friends without much effort. The hungry need to impress them was never there. I can see Heather now, her curls enviously glossy against her deep brown skin, laughing and taking to some other girls. Adrian is already throwing a Frisbee with Justin— good. I let myself breathe. There isn't any danger here.

"We're sitting over there." Hads points to a red picnic blanket. "Justin and Monty have already started pregaming. They don't want to admit that we can't drink like we used to."

I laugh obligingly, grateful but annoyed to be lumped into her *we*. Hads acted like she was *so drunk* every time she exceeded two beers. She and Heather used to get up for early-morning tennis practice almost every day, tiptoeing out the door while I slept. I never saw either of them do drugs or even talk about them. I never tried to corrupt them. I had learned my lesson by then.

When Hadley heads back, I make my way over to the white tents and grab a paper plate. It's a buffet, with burgers and hot dogs under silver domes, heaping bowls of pasta salad and potato salad protected from bugs by mosquito netting. I take a burger that looks more like a hockey puck.

"Ambrosia Wellington." Hearing my name like that, so slow and deliberate, makes me think of the envelope, the careful lettering. I turn around and don't recognize this woman at first, and she must know it, because mercifully she introduces herself.

"Ella. I know, I look really different."

I try not to show her my shock. Ella, the girl I saw my pre-Wesleyan self in but pretended not to. Ella is the one who witnessed what Sully and I did, even though she didn't know we did it.

I help myself to putty-colored pasta salad that I won't actually eat. "Ella. Wow, great to see you. You look amazing."

It's not a lie. Gone are the baby fat, the chubby trim around her face, the softness of her arms, the tacky clothes. She's all wires and sinew, and her hair is blond where it used to be dark.

"Thanks." She touches her bangs. I'm not the first to give her the compliment. Her fingernails are perfect ovals, dark red polish. Somebody that precise pays attention to detail.

Ella disappeared from my life after freshman year. I stopped seeing her on campus and stopped thinking about her altogether. She faded away, a ghost in jeans that never fit right and those god-awful clogs she used to wear, the ones I could perpetually hear clomping down the halls of Butts C.

"What have you been up to?" she says. "God, can you believe we're in our thirties now? I'm an environmental lawyer. A partner now, actually. How about you?"

Lauren became a child psychologist. Ella is an environmental lawyer. I picture them having lunch with Flora, each of them committed to saving the world.

"That's great." I shuffle down the line, grabbing a Diet Coke from a cooler. "I'm in PR. In Manhattan." I'm not sure why I add *in Manhattan*, or why I'm trying to impress Ella at all.

"We're not far away, then. I'm in Tribeca."

"Oh, cool," I say dumbly. I assumed Ella would have moved back to Jersey and settled there permanently, boring and predictable. But I should know that people change.

"I've seen most of the Butts girls here already," Ella says. "Even Sloane. I figured she wouldn't show up. Have you seen her yet? She's right over there. Typical Sloane, she's with a hot guy."

I follow Ella's pointed finger and my chest constricts. Adrian isn't throwing a Frisbee anymore. He's talking to Sully, their heads bent too close together.

"It's not like that," I snap, already on the defensive. "That's my husband. He talks to everyone."

"Oh," she says. "I see."

Ella could have a reason. She tried to befriend me and I chose instead to pick her apart with Sully. If she found out what we did, she could have easily written the notes to summon us here.

And if she did, I'm afraid to find out why.

"Well, I should get going," she says. "But let's catch up some more this weekend, okay? I'm sure we have a lot to talk about." And then she's gone, with a wave and a flick of her perfect hair, virtually the same white blond as Flora's.

14

THEN

I never knew when I met Ella Walden that I would end up ruining her life. I just knew that she wasn't the type of person I wanted to befriend in college. Her cheap, ill-fitting clothes and dated pastel eye makeup reminded me too much of Pennington. She wore openly the same trappings I was desperate to shed.

But sometimes, when nobody else was around, I talked to Ella about our hometowns, about our suburban upbringings. It was comforting, slipping into the past. From her high school stories, I could tell she was someone who was used to being passed up, and I found a counterpoint in her for that reason. But in public, I hated when she acknowledged our similarities and drew attention to the link between us.

Sully noticed, and it didn't take long for her to comment. "Ella seems to think you guys have a lot in common," she said, her lips curling up in a smirk.

"We don't."

"You might want to tell her that," she said, dragging her finger across her throat. So I started to poke, ever so slightly, pushing back against Ella's persistent commentary.

One night, washing our faces next to each other in the bathroom, Ella started talking about Wesleyan. "It's just so different from home." She scrubbed her skin with Neutrogena and a swath of zits poked through the foam, tiny mountains in a cloudscape. "Do you miss it?"

"Not at all," I told her sharply. "That's not who I am anymore."

Ella leaned over to rinse her face, but not before I saw her wounded expression.

"My god," Sully said a few days later, after Ella had accosted us in the lounge, where we were mixing drinks, and desperately fished for an invite to the Nics party we were going to that night. "I can't believe you're still friends with her."

"I'm not," I said quickly. "No matter what I say, she just keeps coming back for more."

Sully took a drag of her cigarette. "You're too nice. That's the problem."

Nice from her mouth was a hard dig, an accusation, something I had to disarm.

"I'm not nice," I said. "She just doesn't care."

"You need to find her weakness," Sully said, blowing a smoke ring toward the window. "We will."

Her certainty was almost chilling. I nodded, already trying to justify what I had to do to earn my place. I didn't owe Ella anything just because I knew things about her life, just because she had chosen to confide in me. I was with Sully. *We will*.

And then we did. Ella told me she was a virgin, something I swore I'd keep between us, something that never should have mattered anyway. I told Sully. I had no idea what she'd do with that nugget of information.

Then there was Ella, knocking on Sully's door when we were getting ready to go out. Sully let her in, then offered her a drink. Ella smiled and took a seat beside me on the bed. I drank faster, trying to swallow what I told myself wasn't guilt.

Sully applied eyeliner in her mirror and randomly blurted out, "I had the most explosive orgasm last night. It pretty much rocked my whole body."

I bit back a laugh. Lauren, who was studying under a blanket on her bed, shook her head and ignored us. Ella stared at the ground.

"From who?" I offered, taking Sully's bait.

Sully pushed the eyeliner pencil into the corner of her eye. She always went right into the waterline, the part that made me tear up. I copied her anyway, forever trying to make my eyes look bigger and more dramatic. "From myself, duh. I haven't met a guy who can do that yet. When I do, it's game over."

Ella's face pinked. She sipped her drink while Sully talked about her vibrator, just like on an episode of *Sex and the City*, which Toni had become obsessed with before leaving for college. I didn't know if Sully was telling the truth, but I hoped she was, at least the part about not having orgasms with guys. I never had either. When Matt and I had started fooling around, he said he wanted to make me feel good and asked me to tell him what I liked, but talking about it was awkward, so I pretended I liked everything, moaning in the dark with his fingers rubbing against me.

The night it turned into actual sex—when his parents were out of town and it was a prime opportunity to ditch my virginity—it felt more like I was being speared than anything else. After that, we did it every chance we got, but I liked being twined with him afterward better than the actual act. I didn't come until one night, alone in the tub, I touched myself until the water went cold, relaxing into my fingers. The buildup, the release, the shaking legs, the skin on my belly reddening. I finally understood the hype, but I could never bring myself to tell Matt exactly what I needed. I couldn't voice all that want clustered in me, tight like a fist.

"We're going to look for a guy for you tonight, Ella," Sully said. "A magic guy. And one for Amb, too. If you come out with us, we'll get you laid. I can find you something to wear."

There was no way Ella would be able to fit into anything in Sully's closet, none of the miniskirts that barely covered Sully's hint of an ass.

"Where are you guys going?" Ella asked. The curiosity in her voice was cloying. It made me flinch, not just from secondhand embarrassment but because that so easily could have been me.

"The Nics," Sully said. "Who have you hooked up with so far, Ella?"

Ella's blush deepened to a blotchy purple. When her eyes flashed to me, I saw something besides humiliation. Hurt. She knew I had told Sully her secret. I made her look away first, even though I wanted to.

"Nobody special," she mumbled. "Just a couple guys."

Sully leaned forward on crossed legs. She wasn't done playing. "Come on, Ella. Tell us their names. Or are you afraid we're going to steal them?"

Ella must have known she was caught in Sully's crosshairs. I willed her not to struggle, because that would just make the trap clench her limbs more tightly. I wondered how long she would try to keep the lie alive.

"Tell us, Ella," I echoed.

"You know, I actually have so much studying to do," she said, standing up. "But I hope you guys have a great time." She put her drink down, unfinished.

To my surprise, Sully let her go. "We're here if you change your mind," she said, and when Ella was gone, her lips trembled with laughter as she put on bright magenta lipstick.

"There. We got rid of her," Sully said. "It really wasn't hard." *We got rid of her.* She made it sound like we had dumped a body. I imagined Ella in tears and waited for the queasiness in my gut to pass.

"Thank you," I said, which was the answer she wanted.

"You guys are awful," Lauren chimed in. "I know she seems kind of square, but she's actually really nice." I had the feeling Lauren was only defending Ella because she had decided to hate me. Or maybe she was spending too much time with Flora and wanted to try *nice* on for size. When Lauren got up and shuffled into the hall with her shower bag, Sully raised both middle fingers at her back.

I reached for the lipstick, but Sully swatted me away. "Have another drink first. And what the hell are you drinking out of, anyway?"

I held up my *Friend* mug. "It was all I could find. Flora gave it to me."

Sully yanked it out of my hand. I thought she was going to throw it on the floor, but she just inspected it, the bubbly font and excessive pinkness, and opened her flask of vodka to refill it.

"Drink up," she said, her voice flat.

I despised the mug in that moment, and Flora for cursing me with it. I figured any headway I had gained in my cruelty to Ella had been lost with an ugly piece of porcelain. I was too scared at the time to understand that Sully wasn't disappointed. She was jealous.

Several drinks and a bump of cocaine later, as the two of us stumbled up Foss Hill toward the Nics, Sully was quiet, and I had to break the silence. "I haven't had an orgasm from a guy either. None of them know how to use their dicks."

She threw her head back and laughed, exposing her milky throat. "Are you serious? That's so sad. I'm the easiest person to get off. I was just making up shit so we could get rid of Ella."

For a second I hated her. The clothes that hung perfectly on her body and the hair she never had to wash and her grades, the way she didn't have to work for anything. She was the opposite of the cool girls from Central, forever trying to cultivate an image.

But mostly I just hated myself. For always slipping, just when I finally thought I had a solid foothold. For my defective body and sluggish brain. I would have to sharpen everything.

"Mission accomplished," I said. "Now I just have to do something about Flora. She's always judging me. Us."

Sully knocked against my shoulder but didn't link her arm in mine like she usually did. "Yeah. She's so goddamn fake. Girls like that are actually the easiest to corrupt."

Ella would have become wallpaper, someone in the background of my college scrapbook with a try-hard smile and dated clothes, if not for what we did. But she unwittingly played a role.

Maybe she's playing a very different one now.

15

NOW

Dear Ambrosia Wellington,

    If you're having trouble relaxing, consider joining us for sunset yoga overlooking Foss Hill. And be sure to gather your energy for the Class of 2007 cocktail reception and party afterward at Eclectic. It'll be like you never left campus, or the Wesleyan spirit never left you!

Sincerely,
Your Alumni Committee

Hads and Heather want me to come back to Bennet for drinks in their room after lunch, but I promised Adrian I would show him around. I take him to Olin and the observatory and we walk down Foss Hill, where a bunch of people in Lululemon are doing yoga, to Fountain Avenue. I point out the wood-frame house where I lived with Hads and Heather during senior year. I tell him I used to study *there* and hang out with friends *there* and eat lunch *there*. I don't tell him what I really did *here* and *there*.

"Sully seems cool," Adrian says when we're heading back. "Too bad you guys didn't stay in touch. What happened?"

His assumption is completely wrong. We didn't lose touch. *There is no us.*

I give him the most generic, harmless answer. "We just grew apart."

He slings his arm around me. "What about the girl you lived with freshman year? Is she here too?"

She's here. I already saw her twice and pretended I didn't. "I don't know. These people—" I start, but I stop myself before I say more.

"What, babe?" Suddenly, his grip on me feels just right—tight but not possessive, loving but not smothering. I lean into him and want to tell him how freaked out I am, but I don't.

"Nothing," I say.

We eventually make our way to Bennet to meet the others. The last thing I want to do is attend another Wesleyan party, but Hadley and Heather are talking like it's going to be *so much fun* and I'm swept along, arms linked in theirs like we're careless again, even though I never was. Being careless, like everything I did, was calculated.

The reception is being held in the Hewitt courtyard and at least has the decency to have an open bar. I'm not going to let Adrian's whispered *you could be*s stop me.

We pass a bunch of older alumni on our walk over, a reunion for a class from before our time. I would never want to show up like that, so far away from who I used to be. Especially when Flora would look the same, preternaturally young and beautiful. *You've aged well,* I would muster up the courage to say. *You haven't,* she'd reply.

I stop walking when I see a tall figure with immaculate posture and a familiar long stride. Along with a familiar uniform.

"Amb?" Heather says, turning back. "You coming?"

I suck in a sharp breath. I would recognize Officer—*Captain*—Tom Felty anywhere. Except now he's three-dimensional, not hidden safely behind a computer screen. I realize, with a pang of fear, that I'm not even surprised to see him here—almost like I knew he would find me when he wanted to.

Please don't see me. I spent years wanting to be the opposite of invisible, but now I wish I could disappear. I can't explain to Adrian why I know a police officer. I can't tell him that I still have Felty's business card at home, kicking around in an old wallet.

Now his hair is almost all white, but his face hasn't changed much, just hardened around the edges. The blue eyes are the same, arctic and intense. If I weren't terrified of him, I would probably think he was sexy.

He never thought Sully had anything to do with it. He somehow knew it was me, even though he never had the evidence he needed to prove it.

Felty could easily be the one who wrote the note in my purse. He could have learned calligraphy. *I'm finally going to get her,* humming merrily as he dropped the envelope in the mail. I know exactly why this case meant so much to him.

His revenge could be almost fourteen years in the making.

"I'm coming," I say, trailing behind the girls, focusing on the back of Adrian's curly head. Felty is mercifully silent as I pass by. Maybe he hasn't seen me.

Then I make the mistake of turning back right before the crowd in the courtyard swallows us up, and those eyes are staring straight at me. There's no hint of a smile, no indication that the past is in the past. Because it's not. I walked right back into it.

16

THEN

If Wesleyan was my universe, Sully was my passport, dragging me not just to regular parties but ones I never would have heard of otherwise. It was like she felt the pulse of campus itself, slender fingers throbbing over Wesleyan's veins. People told her things, wanted her places, maybe because they knew she was up for anything, her excess almost mythical already. She was right when she told me she got bored easily.

Sully was the reason I ended up at the Tomb during the second week of October, answering a bunch of random questions posed by two hooded figures at the entrance. I later learned that only members of the Skull and Serpent society had keys. I liked being part of something exclusive, something not everybody knew about, Sully and I dancing on a ledge in the dark. It was elevated from the regular party scene. This was life with Sully—VIP access, skipping the line, her connections spiderweb sticky.

"Dance with me," Sully said when we finally left at dawn. She held her heels and spun in circles, tilting her face to the sky. "Where can we go now? I'll text Buddy and see who's still partying."

"I can't. I have to sleep before class." Really, I was itching to get back to my room to check my email, where I knew a message from Kevin would be waiting.

Sully stopped abruptly and grabbed my wrist, pulling me in, our arms tacky with sweat. "You're different. Don't think I haven't noticed. It's a guy, isn't it?"

Her crimson-lipped mouth curved downward, pouty and disapproving. I was afraid to tell her about Kevin, afraid it would mean the end of something.

"You're the last person I expected to get sucked in by one of these idiot guys." She pulled away to light a cigarette. "Hypnotized by dick. I thought you were like me."

"I am." In that moment I needed Kevin to not be one of the *idiot guys*. "It's not like that. He's—well, he's not one of them. He goes to Dartmouth."

She yawned and typed something into her phone. She was already moving on. I had to reel her back in. I had to impress her.

"He's Flora's boyfriend."

I was scared when my words landed. I had no idea how she would react, if she would be impressed or disgusted or worse, bored.

But her smile glittered in the dark. "You slut. Fuck him yet? Does Flora suspect?"

I pulled my hair into an elastic on top of my head. Sully had convinced me I could wear it like that and not look stupid. "Not yet. And no. She has no idea."

My feelings toward Flora darkened by the day. She was the worst kind of girl, the kind who intentionally made you sunshine-blind in the prism of her perfection. *Don't even ask. Just take whatever you want,* she had said when we first met, but I was sure she didn't mean it. She just wanted somebody to monitor, an obedient house pet.

I tried every day to break into her laptop and read about Clarissa, my fingers skittering over her keyboard when she was in the shower. But I never managed to guess her password. In my frustration, I stole a picture of Kevin from Flora's wall collage, a recent one that had appeared there, partially covered by a magazine clipping about depression, which she was studying in one of her psych classes. I hid the photo inside my John Donne book. It seemed fitting. John Donne was like a mutual friend, the one who'd set us up.

"So what are you going to do about it?" Sully said.

I shook my head. "I don't know." I didn't tell her about the emails, about how real our connection was.

"You have to commit to it." Sully passed me her cigarette. "We'll figure something out."

She didn't force the issue of going to another party, and when we got back to the Butts, she kissed my cheek. "You better not forget I exist."

"Never," I said. When I washed my face, I saw that her lips had left a red mark.

The truth was, I sensed Kevin's growing distance. His responses that week had been slower to arrive and less effusive. He said things like, *It would be different if u were here.* And I responded, *I wish I was.* I tried to mimic his tone instead of gripping tighter, which was my instinct to stop someone from slipping away.

That morning, as my buzz swelled into a hangover fog, one email waited for me in my inbox. Kevin had sent it two hours ago. *My frat's doing a party this weekend and all I can think is how I'd rather be with u. reading some JD or something*

Instead of replying right away, like I always did, I let the message marinate. Flora's voice was in my head, but it wasn't annoying anymore. *It's not all that far. Less than three hours.* I could go to the party and surprise him. It would be the ultimate test to see how he really felt about me.

I stared at Flora, sleeping on her back, hands at her sides in her manicure gloves, hair twisted off her face. Our *Best* and *Friend* mugs were both on her desk, which meant she had washed them and brought them back from the kitchen. Flora, always tidying up after me. But I was about to make a disaster she would never be able to clean up.

In our Introduction to Playwriting class the next day, we talked about the hero and what happened when the hero fell. Ogden gave a big speech, raising both fists in the air. "To truly destroy a character, you have to know him inside out. You have to know what means the most to him. Take that away, and you can do anything to him. Kill him off, even. Because he has already lost everything that matters."

Sully raised her hand. "So you're saying the only way to dismantle someone is to take away what they love."

He clasped his hands together. "Yes, precisely. We've talked about seeing it prominently in *Othello*. It becomes even more interesting when you take away your hero's morals, along with what he loves. Which, generally, manifests as a person. The love interest."

I was sick of hearing about the love interest, comparing myself to that girl. People told us that comparison was the thief of joy. But the real culprit was competition. They never talked about what happened when we wanted the same thing.

"You seemed really interested today," I said later in MoCon, Sully with a mass of lasagna and me with a burrito that would inevitably upset my stomach. "Do you have an idea for your play?"

She used her fork to pry congealed cheese off her plate. "Not really. I was thinking more about your situation."

"My situation?" The burrito was nearly the size of my forearm, stuffed into its shell like a swaddled baby. The first bite would leave a neon oil slick on my chin, but I was too hungry to care.

"Yeah. With Kevin. I mean, we can eliminate the problem pretty easily."

I kept grinding beef and maggots of rice between my molars, because that was preferable to actually speaking. When I swallowed, I wiped my mouth with a napkin that came away orange. "What do you mean?"

"I mean, it's not that hard to make a guy forget about his girlfriend. It's funny, how they like to pledge their loyalty to one girl. Well, it's not funny, because usually it only happens because a girl makes them do it. Like, she wants legitimacy for sucking him off at a party, so she asks him if she's his girlfriend. And he says yes, because he wants to get sucked off again." She paused to spear a chunk of lasagna, digging her fork through the flesh of the noodles so savagely that I looked away.

She was describing me, the way I clung to the idea of boys in little ways, even the ones I wasn't supposed to care about. How I so easily believed everything Matt ever told me. How I let Hunter call me Amber and didn't correct him, how I had shown up at Drew Tennant's door minutes after his *hey, wanna hook up* text came in.

"Anyway," she continued, "we're the same to them. We have the same parts. It's what we do with them that matters. Why do you think so many guys give in to temptation? Why do you think bachelor parties are, like, a billion-dollar industry? They're pretty much founded on the idea that every man will cheat. It's just a question of when." Red sauce stuck to the corners of her lips.

"So you're saying we get Kevin to cheat?"

"That's exactly what I'm saying." Sully dropped her fork, where it settled on her plate with an indignant clatter. "I mean, I'm sure he's cheated on Flora already. It's not hard for any guy to keep his dick perpetually wet."

"But even if he does cheat on her, Flora gets off looking even more angelic." I could picture her tear-blind face, her pretty sobs, her mourning impeccably neat.

Sully wagged a finger at me. "Ah, you're wrong. I'm not done. The other half of my plan is to have her do the same thing."

I barked out a laugh. "Yeah, right. Who would she cheat on him with? She probably considers masturbation cheating. It's not going to happen."

But Sully wasn't deterred. She smiled her Cheshire cat smile, the one where the edges of her mouth turned all the way up.

"Let me take care of that. You focus on the other part."

So I did. I told her about the party at Kevin's frat, how he had practically invited me.

"Well, that's it. We're fucking going." She leaned back in her chair.

I saw myself with Kevin at Dartmouth, a gauzy fantasy that curtained off the rational part of my brain. I would run to him and throw my legs around his waist the way girls did in movies. He'd hang on, as if I weighed nothing, and kiss me so frantically that maybe our mouths wouldn't even meet. Lips on eyelids, cheeks, forehead, hairline, the clash of teeth. Messy and soft and meaningful, probably underneath a dramatic willow tree, and that tree would be our tree, and maybe he would even propose under it one day. The ring he slipped on my finger would be a solitaire, at least two carats, and the band would be an anemic halo of diamonds struggling to hold its weight.

People thought girls' bodies were our deadliest weapons. They had no idea about the mountains our imaginations could move.

"Why are you helping me?" I said. "I mean, I'm sure this isn't much fun for you."

She slapped the table so hard that I almost jumped. "Are you kidding? It's you. Of course I'm going to do anything I can."

Sully wasn't capable of sweet, but I still savored her words. *It's you.*

I should have known it was never really about me at all.

That night, she knocked on my door and whispered something in my ear as Flora clacked away on her laptop. "I got us a car."

I skipped my Friday classes to pack. I hoped to avoid Flora, but she came back from her morning class early, her usual smile missing in action. My eyes darted to my packed suitcase, the elephant in the room. *She knows.*

"Hey," she said. "I'm having such a bad morning. Poppy and I had this huge argument last night. I told her Kevin was coming for Halloween, and she said it was like I couldn't have fun without him. Like he doesn't want me to go out unless he's here."

My mouth was dry. I never considered that Flora was boring because Kevin made her that way.

"It's so not like that." Flora perched on her bed. "She just doesn't understand. She's fourteen. She's never had a boyfriend."

"Kevin doesn't seem controlling." I regretted my choice of tense—I should have said *Kevin didn't.* I had only met him once.

"Whatever," Flora said, her pained expression morphing into a smile. "I don't want to dump my bad mood on you. I'm just emotional. I blame Aunt Flo."

"Aunt Flo is the worst." I considered what Sully would say about a girl who called her period *Aunt Flo.* "Sometimes it's terrible being a woman."

Flora slumped against her pillow and sighed, theatrical. "Yeah. I would trade these ovaries for a ball sack most days."

The words *ball sack* coming out of Flora's mouth were so shocking that I laughed, an actual laugh, and Flora joined in, and for a minute it felt like we were real friends. Why had I decided not to like Flora? Was it because she had Kevin or because she had everything else? Maybe I had made up the halo over her head. She was just a girl, same as the rest of us, trying to figure life out.

When she flapped her hands against her knees I noticed what was on her nails. Letters. *Kevin*, one letter on each fingernail, *i* dotted with a heart. I let my smile fall. She loved the idea of him. She didn't understand who he really was and didn't deserve him.

"We should eat a bunch of junk food and watch something funny tonight." She pulled on her bunny slippers and her face changed as she gestured at my suitcase. "Oh. Are you going somewhere?"

"It's a last-minute thing. My sister is going home for the weekend, so I thought I'd go too and surprise my parents. We used to go apple picking every fall, so we figured we'd keep up the tradition." The lie was smooth, premeditated.

The apple-picking part was true. My parents loved cheesy traditions, and they were rife in Pennington. The Pennington Day street fair, Easter eggs hidden in Kunkel Park, our annual tree lighting on Main Street, cookies and hot chocolate and my mom's fourth-grade students singing carols, real wholesome community cheer.

"Wow," said Flora. "That's so nice. I wish my parents wanted to do that stuff with us. They can't even be in the same room together."

I had assumed Flora hailed from a family where everything was perfect, where Dad came home from work and the dog ran to the door to greet him and little Flora watched Mom get ready for a night out, dancing in a spray of Chanel No. 5. I figured the people who'd helped her move in were her mom and dad, the traditional family unit.

"I'm sorry. I thought . . ." She hadn't brought this up before. It was intentional, the lack of gory details. This was raw, the most undercooked I had seen Flora.

"It's okay," she said. "It's been that way since I was eight. That's when they split up. Poppy and I got used to the holiday shuffle after that. They both remarried and they're civil now, but for a while it was like Poppy and I only had each other. Maybe that's why fighting with her is so awful."

I could stay. I hadn't done anything yet, and it wasn't too late. I could meet my own Kevin, not the one who belonged to somebody else. I could abandon my daily assaults on Flora's laptop to unearth Clarissa, write her off as a figment of Kevin's imagination.

When my phone went off, I expected it to be Sully, but it was a text from Hunter. *Hey Amber, wanna hang out later?* If I believed in signs from the universe, it would have been a glaring one. I could message him back, agree to *hang out*.

But I didn't believe in signs. The universe where I lived wasn't in the business of giving me anything.

I thought about Sully. About Hunter's crooked dick. Sully's face as she laughed about it. Sully's face if I backed out of this weekend. We'd be over. Dartmouth was for me, but it was just as much for *us*. Sully wanted to see how far I would go. What I was capable of. I would show her.

I put the phone down, finally electrified with the power I wanted. I wouldn't respond to Hunter, and when I saw him on campus, I would pretend he didn't exist.

"I wish I was going somewhere this weekend." Flora stood up and stretched her arms over her head. "I was originally supposed to see Kevin, but his frat is having some big party tonight, and he has to go." She rolled her eyes. "I wish he came to visit more often. He told me he would, but so far he's only come here once. At least he'll be here for Halloween, and we'll see each other at Thanksgiving."

"Yeah, I totally get it," I said, but all I heard was Flora picking at his flaws, expecting Kevin to live up to an impossible standard.

"Anyway, sorry to burden you." She swished her hair back. "I'll miss you this weekend, but I hope you have fun at your parents' house. It'll be good for you to see them, I'm sure."

It was my last chance to back out. But, just as I wavered, there was a knock at our door. I opened it to Sully, backpack slung over her shoulder.

"You ready?" she said.

A tiny sliver of hurt clouded Flora's face, along with something else—anger, maybe, or disappointment. She thought Sully was coming with me to pick apples with my parents and wondered why she wasn't.

"Hi, Sloane," Flora said, almost robotic.

"Hey," Sully said, her gaze dropping to Flora's feet. Sully usually had a compliment for everyone. We were all *beaut* or *darling* or *great tits*. Flora was just *hey*. Sully knew that Flora was resistant to whatever alchemy she worked on the rest of us.

"Come on." Sully gestured to my suitcase. "You're lugging that giant thing all the way to—"

"Pennington," I finished, noticing her smirk and grabbing the handle. "It's really not that much stuff."

"I hope you guys have a good time," Flora said, waving with her *Kevin* fingers. Our door had barely closed when Sully snorted and said, "I had bunny slippers when I was, like, eight. I'm glad we're doing this."

Flora's parents got divorced when she was eight, is what I didn't say. What mattered was what I actually said.

"Me too."

NOW

To: "Ambrosia Wellington" *a.wellington@wesleyan.edu*
From: "Wesleyan Alumni Committee" *reunion.classof2007@gmail.com*
Subject: Class of 2007 Reunion

Dear Ambrosia Wellington,

Let's face it: you came to Wesleyan for the education, but chances are, the killer parties were your real learning experience. Tonight will be no exception. We encourage you to stay after the reception to continue the fun you're bound to be having.

Sincerely,
Your Alumni Committee

I know Felty is watching me, the same way I feel Flora's eyes on me, wondering what I'll do next. It's like a time warp straight back to Dorm Doom, everyone noticing my missteps. Exactly what I wanted when I started at Wesleyan, but for the absolute worst reason. The spotlight I ended up under was more like a torch.

The whispers, the ACB messages, ticker tape in my head. *I saw her in the bathroom. I saw her with him. I swear it was her. I saw her running from the Butts after.*

I stick close to Adrian's side, sneaking glances around for Felty but landing on everyone else instead. Lauren and Jonah are talking to someone who looks vaguely familiar—Hunter, of the crooked dick and inability to learn girls' names. His arm is around a tiny black-haired woman, and when she brushes a thick fringe of bangs off her face, I realize she's Clara from Butts C. She gives me a tentative wave, which I return with a forced smile. Even all these years later, something inside me stiffens. None of them ever picked me, even the ones I didn't want.

I don't see Sully—or more, I don't *feel* her. I know, with a sick rush of disappointment, that she isn't here. Her absence takes up more space than anyone else's presence.

"Babe, you're not being very social." Adrian gestures around. "Aren't we here so you can catch up with these people?"

"I've already said hi to everyone I cared about." It's technically not a lie. I keep talking before he can say anything else. "There's Monty." I point to the bar, grateful that Monty's heavy drinking makes him predictable. "Why don't you go talk to him? I have to go to the bathroom."

I make sure before actually leaving that he's deep in conversation with Monty and not talking to anyone he shouldn't. On the way into Hewitt, I get ambushed by Tara Rollins, who thinks now is an ideal time to plan a potential girls' trip with Hadley and Heather. In my peripheral vision, I keep glimpsing Flora's white-blond hair, but when I turn, she's not there. I'm sure everyone has been approaching her tonight, forlorn eyes and artificial smiles. I won't be one of them. She doesn't want to hear from me.

When I finally get to the Hewitt bathroom, I duck into a stall and text Billie. *I forgot how much I hate these people. This was such a bad idea.*

LOL comes back almost instantly, along with a smiley face with its tongue sticking out. *I'm sure it's better than my night. The kids won't sleep and Ryan is in front of the TV as usual.*

I'd trade if I could, I write back. *Seriously, being here has made me sick.*

Maybe you're pregnant, she says. Billie's canned reply to everything. If I have a headache, I'm pregnant. If I don't immediately reach for the bottle to refill my wine, I'm pregnant. If I don't want to go for sushi, I'm pregnant.

I'm not, I type back.

Boooo, Billie writes. It's funny, how she always wants me to be pregnant, even as she tells me what a horror show her kids are. She assumes Adrian and I have been trying. As much as Billie acts like a free spirit, she would think it was vile, what I did. That the day after I made a big show of getting on board with being a mom and flushed my birth control pills down the toilet, I went out to the pharmacy, refilled my prescription, and hid it in my purse. That was six months ago. I know I should feel guilty, but I would feel guiltier actually going through with it. Some people aren't meant to be mothers.

I stare at my phone. My period actually should have arrived yesterday, but I'm used to its being a day or two late. I take my pill at the same time every evening, always diligent, never forgetting, just like I have every day since I was sixteen.

There's a chiming sound—an incoming text message, but not to my phone. The chime comes from the stall beside me. I ignore it, until the phone starts ringing.

But it's not a ring at all. It's a song.

The opening bars to "I Don't Want to Miss a Thing."

I stiffen, my skin tightening like concrete. Flora, snatching her phone apologetically. *Sorry, it's Kevin again.* But it's impossible. Kevin couldn't be calling her.

"Flora?" I practically whisper. There are no shoes under the door. Nobody answers.

The phone stops ringing and I push my door open, then step in front of the stall next to mine. I nudge the door ajar with my boot. The phone sits neatly on the toilet paper dispenser.

I should leave it there. But it's a silver flip phone. Nobody has a flip phone anymore. I pick it up and open it, which is exactly what she wanted me to do.

Because the image on the screen was meant for my eyes.

I slam the phone down and dart out of the stall, grappling for the bathroom door, tearing into the hall. When I'm back in the courtyard I don't lose myself in the crowd. I run back to the Nics. I need to know if Sully is there. I need to tell her what I just saw.

I'm about to barge into the room when I hear a voice. I walk in quietly, the same way I used to tiptoe past sleeping Flora when Sully and I thundered back from a party at three a.m. The inner door to Sully's room is closed, but a harsh bark makes me jump—Sully's laugh. She's talking to someone. I hold my breath, listening with my ear to the door.

"She has no idea," Sully says. I don't hear another voice—she must be on the phone. "She doesn't suspect a thing about us. I know her."

She has no idea. I know her. There's only one person she could be talking about.

Me.

My bag is sitting on the bed where I left it. I could grab it and go. The fear building like a headache is telling me I should, but I need to know who Sully is talking to, who is the newest member of her sacred *us*.

Somebody replaced me, and I know what Sully demands from the people she lets get close.

I back away and silently leave the room. Outside the Nics, my heart almost stops when I see Flora, wearing the same headband as earlier. It's like she knew I would be here.

"I don't know what you expect me to say." I swallow. "I'm not the only one who was involved."

She doesn't have a response, just the same icy smile. She holds me responsible, and she'll never forgive me. She'll never talk to me again. I walk faster. Away from her, away from Sully and whoever was on the other end of that phone call.

I'm almost back at Hewitt when I see him, a shadow with a lit cigarette, a habit I never expected he had. Felty doesn't say a word to me. I pass by him, keeping my eyes on the ground. It's only when I've slunk away, gratefully unnoticed, that he speaks.

"Miss Wellington." His voice is the same, low and clear. "I thought I might see you back here this year."

I freeze. I don't have the perfect thing to say, and it doesn't matter anyway.

"I trust that life has been kind to you," he says. Now I turn around, my shoe dragging a semicircle in the dirt.

"Things are good." I try to disguise the shake in my words. "How about you?"

He doesn't answer, just asks another question. "Will I be seeing you tomorrow?"

"I don't think so," I answer, defiant. I know what he really means, but I won't acknowledge it. "I have a pretty busy schedule."

I can't read his expression. He lets the butt of his cigarette hit the ground and rubs his boot over it. Felty smokes and litters. I doubt he's as righteous as he wants people to think.

"That's too bad. I'm sure I'll see you around this weekend. Maybe we could grab a coffee. Like old times."

"I don't think so. My husband and I have a full day tomorrow, then we're leaving Sunday morning." *My husband*, the best possible shield, proof that somebody cares enough to protect me. A sense of warmth for Adrian shudders through me.

Felty's eyes bore into mine. He's too intense, always was. "You owe her that."

I cross my arms, my leather jacket riding up around my wrists. "What did you say?"

"I said, I understand that. What did you think I said?"

I'm not going to argue. When I walk away, I'm afraid he's going to yell after me. He doesn't.

Felty wanted me in a very different way than any of the boys I met at Wesleyan.

He wanted me behind bars.

18

THEN

Wesleyan to Dartmouth was basically a straight line down I-91, a drive that MapQuest told me would only take two and a half hours. The car belonged to a DKE boy named Lewis whom Sully hooked up with sporadically because, as she told me, he gave oral sex without just expecting it in return. The farther away we got from Wesleyan, the more real my mission became.

"Thank god we decided to do this," Sully said. "Campus is so boring. I barely have a pulse anymore."

"Yeah," I said, my stomach knotting more each second.

I had considered emailing Kevin to tell him I was coming. Maybe he didn't like being surprised. But it had to be unexpected—I needed him to see that I wasn't like Flora, pushing him to bridge the gaps. I wanted his reaction to be big. I drummed my fingers on my legs as Slipknot's album *Iowa*, which Sully loved, screamed at us through the speakers.

"So Kevin," Sully said, turning down the volume. "Tell me the real story. You met him, like, two weeks ago and decided you were in love with him? Do you guys have a bunch of phone sex, or what?"

"No," I said. "It's not like that. I mean, we send emails."

"Emails," Sully said. She made it sound like a venereal disease. "Wait. So you met him once and haven't talked to him since?"

"We talk. Our emails are really personal. He tells me things about himself." I raked my fingernails across the cuticle of my thumb.

"Why didn't you tell me? I tell you everything." Her voice dropped, as if she didn't want anyone else to hear the hurt in it.

"I don't know," I said. "I didn't think—I guess I didn't want to talk about it until I knew what it was." I left out what I wanted to say. *I was afraid it would change us.* There was a long silence before she finally replied.

"It's easy to hide behind a computer. You can say anything. Just be careful. I don't want a guy to fuck you around."

"He isn't," I said. But she had a point. It was her favorite hobby, taking phones from the boys she hooked up with and sending messages that were bound to get them in trouble. She did it with a hand over her mouth, unable to contain the laughter that spilled out.

"But he has a track record. He's cheating on Flora with you, right?"

"No." I dug my hands into my knees. "It's not like that. It's emotional, not physical."

She cleared her throat. "And you're sure you're the only one?"

A bud of dread burrowed into my gut like an insect. I didn't know how to answer the question. I wanted to defend Kevin, but I suddenly wasn't sure at all.

"Relax." Sully laughed and tugged on my arm. "I didn't mean anything by it. But if he screws you over, I'll have to kill him."

I laughed too, even though I couldn't tell if she was joking or serious.

She drummed her fingers on the wheel. "I mean, hopefully he's better than the idiots we're stuck with. The last Buddy I fucked basically begged me to stay over in his room. Then he said he'd make me dinner. Yeah, no. I don't want your shitty microwave nachos, Hunter."

"Hunter? You slept with him again?"

"I was procrastinating. That always makes me horny. I won't be fucking him again, though. He's so needy. And men think we're the ones who get emotionally attached?"

I was grateful for my sunglasses so that she couldn't see my eyes. Hunter didn't even want me in his room—when we'd had sex, he'd come to my room when Flora wasn't there, almost like the times I snuck Matt in and out of my parents' house before they returned from their infrequent dinner dates. Hunter had told me, *My roommate's always there, sorry, Amber.* But he had no issue remembering Sully's name or making room for her. My personal Holy Grail, casual sex, was a sham. The real power didn't come from being wanted. It came from not wanting anything back. It came from not wanting *anything*, period.

What I understood was that the less Sully cared, the more people around her bent themselves in half to show that they did. And I desperately wanted to crack her code.

"Thanks again for doing this," I said quickly, although the churning in my stomach made me wish I weren't going anywhere.

"Are you kidding?" Sully leaned back, practically vibrating in her seat. "Did I not tell you I get bored easily?"

It was my mission, but now I was the one being pulled along. I was a passenger, in more ways than one.

"Flora needs to see what life is really like," Sully continued. "She's such a bitch. But not in the usual way. She's sneaky. She was talking in the lounge about you with Lauren a couple weeks ago. About how you're always trying so hard, and it's obvious."

"She said what?" I spat the words out, roiling with fresh fury. "What the fuck? She doesn't know me at all."

Sully arched an eyebrow. "I'm telling you, I heard it. She stopped talking as soon as she saw me come in, since she knows how tight we are. If you're going to be a bitch, own it. But she hides it behind this perfect image. I hate girls like that. They're the worst kind."

It was the most terrible thing I thought about myself, and Flora had been luxuriating in it the entire time. The pain on her face from this morning was washed out by the truth. She *was* the worst kind, and I decided I didn't feel bad about what I was about to do.

We pulled onto Webster Avenue, with its mansions and broccoli-top trees, by early evening. Sully parked on the street. She lined her lips with a dark pencil, then turned to do the same to mine. The tights I was wearing under my skirt had holes in them, so Sully told me to take them off.

"Easy access." She sipped from a flask. "You are going to fuck him, right? We didn't come all this way to a frat party for you not to fuck him."

"Yeah," I said. "I'm going to fuck him." I liked the shock of the words in my mouth. My mom used to tell me and Toni to be ladies. She taught us to contain our emotions until we were in an appropriate place to let them out, as if emotions were caged animals and we were the zookeepers.

I wasn't a lady. Sully had shown me that.

"There," Sully said. "Close your eyes." The tug of an eyeliner pencil. "Now open." A shock of wetness as she put mascara on my lashes. Her mouth was close to mine, big and burgundy.

"Look at us." She gestured to the mirror. "We're practically sisters."

When my phone chirped, I assumed it was a text message from Billie, who knew I was trying to make something happen with *Buddy* tonight, although she had no idea how far I had gone, in any sense of the word.

But the message was from Flora. *Miss you. Hope you have fun!* I shoved the phone into my purse without answering.

"Who was that?" Sully asked.

"Nobody." I meant it.

I wouldn't give another thought to Flora, to what she was doing in our dorm room and why she felt the need to verbally strip me down behind my back. I didn't think of her until much later. I had written her out of the movie in my head, even though the script wouldn't have existed without her.

19

NOW

I wake up in the familiar throes of a hangover, with Adrian wrapped around me like a koala. I didn't want to go to the reunion party at Eclectic last night, but Adrian was having fun, and I was too paranoid to leave him alone. Or maybe I was afraid to be alone myself.

In the middle of everything was Sully, crackling with the energy she pulsed into every room, her hands on everyone's backs, her face close to theirs. Whenever we made eye contact, she was never the first to look away, like she was daring me to say something. Or do something.

"She'll never change," Lauren said when we were at the bar, her boozy breath in my ear, a guttural laugh. "She used to have this game, back at Spence, when we'd all go out with our fake IDs. Take a girl's wallet, steal her driver's license, and pretend to be her. Just drinking and flirting with older guys like the rest of us did wasn't enough for her."

I had laughed and wondered if Lauren knew about the many Buddies at Wesleyan whose phones became Sully's casualties. I suppose I never contemplated the origins of Sully's boredom, that it had a life of its own before I met her.

"You awake, babe?" Adrian says, his mouth hot against the back of my neck. "Fuck, I drank a lot last night."

I stay still, hoping he'll fall back asleep and only wake up when it's time for us to leave tomorrow. He doesn't take the hint.

"Did she come home last night?" He rolls onto his back, traces circles on my arm. "I didn't hear her come in. I wonder if she hooked up with someone."

"Probably." I let him kiss my cheek. "It wouldn't be the first time."

When he leaves to take a shower, I grab my phone out of my purse. There's a text from Billie sitting there. *So Ryan says this morning that he wants another kid. He doesn't even pay attention to the ones he has. Maybe we should time it so we get knocked up together?*

No thanks, I write back. *No babies for me.*

Her reply is instant. Billie's phone rarely leaves her hand. *Boo. Did you end up having any fun last night? Any sign of him?*

I told you. He won't be here.

When I put my phone down, Sully is standing in the inner doorway in jean shorts and bare feet. She enters my room without asking and straddles the desk chair, resting her chin on her hands. "Kind of ironic. We're finally roommates, after all this time."

I won't get pulled back in, seaweed in her undertow. I don't return her smile. "I didn't hear you come in last night."

"You guys were passed out. I went back to Clark to have drinks with some of the girls. Ella kept fishing around for details about you. It was creepy. I didn't tell her a thing."

I pause, then decide to give her something back. "I was in the Hewitt bathroom during the reception last night. And I heard a phone ringing in the stall beside me, but nobody was there. I checked it out, and I think it was Flora's old phone."

Sully bites her lip. "Her phone? From back then? How do you know?"

"It was a flip phone. I opened it, and the background picture was of us. You and me and Flora. From Halloween." I don't mention the ringtone, that it was Kevin's. It somehow seems like a betrayal.

"Are you sure? How is that even possible?" Her eyes narrow suspiciously. "Where's the phone? I want to see it."

"I left it there. But I swear, I saw it. She must've taken a photo of the picture."

She twirls a strand of hair around her finger. I can tell she wants a cigarette. "How could you leave it there? We could have gone through it and found something."

"I don't know." I sit cross-legged and tap my knees. "I guess because it wasn't mine."

She understands what I really mean. "That never stopped you before."

"Well, maybe you never knew who I was before. And anyway, I'm not that person now, so it doesn't matter." My irritation is sudden and fresh. I almost expect her to strike back, but she just lets out a sigh, a tiny exhalation through pursed lips.

"I knew who you were." Soft and factual. She can make anything sound like the truth.

"Where were you before the party?" I say, swinging back to now. "I didn't see you at the reception."

"Headache." She stops playing with her hair. "You know how I got those."

She never once complained about a headache, unless she was referring to a person as one. But this is Sully's power—not necessarily making people believe her, but leading them to doubt themselves.

"Felty's here," I say. "I saw him before the reception. Why would a police captain be working event security at a reunion? He was waiting for me."

"I saw him last night too. You really think it could be Felty? But why now? Why here?"

"He's traditional," I say. "Back when he had a wedding ring, it was plain gold. He named his kids Michael and Thomas Jr. Things have meaning to him. He's the type who would like the idea of a reunion. Of it being here, where everything happened."

"Well," Sully says. "You sure know a lot about him."

"I guess." I pick at my thumbnail, suddenly embarrassed. It's hard to articulate how learning details about Felty lulled me into a sense of safety that Sully never seemed to need.

"He's probably worked on, like, a thousand cases since then. Why this one?"

"His sister," I say. "Because of what happened to her. He's taking it out on us."

The email alert on my phone goes off. I swipe to open it and my eyes glaze over as I scan its contents. "These fucking alumni emails. Like, I know we're supposed to be having fun. We're not. Stop checking in."

"They're annoying," Sully says. "But come on. Admit you're having a little bit of fun."

I don't look at her. "I'm not."

"Do you remember all the wild stuff we did?" She stares at her fingernails, chipped and bitten like mine. "Sometimes I miss it."

"Me too." The words come unbidden, because they're true. I miss the lack of responsibility, the weightlessness, damp hair spun into a ponytail to make it last another night, bare legs knocking together, something sweet in my throat, my feet sore from shoes that didn't fit right.

"I didn't mean to be a bitch." She meets my eyes. "I know I was. Things got really complicated. But just know that I never told anybody the truth."

I want to believe her, to trust her. I want to *reconnect*, like the Wesleyan emails keep telling me to. But the past is an electric fence between us, and I would risk everything by attempting to climb it.

The dorm bathrooms at the Nics are different from the ones in Butts C—they're bigger, with multiple shower and toilet stalls. I step into a stall and turn the hot water on, letting it beat against my back.

Sully used to think it was funny to peek under the door when I was showering and yell, *Surprise!* The first time, I covered myself with my hands as best I could. Then I stopped thinking it was strange when she darted into the stall with me, sharing my water stream, reaching over to use my body wash. It was like she never wanted us to be apart.

When I'm done showering I dry off and step back into my pajamas, wrapping my towel around my hair. I move over to the sinks, and my eyes lock on something that wasn't there when I walked in.

A hairbrush, the round kind, fat with someone else's hair, wispy white-blond strands. Flora's hair, almost always worn down and straight. And beside it, a pink mug with one word on it. *Friend*, the letters dressed in purple-and-white polka dots.

I crouch down, spinning with nausea. The hairbrush could be a coincidence. Lots of people have hair that color. This isn't Flora's doing.

The mug, though. The mug isn't a coincidence. I creep up, slowly, like it might explode any second. Who would know that Flora gave it to me, or that hers was its matching *Best*? Ella would know—she was in our room more than once. The other Butts C girls, who came to Flora when they wanted something. Shampoo. Makeup remover. Advice. Someone to proofread their essays. Someone to tell them they were pretty. Those girls knew.

And Sully. Sully definitely knew.

I don't touch the mug. I don't want my fingerprints on it. At least, that's the plan, until I see what's inside it. Blood, a chubby trickle from rim to bottom.

I get closer. I pick it up, run it under the faucet. The blood doesn't budge. It's too red to be blood. Wesleyan red. Nail polish, already dried, a snake gripping pink ceramic. My hands shake as I put the mug back down.

The note. The bathroom stall in Hewitt. Now this, my mug and her nail polish. I've been on campus for almost an entire day now and nobody has come forward and told me we need to talk.

It's suddenly obvious: whoever wrote *We need to talk about what we did that night* may not want to talk at all.

20

THEN

Webster Avenue was Dartmouth's fraternity row, Alpha Chi a rambling green-shingled mansion. Girls drink free, we were told at the front door, except the boy who said it had a glint in his eyes, like we were expected to pay in some other way.

"This looks promising," Sully said with an exaggerated eye roll. "I'll get us drinks. You should look for Kevin, and we'll meet back here."

Here was a big gas fireplace that wasn't actually turned on, bordered by a mantel with pictures of sports teams, golden boys in brass frames. I moved quickly to the stairs, tottering in my heels. I expected to find Kevin up there, in one of the bedrooms, maybe with a book, because parties weren't his scene and he needed the alone time to recharge.

"Have you seen Kevin McArthur?" I asked a boy with a shock of blond hair in a Manchester United jersey.

"Mac Daddy? He's around here somewhere. Or he will be. Why're you wasting your time with that fucker? Come hang with us instead."

I ignored his leer, his flippant *Mac Daddy*, then turned around and got out of his gaze. Kevin wasn't upstairs, but lots of other boys were, all wearing jerseys. I was very aware of eyes on my bare legs, the expanse of flesh. I tried to look like I was enjoying the throb of the music and the cup of cheap beer somebody pushed in my face. The thud of a hand on my back made me whirl around. *Kevin*, I thought, but it was just Sully.

"I can't find him anywhere," I said, frantic. "What if he isn't here?"

"If he's not, somebody else is." Sully poured the contents of her cup into mine. "Let's explore. This place is actually kind of cool."

I followed Sully back downstairs and through a concrete hallway into another part of the house—later, I would learn that it was known as the Barn.

The party got a lot louder when a bunch of guys wearing jerseys thundered in, fists in the air, green and black stripes under their eyes. Every school had its kings, the guys everyone watched and worshipped. Then one of them became Kevin.

I was sure it was some kind of mirage, that I'd had too much to drink and hallucinated his face on this jersey-wearing body. Kevin would wear button-down shirts, like Pacey from *Dawson's Creek*, a show Billie and I used to watch religiously. And his jeans wouldn't be falling off his ass like this guy's were, complete with chains coming down to the knees. The pack turned and made a beeline for the keg. They were messy, sloppy, taking up so much space.

"It's him. There he is." He hadn't seen me yet.

"Which one?" Sully said, stifling a yawn. "I can't remember. They all look the same."

Kevin stood behind a beer-pong table, giving out high fives. Maybe I had forgotten what he looked like and started replacing parts of his face with whatever my brain wanted to summon. His nose looked bigger and his lips thinner, and his hair wasn't long, no ringlets curling around seashell ears. He was just a boy, a mortal.

"That one," I said.

She leaned into me. "Well, are you going to stand here all night with me or actually talk to him?"

I took a deep breath. "I'm going to talk to him."

I walked up and tapped him on the shoulder, an approach I instantly regretted. There was nothing sexy about a shoulder tap. It was what you did to get a rude person to move out of your way. But when he turned around and saw me, his smile was worth the stress.

"Holy shit," he said. "Ambrosia. What are you doing here? I mean, I'm glad you're here. But—am I super drunk, or are you actually standing in front of me?"

I smiled back. "It's me."

I don't know what I expected—that he would kiss me, maybe, drop his beer and put his hands on my cheeks to see if I was real. But instead, he gave me a hug, the same casual hug I'd just seen him give a bunch of his jerseyed buddies.

"Why are you here?" he said. Paint was smeared across his cheek-bones. Flora wouldn't approve of this—Kevin in his red-blooded jock glory, me with my short skirt in front of him.

"I'm—it's a long story." I had planned to tell him the truth. That I was here for him. But it felt like too much, so I took the safe way out. "I have some friends who go here."

He nodded. I wasn't sure if he was disappointed or relieved. "Yeah. That makes sense. But I thought you had a big assignment you were working on this weekend."

"I did," I said. "I mean, I do." *It was this. Finding you.* All of the lines swirled in my head, a veritable potpourri of every cheesy bit of dialogue from romantic comedies, but I didn't have the courage to say any of them. I didn't need another excuse to cringe at my own desperation.

"You know, we should—" he said, eyes on my face like he was studying it.

I didn't get to hear the rest because Sully chose that moment to sweep in and wrap her arm around my waist. I bit back my annoyance. She knew what I was doing but interrupted regardless.

"Hey." She clutched my side. "Are we going to turn this into a real party, or what?"

"Sully." I silently prayed she wouldn't tell Kevin what a *real party* was. "You remember Kevin, right? He goes to Dartmouth too."

"Of course," she said. "You poor boy."

I wanted to smack her. The guys were passing out shots, and Kevin looked at his like he shouldn't drink it. Flora was in our room, cross-legged on her bed, cell phone beside her on her duvet like a beloved pet. When it didn't ring, she would call Kevin herself. She pictured

Kevin's car in a ditch, Kevin on the floor of his room, unable to call for help. When she pictured the worst, she didn't see me and Sully. But she should have.

Kevin's friends were just like everybody at Wesleyan, letting Sully suck out their energy. She indulged them, grinding her hips against theirs and leaning in when they talked, slipping her bra strap off her shoulder. Kevin and I hung around the periphery, him eyeing Sully and the thickening dance floor, never touching, like a kid in a store whose mother strictly forbade him to put his hands on anything, because if you break it, you buy it. He checked his watch. I was sure Flora had gotten him the watch. She was the kind of girlfriend who would buy a watch, and maybe even a ridiculously expensive pen.

"I still can't believe you're here," Kevin said. "I didn't even want to come to this party. But, you know, this is my frat. I kind of have to show up."

"I get it," I said. "I'm sort of over the party scene at Wes. I'm looking for something more meaningful."

His hand brushed mine. "I know you are."

"I never got the grand tour. Want to show me around?" He hadn't asked about my fictitious friends I was supposedly here to visit, like he knew I had made them up.

"Yeah," he said. Relaxed, easy. I let myself relax too.

We ended up in his room, on the second floor of the Barn, which was gratefully unoccupied by the two brothers he said he shared the space with. We sat down on his bed, neatly made, his nightstand heaped with books—and, I noticed with satisfaction, bereft of any photos of Flora. The room was what I'd pictured from Kevin, and the fact that this one bit of reality aligned with the boy in my head fueled me. I sipped my beer until he reached over and took my cup, bringing it to his lips.

"This is weird," he said. "I mean, we talk about everything in our emails, but I don't know what to say to you."

"You don't have to say anything." I waited for him to go in for the kiss but he didn't, so I did.

He didn't react at first, and panic coursed through me. He was another fantasy I had concocted in my head, a fairy tale that could too easily be slammed shut. Then his mouth covered mine and one of his hands went to the base of my skull, his fingers sifting my hair like it was sand. I had never been kissed this way, by somebody who knew my insides without ever having been inside me. I had kissed Matt hundreds of times without feeling *this*.

But just as I fell deeper, it was over.

"I can't do this." He jerked away. "I'm sorry, Amb. It's just—I have a girlfriend. Obviously. She's already on me about where I am all the time. I can't give her a reason to be more paranoid. And you're—you're special."

I didn't like the *obviously* or the way he wiped his mouth.

"Sorry, I'm not trying to be an asshole. But you deserve someone who's all in, and I can't be. I don't cheat. I could never get into something like this."

"We're not—" I started.

"You should know," he said. "I mean, you were cheated on. You know what it feels like."

It was almost a warning—almost. I wasn't sure if he was trying to convince me or himself. I wasn't mad that he'd brought up Matt as much as I was furious that precious Flora couldn't have her perfection marred by suffering through what I had.

I managed to smile weakly. "I know. You're right. I'm sorry."

It was hearing those two words out loud—*I'm sorry*—that made me say the next part. I was sick of apologizing. I thought about what Sully would do. She had shown me it was okay to be selfish, that just because the world wasn't willing to give me something, it didn't mean I couldn't take it anyway.

"Look, there's something you should know." My voice trembled. It would have to be a convincing performance, the best acting I had ever done. "I don't know if I should even tell you. But we've gotten to know each other so well, and I'd want you to do the same for me."

"What?" he said. "What is it?"

Showtime. "Have you ever thought about why Flora is so intent on knowing where you are all the time, even though you haven't done anything wrong?"

"What do you mean?" He tugged on the ends of his hair, as if that would help his brain figure it out.

"There's a guy." I rubbed my hand over my face. "This is so awkward. It's really not my place to be saying anything. But like you said, I got cheated on. I know how much it hurts. There's a guy she flirts with, and it might be turning into more."

"No way. Flora's a—she wouldn't be hooking up with other guys."

I let a rattling sigh escape my lips. "I saw them together, in our room. It's a guy from our dorm. Hunter. She tried to say they were studying. Then later, she asked me not to tell anyone he was in our room. Like she was afraid her reputation would be ruined."

He clenched his jaw. I wanted to add more incriminating details, but I let what I had already said marinate between us.

"I heard her on the phone with her sister, saying something about him. But she hung up really quickly when I walked in."

"Her sister doesn't like me," Kevin muttered. "Never did."

I smiled tightly. Poppy was a fissure between Flora and Kevin. It was something I'd learned from Sully—where to pick to make it bleed.

"We talk on the phone almost every night," he said. "She wants us to tell each other everything. She asks about who I'm hanging out with."

"Because she doesn't want you to know what she's doing. It's reverse psychology. Look, I'm sorry to unload this on you. I like Flora, but she has this whole other side." It felt good, cutting into Flora's veneer, chiseling away at it.

Kevin stared at the ground. I almost caved. But I had to finish what I'd started. I couldn't leave it, like a wounded animal beside the road.

"Things have changed. You sense it. I mean, it's partly why we write to each other. You need someone who understands you."

"It's not true." His voice became both softer and harder. I had planted doubt, and doubt is the mint of the emotional world. It takes over the entire garden, choking out everything else. "I'm supposed to call her when the party ends. I'm going to ask her."

"No. She'll just deny it. I mean, she's in denial about it too—you know how Flora hates to admit when anything's wrong. And she'll know you heard it from me, because nobody else saw Hunter in our room."

"Fuck." His eyes pleaded with me. "I mean, I know you're honest. I just don't want this to be true."

I do. "She calls him Buddy. It's like a pet name or something."

"Fuck. I don't know what to do."

"If I were you, I'd think about what you really want. What you deserve. Because it isn't that."

He nodded. Then he reached for me and pulled me into a hug. It had been so long since anybody actually hugged me, especially with the kind of intensity that made my body quake. *I'm going to make it. I'm an excellent fucking actress after all.*

"I worried about this," he said. "That she'd realize she was out of my league and find someone else at college."

"I'm sorry." I smiled into his shoulder.

My story had implanted, the same way a tick latches on to a dog and buries its whole ugly head in its skin. Kevin was revisiting every conversation he'd had with Flora, every call where it took her longer than usual to pick up, and each silence where she seemed distracted. It was a tale as old as time. Iago did it to Othello and I was doing it to Kevin. I couldn't be the main character in our fucked-up soap opera, so I would have to be the villain. For now.

"I have to figure stuff out," he said when he finally let me go. "This isn't easy. We have a lot of history."

The way he said *history*, like it was more than just a timeline of chaste dates and corsages. I hated *history*, the rich families writing it. The Fairfield golf club would be so disappointed by the fallout.

"Of course." I stood up and pulled my skirt down. "Just don't tell her I was here, okay? Not that you would. But she'd get so mad if she knew I told you. She already doesn't like me."

Kevin scrubbed a hand over his mouth. "I'd never put you in that position. But you're wrong. She's always talking about how great you are."

I sucked in a breath. Kevin had no reason to lie. Maybe Flora had told him I was great, but it didn't matter. Sully had heard the real Flora, talking behind my back, an image so visceral I could almost see it myself.

"She has a snarky comment every time I stay out late. She monitors who I hang out with. I guess she's lying to both of us." I surprised myself by how pissed off I actually was—not at Kevin for being afraid of hurting Flora, but at Flora for not being afraid to hurt me. Her judgment was just another microscope I had never asked to be inspected under.

"I'll talk to you later," he said. "Once I have things figured out." His fingers grazed mine as I walked out the door, not letting myself turn back.

I found Sully and the boys and drank and danced. Kevin never resurfaced—he must have been *figuring stuff out*. I eventually surrendered to sleep on a couch that smelled like old basement, the party swirling around me. I vaguely sensed Sully nestled in behind me, hands snaking down to my stomach and curling up there like a housecat, and the absence of her when I woke up later. My thoughts glowed, phosphorescent. It wasn't a level playing field, me and Flora. I had to play dirty. But that was the difference between us. I never minded having dirty hands.

NOW

To: "Ambrosia Wellington" *a.wellington@wesleyan.edu*
From: "Wesleyan Alumni Committee" *reunion.classof2007@gmail.com*
Subject: Class of 2007 Reunion

Dear Ambrosia Wellington,

There's no better place than Foss Hill to take in the view, and our festival this afternoon is not to be missed. Sure, this reunion is all about revisiting the past, but there are ways of finding out what the future holds too (see one of our expert tarot card readers)—and it may not be what you expect!

Sincerely,
Your Alumni Committee

I need to tell Sully about the mug. If she doesn't believe me, she can go back and see it for herself. But when I spill into our room, breathless, I can't say a word, because Sully is with Adrian. Not just talking to him—she's behind him with her hands in his hair and he's laughing, his eyes cast up.

"What are you doing?" Fear buzzes at the base of my spine.

"Sully was trying to get rid of my hangover," Adrian says. "Apparently there are all these pressure points in your scalp that release the toxins. She might be onto something. I swear, I'm feeling better."

Sully hasn't moved her hands. She's staring at me, hair swishing against Adrian's neck, challenging me to find something wrong with what she's doing. That's her—always blameless, an expert at shifting the weight to somebody else.

"Fine. Adrian, can we talk for a minute?"

"I'm meeting up with some people anyway," Sully says, releasing her grip. "I'll see you guys at Foss. If we even find each other. It's going to be a madhouse."

As soon as she's gone, I turn to Adrian and rest my hands on his shoulders, claiming back my territory. "Look, I think we need to leave. I'm not feeling well at all. It's better if we just head home. I'm not going to be any fun."

He stands up and wraps his arms around me. "I think that's a bit extreme. You've been kind of off since we got here. Do you not like me talking to your friends?"

"Of course not," I say into his chest. I hate how he has made it all about him—he's right in a way, but not the way he suspects. "Just be careful with Sully. She's not . . . she's not always someone you can trust."

"Chill, babe," he says, his mouth humming against my neck. "I'm just being friendly. What do you not want me to know?"

"Nothing. She's just kind of difficult."

He shrugs. "She seems fine to me. Why don't you take a nap and see if you feel better when you wake up? We're having such a good time."

I grit my teeth. It's typical Adrian. *We're having such a good time.* His stock line whenever I want to leave and he isn't ready to call it quits on a party.

"I can hang out with Justin and Monty. You don't need to worry about me feeling abandoned or anything." He tries to pull away, but I hug him tighter, not wanting him to see my face. *Trust me*, I would say if I were honest. *That's the last thing I'm worried about.*

I could insist that we leave now, which will inevitably end in a huge fight. I can stay here and let him go to the festival alone and hope that no incriminating details find their way into his ears. Or I could go with him and pretend everything is okay, knowing that whoever is behind the note and the mug will probably be watching me.

It's not really a choice. I'm trapped. I try to banish the ugly thought that I might have been summoned back here for that very reason. So I could never leave.

Foss Hill is packed with bodies, with music and noise, harsh sun nestled in gauzy clouds. I squint from behind my sunglasses and shiver despite the rising heat. I'm straddling two worlds—my comfortable one, with Hadley and Heather beside me, drinking wine on a blanket, and the other one, Butts C girls standing in a clump, *catching up*. Hads and Heather seem happy to spend the entire weekend as a trio, almost like it's another girls' trip, but I can't let my guard down. Just when I start to feel safe is always when the world shows me its claws.

Adrian pinballs between Justin and Monty and the husbands of the other girls. He's currently locked in a conversation with Jonah Belford—they're talking about stocks, something Adrian pretends to have firsthand knowledge of, even though I'm the one who takes care of our finances. I keep one ear on his conversation and another on Gemma, who is regaling the girls with the details of her Hollywood Hills bungalow and her casual friendship with Jason Statham.

The only girl from our floor at Butts C not sitting with us is Flora. I know she's here—I feel her gaze, still holier-than-thou—but I refuse to look up and truly see her.

"What a night, right?" Lauren brings her plastic cup to clink against mine. "I haven't drunk that much in years. Actually, I barely drink at all anymore. It's not responsible with the kids. But they're with my parents, so I think I deserve to let loose."

"Sure." I swirl my wine around, not even wanting to drink it. "What dorm are you guys in, anyway?"

"We're in the Nics. How about you?" The way she looks at me makes me think she already knows.

"Us too," I say.

"Sully hasn't changed much," Clara says. "Does anyone know what she's up to now? I lost touch with her when I did my MFA."

"No idea," says Gemma. "She said something about acting, but we've never crossed paths."

"Not surprising," Lauren says with a derisive snort. "She thought she was so talented. I remember when she'd get coked up and convince guys she was an heiress. She was always somebody else. Does anyone know who she actually is?"

That was lobbed at me, underhanded, exactly what I expect from Lauren. I don't give her a reaction, instead looking into the crowd, directly at the girl everyone is talking about.

Sully watches the band, swaying her hips lightly, as if the music is for her alone. Every so often she looks back at us, like she wants to make sure she isn't missing out on anything.

"You know who looks incredible? Ella," Lily says. "I barely recognized her."

"I know, right? We were texting before coming here and I told her to go for it and go blond. She said she always wanted blond hair." Lauren pushes her own hair off her face. I make a mental note that they're friends. They could have written the notes together. Lauren was the ringleader back then, the one who left *SLUT* Post-its on my dorm room door and wrote on the ACB junior year, *AW is pathetic trash, she's so evil she's barely human*, even though I could never prove it.

"She had a hard time," Gemma says. "It's good to see her doing well."

"Yeah. She was actually really mad at Flora," Lauren says, louder now, aware that more people are listening. Just then, Adrian and Jonah stop their conversation and turn toward our group.

"Who's Flora?" Adrian hugs me loosely from behind.

All eyes on me. Everyone waiting for my explanation. When I don't have one, Lauren does. "She was Amb's roommate freshman year."

"Cool," Adrian says. "Where is she?"

She's over there, I want to say, and point to her blond head, cresting over the crowd like part of the sun, right beside the tent where they're giving out temporary tattoos. But if I do, he'll insist on marching over there, where he'll inevitably gawk at her perfect face.

I wait for my world to detonate, but it doesn't. The girls have turned away from us, breaking off into little satellites, casting their eyes at me every so often. It's a move I'm familiar with. Nothing solidifies a group like casting someone out and having a common enemy.

I know what they're saying. *I can't believe she didn't tell him. That poor guy.*

"I don't think you'll meet her this weekend," I tell Adrian. *Or ever.* I turn around and search for Sully in the crowd, but she's not watching the band anymore, and I don't see her near any of the tents. I scan Andrus for her—tomorrow, it will be clogged with graduates and parents, never-ending rows of chairs and cheers.

I look behind us, back toward the Nics, just in time to see her emerging from a thicket of men in cargo shorts. I have to decide if I'm more desperate to know where she's going than I am terrified to leave Adrian here without me. But I always choose her.

"I'll be right back," I mumble, and before I can lose sight of her, I take off, clutching my half-full cup of wine.

She's walking down the paved path past the observatory, heading for Hewitt and McConaughy Drive. I keep a safe distance behind her, trying to stay hidden behind people dotting the space between us. Then I realize where she's going. Toward V Lot, where we parked yesterday.

She's leaving.

I stand back as she darts across Vine Street, her purse flapping at her side. She doesn't have her luggage, which means something scared her enough to make her take off without it, or her plan is done and she's wiping the mess off her hands like dust.

"Sully," I yell. A rumbling truck drowns out my voice. I cross the street as soon as traffic clears, dropping my sloshing cup on the road. I didn't make her answer to me then, but now I'm not letting her get away without an explanation.

She jumps into the passenger seat of a rusty brown truck parked in the lot. There's somebody in the driver's seat already—a man, broad shouldered. He's wearing a red baseball cap, so I can't see his face. Sully's hands are immediately in the air, like they always were when she really needed to make a point, as if by taking up more space she could prove anything to anyone. As if she needed to.

Now the man seems to have deflated, with no fight left, slumping against the wheel. He takes his hat off and slides his hand through his hair before putting it back on, and it's in that one second, maybe two, that I know who he is. A scream splits my head in half.

Sully is with *him*. Sully is in his truck. He's here. Of all the people who shouldn't have shown up this weekend, he's at the top of the list. There wouldn't even be a list without him.

Another sick thought unfurls like a flag. He was the one she was talking to last night. *She has no idea.* The two of them, with their own plan. Sully wouldn't do that to me.

My brain commands the rest of me to leave, but my body doesn't get the message. I turn around too late. Because now they're both looking straight at me.

Sully and Kevin.

22

THEN

Things changed in the days after Dartmouth. Whatever power I held in my original emails to Kevin—whatever element of mystery I wielded—was replaced by a neediness I hated but couldn't shake. My emails were tinged with urgency. *Just thinking about you, I'm here if you want to talk!!* His replies were sluggish and vague, a handful of words where I used to get paragraphs. *I'm good thanks well talk soon*

Then there was the thing Sully told me on our drive down I-91 after the party at Kevin's frat, both of us mainlining cheap coffee to keep from falling asleep. "I got his phone, Amb."

"What? Please tell me you're lying." The panic was instant and acute.

"Relax. I just wanted to have a look. I gave it back. Don't you want to know what was on it?"

"No," I said instantly, trying to focus on the road. "Yes."

She propped her feet up on the dashboard. "You said you emailed him. Well, he texts other girls. Look, I'm sorry, but you know I wasn't going to let him pull that shit. Now you can write him off as another douchebag and move on."

I was silent for a long time. When I did find my words, I said the wrong thing. "Maybe they're just friends. What did the messages say?"

Sully's sigh was heavy. "I didn't read them all. I just thought it was a pretty big coincidence that he had so many girls in his phone."

I decided it *was* a coincidence, no matter how big. Sully was annoyed that I was making excuses for him, and even more annoyed when she found out I was still emailing him a few days later.

"You're wasting your time," she said. "He's not a good guy. I'll prove it to you. You're going to look back and feel like an idiot."

I knew that feeling well. But I heard Kevin's voice in the Barn, felt his kiss. He was in love with me. And I had work to do.

I was supposed to go home that weekend for fall break, but I told my parents I wanted to stay at school and get caught up on my reading. Billie was harder to pacify. "Is this because of the guy?" she asked over the phone. "What's even happening with him after you guys kissed? I feel like you're not telling me everything."

"It's kind of complicated," I replied. My eyes strayed back to my laptop.

Just super busy lately with classes I hate, Kevin's last email said. It was sent at five a.m., which meant he was either just going to bed or just waking up. If it was the former, I had a real reason to worry.

That's the worst, I wrote back feverishly, deciding to cut to the point. *When do you think you'll talk to Flora?*

I knew I should be studying—most of the girls had gone home for break, including Flora. Sully was going to stay on campus with me, but at the last minute she'd changed her mind and caught a train back to the Upper East Side, kissing me on both cheeks before she left.

"Don't do anything fun without me," she said.

"Same," I told her, even though I was sure Evie would be there, willing to do everything I wasn't.

I didn't hear from Kevin for an entire day. Fear plucked at my skin like an insect. When an email did come in, I could practically feel his frustration.

Sorry can't really deal with this right now got so many exams to study for. We can talk later OK?

But we didn't talk for the rest of fall break. I couldn't concentrate on my reading, so I spent the time trying on Flora's clothes, painting my stubby nails with her rainbow of colors. I had sunk to a new low, but I still had a long way to fall.

Flora came back from Fairfield visibly upset and I was sure that Kevin had called her and finally said something. I tried to quell the heat rising in my chest and play the doting friend.

"What's wrong?" I asked. "Did you not have a good break?" *Or breakup?*

She flopped onto her bed, hair thatched across her pillow. "I hate going home. All my parents ever do is fight. Now my mom and my stepdad are fighting all the time, too. She snaps at him for every little thing. I feel awful for Poppy. She cried when I had to leave. I honestly wanted to smuggle her back here with me."

"I'm sorry," I said. "Want me to make us some hot chocolate?"

She gave me a wan smile. "I'd love that. Honestly, I just want to forget this ever happened and focus on something good. Like Halloween. It feels like I haven't seen Kevin in forever."

"It's going to be fun," I said. It was. Sully and I had bought our tickets to the huge Halloween party at Eclectic already, and I knew Flora had bought them for herself and Kevin.

"It'll be my first frat party," she said. "I'll get to see what I've been missing."

My smile hurt. I decided Flora deserved what was coming to her. She was always so *righteous*, makeup off and tucked into bed, never in a rush for class, always measured and calm and so damn *nice*. She existed in a state of silent gloating.

"You're not missing out on much," I said sweetly.

Kevin didn't call her that night, or the next night. I stayed home just to monitor what was happening, observing Flora like she was some kind of exotic species at the zoo.

She cried the next day in our room, the tip of her nose petal pink. "Maybe I'm just being paranoid. But you know how Kevin calls me every night? Well, he keeps blowing me off. Says he's busy studying for midterms, but I think it's more than that." Her blue eyes, wet and watery. "What if he's sick of me and found someone else?"

I rubbed her back in circles, like my mom did when I was upset. "I'm sure there's no other girl. He's totally into you." Inwardly, I beamed. *Who's trying so hard now?*

Flora pushed her bangs off her face with a plastic headband. "I'm not adventurous enough. Or smart enough. I always knew he could do better. After his graduation, I overheard these girls talking about me. They were saying how they were surprised a guy like Kevin could end up with a girl like me."

"That's not true," I said, shocked that Flora had an insecurity. "People love you."

"People like me. There's a difference. I just—I thought Kevin and I would be together forever."

I stared at the girl in front of me, with her hands on her blotchy cheeks, and tried to reconcile her with the Flora in my head. She wasn't perfect, and she wasn't pretending to be. Maybe her struggle was the opposite of mine. I fought to make myself look flawless. She fought to get people to see under the flawless veneer.

"Do you think I should ask him? We've always been able to talk about everything, and we promised each other that we'd be honest, even if it hurt the other person to hear." Mascara pooled under her eyes, enough to make her tragic.

"No. Don't ask him. You don't want to seem suspicious. He'll be here soon for Halloween. If things still seem weird, you can bring it up then. I feel like you only get a good read on someone when you see them in person."

It was important that Flora didn't call Kevin out, because under her glare, he might break down and tell her everything I had said. So much hinged on their not communicating. Every time guilt crept in, I reminded myself that it was love, this willingness to hurt anyone necessary. Flora was a casualty.

She nodded, perking up. "You're right. Halloween isn't too far off—I can wait to talk to him then. I'm probably being paranoid. I swear, my brain is a scary place sometimes. It gloms on to one bad thought and turns it into a flesh-eating virus."

I rolled that line over and over in my head. Of all the things Flora said to me, it's what I remember most.

Sully asked me repeatedly if I was still in touch with Kevin. I didn't lie. "Is he going to dump her?" she said the morning of the Halloween party, impatient, while we were sitting in Olin. "If he's so into you, why is he taking so long?"

"He's going to dump her," I said. "I just don't know when."

"Well, is he coming today?" She inched up her skirt as a group of boys walked past.

"I don't know," I said. "He told Flora he was."

"If he really cares about you, he'll show up." She bit the end of her pen. "This should be interesting."

I didn't tell her that I had emailed Kevin last night to ask if he was coming. He and Flora had spoken on the phone—I'd had my headphones on and pretended not to pay attention, but I knew from her repeatedly pleading, "Just tell me what's going on," that it hadn't gone well.

"He'll be here," I told Sully.

But when I checked my email after lunch, I knew he wasn't coming. *I can't do it yet, need more time and space to think thru it all.* It was a message that made me want to shatter my laptop screen. *Don't you want to see me?* I almost wrote back, but I stopped myself.

I totally understand, I replied. *I'm here anytime. You can call me if you're sick of typing.* I wanted to hear his voice, but he didn't take me up on my offer. Disappointment shuddered through me, but so did realization. I could use his absence, make it a weapon in my arsenal.

That evening, Flora wouldn't stop crying. She had veered beyond smudged mascara into big tears, each one rolling down her cheek in slow motion. "He says he's studying, but you know there's going to be some huge Halloween party at his frat, with girls wearing next to nothing. I keep picturing him taking one of them up to his room. You know, I haven't even been in his room this year. Why doesn't he break up with me and put me out of my misery?"

"I'm sorry," I said. I wasn't.

"It's like he's a stranger. We barely ever talk anymore and when we do, we fight. I'm sure you've noticed. I'm sorry you have to hear that."

She was apologizing, but I was the one with a running tally of missed calls and angry conversations in the margin of my Acting I notebook. "Look. It's Halloween. You can't stay in alone. So forget about him for the night, and come to the party with me and Sully."

"I don't know," she said. "I should just stay here. In case he calls and changes his mind."

"Stop giving him so much power. We'll go, have a few drinks, and come home. It's what you need." Flora always seemed to know what I needed. This was me turning the tables.

Someone knocked on our door. Sully, already wearing her slutty blue-and-white dress. She was Belle, the "Provincial Life" version, except instead of carrying a basket and a book, she had a bottle of Stoli.

"Time to start this party, slut," she said. Her eyes swept the room, obviously looking for Kevin. "Why aren't you dressed?"

Flora wiped her face. She didn't trust Sully to see her undone, but she trusted me. That made me soften, briefly. I shook it off.

"Flora's coming with us," I said. "Her boyfriend is being a dick."

I worried that Sully would be disappointed, but if she was, she didn't show it. If anything, she seemed excited. I couldn't make Kevin show up, but I was bringing the ultimate lamb.

"They all are," Sully said. "If you're coming out with us, you need to drink."

"She doesn't drink," I said, unsure of where the instinct to protect came from, but Flora had already accepted the bottle in Sully's outstretched hands, unscrewing the cap and bringing it to her lips. Her face contorted immediately.

"God, this is awful," she sputtered.

"Just wait," Sully said. "It'll get better."

I put on my own costume—slutty Cinderella, a dress I had found in a thrift shop that I was pretty sure had once belonged to an eight-year-old trick-or-treater, paired with plastic heels undoubtedly worn onstage by a stripper. Sully insisted on sweeping my hair into an updo, her hands lingering at the base of my neck. She whispered something in my ear. "Showtime."

"So your boyfriend's an asshole," Sully said to Flora. "What did he do?"

"Nothing." Flora tucked her legs underneath her. "We're just dealing with long distance. It's hard."

Sully ran her fingers through Flora's hair. At first, it made her flinch, but I saw her settle into it. Her immunity to Sully's charm was wearing off. "He's an idiot, then. He doesn't know how good he has it."

Flora didn't want to wear her Scarlett O'Hara costume. "It doesn't make sense without Rhett Butler," she said.

"I have an idea," Sully said. "Let's ask Gem." It was widely known that Gemma had the most expansive closet of any girl on our floor, a wardrobe that took up all of her closet plus half of Clara's, frothy dresses that peeked out from suitcases still covering her floor.

Gemma did have something for Flora. A pink open-backed dress that Sully decided would be perfect for Sleeping Beauty. Flora said it was too short, but we convinced her to wear it anyway. There was a moment, when Flora was checking out her reflection in the mirror, that I saw in her eyes what I knew lived in mine. The realization that she could get away with things. The knowledge that she was attractive, that her legs looked amazing, even better with a pair of Gemma's towering heels.

We drank in Sully and Lauren's room. Lauren was dressed like Uma Thurman from *Pulp Fiction*, a costume that looked ridiculous— her face was too round to pull off the black wig. Sully did bumps of cocaine off a key. I snorted a tiny line away from Flora's prying eyes, and when Sully offered some to her, Flora shook her head adamantly. After she'd had a few increasingly less modest sips of vodka, I could tell she was drunk.

"You should probably slow down," Lauren said, almost maternal. When Flora ignored her, I wanted to gloat. Lauren had tried to exclude me, and now she was the one being boxed out. When she left to meet some of the Butts A girls, I was glad to see her go.

"Take care of Flora," she told me and Sully. She must have known we would do the absolute opposite.

"I heard that," Flora muttered when Lauren was gone. "I'm so sick of people treating me like a porcelain doll. Everyone knows what's best for me but none of them listen."

We're the same, I thought briefly in my coke-spun high. I never said it out loud.

The three of us took pictures with my camera, Sully in the middle, me on the left because my arms were the longest for picture taking. We smiled and pouted and made silly faces with our tongues out, and in the last photo, Sully kissed me on the cheek. "I'm sorry," she said. She was drunk too, because she never apologized for anything.

Later, when I had the roll of film from that camera developed, I had forgotten about those stupid pictures and was unable to breathe when I saw them in their glossy four-by-six form. I couldn't bring myself to tear them up, but I really should have.

At Eclectic, we gave our tickets to a boy dressed as Chewbacca, then had our hands stamped and wove ourselves into the tapestry of the crowd, a daisy chain of girls linking arms. Flora's grip was hot and unrelenting. The ballroom was glitter and lights, legs and boobs and asses glistening, lipsticked mouths wide, guys watching us, their gazes more expansive than our costumes. There was a band onstage, boys with spiky hair and dog collars. Flora wanted to dance, and she did, with Ella, who managed to make Penny Lane look completely uncool.

"She's had way too much to drink," Ella said a few minutes later. "We should get her home."

"Relax," I said. "She's having fun for once."

"She's wasted. I have a bad feeling about this."

"Stop being such a buzzkill," Sully chimed in. "She's loving this."

Flora liked the attention, liked the eyes that detoured to her body. I could tell by the way she tossed her hair back over her shoulders, the way her fingers went occasionally to her mouth, as if to make sure her lipstick was still there. Sully slung her arm around Flora. I swallowed a current of jealousy. Flora wasn't one of us. She was just pretending, wearing our costume for one night.

We made our way into the lounge. Sully and I snorted the rest of her cocaine—she would get more, like she always did, never asking me to pay a cent. Flora drank. I kept filling her cup, making sure it was bottomless. I wasn't going to be the friend who told her she'd had enough to drink. I was going to be the other friend, the one who wasn't a friend at all.

Suddenly, there were three of them and three of us. A pilot, a lumberjack, and Slash. I didn't know how long they had been watching, waiting for the perfect group of three girls. They probably assessed each trio, determining ours had the right ratio of hair to lips to ass to boobs to legs. When Slash leaned in and kissed me, I let him, because it was easier than pushing him away, even though *Kevin* pulsed in the back of my head like a second heartbeat.

Flora stiffened, visibly uncomfortable. The pilot was dancing behind her, arms circled around her like a life preserver. I could practically read her mind. *Is this cheating or just being friendly?* I made eye contact with her, briefly, before going back to Slash, whose name I didn't know. Whose name I would never know.

Sully was draped over a couch, her Belle dress riding up to show the garter belt holding up her fishnets. She never went anywhere without the right lingerie. The lumberjack, perched beside her, was the best-looking of the three guys, his dark complexion smooth yet impressively bearded.

The next time I looked over at Flora, she was turned toward the pilot, chin tilted up. He was kissing her, with his hands cupped around her ass. I couldn't tell if she was kissing him back but something released inside me, a warmth in my rib cage. She was ruined. She had done something to Kevin that she couldn't take back.

I pulled out my cell phone and took a picture. I hardly ever used the camera on my phone, since the pictures always turned out so blurry.

"What are you doing?" Slash asked. I kissed him again to shut him up.

Sully hooked her arms around my waist and I sank into her bony grip. "Buddy wants to know if we want to get out of here and go back to his place for some more drinks."

I knew what "more drinks" meant. I didn't exactly want to have sex with Slash, but I didn't want to end the night, either. If I said I wanted to go home, Flora would leave with me, and her self-destruction wouldn't be complete. We'd received a lecture from RA Dawn in the first week of school. "Use the buddy system, guys. Always stick with a friend." Flora had looped her arm through mine and smiled, as if to say she would always look out for me.

But I hadn't smiled back. I'd never promised anything.

The guys shared one of the wood-frame houses on William Street, white with green shutters. We walked behind them in a pack of exposed collarbones and jutting spines. Slash hung back to share a cigarette.

"You an English major?" he said, as if he actually wanted to get to know me, as if his slug of a tongue hadn't been in my mouth for the past hour. When I didn't reply right away, he continued to talk about himself. They were all the same, everybody I had hooked up with. Even when they did ask, they never cared to listen for the answer.

Flora's buzz was wearing off. I could tell by the way she sucked in deep, shaky breaths, gulping them down like water. I kissed her on the cheek, that strange protective instinct making an appearance, like a glitch in my system. She snuggled into me, her head in the crook of my neck.

The boys lived in the first-floor unit and when we were inside, Sully grabbed Buddy the lumberjack's hand and pulled him into the kitchen, where he pressed her up against the counter. Her hands slipped under Buddy's jacket. He thought she wanted to get closer, but I knew what she was really doing. She would emerge with his cell phone, her desired treasure.

We paired off, like we were getting on Noah's ark. Sully and Buddy went into a bedroom. Slash tossed off his top hat and led me to a futon in the common area. Flora's pilot sat down on the couch across the room, pulling her onto his lap like she was some kind of throw blanket to keep him warm. Her legs swung over his, crossed at the ankles. I fixated on her ankles because she kept bob-bing them, even when Slash started kissing me and Flora's pilot started kissing her.

I kept my eyes open—I knew Slash would barely notice, anyway. Flora's pilot swept his arm around her lower back, rubbing the swatch of exposed skin there with his thumb. He whispered something in her ear, moved her hair behind it. She laughed. That laugh was all I needed to hear to convince myself she was enjoying it. She was the one who wanted to be one of us. She was the one kissing back.

Slash's hands did the inevitable creep up my leg, under my skirt, to the outside of my underwear. I hadn't worn cute ones or even shaved. Sully wouldn't have approved.

Somebody dimmed the lights—Sully, maybe—and I finally closed my eyes.

Slash moved on top of me. I could feel his dick pressed against my thigh and thought it was only a matter of time before he unzipped his pants and wanted me to do something with it. But instead, he pulled away, pushed up my Cinderella dress. I jerked upright. The only guy who had ever gone down on me was Matt, and it had only happened once, which was awkward at the time but worse after, when he never expressed interest in doing it again. Sex with Wesleyan boys had been perfunctory, my head bobbing when it was their turn, my turn never coming.

I was vaguely aware of Flora and the pilot across the room. I heard a zipper, the shifting of fabric, something like clothes dropping to the floor, but my eyes were shut, and even if I had opened them, it was too dark to see much beyond the outlines of people. My legs dangled over Slash's shoulders and he gripped my butt with his hands. I would have to fake an orgasm. It was too foreign, having some random person's tongue darting in and out of me, his mouth opening and closing like a machine.

Then I promptly stopped caring, stopped hearing anything, because my guy was good at what he was doing, much better than Matt had been. I let myself fall back on the couch, legs trembling. This was different from before, when the guys didn't care about my pleasure.

This was a dull throb building, my entire body tingling, a total loss of control. When I came, it was loud and ugly and I didn't care.

I finally cracked my eyes open long enough to see Flora's pilot moving on top of her, shifting her head to the arm of the couch. She was turned away from me so that I could only see her hair spilling onto the parquet floor. She wasn't making a single noise. That didn't mean anything, of course. She hadn't made any sounds in bed with Kevin either, aside from a few giggles. Girls like Flora didn't have to shout to make themselves heard.

I expected Slash to clamber on top of me, or at least sit down beside me and pull his dick out of his pants, because boys never did anything without expecting the same or greater in return. But he got up and kissed me on the cheek, then padded away. I heard the tap running a few seconds later. "Want some water?" he said. I nodded, even though he obviously couldn't see me.

I crossed my legs, my body humming, waiting for Flora and the pilot to finish so we could laugh about this. But the couch kept creaking, the pilot making occasional quiet grunts. I was sure he wished he had synched it so that we finished at the same time.

I got up, groping my way to where a bathroom must have been. That was when I heard Flora. It sounded like she was crying, or whimpering. But the noise stopped before I could decide if that was what I'd heard. I found the bathroom—filthy, the toilet freckled with shit—and sat down, even though I didn't really have to go.

By the time I flushed the toilet and opened the bathroom door, Sully and Buddy were sitting on the couch on either side of Slash, whom I couldn't look in the eye with the lights on. Flora was on the love seat, smile placid. The guys would celebrate this later while we stayed mute. I would be called a slut if anyone found out. But so would Flora, and that made it okay somehow.

We got stilted hugs at the door. Slash actually said, "We should do this again sometime." I was no stranger to that line. He never bothered to ask for my name, much less my phone number.

Sully talked the entire way back to Butts C, but Flora was silent. The campus was peppered with costumed students. A pack of Crayola crayons ran down High Street, a whorl of shrieks; a boy dressed as a centaur was almost completely naked.

"Flora, you've been holding out," Sully said, tugging on the ends of Flora's hair. "I had no idea you were so wild. I like it."

Flora didn't have a response. Sully winked at me over her head.

When Flora and I were in our room, I got into bed without taking off my dress or makeup. Flora did the same, which was maybe the most shocking thing of all—she followed a skin-care regimen every single night, cleanser-toner-moisturizer. I had almost dozed off when I heard her voice in the dark, small and scared.

"I didn't want to do that."

I pretended I was asleep.

23

NOW

To: "Ambrosia Wellington" *a.wellington@wesleyan.edu*
From: "Wesleyan Alumni Committee" *reunion.classof2007@gmail.com*
Subject: Class of 2007 Reunion

Dear Ambrosia Wellington,

  The people you grew close with during your time at Wesleyan knew you at your best—and sometimes even your worst. We all have things we wish we'd told our friends back then. There's no better time than now!

Sincerely,
Your Alumni Committee

Kevin McArthur looks the same, at least through a windshield. I can't stop staring at his face, even when Sully gets out and makes her way toward me. As she walks over, I realize that maybe she said *There is no us* not because of what we did, but because of what she did when I wasn't looking.

"Amb," she says, her voice forceful. My eyes flit back to Kevin, who is watching us. I can't read his expression. "Amb, wait. I can explain, okay?" Her hands are on my wrists. I want Kevin to get out of the truck and complete our fucked-up trio, our walk to the darkest parts of memory lane. But he stays where he is.

"Amb, hear me out, okay?"

"I don't know what to say." My teeth chatter, like they did the night of Dorm Doom, even though it's warm out. "Why is he here? Why didn't you tell me yesterday?"

"He reached out to me," she says. "A few weeks ago. He got a note too. I should have told you, but I didn't know if we could trust him."

We. We're *we* again. I watch, powerless, as Kevin starts the truck, wishing it weren't so easy for him to leave all over. But he pulls onto the road without so much as a glance. I wonder if I'll ever see him again, and what I would say to him if I did.

"How did he even know where to find you?" I ask.

"It's a long story." She drops her hands to her sides. "I'll tell you later. You just have to believe me that everything I've done has been for us."

There's only an *us* when it's convenient for her.

"Can we?" I sputter. "Can we trust him?"

She nods, her face solemn. In the hard afternoon sun, I can see that age has played with her after all. It's there in the lines around her mouth, in the light waves creasing her forehead, the pucker between those eyebrows I used to envy. "I think so. He said he didn't know who else to reach out to, and he found my email address."

"But it doesn't even make sense. He must have received hundreds of letters just like that. Hate mail. Death threats. Why would he do something about this one? Why now?"

"I don't know why. But I obviously didn't tell him. He doesn't know what we did."

"Unless he does, and he's the one who sent the notes. He has more reason to hate us than anyone. We ruined his life."

She plays with her tank top strap. She knows more than she's telling me. I want to shake the information out of her, turn her upside down like she's a saltshaker and watch her insides spill out.

"He has no clue, Amb. I swear, he doesn't suspect us."

"I want—" I want to see him, but I'm not sure I do. After everything,

I was lovesick over the loss of him, then I went into self-protection mode. I reread the emails once, twice, countless times. I saw us differently. Both of us self-absorbed and desperate for an excuse to talk about ourselves. Both manipulative. Even now, I have a complicated relationship with his memory. Sometimes he's the sun and other times a thunderhead, scabbing out the light.

I want to know if he ever actually felt it. If we ever would have had a chance. But I can't ask him that. Not when I can barely ask myself.

"Flora," I say instead. "Have you seen her? Has . . . has Kevin seen her?"

Sully's lips form a scowl. "Of course I've seen her. You can't miss her."

"Where's Kevin staying? He can't be here on campus."

"Somewhere in Middletown. I think he mentioned the Super 8."

Were you talking to him last night? Are you playing your own game with him? I never let myself consider back then that Sully might have felt the same way I did. Kevin was easy to fall in love with. So was she. But they had barely known each other—they were in the same room only a few times, although that could also be said for me and Kevin. Sully had been skeptical when I told her about the emails, but suddenly I understand that she and Kevin could have been doing the same thing.

The wind churns her hair. She pushes it back impatiently. "We have to stay strong, okay? It's you and me."

It's you and me, as if it always was. *Real friends are the ones you don't see as often as you'd like, but it feels like old times when you do!* Billie wrote something like that on one of her Instagram posts, accompanied by a picture of us from high school, hair knotted on top of our heads, baby Gwen Stefanis. Sully was there for my worst moments, but the worst moments only existed because of her.

"Kevin must have suspected. We were the only ones who got close enough to take it. He's had a long time to figure it out. He could have lured us back here to get revenge."

"Yeah, but, Amb. He was just as guilty as we were. Don't let him off the hook."

It's a strange thing to say, but she has a point. Sully and I didn't go into the night thinking it would end the way it did. Kevin didn't either.

A car horn blares from the street, making us both jump. "We should get back," I say, my panic shifting to Adrian. I left him there, where anyone could say anything. *AW is a slut who deserves to actually die.* The three-dimensional version of the ACB, surrounding my husband on Foss Hill.

Sully's eyes are on me as we walk past the Nics, that hypnotic seafoam gaze. "You don't still love him, do you?" She makes *love* a dirty word.

I used to think love was a permanent haze, cobwebbing a person's sanity. That's how I justified what I did to Flora. I clung to the connection I had with Kevin, retracing our actions, rereading the emails. It was embarrassing. My want was baked into every word. And he loved it, because he hungered for attention as badly as I did.

"No," I finally settle on, because I don't trust Sully with the enormity of my emotions. I can't possibly explain to her what seeing Kevin has done to me, what choked feelings he has unspooled.

"We need a plan." She casts a look behind us, like she's afraid somebody is listening. "None of us will be able to move on with our lives until we figure out who's behind this and what they want."

"Maybe it's more than one person," I say. "A lot of people hated us." In my head, she's still a suspect.

"Well, what did I always tell you back then?" Sully says, her voice slipping into its natural velveteen. "We're together, and we're worse."

It was something we said to each other whenever we approached a pack of boys. I would hesitate, like their thick cluster of bodies was impermeable.

"They're together, and they're bad," I'd say, as in, *Let's pick someone else.* Someone without a herd, the baby elephant toddling after the stampede. Sully would whisper, all Stoli and Burberry Brit, "We're together, and we're worse."

We're almost back at Foss Hill, the festival still in full swing. It seems like everyone has a fun memory to smile about. It's a gigantic, throbbing lie. All of them have secrets. Most of them have hidden behind a computer, written something horrible about someone else. And they're acting like being back at Wesleyan is *just so nice*.

For a moment, I'm relieved to see that Adrian is where I left him, but then I notice that Lauren and Ella have replaced Justin and Monty. Ella's hand is on his back and she's leaning in. I break away from Sully and catch up to them before Ella can say anything else to incriminate me.

"I'm sorry I was gone so long," I say quickly, grabbing Adrian's arm. "I told you earlier, though. I'm not feeling well today."

"Okay." He doesn't look directly at me, and I can tell immediately that he knows something. I swallow the panic as it swells up. I should have told him our side of the story first. *My* side. The shape of it, forever changing.

He continues before I can find the right words. "Why did you not tell me about Flora? Seems like kind of a big deal to leave out."

White noise roars in my ears. I didn't keep him close, and now I'm going to pay for it. "I did tell you. At least, I thought I did last night. I guess we were both wasted." It's an excuse I've used before. *You were too drunk to remember*. This time, he knows it's a lie.

He arches an eyebrow. "No. You said you weren't really friends, and that I probably wouldn't meet her this weekend. But you made it sound like she's still—when she's not."

I don't want him to say it. Hearing it out loud makes my skin twitch. But he's going to say it, because that's what people do with tragedy. They talk about it because it's too big to be contained, and talking breaks it into manageable pieces.

"You could have told me," he says. "I looked like an idiot when Ella mentioned her memorial. You could have told me she died."

There's that word, in all its finality. I know she's dead. I've known for so long. But hearing it never gets easier. Those words never fail to open the same jagged guilt.

"I don't like talking about it." Nausea burns in my gut. "It was a hard time for me."

Adrian opens his mouth, then envelops me in a hug, and I let myself breathe. He doesn't know what I am, and I'll make sure he never has to find out.

I don't like talking about it.

Because then I'd have to admit that I'm the one who killed her.

24

THEN

We destroyed Flora twice. We ruined her on Halloween, the night she cheated on Kevin. But what killed her came later.

I asked her, the morning after Eclectic, if she was okay. She was still in bed, not up with her usual seven o'clock alarm.

"Why wouldn't I be?"

It wasn't her voice. It was flat, no bounce, none of the typical Flora inflections. She didn't want to talk about what had happened. She didn't want to talk about what she'd done to Kevin. She didn't want to talk at all.

That week, she studied with headphones on and barely acknowledged me with anything bigger than a nod. The doors on our floor were bare without her Post-it affirmations. She started leaving at night, which made me paranoid, because she could have been talking to Kevin. Once, I walked into our room when she was on the phone, and my heart could have punched through my chest. But it was just her sister on the other end. "Love you, Poppy," Flora always ended her calls.

She was counting down to Thanksgiving. I knew she wanted to see Poppy and Kevin. I was counting down, too. He would break up with her. His emails had lately become more decisive. *I know ur right, we've grown apart and its like I'm pretending we haven't because people expect us to stay together. Just be patient OK?*

I didn't like being told what to do.

What do you mean, be patient? I just want to know how you feel about me. I was losing control and sensed that any thrall I'd once held him in was dissolving.

You know I think ur beautiful Amb. But this is a mess and I need to figure shit out before this can go anywhere OK?

I started to wonder if *beautiful* was all he had to offer. Its impact had dwindled, and I needed more. It was always *later, later, I'm figuring it out, I need to find the right time.*

Then I remembered the picture of Flora I had taken on Halloween. Her short pink Sleeping Beauty dress bunched up at the back, her mouth all over the pilot's. The boys I would never know out of costume, three Buddies who roamed campus and knew the skin under our clothes.

The boys didn't matter. The picture did. I would use it if I had to.

The week before Thanksgiving, Ella caught up to me when I was walking through the CFA on my way to class. "Amb, we need to talk about Flora." She sounded like she was on the brink of tears.

I rolled my eyes behind my sunglasses. I resented that Flora had become the focal point of my life. Flora and Sully were like the sun and moon, me an obedient satellite orbiting around them.

"What about Flora?" I walked quicker to make Ella jog, her stubby legs straining to catch up.

"I'm sure you've noticed how weird she's acting. And this morning I saw her crying in the bathroom. She didn't even see me come in—she was, like, bawling over the sink. She said she has allergies."

"So maybe she does."

"Come on, Amb." In her mouth, my name was a stab, an accusation. "Ever since Halloween, she hasn't been herself. You're the one who lives with her. There's something seriously wrong."

I spun around so fast she almost crashed into me. "Don't be so dramatic. She's probably stressed about classes. Who knows? Not everybody has to be happy all the time. If you're so worried, you talk to her."

I don't know if she ever did. What I do remember is what she shouted after me as I retreated into the theater building. "I told you she had too much to drink. You didn't listen."

After class, on a bench in the green space sheltered by the CFA, I told Sully about the exchange, complaining about how annoying Ella was.

"Yeah, she's a cunt," Sully said. "This is Flora's problem, not ours. She feels guilty. There was this girl at Spence who got wasted at a party and fucked two dudes, even though everyone knew she had this long-distance boyfriend. Evie heard her call him from the party and confess, all wasted, and he dumped her on the phone. Then she went and OD'd to make him feel bad about it."

I soured on the mention of Evie's name. I didn't like when Sully talked about her.

"What a slut," I said. Sully always warmed to my profanity. I was careful not to react to the OD. Shock would be too predictable.

"Yeah. So what's happening with Kevin, anyway? Has he dumped Flora yet?"

I told her about the latest emails. That he was *figuring it out.*

"You need to help him figure it out." She lit another cigarette. "Otherwise she'll convince him to stay with her. Guys are idiots. They like a sure thing."

"What else can I do? He already suspects she has something going on with another guy. Their phone calls have pretty much stopped."

Sully tapped her cigarette with her long index finger. "We need to up the stakes. Get him here. Fuck him senseless."

There was her *we*, almost majestic, lingering in the cold air like smoke. I was buoyed by the challenge. I had the picture and I had my imagination, and I didn't know which could yield more damage.

"I don't know how to get him here," I said.

"Ask nicely. Better yet, tell him."

"I have an idea," I said.

Sully gave me her cigarette. "I want things back to normal," she said, pouting. "It feels like they're all we ever talk about anymore. Kevin and Flora. It's getting boring."

I took a drag. "I know. I'm sorry. It'll be different once they finally break up, I promise."

Her lips puckered into a smirk. "Good."

She's cheating on you, I wrote that evening as Flora slept in her bed beside me, pink satin mask pulled over her eyes. *It happened on Halloween. I have proof.*

Show me

Come see it in person. This weekend. I can't keep all these secrets anymore. I let myself be guided by Sully's heavy hand. I asked nicely and let him read between the lines.

The next morning, he wrote back, *I'm coming tomorrow*

No period, no punctuation, no ending. I was surprised by how easy it was. I had poisoned the relationship from both sides, and now it was time to suck the poison out of Kevin. He was the gentleman I deserved. Now it was my turn to be his leading lady.

The next day, I was surprised when Flora took her headphones off and came to sit beside me on my bed. I put my notes aside—I couldn't concentrate on anything but our fucked-up diorama anyway. My grades were plummeting. My real education was taking place outside the classroom. My life was Method acting.

"Kevin's coming here. Tonight," she said. "But he didn't even call me to tell me. He sent me a really weird text. I have a feeling he's going to dump me."

"I'm sure you're wrong," I said, marveling over my own power to make things happen.

She shook her head, tears wobbling in her eyes. "I'm not. He's been distant. And I mean—I can't really blame him. I've been acting strange since—well, I was actually hoping I could talk to you about something. I think there's something Kevin needs to know."

No. *No.* I couldn't become Flora's receptacle. It was too late for that. I knew I should feel sorry for her—she looked exhausted, with bruise-colored circles under her eyes, shirt slumping over sharp collarbones. But instead, all I felt was a sick satisfaction.

To my relief, someone started pounding on our door. "You locked me out again," Sully yelled.

"Don't," I said quickly. I didn't even know if Flora heard me.

I let Sully in, and she sat cross-legged on our floor. She cast an irritated glance at Flora, as if Flora were the one who had intruded on us. "I got another bottle. We should start drinking soon. Showtime."

I glared at her, but she either didn't notice or didn't care.

Flora interjected. "Where are you guys going tonight? Kevin is coming for a visit. Maybe we can go too."

There it was again. She had just told me Kevin was breaking up with her and now she was pretending for Sully that things were normal. She was the reason the rest of us lied. Because she made her halo look so goddamn easy to wear, even if it weighed her head down.

"Beta." Sully raised her eyebrows. "Yeah. Bring him. Dress like twins. It should be an interesting night."

Flora's smile was automatic, as if jerked into place like a marionette. "We'll try to make it."

A moment passed between me and Sully where I knew something big was going to happen. Tonight could be the beginning of a dream or the start of a nightmare.

The Double Feature meant everyone was supposed to come dressed identical to someone else, so Sully and I were both in mesh tops and leather skirts, chokers circling our necks. We got ready in her room, flat-ironing each other's hair while doing shots of Stoli, the bottle's mouth becoming as red as ours. We took turns pressing our ears to the wall she shared with my room, waiting to hear something, anything, some hint that Kevin had arrived. I had agreed to let Flora have our room so that they could *be alone*. But all we heard was music pumping from somewhere else, the hallway throbbing with shitty bass.

Part of me wanted to stick around Butts C to see if Kevin showed up, but Sully convinced me that was the wrong move. "They'll be at the party. Maybe she told him to meet her there to delay the inevitable."

I didn't know how she could be so sure. I still entertained the possibility that Kevin would change his mind and not show up at all.

Lauren, who was staring at her phone, suddenly removed her headphones and looked at us like we were crazy. "You guys are being so loud. Why are you spying on Flora? What are you trying to overhear?"

"Maybe I just like hearing people fuck," Sully said. "Where's your twin, anyway?"

"I told Ella I'd go with her, but now she's sick and isn't coming at all. Can I third-wheel it with you guys?"

"That's not exactly the point," I said. I didn't want Lauren to tag along. Lauren, who had called Sully insane, who had purposely left me out of her Hamptons weekend. "You're supposed to come with a twin, not a triplet."

"Who really cares? It's just another dumb theme party."

"I don't want to share my hot date," Sully said, wrapping her arms around me. "If you want to come, whatever. But we're on a mission."

I swatted her away. *Don't say that.* I didn't want Lauren to suspect anything. I could see her running back to Flora, making herself comfortable under Flora's feathered wings.

I cast a glance at our door as we left. I wanted to go in, but Sully yanked me away.

At Beta, Sully and I clutched each other's arms as Lauren strode behind us in her pleather pants. People were packed everywhere. Standing beside a keg, playing a giant game of beer pong, making out in corners, groping in the open. A disco ball spattered the room with ghastly neon.

My cell phone was in my purse. On my phone was the picture of Flora and the pilot. I would wield it like a weapon if I had to.

"I don't see them," I shouted at the same time as Sully leaned in and said she would get us a drink.

"Who are you even looking for?" Lauren asked. We both ignored her. It felt good, rendering her invisible.

A hand gripped my ass cheek under my skirt but when I spun

around, nobody was there. I walked the main floor in a figure eight. Lauren stuck to me like glue, the personal chaperone I'd never asked for. "Have you seen Flora?"

I whipped back to face her. "No, why? Am I her babysitter?"

Lauren curled her lip. "You're her roommate. And she seemed weird earlier. We were supposed to meet at Olin to study, and she blew me off. It's not like her."

"Well, I haven't seen her. Try texting her or something." I wanted to add, *If you're so close, you should know where she is.* It was a Sully thing to say. But I wasn't Sully.

"I did. She's not replying. What's your mission tonight, anyway?" She tapped her boot, waiting for my answer.

I decided to give her something—she would never piece it together anyway. "There's a guy I've been talking to who might be here. I think he's in love with me." I liked how it sounded.

"Who is he?" I liked the hint of jealousy in her voice too.

"Nobody you know."

She didn't have a reply. Instead, she said something totally random. "She's dangerous, you know. Sloane. You don't know what she's capable of."

I thought I must have misheard her over the music. "What?" I shouted, but then Sully appeared behind her. I took the drink she handed over and accepted the bump of cocaine she offered me off one of her keys. Lauren stalked away, shaking her head.

Sully's mouth curved into a smile. When I revisited that night— and I did, often, as much as I pretended I didn't—that smile jutted out first, the biggest picture on a collage.

"Look over there. I told you he'd be here."

Over there was Flora, dancing in front of the mantel, hair flying, jeans sagging off her skinny ass. She was wearing flip-flops, the same pink polka-dot ones she wore in the dorm showers. She hadn't even attempted to match Kevin, in his green Dartmouth cap, handsome and completely bewildered, his mouth a flat line.

"Is she drunk?" I yelled, turning to Sully. But I didn't get an answer, because there was that smile again, except it was even bigger now, carving a path to her cheekbones. I turned back to see Kevin trying to extract Flora from the dance floor. She shoved him away, her eyes blurry with smeared mascara.

"She's done," Sully said.

Those two words, over and over in my head. Like Flora was a piece of meat, cooked too long.

25

NOW

Dear Ambrosia Wellington,

Things are gearing up. If movement is on your mind, lace up your shoes for a campus fun run. No competition, just fitness between friends. Don't look over your shoulder to see who's behind you—what matters is the finish line!

Sincerely,
Your Alumni Committee

We have to walk past Flora on our way back to the dorm. Somebody has plastered her on the side of the Nics, her blue eyes boring into us. The same life-sized poster that's hanging all over campus. *Flora Banning Memorial Foundation—Support Mental Health!* I don't look at her, like I tried not to look at her name on all the emails, the Flora Banning Memorial Foundation, right underneath the names of the Alumni Committee. If she were alive, she'd be one of them. She would have married a boy from a good family, worn headbands and pleated skirts to church. She would have been a child psychologist and a patient mother. She would have been everything I'm not. Maybe that's why I hated her—not because she had who I wanted but because she had *what* I wanted, qualities I could never embody when I tried. Because she was nice, and that was its own power.

I tell myself that I won't leave Adrian again. I'll go on the stupid campus fun run, even though the only running I feel like doing is back home, to our apartment and the warm buzz of Astoria.

But now that I've convinced him I'm sick, he won't let me do the run. He insists that I lie down, claiming he wants to run with Justin and Monty anyway. And Jonah, apparently, his new friend, who Adrian says is "super chill." My own lies have boxed me into these four walls.

"I'll stay here and take care of Amb," Sully says, lips scrunching into a smile as she retreats into her room. "You go and have fun."

I don't like the way she's practically pushing him out the door, like she wants me all to herself. But there's nothing more I can say.

"Hey," he says, finger to my cheek. "Do you think—do you think you're not feeling well because—you know?"

I shake my head. "I doubt it."

When he's gone, Sully hovers in the inner doorway. "Because what? Does he think you're knocked up?"

I suppose we're both aware of how thin the walls are. "Maybe. But I'm not."

"Good. I never want kids." Sully sits next to me on the bed, which jars me back to our getting ready for countless nights out, side by side. "Some people aren't meant to be mothers. Especially if they have daughters. The last thing I need is another girl like me in the world."

There's Billie, who always proclaimed that she wanted kids but yanks a brush through Sawyer's hair impatiently. *Sometimes all I want is my old life back*, she says when she drinks. And then there's me, who wants a life I never even had to begin with.

"My mom couldn't handle me," Sully continues. "I got away with so much. She thought having me at Spence would help. No boys around to distract me. As if I couldn't find them elsewhere . . . among other distractions."

Her own words. *I get bored easily.* I was a toy, convenient for her to bat around. We all were.

"Anyway. What are we going to do about Flora?" Sully tucks her knees into her chest. "We need to figure out who's sending these notes and what they want. When you saw us in the truck, Kevin and I had been talking about meeting at Friendly's to make a plan."

What are we going to do about Flora? The same conversation we had back then. The knowledge that something had to be done.

"I guess that makes sense." Despite all the time I spent getting over somebody I never had, I want to see him again. Not on TV or in shitty Internet photos or through a windshield. I want to ask him the question I've been holding in for almost fourteen years. *Did you really mean it?*

Sully gets up and wanders into her room. "I didn't know you ever talked to him," I call after her.

"Relax. I don't." She emerges at the doorframe in jeans and a bra, as nonchalant as ever about her body being on display. "I told you, he's the one who reached out."

"I know. It still doesn't make sense, though." *Why didn't he reach out to me?*

"You can't possibly be jealous," Sully says softly. She turns around, giving me her back. I want to ask how he even found her email address, but I have a feeling she would twist the answer. "If you're coming, you'd better get ready."

We both end up in dark denim and heather gray, almost like we planned it. Almost like the grown-up version of Double Feature. If I believed in signs, this would be the worst one.

Sully's car is a black Toyota Echo, older and plainer than something I'd imagine her driving. We used to talk about taking road trips together. Feet on the dashboard, Slipknot on the radio, probably heading toward the ocean.

"I don't know about you," Sully says as she pulls out of V Lot, "but being back here has really fucked with my head. Maybe it's that no-body seems to have changed, just gotten older."

"Yeah. And they all still hate us. At least, they hate me."

"They're idiots," Sully says.

"I thought you hated me too." I sound wounded and pathetic.

"I never did. You know that. But it was a weird time for me. I couldn't really be myself."

I nod, but it doesn't take away the chasm of loneliness I spun into without her. When Sully and I started spending all of our time together, I stopped needing to befriend the other girls. Sully picked them apart, a vulture on fresh carcasses. I only saw their flaws and insecurities and couldn't believe I ever cared about their approval.

After Sully, nobody wanted to know me. When Wesleyan's ACB started up on LiveJournal during my junior year, I knew my name would be on it. I knew people would say horrible things, and I read every single one. *I saw AW running from Butts that night in a slutty outfit—she did it. She hated Flora.*

Sully had her own thread, too. And I remember what somebody wrote on it. *This bitch is not only insane but may also be a sociopath capable of killing people! Just saying!*

"Did you keep in touch with anyone after graduation?" I don't know why I ask, except it suddenly seems important. "Do you still talk to any of the girls?"

"No," she deadpans. "Definitely not." I think about the girls I used to see her with on campus, the ones who came before and after, my bookends. She snipped so easily, cut out everybody she pretended to care about and hurt at Wesleyan. I was just another hanging thread.

I cough into my hand. "They're all the same. They love the drama. You know they're going to be at the dedication later, with their fake tears. As if they ever really cared about Flora."

"They didn't." Sully laughs, still at her most relaxed when she's getting dirty. "But you know, death makes everyone best friends. You were brave to bring your cute husband here. I always wondered if you'd find someone."

Normally that might be insulting, Sully calling my husband *cute,* but what she said isn't about Adrian. It's about me. She thinks I settled, and I'm torn between wanting to defend Adrian and wanting to agree with her.

"You better keep an eye on Lauren," she continues. "There's something about how she's been looking at you. And Adrian."

"I don't trust her. She was there, at Double Feature. And she's the one who told the cops that she heard us talking about Flora, and that we were looking for a guy at the party."

"Lauren's the worst," she says. "She just wants to stir up shit. Don't believe a word she says. She thought she was such a mastermind, pitting people against each other." She turns her head to look at me. "I thought maybe she had something to do with this, but she's too dumb to pull it off."

Pull what off? I almost say, but now we're rolling into Friendly's, and I'm suddenly shit-scared. I have so many questions for Kevin that I never thought I would get to ask, and now it's like an exam I didn't prepare for. *Did you mean what you said about me? What you said about her?* His promises changed my life, and I don't know if they were ever real.

He's sitting in a booth, red cap pulled down, hair flattened out at the ends. He's in a sweatshirt, not a Dartmouth one. He never graduated from there. Maybe he never graduated from anywhere. Just like Sully fell off the face of the earth after college, Kevin disappeared too.

Sully and I slide into the bench across from him. "No need for introductions. You obviously remember Ambrosia. This is the real reunion, huh?"

He looks up and I lose the generic greeting that was building on my tongue. The same eyes, same mouth. There's shadowing on his cheeks and chin that I didn't notice through the windshield. He probably has to shave every day. Adrian can't grow a proper beard. Kevin looks handsome and tragic, somehow, a hurt built into the structure of his face.

"Hi," he says. "Amb. You look great."

After all that, *You look great.* A downgrade from *beautiful.* I play with his words. I'm sure he says them to everybody, because it's the nice thing to say when you haven't seen someone in over a decade, even if it's not true. It's the nice thing to say to the last person you slept with before your life imploded. And Kevin always had the right things to say.

"You too," I manage. I can't decide if he actually does. If he ever did, or if he only did when Flora had him, her ownership branding him as someone worthy.

"Okay, we all look great. Let's get right to it," Sully interjects hastily. "We came here because we all got notes, so now we have to figure out who sent them and what they want. Amb found a cell phone last night in the bathroom with our picture on it. She thinks it might have been Flora's phone."

Kevin's voice is gravelly when he speaks. "I was telling Sully that I've gotten this note before. Not the exact same, but pretty much. It's from the same person. I'd know that handwriting anywhere. Most of the other threats I've gotten were typed out, like they were afraid I'd go to the cops and figure out who it was."

"Did you keep them?" I ask. He shakes his head. Of course he didn't keep them. I'm sure he didn't keep my emails either.

"I thought it could be Felty," I say. "He questioned me—us. He suspected that we had something to do with it."

Kevin, softly. "We did, didn't we? I mean—you and me." *You and me.* My legs, under the table, are drumming. Time away hasn't made me any less pathetic. I still cling like Saran wrap to any form of attention.

"Felty questioned all the girls on our floor," Sully says. "Some of them totally lied. Like Ella Walden. She made it seem like Flora was her best friend. And this Lauren bitch that Amb and I were just talking about on the way here. She was my roommate, and that night, she basically followed us around the party like a lost puppy."

"I don't think Flora talked much about Ella," he mumbles. "Or Lauren. Just Amb."

Just Amb. There it is. The guilt, the same guilt I hold so easily at bay most of the time, because most of the time I can honestly convince myself that we weren't friends. The details Flora told me about her life, her family, her ambitions, have been fuzzed out. She wasn't innocent. She did what she did. Then there are the days when I hear her desperate pleas and can almost feel her tears on my skin.

"I'm surprised she didn't mention me. She sure judged me enough." Sully is obviously annoyed, not used to having her name left off any list.

"I don't know how they found out where I live," I say. "I don't have the same address I had in college. The alumni magazines go to my parents' house, but the note came to my apartment."

"Whoever it is, I'm sure they're here this weekend," Sully adds. "That still leaves a lot of possible suspects. Who has something to gain by getting us here?"

"I don't know," Kevin says. He rubs his forehead, takes off his baseball cap long enough for me to see that his hair is graying under it. "I have a different theory. I think whoever sent these notes is the person who murdered Flora."

My entire body goes cold. Beside me, Sully laughs sharply. "You don't actually believe that."

"I do. That's why—that's why I came here. Not because I was threatened by the note. But because I need to know. I owe it to her."

I didn't want to believe that Kevin ever really loved Flora. But this is bigger than love. This is guilt, the thing I always turn my back on. If Kevin feels a duty to avenge Flora's memory, there's no telling how deep he'll dig for the truth.

"Okay, your interesting theory aside, we're all here for the same reason." Sully clacks a saltshaker against the table. "Because we want to know who's targeting us and move on."

The three of us had one thing in common back then. Flora. And she's all we have in common now.

"So when do they make their move?" Kevin says. "And how do we figure out what it's going to be and catch them in the act?"

"There's the dedication this afternoon," Sully says. "Whoever wrote the notes wants us to be there. I think that's where it's going to happen, whatever they have planned."

"Maybe," Kevin says. "I don't know what they have planned for me."

A waitress finally comes by, asks if we want to order. "We'll be leaving soon," Kevin says, his smile rising from the ashes, that gleaming white phoenix—and there it is, the familiar grip of jealousy, because Kevin could make any girl feel like the center of his universe.

Sully glances at her phone. "The dedication starts in a couple hours. I'm sure we'll get an email reminding us about it soon."

"I think you two need to stick together," says Kevin. "Keep track of who's always around and who's asking questions. Who's watching you."

Sully snorts. "Everyone's watching us. Nothing has changed."

"I'm serious, Sully. I'm going to be around. I mean, I can't be seen on campus, but that doesn't mean I won't be looking too. I'm not going home until I figure out who did it."

Who did it. Who sent the notes, or who killed her, because he doesn't believe it could have been me.

"Me either." I clamp my teeth together. "We'll go to the dedication."

"Don't trust anyone," Kevin says, paranoia etched into his frown. "You don't know what this person is capable of, if they did—if they did *that*."

I meet his eyes, and it's like they're pleading with me to believe him. I used to be scared that if I ever saw him again, he would read the truth on my face. But he only wants me to read the truth on his.

"You guys don't understand. I tried to get them to figure it out. The cops and detectives. But they were always satisfied for it to have been me. That I was the only one capable."

Sully's expression has become strained, and she's tapping her foot impatiently, like she wants to leave immediately. "We'll find whoever wrote the notes. Amb and I—we won't let them get away with it."

Before Sully ushers me out of the booth, I reach over and touch Kevin's shoulder. He doesn't move—doesn't stiffen away or lean into me. I don't know what I expected, that a touch would validate me somehow, but it's just fingertips on a sweatshirt.

"Can you believe him?" Sully says as we stride across the parking lot. "He actually thinks someone—I mean, I had no idea he was so wrapped up in conspiracies."

"What if he's right?" I say in a small voice. "We don't know what really happened." I don't tell her that as terrifying as Kevin's theory is to contemplate, it might absolve us. *Me.*

"I'm pretty sure we were there," she snaps. "We know better than anyone." When we get back into the car, she jams the volume button with the heel of her hand. I guess we'd both rather listen to the radio than play tug-of-war with those memories.

"What now?" I say when we arrive back on campus.

"I think we should split up." Sully slams her car door. "Everyone's at the run. It's the perfect time to look around. I'm gonna try to get into Ella's and Lauren's rooms and see if I can find anything."

"Okay," I say. "I doubt they just left their doors unlocked, but we can try. I'll go with you. Kevin told us to stay together."

She arches an eyebrow. "Are you seriously going to listen to him? We don't have much time before the dedication. We need to separate and cover some ground. You should find Felty. Keep an eye on him."

I watch her walk away, with her hands jammed in her pockets, her familiar swagger imbued with tension. I reluctantly set off in the other direction, with no intention of looking for Felty. I pass people setting up tents on Andrus for some of the reunion dinners and side-step Olin out onto High Street, where Beta stands behind immaculate hedges, windows glinting in the sunlight. There's the roof where Sully and I sat, legs dangling and heads bowed over, our laughter spraying the air.

I suddenly can't breathe. I need to get off campus, out of the purgatory of memories that share the same source: Sloane Sullivan.

I walk until I'm at a Rite Aid, where I stop to buy a bottle of water and a magazine and pick up something else at the last minute, a First Response that I shove in my purse, not making eye contact with the cashier. I've taken them before in the dorm bathrooms, the surge of fear, the thumping heartbeat and sticky armpits followed by relief, the promise to myself that I'd be safer next time, that I'd make them wear a condom even though I was on the Pill. I don't think I'm pregnant—I'm sure the sick feeling in my stomach is just the stress of being back here—but I'll feel better when I know for sure.

Lauren jogs up to me when I'm headed back up Foss Hill toward the Nics, which means the run must be over.

"How are you feeling?" she chirps. "Adrian said you were having a nap. I remember those days, having to sleep off the hangover."

"I'm fine." I don't give her any more. I wish I could know what Lauren told Adrian during the run. Her fanged comments, always calculated, biting into unsuspecting victims.

"That's good. You know, I was saying to Gemma that it almost feels like old times. With you and Sloane hanging out." She always insisted on calling Sully "Sloane" even when nobody else did.

"I don't know," I say. "I think everything is different now."

"A lot of us thought Sloane had something to do with it." She takes a drink from a pink water bottle. "With getting to Flora. Getting in her head. You know, I only found out the weekend of graduation that Sloane slept with my boyfriend during freshman year. Remember Charlie, who I started dating after Thanksgiving?" She pushes sweaty bangs off her face. "I told you guys about him. At that Psi U party."

"Maybe she didn't know." I'm sick of Lauren. She's the type of woman who insists that we have to empower other women, only to peel them apart and chop them up.

"She knew. She went after him on purpose. She was all over him at a party in one of the wood-frames. Clara and Dora saw. I guess they went into a bedroom together."

"So what? He was the one cheating."

Even as I say it, I flash back to being seventeen and freshly betrayed, the image of Matt with Jessica French never fully leaving my brain, no matter how hard I tried to exorcise it. The bitterness of seeing them together at senior prom—a prom he had talked endlessly about taking me to—is still on my tongue.

But I can't feel sorry for Lauren. My mind so easily conjures what she wrote about me on the ACB and the rumors I know she started. As soon as we part ways, she'll go to the others and tell them I'm a bitch. Nothing has changed.

"Before you go defending her, hear me out. You know I went to

Spence with her. Well, there was this girl Evie, who was Sloane's best friend."

"Yeah, she told me about Evie. What does it matter?" I don't want to hear her name again. I'm sure Sully raced back to her after I couldn't keep up.

Lauren's forehead creases. "Well, she probably didn't tell you the whole story. There was this party senior year, and Evie got wasted. Then a bunch of girls started screaming, and turns out Evie was in the bathroom, slumped over the tub. Apparently she'd OD'd on Oxy. She went into a coma and was, like, brain-dead, and her parents took her off life support a couple weeks later."

My first reaction is that it's not true. I open my mouth to tell Lauren off. Evie was alive—Sully talked about her. I compared myself to her.

But maybe I wanted to one-up a ghost.

Lauren waits for my shock, smiling smugly. I won't give it to her. "That's really sad."

"Yeah. Sad." Lauren pauses for dramatic emphasis. "Evie wasn't even into drugs, just pot sometimes. And the day before that party, Sloane hooked up with Evie's boyfriend. She obviously has a history of doing this. A lot of people pointed the finger at you with Kevin, but some of us thought it was Sloane the whole time."

The SS thread on the ACB. *This bitch is not only insane but may also be a sociopath capable of killing people!*

I thought the person who typed it was jealous. I never thought they were right.

"I tried to tell you back then," she says. "But you never wanted to listen."

"I already knew." I struggle to keep doubt out of my voice. "We all did things we're not proud of." I want to say more to defend Sully, but my brain starts spiraling somewhere dark, to a day when Sully told me a story about a girl who overdosed at a Spence party. At least, that was her version of events.

"Nobody's perfect," she says. "But she has a pattern. The girls and I saw the way she's been looking at your husband. Just watch out, okay?"

Almost a threat, except for the question at the end. She's not worried about me and she never was. She loves the drama, loves to find the fissure between two people. She liked when Sully and I stopped being friends. She's trying to do the same thing now—put a wedge between us.

I won't let her. Sully didn't do anything to Evie. It's not like she could make a girl take too many drugs. I know Sully's brand of persuasion better than anyone. She could put ideas in someone's head, but it was up to everyone else to follow through.

Just like I did.

"See you at the dedication, right? Then you'll be at dinner? We should all sit together. Like old times." Lauren's tone is light again.

"Maybe," I say. Except in old times, she would have made sure I knew my spot was at the very end of the table.

She actually has the nerve to blow me a kiss as we enter the Nics, and that's when I decide to bring it up, no matter how much I know I shouldn't.

"Why are you pretending to like me? You stopped talking to me freshman year. And you called me pathetic trash. On the ACB."

She pauses in front of the stairwell but doesn't turn around. "I didn't write anything about you on there. It must have been someone else. A lot of the girls were pretty angry at you after. And you're the one who stopped talking to me."

That's not what happened. Lauren wasn't the only girl who turned on me, but she's the one who had the social prowess to take gossip and spread it like a disease.

"Sloane plays with people, Amb. It's what she's always done. She doesn't know any other way. When you're in her inner circle, that's when you're being played the hardest. I don't even think she's capable of feeling bad about it." She pauses. "Maybe she's the one who started the rumors about you and Kevin. I wouldn't put it past her."

She thumps up the stairs and I sink down against a bank of mailboxes, remembering how Billie and I used to mail each other the dirtiest and most disgusting postcards we could find. How my grandma wrote me letters asking all about college. I'd write lies back, telling her classes were interesting and the weather was great and of course I'd made some friends, the girls are all so nice here.

I don't know what's true. If Sully stole Evie's boyfriend. If she played a part in her death. And, if she did, what else was she capable of?

26

THEN

Kevin saw me. He pretended not to, which stung like an open-handed slap, but I convinced myself he had to deal with Flora first. It was almost like he was afraid to come near me. But the more times Flora pushed him away, and the longer he watched her like a worried parent, the closer he crept toward me and Sully. Then, finally, he was in front of us, hands clenched, asking us what to do.

"She won't talk to me," he yelled over the music. He shuffled over to an alcove away from the sound and we followed him. "She begged me to come see her, then broke down crying." I noticed his shirt was buttoned unevenly, as if he did it up in a rush. "This isn't Flora. She's out of control."

"We tried getting her help." Sully placed her hand on Kevin's fore-arm. "She copes with stress in such unhealthy ways. I told her to see the guidance counselor, but she wouldn't do it."

I would have marveled at the lie if I hadn't known Sully could do so much worse. I didn't like Sully's making Flora the victim. She needed to be the monster in this story.

Kevin looked terrified, which was disconcerting, and up came the guilt, an acid burn in my chest. "I don't know what to do. I came here because . . ."

He trailed off, never finished that sentence. I finished it in my head. *I came here because I wanted to break up with her in person.*

When he went back to the ballroom, presumably to keep an eye on Flora, we followed him. We had nowhere else to be. Well, I didn't. Sully could have spent the party finding her own guy to hook up with, another Buddy for another night. But that wasn't enough anymore. We were storming the castle, and she was leading the charge.

Flora kept dancing. Under the harsh lights, her skin was shiny and unnaturally pallid, and she was bumping into everyone. People gave her a wide berth, like she might spontaneously combust. Kevin tried to step in and take her away once, twice, but both times she slapped his hand like it was on fire. The third time, she screamed and shrugged away from him, prompting a big jock in a wife beater to get in front of Kevin and poke him in the chest, as if to say, *What gives?*

"This is a mess," I said. We looked like spectators, but this disaster was entirely my own making.

"It's what you wanted," Sully said. "God, I'll be glad when he finally dumps her and this dumb drama is over."

It wasn't exactly what she said but the way she said it. Like when this dumb drama was over, she'd be looking for something—or some-one—else to entertain her.

Flora pushed a stringy piece of hair behind her ear. I was close enough to see that her fingernails weren't painted but totally bare, bit-ten into ragged red zigzags. That detail almost made me want to take back everything I'd done. But I didn't. To become the heroine, I had to push the queen off her throne.

Flora suddenly shoved her way out of the room, darting around the corner like a wild animal. Sully and I followed her without exchanging a single word.

She ended up in an upstairs bathroom, hunched over the sink, spitting something red into it. *Blood.* Or vodka cranberry.

"Flora," I said. "What's going on? Are you okay?"

She glared at us, or maybe it just looked that way because her eyes were little slits, puffy from crying or lack of sleep or both.

"Why did you do it, Amb? You told him there was another guy.

He mentioned the name Hunter—you're the one who had that guy in our room. But he doesn't believe me. Then you two took me out on Halloween and—everything is ruined."

"You know that's not true," Sully said, cool and calm, a parent handling a child's emotional outburst. "You're not thinking straight."

"Fuck you," Flora spat out. The words sounded completely wrong coming from her mouth. She turned to me, reaching out her hands, and I thought of the first manicure she had given me, how gentle and precise she had been. Her eyes pleaded with me. "Amb, you're my best friend. Tell me you didn't do this."

I stood rooted to the ground, unable to move. Sully and I had successfully dismantled a girl, stripped her down to bits and pieces. It was easy for Sully to think of our plot that way, with a character at its center, not a real person. Flora meant nothing to her, but I meant something to Flora, maybe something more than I would ever mean to Sully. The panic surged so quickly and violently that I felt lightheaded.

"This is hard to hear," Sully said, even calmer, like the angrier Flora got, the mellower she would get in return. "But your boyfriend is just like every other guy. Always looking for something better. He's in love with someone else." She crossed her arms over her chest, black bra on display under her mesh top. "Meanwhile, you got bored and fucked a stranger. I don't blame you. Just own it."

Flora's mouth opened and closed in quick succession. I was pissed that Sully had gone so far without checking in with me first.

"Sully—" I started, but Flora cut me off before I had time to decide if I would defend myself or lean into the lie.

"I didn't fuck a stranger. I didn't want to—I never said—he just—"

But she never said it. She didn't know how to, or she wouldn't let herself go there, because her brain was protecting her from the truth. I knew exactly what she was trying to say, and I was sure Sully did too, even though Sully hadn't been in the room that night, able to stop it but unwilling to.

"Flora. Honestly. If you're going to make excuses for yourself, you might as well tell Kevin what happened. You can go your separate ways, and we can find you a different guy to fuck tonight. There are tons of guys out there who would gladly fuck you. You'll feel better, you know. Being free."

Flora was beaten down. Sully had already slung so many barbs at her, punched so many holes in her perfect existence, that she was less girl and more gaping wound. There was no way she was getting back up. But what she said next surprised me.

"We can get through this," she said. "If he understands what happened—" This was when she fixated on me again, eyes watery, waiting for some kind of validation. "Amb, please, you know what happened. You could tell him. This isn't who you are."

I was pinned between two sets of eyeballs, two girls, each wanting something very different from me. My stomach lurched. I hadn't expected this guilt, this eleventh-hour sensation of being torn in half. But it was too late to turn back. The choice had already been made, the damage done. If I defended Flora, Sully would cut me loose. It was easy for her to discard people, like dolls she was finished playing with. I didn't want to be one of those dolls. I wanted to be the person throwing them away with her.

And it was more than that. This was Flora crawling on the ground, finally no longer immaculate. This was revenge, not even against her in particular but against a universe that let some girls have everything.

I grabbed my phone out of my purse and found the photo, the one I had taken of Flora kissing the pilot on Halloween. I held it up to her, not letting her touch it when her hands reached out, afraid she would smash my phone to obliterate the evidence.

The color drained from Flora's face, like somebody had pulled a plug deep inside her. She was done fighting. My breath came in short bursts. I was sure I would pass out.

"How could you do that?" she practically whispered. Big Disney eyes, Bambi's mother before the shotgun. "I trusted you."

"I trusted you too." My voice was tinny and uneven. "But it wasn't right, what you did. I've been cheated on, so I know how it feels. I don't think you're the kind of person who can live with this weighing on you. You should tell him yourself."

Her tears started coming, fast and furious. She rubbed her eyes, smearing away what was left of her makeup. She muttered something under her breath, something I wish I had never heard. "I want to die."

Sully grabbed my arm. "Come on. We should go."

So we did. We left what remained of Flora hunched over the sink, not looking at the ghost in the mirror.

Kevin was downstairs, standing by the dance floor. This time he had a drink in his hand.

"What's going on? Where is she?" I couldn't tell if he was annoyed or actually concerned. His facial nuances meant nothing—I only knew the written version of him.

"She's upstairs," Sully said. "She's acting like a drunk idiot." She paused, deliberately, as if she were considering which ingredient to add to her recipe next. "She does this a lot. Gets remorseful, then pukes all over."

My nod was automatic. It was over; we had won. But Sully was still swinging, still fighting. It was one of those movie scenes where somebody is on the ground, unconscious, but the other person keeps kicking.

"Amb, why don't you go get us another drink?" Sully said, her touch light on Kevin's arm. "We could all use it."

Suddenly it wasn't us versus Flora anymore. It was like I had been bumped from the adult table to the kiddie corner, but I dutifully went, trying to steal glances as I headed for the keg. Sully leaned in and said something to Kevin that made his jaw stiffen. Her nods were sympathetic, the concern on her face genuine, like we hadn't just conspired to ruin his relationship.

I had a thought. *This is a game for you. Everything is a game for you. School, boys, other girls. Maybe even me.* Sully pretended she didn't care about rules. But really, it was that she learned them too quickly, picked them up the same way some people did a second language. She knew all the rules already, so she made a game out of breaking them.

Sully joined me in the line for the keg a few minutes later, her fingers creeping under the mesh of my top, drumming on my spine. Her territory, all of me. I let myself breathe. The worst of it was over.

But my head spun anew as she pulled something out of her purse. A cell phone, not hers. A black one, a plain lump.

"We could have some fun with this," she said.

"Whose is it?" But as soon as I asked, I already knew. "How did you get it?"

"When you get close enough to a boy, you can do just about anything." Her breath on my face, somehow sweet and not beery.

"What are we going to do?"

Sully shrugged, as if all of this was an impulse. "We're going to do what he didn't have the balls to do himself. We're going to break them up."

27

NOW

To: "Ambrosia Wellington" *a.wellington@wesleyan.edu*
From: "Wesleyan Alumni Committee" *reunion.classof2007@gmail.com*
Subject: Class of 2007 Reunion

Dear Ambrosia Wellington,

   Please join us for a tree dedication to celebrate the life of Flora Banning, who was taken from us far too soon. Those who knew Flora are aware of exactly how many lives she touched during her short time at Wesleyan. All are welcome to join Flora's friends in a gathering behind Butterfield C to talk about the girl whose memory lives in so many of us.

Sincerely,
Your Alumni Committee

My back is clammy with sweat and the sundress I just changed into clings to my thighs. The First Response has two lines—two lines that showed up almost instantly, like big middle fingers. *Fuck you. Yeah, you took your pills, but karma has been waiting to catch up with you for a very long time.*

   I wish I didn't know that there were no false positives, something I learned when Billie took her first test, the first time she and Ryan had ever skipped the condom. Toni was different—she had trouble getting pregnant. It took her and Scott six months of obsessively tracking her cycle. I assumed if I ever wanted kids it would be the same thing. But here I am, the unlucky 1 percent.

I don't know what this means, but I do know that I can't have a baby. I can't watch my stomach grow, watch my boobs get huge and veiny, see my feet inflate out of my shoes, and be happy about it. I want to text Billie and tell her, *You were right,* but she'd be thrilled that I'm joining her team. She'll want to pass down her maternity clothes, stretchy dresses pilled at the arms, leggings she constantly tugged down from her rib cage.

I can't tell Billie. I'll have to tell Adrian. He'll cry and instantly drop down to kiss my belly. I can't think about that now. Not until I know who is behind the notes and what they want from me.

I flush the offending pee down the toilet and throw out the test, then go to wash my hands at the sink. It's only when I look up that I see the message, neat letters in waxy red lipstick.

Stay—you owe her that.

My hands are clenched by my sides, fresh fear rooting me in place. I didn't hear anyone come in while I was in the bathroom, but how long did I sit there, staring at the test, praying for it to somehow change? Or has the message been waiting for me all along?

I need to tell Adrian that we're leaving, and this time I need to explain why. Not everything, of course. But enough to get him in the rental car, with Wesleyan in the rearview mirror forever.

I jog back down the hall to our room, trying to decide what I'm going to say. *There's something you don't know about Flora Banning. A lot you don't know. I did something to her.* I have no idea how I'll make it digestible. But when I open the door, I hear their laughs in sync. Adrian and Sully. They're sitting on our bed, their heads clustered over something, Adrian's hair still wet from his post-run shower.

"What are you doing?" I tug on the hem of my dress.

Sully rolls her neck and winks at me. "I'm showing Adrian some old photos of us."

Now Adrian turns around. "You were hot. I totally would have wanted to ask you out, but I wouldn't have had the balls."

Sully is holding a small album, like the one Toni made for my parents when Layla was born. I hover over Adrian and survey the damage.

"You guys look like sisters," Adrian says. There's Sully and me in our princess outfits, more leg than dress. Flora isn't in it because she took the photo. *Smile, girls,* she'd said, but I hated how smiling made my eyes crinkle up.

I grab the book and flip through the pages. Flora is in most of the other photos, Sleeping Beauty pink, forced cheer on her face. She was so upset that night. She never should have come with us.

"She was really pretty," Adrian says softly.

"Where did you get these pictures?" I snap the album shut.

"I borrowed them," Sully says. "I always meant to give them back. I thought I'd bring them to the dedication. Lauren mentioned that some of the girls were bringing photos and stuff to share memories."

I glare at her. "No. That's—" I can't finish the sentence with Adrian right here. *That's sick. That's morbid.* But that's Sully.

Sully cocks her head. It's like she knows I need to talk to Adrian and is making sure I don't get a chance. Her lips twist into a smile. Her red lips. It would have been easy for her to leave the message on the mirror.

She has photos from back then. She could have planted the cell phone. She knew Flora's ringtone for Kevin—she used to put a finger to her temple every time she heard it.

"Justin wanted to go for drinks somewhere, but I told him we were going to the dedication," Adrian says. "I assume we are. It seems like the right thing to do. Ella said during the run that she'd see us there."

What else did Ella say during the run?

The only place I want to go is back to Astoria, to smudgy skylines and Greek takeout and shitty live music at happy hour and our apartment, where there's never enough room. But someone is making it almost impossible for me to get there.

"We should actually head out so we're not late." Sully gets up—Adrian's eyes linger a beat too long on her body—and slips on a jean jacket before pausing at the door. "Are you guys coming?"

When she swings the door open, Ella is right behind it, eyebrows raised in surprise. There's a piece of paper in her hand—a card, thick and off-white. The same as the notes we got.

"Oh, hey," she says. "I figured you guys were out. I just wanted to leave this here to invite you to a pre-drink I'm hosting in my room before the dinner tonight. A bunch of us are going to share some Butts stories and toast Flora."

I jump up and snatch the card from her hands. The lettering isn't fancy or sculpted—just basic black pen, like a note you'd take in class. I hand the card to Sully.

"That's nice of you," Adrian says, zipping up his jacket. "I'm down for that."

Ella smiles. She's genuinely pretty—proof that college isn't everyone's prime. Or maybe she was always pretty and I just didn't notice because I was laser-focused on disassociating myself from her and our suburban similarities. Now I wonder why I cared so much.

"Shouldn't you be getting ready to dedicate a tree or something?" Sully says.

Ella's expression doesn't falter, but her eyes narrow ever so slightly. "I just wanted to get these invites out before everyone made their own plans. It was kind of a spur-of-the-moment thing, but when's the next time we're all going to be in the same room together?"

Never, I want to scream. *It's never going to happen again.*

"It's pretty old-fashioned handing out actual invitations," I say instead. The snark slips easily into my voice. It's not the place making me eighteen again but the people. *These* people.

Ella retains her smile. "Flora used to put Post-its on our doors to invite us to movie nights, remember? She would appreciate what I'm doing."

What I'm doing.

"Movie nights. Cool. Sounds like you guys had some good times," Adrian says.

"It wasn't all fun and games here. Ambrosia could tell you that," Ella responds.

"No, it wasn't all fun and games." Sully shoves the card in her jacket pocket. "But some people at least knew how to play the games." She starts down the hall, and Adrian and I trail after her. I only notice when I look back that Ella is wearing red lipstick too.

"Some of us made up the games," I half-shout.

Sully spins around. She looks genuinely pissed off. "We all did."

"What are you guys talking about?" Adrian says.

It's a standoff, no weapons, just words. Sully's expression is somewhere between defiant and angry. As I stare, the fight leaves me. Sully used to seem so complicated, an impossible code to crack. But she wasn't. She was simplistic, in a way. She showed people what they desired and watched them bat helplessly at a toy she could have easily clawed from the air herself. She made us feel special when it was finally in our hands.

Then made us realize it wasn't worth wanting anyway.

In this moment I feel sorry for her. Wanting something means accepting the possibility that you may not get it. But wanting nothing is worse.

"Did I say something wrong?" Adrian asks. "If I did, I'm sorry."

Adrian is obviously afraid this is going to become an argument—I know how much he hates public confrontation. But Sully's face softens and she musters a smile.

"Of course not. Nobody said anything wrong."

She looks directly at me when she says the last word.

We walk past Exley on our way to the Butts. I keep my eyes down when I see who is standing out front: Felty and a woman cop I vaguely recognize from the night of Dorm Doom. She was sympathetic, offering us tissues, which I used to dry up the tears that kept coming, the ones I let Sully think were a performance.

Felty stares. Sully actually waves to him, which he tentatively returns. *We're together and we're worse.* His eyes are on me as we walk by, trailing up my body, honing in on the back of my head, like I'm a target at a shooting range.

You owe her that.

Before those words appeared on the mirror, Felty said them.

We're some of the last people to arrive. Everyone else is clustered around an uninspiring tree, recently planted, parched brown stem and sparse head of leaves. It doesn't stand a chance against a world of wind-whipped cruelty, just like the girl it was planted for. We stand behind Lauren and Jonah, whose hands are locked together. Sully whispers in my ear.

"There was writing on the mirror. In the bathroom."

I keep my voice low. "I know. I saw it."

"Saw what?" Adrian says.

"Nothing," I say, too loud.

Lauren and Jonah turn around briefly, then look away. Across the circle, Clara and Hunter watch the tree intently, like it's going to up-root itself and start moving any minute. Gemma is dabbing her eyes already. At the very back I spy Hadley, saying something to Heather. I haven't responded to their texts from the past couple hours. *Where are you? What's going on?*

I let a message in lipstick bring me here, where all the girls are talking about us. Whispers rise, circulating in the air like pollen. I can tell by the lowered chins, the eyes peering out from behind bangs. What else is there to talk about? Their husbands, their looks, their glittering careers that started here. Clara's MFA and Lily's SoHo gallery and Dora's Broadway roles and Gemma's celebrity acquaintances. They're polished and accomplished, but they still have claws that need to be sharpened. Even now, I'm their favorite scratching post.

Soft music starts to play, something classical, like what Flora listened to when she studied, the swell of it floating out from her headphones. The circle breaks up to let Ella in. Ella, and someone else. White-blond hair, gingham dress, Mary Janes, slick of red on her lips.

"Sully." I grip her arm instinctively, because I'm falling, my legs incapable of supporting my body and all the lies within it. "Sully, it's her."

Because it is her. It's Flora.

28

THEN

We brought Kevin's phone to the roof, where we sat on the edge, legs hanging down, as Sully pulled up his text message history with Flora. "This is gold," she proclaimed.

All it took was a brief scroll for us to see how the relationship had started to fray. Her desperation its own beast, her panic something palpable. *Where were you? Who were you with? Why didn't you call me back?* His excuses, always generic, his patience losing steam as her insecurities hit a crescendo. *I went out with the guys just Aiden and Martin. It was late, didn't wanna wake u*

Who are Aiden and Martin? Do they really exist?

She must have sensed herself losing him. You had to cup boys in your palm ever so gently, like you would when you found a frog in the woods, frozen on your path. If you closed your hands too tightly it would panic and thrash against your fingers until it either found a way to jump out or suffocated.

"This is sad," Sully said. "She's so desperate for him to be a certain kind of guy."

I felt like she wasn't just talking about Flora anymore.

She started typing something, then handed the phone over to show me. It said: *Hey babe where are you? Are you okay?*

"Hit send," she said. I did.

Not okay. I'm sorry. In my room, please come

The response was almost instant, which made me angry. Flora had run away from the party for attention. She wanted Kevin to follow her, to fold her into his arms and apologize, even though she was the one who had fucked up.

And because I was pissed off on behalf of girls everywhere—annoyed that Flora was just so good at playing the damsel in distress, and angry that a white knight had always been there to rescue her when she should have saved herself—I snatched the phone and typed something back.

I'm not coming. I know what you did.

"Oh, that's good," Sully said, her fingers like talons on my shoulder. "Short and sweet." She sputtered on a laugh. "Okay, not sweet. But it's perfect."

We stared at the phone, waiting for Flora to respond, both of us watching the screen with glazed eyes. This was our entertainment, better than actually being at the party. It was the logical next level in whatever game Sully and I were playing.

I didn't even know where Kevin was, whether he was still downstairs. I should have tried to find him, played the normal, drama-free girl to Flora's mess. But in those moments, breaking Flora down was more important. Because it was never just about the boy. It was about the girl standing in the way of the boy. Maybe it had been about her the entire time.

The message that popped up on Kevin's screen wasn't at all what I expected. It made me hold my breath, like a balloon that had become too big to fit inside my chest.

If you don't come I think I might do something bad

"Oh, come on," Sully said. "What a fucking drama queen. Evie was like that. She always threatened to do something to herself whenever we had a fight."

It was a puncture in another girl I needed to beat. If I could pull off what Sully expected from me, I wouldn't have to compete anymore.

"Flora isn't going to do anything," I declared. "Besides put on those god-awful bunny slippers and cry herself to sleep."

Sully snorted. "She's acting like she did nothing wrong. She's the one who had a stranger's dick inside her."

I didn't answer, because I didn't want to think about that night. Instead, I thumbed out a reply.

You need to take care of yourself. I'm not going to be around anymore. We shouldn't be together.

We both stared at the message. "It's too formal," said Sully. "Change the last part to *I need to figure shit out.* It's totally a line a guy like Kevin would feed her."

I did what I was told. After I hit send, I realized it was something Kevin had actually said to me. I had seen it as a promise, but maybe it was an excuse the whole time.

"There you guys are. This party sucks," Lauren said, suddenly hovering over us. I buried the phone in my lap. "What are you doing? Did you see Flora? She looked so upset. I think we should go and check on her. I'm pretty sure she left."

"You do it," Sully said. "If you're so concerned. We're having fun." She stood and grabbed my hand, pulled me up and led me through a clump of smokers and back indoors. We ended up in the same bathroom we had followed Flora into and locked ourselves inside.

"What if he's already back at the Butts?" I said, my grip sweaty on the phone. "What if Flora knows they're from us?"

"He's not back there. I guarantee he's downstairs having another drink. And she's probably already in her pajamas with some fucking hot chocolate."

Vegan, I almost added. *Vegan hot chocolate.* Guilt bubbled, but only for a second, when I remembered *Best* and *Friend.* I glanced at the phone. "Shit. She wrote back."

I don't know what you heard about what I did but it wasn't like that, I swear I can explain, just please come here now

"No dignity," Sully said. "This is pathetic."

Her disgust was the fuel I needed.

I'm not coming. We're done. I've known it for a while, but I just don't love you anymore.

It felt good typing those words, sending them. I didn't even wait for Sully to give me the okay. I was playing a role, and I was good at it.

While we waited for the reply, Sully had to pee. I leaned against the door, stretching out my legs. I saw the words first.

You don't mean that. Please come, we can talk. I want to kill myself right now

My first thought: *We've gone too far.*

My second thought: *We could go further.*

Before Sully could say anything—before she had time to wipe and get off the toilet and tell me what to do—I had already done it. Not because I was her puppet. Because, head inflamed with vodka and drugs and rage, I wanted to.

Just do it, then, and stop talking about it.

The toilet flushed. I hit send. Sully clapped a hand over her mouth when she saw the screen. It was the mixture of surprise and awe that I had been waiting for. Since the day we'd met, I'd wanted to shock Sloane Sullivan.

"She's not serious," I said. "She's just being dramatic. She's one of those people who needs the attention."

Sully laughed and slung her arm around my shoulder. "I had no idea you were capable of this. It's pure evil."

Pure evil was her highest form of compliment. I was drunk on power. "I should go find Kevin."

"One sec," she said, grabbing the phone. "Before you do that, let me show you something."

I waited as she fiddled with the phone, figuring she might be writing something even worse than I had. But after a minute, she handed it back to me. "I told you I'd prove it to you."

I was staring at the messages. The texts that Kevin had written to other girls, the ones I hadn't believed Sully about. They were real.

Hey Lisa, was thinking about u earlier

Hey Tammy hows ur essay going

Hey Britt loved your Halloween costume

I only had to click briefly on each message to know that I wasn't special. That Kevin indeed saw me, but the same way he saw other girls. I wasn't unique. And in that moment, I wanted to pull back what I had just sent to Flora. I sucked in a breath, lightheaded. I needed it to be for love. I needed it to not be for nothing.

My eyes flitted up to Sully, who was smiling pointedly. *I told you so.* Suddenly she was the one I was angry with, even though she had warned me—I had just refused to believe her.

I still wouldn't give her my outrage, and I wasn't ready to let my fairy tale die. I slipped the phone into my purse.

"This doesn't mean anything. So he hangs out with other girls. This doesn't mean he's sleeping with them."

"Stop making excuses for him," Sully snapped. "He isn't worth it."

"I still want to talk to him," I said. "I can give him a chance to explain."

Sully was silent for a long time. Finally, she shrugged. "I guess you do need to find him. Give me that phone. I'll make sure he never knows it was missing."

I gave her my purse and followed her out of the bathroom, then accepted her arm and skipped down the stairs. I cleared the heaviness from my head. We just wanted what every other girl wanted. To get laid, to get loved, to conflate the two into something beautiful. We found Kevin pretty much right where we'd left him, talking to two girls in lace dresses. My heart was a hot fist in my chest.

But he turned away from them as soon as he saw us. Saw *me*. Sully slipped an arm around him, which wasn't part of the plan, but she was making up the plan as she went. She whispered something in his ear that made him pull away. A threat, probably, or a warning, wrapped up as something sweet.

I moved in and swayed against him. He mumbled something that I didn't quite understand—I could tell he was drunk. My lips found the side of his face and I left a kiss there, hoping my lipstick would leave a mark, proof that it was real. He opened his mouth, cupped it almost directly over my ear. The heat made my whole body shiver, then freeze when I heard what he said.

"This can't be serious right now, okay? It's all fucked up. But you're so cool, you understand, right?"

"You think I'm beautiful," I said. I hadn't seen that word in any of his texts to *Lisa, Tammy, Britt.*

"Yeah," he said.

It was a truth I had learned even before Sully drilled it into me. Being wanted is what sets some of us apart from the rest. The world makes it goddamn clear that no matter how much a woman does, she's nothing if she's not also some man's *beautiful.*

I should have let Kevin go when I found out who he was, written him off as another asshole. But I didn't. So I ignored any lingering thoughts about Flora, the texts I'd seen. What Kevin had said about everything being *all fucked up*. I put my hands on the back of his head and kissed him hard, because I had shocked Sloane Sullivan, and I was capable of anything.

And because boys were one giant contradiction, or because his dick was doing the thinking, or maybe because he decided I was worth it after all, he kissed me back.

Flora was the reason we ended up in the upstairs bathroom, the same one where we—I—had sent that final message. I couldn't exactly take Kevin back to our room in Butts C. Had she replied? I didn't spend much time thinking about it because Kevin's hands were all over me, skimming my breasts, hiking up my skirt. He *did* want me.

I had pictured sex with Kevin many times. It was what I fantasized about when I was supposed to be studying, when my fingers wandered distractedly into my jeans. Sex with Kevin in reality was a spurt of frenzied jackhammering, the same as sex with any other boy. There was no foreplay. We barely kissed. I focused on his hand, a warm starfish on my back. His breath cascaded by my ear in short bursts. This wasn't worship. Not even close.

He barely made any sound, so I had no idea if he had come or not until he pulled out of me. We hadn't used a condom and he hadn't brought it up. I was on the Pill, but, for a brief, psychotic flash, I almost wished I weren't. I didn't want to make it easy for Kevin to walk away.

His pants were up and he was washing his hands before I even had time to unstick my ass from the counter. I was unnerved by his silence—behind a computer, he told me everything, but in person he had nothing to say.

"So," I said, trying to make my voice light. "I mean, I kind of can't believe we just did that. I don't do this kind of thing."

A variation of the excuse I used every time I had sex. Now, when I needed Kevin to believe that I wasn't the carefree slut I had so badly tried to become for everyone else, it finally sounded like a lie.

"I know," Kevin said. He washed his face and rubbed the wet skin with his hands. "I don't do this, either. I mean, I don't cheat. You know that. I need to find her and deal with this."

It was my chance to ask about *Lisa, Tammy, Britt*. I didn't.

"I guess—" I started, but he cut me off, his fingers at his temples like twin guns.

"I really like you, Amb. A lot. But I need time." His face was so earnest that he couldn't be lying. I seesawed between hope and anger.

Hope felt better.

"I can give you time," I mumbled, leaning into him. His lips brushed my collarbone. That wasn't an accident.

"I'll see you later," he finally said. I watched him leave, unaware that the next time I saw him in person, it would be through a windshield nearly fourteen years later.

I needed to find Sully. My body twitched with its knowledge of Kevin. As I walked down the stairs, I rolled his words over, like I would for years. *I need time.* I could give him that. I had given more valuable things to boys who meant less.

I wouldn't tell Sully the sex was just regular, drunken sex. By that time, I had already convinced myself that it was some kind of transcendental experience. "We just fit together perfectly," I'd gush. I had to prove a point. I had to resuscitate the fairy tale.

Sully found me first, twisting my arm, her face a scowl. "Well? Did you get what you needed?"

"I was with Kevin," I said.

"You fucked him," she said flatly. "Wasn't it fucking amazing?"

It bothered me that she took the words out of my mouth and made them crass. It bothered me that all I could do was nod.

"Good, then," she said. "It's done. We can go back to normal now. Let's get some drinks, okay? I just let some meathead in a bow tie finger me and it feels like my clit got burned off."

"Yeah." I felt myself relax. Sully wasn't mad. She hadn't accused me of picking Kevin over her. I could have them both.

It was late, probably close to midnight. I could tell by the way people were dancing, slow and sloppy. The energy from earlier had dissipated, leaving a funk of spilled beer and body odor in its wake. When Sully passed me a drink, it sloshed all over my shoes.

"So did he go down on you?" Sully asked. I shook my head, trying to make it seem like I didn't care. I had no idea he was supposed to go down on me, but the way Sully said it made it sound like he should have. I'd misread the power dynamic, same as when Hunter wanted to make her dinner but wouldn't bring me back to his room.

"Oh well," she said. "Next time. Did you blow him?"

"No, I didn't blow him." My words were sharp. I didn't want her to talk about it as if it were just another random hookup.

"You were gone for a long time. He can obviously keep it hard for a while." She sipped her drink. Her choker was missing. We weren't twins anymore. "I got bored."

I didn't think I'd been gone for very long, but maybe she was right. I didn't wear a watch. It wasn't like there was a clock on the wall. Maybe the sex had taken a lot longer. Maybe I only thought it was mediocre because I was drunk.

"Sorry you were bored," I said. "That explains the terrible finger fuck."

"Where is he now?" she said.

"I'm not sure, actually. He went to find Flora. To break up with her. He told me he needs to deal with this. That must've been what he meant."

Sully led me back onto the dance floor. "Sure. That must have been it."

I tried to shake off her weird mood and focus on the fact that I had gotten what I wanted. Kevin and I had had sex. He wanted nothing more from me than time. Sully was a skeptic, but she was skeptical about everything.

As we danced, Kevin reinflated in my head to Prince Charming proportions. I hadn't seen the dates on his messages to *Lisa, Tammy, Britt*. They were probably from before he met me. Plus, he probably wasn't sending them long emails every night.

People started leaving in clumps, only stragglers remaining. Sully's coke was gone. She must have snorted the rest of it without me, because her energy was almost manic, her eyes wild and unfocused. Her hands, when they landed on my shoulders, were clammy. She wanted to keep dancing, but my feet were numb in my shoes.

"We should go." The noise had died and I didn't have to shout anymore. "My feet really hurt."

"Fine." Sully huffed out a breath, like she was annoyed at me for ruining her fun.

We walked home arm in arm. Home—I had no idea when Butts C, with its loudness and smells, hairspray and Marc Jacobs and beer, had become my home. Next year, Sully and I would be roommates, and I could pretend Flora didn't exist. Flora, who would undoubtedly never speak to me again anyway. Maybe I could ask to be transferred to another room. Lauren and I could swap. Maybe it would be that easy.

Something was different tonight. Butts C was lit up like a Christmas tree, noise strung out around it. There were two fire trucks and several police cars parked near the front entrance, blocking our way, sirens flashing like strobe lights.

"Great," Sully said with a yawn. "Somebody must have pulled the fucking fire alarm again."

That was when I saw them, being ushered out the door. The Butts C crew. Some of them in pajamas with blankets draped over their shoulders like capes. Some wearing their slutty twin outfits. Gemma and Sienna in green bra tops and jean skirts, faces red and blotchy. Dawn the RA in a bathrobe, rubbing her eyes. Lauren's hair disheveled, her face a mask of shock. Lily in terry-cloth shorts, biting her lip.

Clara was with a guy whom she had obviously been in the process of fucking, except his arm was around her and she was crying.

Most of them were crying.

I didn't notice the police tape until we practically tripped over it.

I didn't see the stretcher at all. It was already in the back of an ambulance, which was already on its way to the hospital, even though everybody must have known there was no reason to take her there.

A policeman held out his arms when he saw us standing behind the tape, staring at the whole scene like it was something out of a movie. Bright blue eyes, graying hair.

"You're going to have to stay back, girls."

"What happened?" I blurted out at the same time Sully said, almost defiant, "We live here."

The cop frowned. "Don't go anywhere. We're going to be questioning everyone who lives in this building."

"Questioning us about what?"

He didn't answer. Somebody barked something through the device on his belt and he picked it up and walked away. Sully's hand slipped around mine and enclosed my fingers. Her thumb rubbed the inside of my wrist.

"Ella!" I called when I recognized her back, her stupid Posh Spice haircut. "Ella, over here."

She turned around, sniffling, her eyes and nose red. She actually was sick. But no—this was different. She was crying, her entire face contorted. I stepped over the police line, dragging Sully behind me.

"What happened?" I looked past her, to where everyone's heads were haloed by flashing lights, like the black sky was dropping its own disco ball. The boys, mostly in boxers and sweatpants, offering their arms. The girls, crouching, leaning. All the girls except Flora, who wasn't anywhere.

"Amb," Ella said when we were in front of her. She practically fell into me, resting her wet face on my shoulder. "She's dead. She's dead."

A dam didn't burst behind my eyes. I didn't cry. This was some kind of joke, some elaborate hoax, a hazing ritual the whole dorm was in on.

These weren't police officers. They were actors, probably Wesleyan boys, which explained why they looked so young. Nobody was dead. But I couldn't find the words to actually say that.

Ella was practically hyperventilating. I could barely understand her, but she choked out the name. "Flora. I saw her. I saw the—what she did." She bent down and put her head between her knees, like she was going to throw up.

I was going to throw up too, and I did, vaguely aware that Sully was still holding my hand, as vodka and beer burned my throat. The things we'd said. The things we'd done. The messages we'd sent.

The last message I'd sent.

It couldn't have been what happened. My fingers, the phone. They weren't murder weapons. It must have been something else. Kevin, maybe. *I need to find her and deal with this.* Where did he go after he left me?

Sully pulled my hair back from my face and stroked it gently, whispering calmly in my ear. "You're going to be fine. I'll make sure of it. We were together all night, okay? You didn't leave my side."

She was here for me. She would keep me safe. I bit the insides of my cheeks and nodded until I believed it.

29

NOW

To: "Ambrosia Wellington" *a.wellington@wesleyan.edu*
From: "Wesleyan Alumni Committee" *reunion.classof2007@gmail.com*
Subject: Class of 2007 Reunion

Dear Ambrosia Wellington,

The birch tree signifies truth, new beginnings, and the cleansing of the past. Share your memories of Flora's beautiful spirit and her reverberating impact on those who knew her. Flora's positivity was a rare quality in a world that presents so many challenges, and the Flora Banning Memorial Foundation, created in her honor, strives to keep doing her good work.

Sincerely,
Your Alumni Committee

"It's not Flora," Sully says. "Flora's dead." But she doesn't sound so sure.

The girl takes her spot beside Ella. She doesn't smile. I finally let myself breathe because of course she's not Flora. But she looks almost identical. Her eyebrows are a bit different, darker and thicker, and her mouth is wider. She's willowy, like Flora, the same thin limbs and dainty collarbones. Younger than us, but older than Flora was when she died. She's the girl I see everywhere, Flora's ghost chasing me around. Or maybe every girl has become Flora to me.

No, I have seen this girl before. I've *met* this girl before. In Butts C, clinging to Flora, face mobbed with tears. In pictures on our wall, little girls with swan necks and sun-whitened hair. In news footage, holding Flora's mother's hand.

"It's her sister," I say. "It's Poppy."

"I didn't know she had a sister," Sully says.

"She talked about her all the time," I say. "You must have known."

Sully shrugs. "I had no idea." Her nonchalance makes me wince, not because it's mean but because it proves my crime was always worse. Flora thought I was her best friend.

Poppy's eyes scan the crowd, looking for somebody. Maybe she's looking for us.

"What if it's her?" I practically whisper.

I never considered that Poppy could be behind the notes. She wasn't there. She had no cause to suspect anyone but Kevin. He was the only reason she and Flora ever argued. She even spoke out against him, in the media shitstorm that followed. Her statement to the press was tearful, a stark contrast to her father's angry missive. She couldn't even finish without sobs overtaking her speech. *You took my sister away, and I'll never forgive you.*

"It's not her," Sully says. "I mean, she barely looks old enough to drink."

She's twenty-seven. Four years younger than us. Sully doesn't know, but I do.

"Thank you so much to everyone for coming," Poppy says. Her voice is almost identical to Flora's. High and airy, probably susceptible to bursts of giggles. Flora told me Poppy wanted to go to Wesleyan too. *I told her she could come visit, stay with us for a couple nights. She would love it here.*

Flora told her sister about me, the girl who slept a few feet away. But she got it wrong.

"My sister would have loved to be here for the reunion. And she is here, in spirit. It took me a long time to come to terms with what happened to her, and I always knew I wanted to do something to honor her memory. After I did my undergrad here at Wesleyan, I started this foundation to raise money for mental health awareness, so girls like Flora don't suffer alone. It's my mission in life to make sure women feel more supported. We're in this together."

Poppy during the investigation, so certain. *Flora would have left a note.*

"Flora was more than just a sister to me. She was my best friend. She would have done anything for me. Now it's my turn to do something for her."

"See?" I hiss to Sully. "It's her *turn*. This is a threat."

"There's no way she could know it was us," Sully murmurs, like she's trying to convince herself.

"Flora loved nature," Poppy continues, her voice fraying. "Her dream was to have a house with a garden and a lot of trees. She had so much love to give, not just to everyone but everything. She took care of the earth. She took care of people. I wish I could have taken care of her. But this is the next best thing I could do. She would have wanted this."

Wanted what? I think. Adrian shoots me a bewildered look and I wonder if I said it out loud.

"I encourage you, her former friends and classmates, to share your memories of Flora. To keep her legacy alive. If you're able, please consider donating to the memorial foundation in her honor. But above all, listen to each other." She blots underneath her eye with her fingertip. "Thank you to everyone for coming. Looking around, I can see exactly how loved my sister was."

People clap lightly. Ella embraces Poppy, then turns to the crowd, wires her mouth into a smile, and clears her throat. "Flora was genuinely kind to me when I got here. She made me feel like I could just be myself. I can't even begin to stress how much that meant to me."

I stare at the grass under our shoes. I could have been kind to Ella, but somehow it was easier not to be.

Ella continues. "Sometimes people can look like they're totally okay, but they're not. This is why it's important to check in with your friends.

"I want to open this up to all of you." Ella focuses her gaze directly on me. "That's why we're here. To share and grieve together. I'm sure a lot of you have something to say about Flora Banning."

Gemma wanders into the center of the circle and starts telling a story about how Flora was there for her during her dad's cancer diagnosis. Sniffles travel through the crowd, but Sully huffs out a frustrated breath.

"Please. Her dad never had cancer. She's just too embarrassed to say that Flora went with her to get tested when she thought she had gonorrhea. Gem told me Flora was a total prude."

It would have been easy to nod in agreement if I didn't know Gemma's dad died during our junior year. I shift uncomfortably, wishing I could be buoyed by Sully's version of the truth.

Lily shares a memory of Flora's bringing her candy from Weshop when she was particularly stressed about a paper. Clara tells us Flora helped her end things with her toxic high school boyfriend.

"Saint fucking Flora," Sully snaps. "This is ridiculous."

But I'm wondering if maybe the girls really did love Flora. They were drawn to the very warmth they lacked. They let her be their personal sun, under which they could bloom without competition, the opposite of my mom's sunflowers. That was why they formed a phalanx around her memory after her death.

Sully and I hated that a girl like that existed. We were too cynical to believe in her goodness. But maybe Flora actually was that nice. Maybe I aligned myself with the wrong person, and a girl died because of it. Nausea rises, sudden and acute.

"I have to go." I turn away, ignoring Adrian's concerned "Where are you going?" and Sully's outstretched hand. I shove my way out of the circle and break into a run on High Street. I need to get away from campus, no matter how bad it looks. No matter what they all think. I run away from the noise, from the starbursts of alumni and graduates everywhere. Nobody can stand in my way.

Except for the last person I want to see right now. The last person I ever want to see. Felty, looming with his hands on his hips, like he has been waiting for me. I do think he has been waiting. For a very long time.

"You went," he says. "Did you get to share a favorite memory? I'm sure you have lots to choose from."

"What happened was a tragedy." I keep my chin raised. "I'll be making a donation to the memorial foundation."

He doesn't break eye contact. "You think I was hard on you. And I was."

I never thought Felty would apologize. I didn't think he was capable of *I'm sorry*. But this sounds like a lead-up, an introduction. His eyes bore into my face.

"I wasn't hard enough."

"I didn't do anything."

He shakes his head, more like a twitch. "All that, and you never even got what you wanted from it, did you? You never got the guy. Or the career. I guess I should be happy about that, but it isn't enough."

"You aren't allowed to talk to me like that." My voice breaks. "I'll report you for harassment."

He laughs now, not loud and booming, but quietly, which is more disconcerting. "To who? And tell them what? If you want to rehash the past, please do. I'm more than ready to play that game. Your file has never left my head."

Your file has never left my head. Maybe I was right when I thought it was Felty. I picture him now, hunched over that card stock. Our case was personal to him. He couldn't save his sister but he could make it right through Flora Banning.

"You wanted to get us here this weekend. You want something to happen."

He loops his thumbs into his belt. "There's a lot I want to happen. But I didn't have to do anything to get you here this weekend. I knew you'd be here. You wouldn't be able to resist coming back to see what you've done."

My jaw trembles and I remember that night, how I couldn't stop my teeth from chattering. I turn to leave.

"Ambrosia," he calls after me. "You're wrong. There is no us. Just you."

Now I'm running, my wedge sandals making *thunk* noises on the sidewalk. Sully and I went over our story so many times, diligently, the same way we once memorized monologues for class. *We have to stick to the same story.* Those were her words. We sat across from each other and repeated the same lines, staring into each other's eyes.

I didn't turn on her.

But maybe she turned on me.

There is no us. She said that, and Felty somehow knows.

I slow to a walk through Andrus and up Foss Hill, but I don't stop at the Nics to see what might be waiting there for me. I head straight for V Lot and get into our rental car, then use my phone to pull up directions to the Super 8. To the only person who can give me the truth about that night.

Even though I can never do the same for him.

30

THEN

Kevin was the one who found her, but nobody felt sorry for him. It was already his fault.

"He might as well have cut her wrists himself," Ella said when we were in the Butts A lounge, huddled together on couches, the boys with their arms around us. I leaned against Sully, our hands knotted together. "I hope he rots in hell."

Gemma wiped her face. "I thought they had this perfect relationship. Does anyone know what happened?"

"Amb, you must know something," Lily said. "Did they break up?"

"I don't know anything." My tone was curt. I was already sick of being asked.

"So they had a fight?" Lauren passed me the flask of vodka that was being shuffled around without looking at me. "And that's why she—"

When she did meet my eyes, there was anger in hers. Anger, and something else. Suspicion. Maybe I was paranoid, but she had been there. She'd seen me and Sully. She knew we were looking for a boy I thought was in love with me.

Ella jumped in. "Why else *would she*? He let her leave that party drunk and alone. He must've known she was really upset. If he would have been with her, she wouldn't have—"

She squeezed her eyes shut. She did that every few minutes, like she was remembering something so harsh she couldn't look directly at it. Ella hadn't gone to the party because she was sick. She was asleep when Kevin's scream woke her. She ran into the hall out of instinct. She hovered by the open door, probably thinking she was about to secure her position in Flora's good graces.

"Blood," she told us when we asked what she saw. "So much blood. Like, how did someone her size have all that blood? And she was—her eyes were open. But she didn't even look human anymore. I was sure it was some kind of prank."

Sully and I hadn't been questioned yet by the police—if they were even going to bother questioning us—but Sully was a step ahead. She had ushered me into the bathroom and used a wad of damp toilet paper to wipe my smeared makeup.

"We don't know what happened," she said. "But don't mention Kevin. Or Dartmouth. Or the phone. Don't worry, I wiped it off on my skirt before I put it back in his jacket."

My brain was too scrambled to understand. She wiped our fingerprints off, but our messages were still there. She wasn't protecting herself. She was protecting *me*. I was the one who'd sent those texts. I was the one who'd told Flora to *just do it, then, and stop talking about it*. Kevin might not have even known his phone was missing.

"We didn't delete the texts," I said. "We have to—"

"It's too late." She smoothed my hair. I heard her subtext. Kevin was going down for this, not us.

I waited for the police to barge into the lounge and arrest me, bind my hands behind my back with a pair of cold handcuffs. But that didn't happen. In the morning, after we had bunked up in Butts A, the police wanted to talk to anyone who had seen Flora at the party.

"Why are they asking so many questions? Didn't she kill herself?" I whispered to Sully. The mental image of Flora's wrists, ribboned with blood, made me dizzy.

"I don't know. That's what Ella said. I guess they're trying to figure out why." She sounded different. I realized Sully was scared, which made me terrified.

"I'm going to say something," I said. "How can I not say anything? We had something to do with this—"

"Don't say a fucking word. Remember, we were together all night. We have to stick to the same story. Just say we saw her and she seemed really drunk." She gripped my wrist tightly. "This is fucked, okay? But you didn't do anything. You didn't put the razor blade in her hand. You were just joking around." I noticed, acutely, that it wasn't *we* anymore. It was *you*.

It was me.

Later, when we got more details, we would learn that it wasn't a razor blade at all.

"I can't do that to Kevin." But part of me was sickened by him. If he had just broken up with Flora like a decent human being, this never would have happened. It was easier to blame Kevin than actually turn the lens on myself and see the monster that my obsession had turned me into.

An even uglier part of me—the most hideous part, which not even Sully could know about—was mad at Flora for killing herself. She had ruined any chance I had with Kevin. He would never forgive himself, or me, for what we did while she bled.

"You can," Sully said. "He's just a guy. There are lots more of them. He sent those messages, not you. We saw them together. It looked like they were arguing." She narrowed her eyes. "Remember that you weren't the only girl he played. You don't owe him a goddamn thing."

Maybe she was right, but I didn't need another reminder that I wasn't special.

"What if Kevin mentions me? He might already know we took his phone." I was still using *we*, but Sully had been the one to take the phone. If she hadn't slipped a hand inside his jacket and stolen it, I never would have sent those messages. And Flora would have been alive.

"He's not going to mention you. Come on, Amb. It would make him look really bad. A guy isn't going to talk to the police about a girl he fucked at a party while his girlfriend sliced her wrists."

I winced. When Sully became weaponized, I never knew which weapon she'd become.

I was sure we would see Kevin at the police station. That was how it was in the movies, passing in the hall, a furtive glance that carried more than words. But we didn't see him because, as we later found out, he wasn't even there. He was out in the world again, because there wasn't enough evidence to prove he was involved in his girlfriend's suicide. Even after the police took his phone and found the messages. Even after they didn't believe him when he said he didn't send them.

Sully and I got separated at the station, but it didn't matter. We had rehearsed the story ahead of time. My mom had made it known that she thought studying theater and acting would never lead to a practical career choice. But it led me to that moment, in that room at the Middletown police station, in front of a cop with piercing blue eyes and a badge that read FELTY. I recognized him from the crime scene.

"You lived with Miss Banning—Flora," he said. Straight to business.

I nodded. Flora would always be Miss Banning, never Mrs. Someone Else. Never Mrs. McArthur.

"And you were friends."

"Yeah. Sort of. I mean, I guess we were friends."

"Did you notice any changes in Flora's behavior leading up to yesterday? Anything that would lead you to believe she was depressed?"

I thought back to Halloween. Slash and the pilot. Hair spilling onto parquet floor. *I didn't want to do that.* Flora, pulling away from everyone. Trying to tell me something I already knew.

"No. Nothing really. Although—" I paused, deviating from Sully's script, but for a good reason. "She had an article about depression on the wall in our room. I figured it was because she was studying psychology."

"Were you aware she hadn't gone to classes for over a week before her death?"

I shook my head. The lump of Flora in her bed, her perpetually watery eyes. "We didn't have the same classes. I'd have no way of knowing."

"Did you know she was having trouble with her boyfriend?"

"No. We didn't really talk about that stuff."

"But you met her boyfriend. Is that correct?" He folded his hands on the table. He was wearing a wedding ring. His nails were in better shape than mine.

"He came to visit her once. I met him. But we didn't spend any time together." I was tacking on too many words.

"Kevin McArthur." His name reduced to a weary breath. "You didn't notice anything about Kevin's behavior that would lead you to believe he was violent? Or aggressive with Flora?"

I shrugged. "No. But I really didn't know him. I just know they met in high school and that he went to Dartmouth. I think." Felty squinted at me, like he was deciding if I was telling the truth. Maybe he already knew that Sully and I had been to Dartmouth. Maybe he knew everything. The room tilted with my hangover.

"Dartmouth. That's right. And he came to Wesleyan yesterday to see Flora."

"Yeah. I guess so."

"You didn't go to the party with Flora," Felty said. It wasn't a question.

"No. I went with Sully. Flora wasn't really into parties."

"Sloane Sullivan." Her real name sounded foreign, how an adult said your name when you were getting in trouble. "And you saw Flora and Kevin there together."

"Yeah. It looked like they were arguing about something. We didn't want to get involved with someone else's business, so we didn't think much of it. Lots of couples fight when they drink."

"Were they fighting, or just arguing?"

I picked my cuticles under the table. "Arguing. Nothing, like, physical." I paused, then added something to appease Sully. "That we saw."

"And you didn't talk to either of them all night."

I shook my head, not wanting to give an actual answer, because I had a feeling Felty was waiting for me to say the wrong thing. Maybe I was already a suspect.

"Someone at the party says you and Sloane were talking to Kevin. That you went into a bathroom with him and locked the door. Someone saw a girl fitting your description running from the Butterfields dorm later that night."

Of course somebody saw us. There were probably hundreds of people at that party, and discretion wasn't on my mind. Girls banging on the door while I was in that bathroom with Kevin. A chorus of *hurry up*, eyes on me as I staggered back downstairs, gripping the railing, underwear damp.

Sully and I hadn't talked about this part. I didn't have a rehearsed answer ready.

"That's impossible," I said. "I mean, of course I talked to guys. It was a party."

"So you didn't go into the bathroom with Kevin and lock the door?"

"No." I shook my head profusely. "The only person I went into the bathroom with was Sully. Sloane. And we didn't lock the door."

I could tell Felty didn't believe me. I hadn't showered since yesterday. Maybe he could smell the boy on me. But what could Felty possibly care who I had sex with? Or who Kevin had sex with? People cheated every day. On their diets, on tests, on their girlfriends and boyfriends. It didn't come with jail time.

I was ready to go on the offensive, to spring into a tirade at his next question. But to my surprise, he folded up those smooth hands and thanked me for my time.

"One more thing, before you go," he said as I stood up on wobbly legs. "A search history of Flora's laptop revealed she recently looked up how to know if you've been raped."

I stared at my feet. I was wearing Sully's Uggs, and they were too big. That was what my brain held on to instead of the word Felty had spat out. *Raped.* That wasn't what happened. I thought it hard enough that I actually believed it.

I looked up at Felty. "I don't know anything about that. We lived together, but to be honest, we were never really friends."

After Thanksgiving, we were allowed to go back to Butts C. President Bums sent a long email about the warning signs of needing help and made sure we all knew where we could go for support. Some of the girls requested to be transferred elsewhere, but there wasn't any room on campus. Except for me—a single in Butts A, which was only available because another student had recently dropped out. I reluctantly trooped over with my belongings packed in cardboard boxes I'd procured from the cafeteria. I threw most of my clothes out, certain I could smell Flora's blood on them. I got called *lucky*. The other girls said they couldn't sleep, couldn't study, couldn't concentrate in a dorm that was haunted. Somebody called it Dorm Doom, and the name stuck.

Nobody knew what was going to happen to our room, the door to which remained locked. The flooring would have to be replaced, the walls and ceiling painted, probably several coats. Maybe that was all it took to erase the traces of a girl who had lived and died there.

The facts started to emerge, kicked up like leaves in the wind. We read the news online. Flora and Kevin, high school sweethearts unraveling with the demands of the distance between them. Flora's speechless mother and furious father. Flora's high school friends, revealing that they'd heard from her less and less. Flora's little sister, who said Flora had seemed sad the last time they talked on the phone. The story of a girl who covered the wreckage of her truth with a smile.

Kevin was cast as the asshole. Kevin was the murderer. He never went back to Dartmouth. The media would have followed him. Death threats popped up in the comments of articles posted online. *Die, motherfucker. Kill yourself. If you won't do it, I will. The world would be better off.* Our own ACB, two years after Flora's death, was the worst of all. Flora's thread was its own beast, hijacked by mentions of Kevin. *We should all make KM pay for what he did.*

He was drunk that night. Most people thought he had come to Wesleyan to break up with Flora, and the Double Feature party was a good setting for a breakup, with alcohol as the airbag. Except things got nasty. They fought, a public spat that suddenly everyone made sound a lot worse than it actually was. Kevin got aggressive with Flora on the dance floor, prompting several guys to tell him to back off. Flora ran away, clearly upset. Kevin didn't reply to her pleas, instead sending her increasingly horrible messages, including one explicitly telling her to kill herself.

All she did was listen. All she did was take his advice. Flora was a people pleaser.

Flora didn't do it with a razor blade, or even a knife. Apparently it was a shard from a broken mug, other pieces of which were later found near the drain of one of the dorm showers. The sequence of events played in my head like a horror movie. Flora, shuffling into the bathroom in her fluffy robe, eyes red and cheeks ashy from leftover makeup. Turning on the shower, heaving the mug she had hidden in the pocket of her robe against the ground. Scouting out the biggest piece, the sharpest one that would do the most damage, and leaving the others.

Clara had seen her heading to the bathroom. They made eye contact in the hall, Clara said. She didn't notice that Flora was upset because Clara had a guy with her. She had, as they passed each other, put her finger to her lips and giggled, and Flora had mirrored her. *Our little secret.*

Clara saw the shards later, when she went to shower. Apparently the guy she was with would only go down on her if she was freshly showered, so she scrubbed herself with a washcloth and hastened back to her room with a towel wrapped around her waist. She didn't think anything of the fact that there was a broken mug in the shower. Probably an accident. Probably someone getting ready for the party who brought some vodka in with them. We had all done it.

I was mostly surprised that Flora had left such a mess. She was immaculate in her neatness, the only girl out of all of us who ever brought a garbage bag into the lounge and collected the chip bags and paper plates and sticky Solo cups.

But she sat down on her bed with the shard of mug clutched in her fingertips. She read Kevin's—my—message one last time, to prove to herself that it did exist, that it was real, that he was actually that cruel, the boy she had spent four years loving. That the world had turned on her.

She did the left arm first. She started at the wrist, where tiny blue veins emerged like rivers under the fog of her skin. The sharpest edge of the blade hooked in, a puncture wound. She could have stopped there, held a wad of toilet paper over the bloody dot. The skin would have filled in around it and nobody would have known. It would have been her dark secret, the one she guarded.

But she didn't stop there.

Most people who slit their wrists don't actually die. I looked it up online after, consumed with the gore of what Flora had done. Most people don't manage to find both arteries. Most people don't have the precision, the conviction needed to go that deep. Most people get found in time and wake up in a hospital room with gauze around their wrists and a stern-faced nurse looming over them. Most people realize that they have something to live for.

She must have made a sound, because it must have hurt. But if she did cry out, nobody was around to hear it. Everyone was either asleep or at parties. RA Dawn, always nocturnal, was writing an essay with Kurt Cobain screaming in her ears, and Clara was getting fucked to a soundtrack of heavy metal. Maybe Clara did hear something—a whimper, the beginning of a scream—but the music was loud, and orgasms have a way of drowning out everything you don't want to hear. Didn't I know that firsthand?

And Ella. Ella was fast asleep, practically comatose on account of the Theraflu she had used to chase two Tylenol Cold and Sinus.

According to the police report, it took Flora approximately five minutes to bleed out, for her blood to turn her pink duvet crimson and spray on the walls and ceiling like some kind of demented graffiti. The Internet let me know that usually it took hours, because the human body is equipped to not want to die. Flora's body barely put up a fight. She died between eleven and eleven thirty, and somewhere in that thirty minutes existed the time that Kevin had spent in the bathroom with me.

If I hadn't followed him up there. If I had kept everything closed. My mouth. My legs. My heart.

If I hadn't. If I hadn't. If I hadn't. He would have gone after her, and maybe he would have found her in time.

Her arms were splayed out by her sides when he finally did find her, in the middle of her comforter, glassy eyes trained on the ceiling. Maybe it looked like she was making a snow angel, before he noticed all the blood.

Ella said she heard him scream, and that was what woke her, what made her jump out of bed and race down the hall. That scream was what ruined her life, because she had to see it too, the dead girl under the lights. Kevin had flipped them on by then. Flora had cut herself in the dark, in the glow of the stick-on stars on our ceiling. Maybe she was thinking about the person who would have to find her. In her final magnanimous act, she wanted to soften the blow.

She must have known Kevin would find her. Part of her still loved him. Maybe that was why she cut so deep, to be sure the last traces of that love would drain out of her.

The news called it the Wesleyan Suicide. To us, it was Dorm Doom. Flora stopped being a girl and started being a cautionary tale as soon as the media saw her pretty face.

"My daughter didn't want to die," Flora's mother said in an interview, her voice wavering. "She was crying for help. And his message killed her."

Flora's parents demanded an investigation. Her father's face, marbled like a steak, angry in a way Flora never was. They wanted Kevin put away for what he wrote. What I wrote.

Kevin denied ever sending the messages. He apparently never saw them until some unspecified *after*, sometime after he whipped out his phone to call 911. His reaction to what he must have seen haunted me. Maybe there was a moment where he thought he'd actually sent the texts.

"Someone must have stolen my phone," he told the press. "It wasn't me."

It wasn't me. Three words made famous by men.

I lived with knots in my neck, waiting for them to come for me. I didn't even know who *they* were. The police, probably, barging into class, telling everybody to put their hands up. Reporters, maybe, wielding badges and microphones like deadly weapons. "It's her!" they would shout, chasing me through the CFA, accusations sharp in their mouths.

But the other girls were the ones who ended up coming for me, not the police. Felty wasn't wrong. Someone did see me and Kevin at the party, closing the bathroom door, and pretty soon everyone knew. It must have been Lauren, because the rumor sprouted new heads the more it was repeated. I'd plotted to steal Kevin. I'd looked for him at the party. I'd been on a mission. For the rest of my time at Wesleyan, a good chunk of the student body would see me as the girl who fucked Kevin McArthur while his girlfriend killed herself.

And another, smaller contingent had an even more menacing theory. That I had done it myself. I had been spotted running through the Butts C courtyard, hair swishing in the dark.

There would be an investigation, and it would open up a question nobody had thought they would ever have to answer: can you kill a girl without actually killing her?

It was Kevin's public reckoning. But it was just as much mine.

31

NOW

To: "Ambrosia Wellington" *a.wellington@wesleyan.edu*
From: "Wesleyan Alumni Committee" *reunion.classof2007@gmail.com*
Subject: Class of 2007 Reunion

Dear Ambrosia Wellington,

Our Red and Black Alumni Dinner for the Class of 2007 is the event that caps off a truly enlightening weekend. Please join us in the West Wing at Usdan for a three-course meal, drinks, live music, and more. This is a dinner you won't want to miss. We'll be talking about it for the next ten years.

Sincerely,

Your Alumni Committee

I consider not going to the Super 8. It would be easy to get on I-91 and keep driving back to Astoria, where I can worry about the consequences later. But if I don't do it now, I may never get a chance to talk to Kevin. I may never get a chance to ask him what makes him so sure that somebody killed Flora.

The clerk at the front desk, a girl with a perky ponytail, tells me there is no Kevin McArthur staying here. I briefly wonder if Kevin called her beautiful.

I know Kevin is here. Maybe he's just not here as himself. If he wanted to hide his identity, who would he become?

I paste on an apologetic expression. "I'm sorry. I meant John Donne."

"Okay, let me check." She types something into her computer and flashes me a white smile. "Mr. Donne's in room one twelve. Have a nice day." As if anything about today is *nice*.

I lose momentum when I get to his door. I knock quietly, almost hoping he's not inside, because I have no idea what I'm going to say. Eventually, the door inches open, and he peers out hesitantly. "Amb?"

"Hi," I say. "I took a chance that you still like John Donne."

"What are you doing here?" He squints at me like I'm a stranger. I suppose I am.

"I'm sorry to just show up. But I feel like—I think we need to talk."

"Okay," he says flatly. "Did something happen? Did you guys find anything?" He's wearing a white T-shirt and no hat this time. Without the sweatshirt on, I can tell he has been working out, keeping himself in shape, fighting the self-proclaimed fat kid who used to inhabit his skin.

"Flora's sister is here. On campus. I don't know if she has anything to do with it or not, but she's here. We saw her at the dedication."

Kevin blows out a breath. "Shit. Poppy never liked me. But she was a kid. I don't see her doing something like this." He looks down the hall. "You should come in."

As he opens the door, I see it. The lazy tilt of his head, the barest hint of a smile. He's under there, the boy who made me feel like I was unique. I follow him inside and we both sit on his bed. The curtains are drawn, pale light framing the window.

I start talking. "You said something earlier. About the person who wrote the notes being the person who killed Flora. Do you honestly think she was murdered?"

He digs his fingers into the duvet. "You didn't see what I saw. Somebody killed her. It was plotted out—someone used my phone, then followed her back to the dorm. Flora wouldn't have killed herself. She wasn't—she wouldn't have done *that*. And she would have left a note."

"Did you tell the police?" A flare of heat engulfs my neck.

"Do you think they wanted to hear me? Her fingerprints were on the mug. Nobody was seen entering the building. No signs of a fight. I tried to tell them maybe she wouldn't have put up a fight, because she was so upset. Or if it was someone she knew coming in."

"But who would have done that and made it look like a suicide?"

"Somebody who knew it could be pinned on me." He gets up and picks up his wallet from the nightstand, then pulls out a wrinkled piece of paper that has been folded several times. "I showed this to the cops. Sorry. Your name is on it."

My name. I realize, as I take the paper, that I've never seen Kevin's handwriting before. It's big and blocky, letters bleeding together. It's a list—me and Sully, and some of the Butts girls, plus Hunter, who Kevin believed Flora was cheating on him with.

"What's this?" I ask. The paper is soft and worn, like Felty's business card. Kevin's personal albatross, the weight he has carried because of me.

"People she knew. People I saw that night. People who could have wanted to hurt her."

"I didn't want to hurt her. She was my—she was my best friend."

"But you showed up at Dartmouth and told me she was cheating on me. Then I came to see her, because Flora begged me, and you and me—I wasn't planning on hooking up with you. But I wondered after if you planned it. The way we just ended up in that bathroom. You had this look, like you won something."

A blast of terror snakes up my spine. "I didn't plan any of it, Kevin. I swear. I had no idea any of this was going to happen. That night, you and I just got carried away." I scrape at the already torn skin on my cuticles.

"Did you write those messages?" His eyes bore into me.

"Of course not." My heart is a rapid drumbeat, panic making me dizzy. "Besides, you think someone murdered her. How could I have done it? I was with you."

He rubs his hair. "I know. I just keep trying to make sense of it, and I never can."

"She was drunk and heartbroken. Why did you even stay with her?" I snap, because the memory is an emotional conflagration, even now. "Why didn't you just break up with her so you could both move on?"

"You don't get it," he says. "It was complicated. Our dads golfed together. My mom and her stepmom were, like, best friends. They were practically planning our wedding."

I put the paper down and cross my arms. "So you strung me along. And you strung her along."

"It wasn't like that. It sounds bad. But hear me out. Flora was always there for me. The one constant thing I had. I knew she'd always be there. So yeah, I wasn't in love with her anymore, but I wasn't looking forward to breaking her heart either. I had to do it the right way."

"You didn't." My voice is ice.

"No." He rubs his jawline. "I didn't. I ruined everything."

He walks over to the desk, where a bottle of Jack Daniel's sits beside a coffeemaker. "Do you want a drink? I need a drink." He tips the bottle into a flimsy paper cup. When he swallows his first pour and goes for another, I can tell he drinks a lot, and often.

"Were there other girls you were emailing?" We're veering far off track but I'm desperate to finally hear the truth.

He doesn't look at me. "No. It was just you."

"How about texting?"

His response is slower. "No."

I'm collecting my frustration, trying to mold it into the right missive. He starts talking again. He knows I know he's lying.

"I thought you blamed me like everyone else did. I mean, I never heard from you again."

I soften against my will. "I sent you an email, but you never replied."

He takes a sip of his drink. "I shut that account down. What did it say? The email?"

"I asked how you were doing." I remember exactly what it said. It was half-drunk and sloppy. *Hey, I'm so sorry this is all happening to you, I'm here if you want to talk, I still care about you a lot and that won't go away.*

"What do you think the answer was?" He laughs, a sound twisted and unholy. "You wanted to be an actress. I thought maybe you were acting the whole time with me."

"I wasn't. And I'm not an actress. Did you ever become a writer?"

He drains the rest of his cup. "I work for my dad. I didn't do anything I said I would."

I steer us back to the past, because talking about our failures is getting us nowhere. "Were you going to break up with Flora? You told me you needed time. And then . . ."

He blows out a breath. "And then I had to find her like that. It was—I can't even describe it. And I won't, because you can't unsee it. I was going to let her know it was over."

"So you could be with me." I hate how I sound, eighteen and in desperate need of validation. Sully would crucify me for wanting to believe him, but I have to know it was all worth something.

"Yeah." It's more a grunt than a word. I wonder if he was like this on the phone with Flora, dodging her increasingly probing questions. I wish I believed him—no, I wish I had believed my own instincts the day Kevin and I met. I wish I had shredded his email address and zoned out when Flora bubbled over about their *connection*. But it's too late for that.

"You went back to the dorm that night, but you didn't see anyone around? Like, nobody in the halls or anything?"

"No. I could hear some music and stuff, but I didn't see anybody." He inches closer to me. "Look, when Sully called to tell me she got a note—"

Her name makes my ears ring. It's not that he called her *Sully*, because everyone does. It's that *she called him*.

"She told me you emailed her about it," I say. His blank expression speaks volumes. "How did she get your phone number?"

The silence is horrible—it's the same white noise from the aftermath of Matt and Jessica French. I know something hideous is happening but can't fully process it.

"I guess she must have got it somehow," Kevin mumbles.

Sully and Kevin. The screaming truth of them, right in front of me the entire time. I didn't find him after Flora was gone, but she could have. She was always more creative, more resourceful. When I stopped being fun, she needed somebody new to play with. Rage sears my skull, but I'm almost angrier at myself than I am at Sully. I should have known.

Her words rush back, the night of the Double Feature party. *You fucked him. Wasn't it fucking amazing?*

"You and Sully," I say, my tongue heavy. "You slept with her."

"Um." He coughs. "A really long time ago. I figured you knew, but then she just told me you had no idea, and she wanted to keep it that way."

She has no idea. Sully was talking to Kevin last night. I'm almost scared to ask the next part. "Are you with her?"

He sits down next to me, almost hesitantly. "No. God, no. She was a mistake."

I can't deny that hearing Sully described as somebody's mistake fills me with satisfaction. She was an easy mistake to make. "But you talk to her."

"Until she called me about the note, I hadn't talked to her in forever."

"When were you with her?" *I need to know.* "When did it start?"

He sighs. "She was just there. That night you showed up at Alpha Chi, she came up to my room, and—well."

That night. Waking up on a moldy couch, Sully there, then gone. An absence she never bothered to explain, even when I asked.

"So you still expect me to believe there were no other girls," I say flatly.

"I regretted it," he says. "I wish I would have told her to leave, but my ego was, like, this hungry monster. It took what anyone fed it. And after Flora—well, everyone else wanted to see it starve."

"What happened after Flora?" There's the *need* I always try to keep at bay, warping my voice.

"She found me in Fairfield and told me she believed I didn't send the texts. You have to understand, I was so messed up, and nobody even wanted to look at me. Then she got bored, I guess, and took off. I didn't think I'd hear from her ever again. And I didn't, until she called about the note."

"So you were her boyfriend." I don't know what's more impossible to digest. That Sully was with Kevin, or that she was with anyone.

"No." His hair falls in his face. "I really knew nothing about her. And sometimes . . ." He trails off.

"Sometimes what?"

"Sometimes it was like she just wanted to keep me in her sight."

I know the feeling, I could say, but I swallow the words as his fingers brush up my arm. I don't stop him. Because Sully isn't here, and Flora isn't here, but I am.

"Did you ever think she did it?" My skin is hot with anger. I want him to say yes. I want somebody to hold her accountable for something. And as the question leaves my mouth, I realize it was exactly what I came here to ask.

"Yeah," he says. "At first, I suspected everyone. But I don't think she cares enough about anyone to do something like that."

I blink furiously, my brain catching on an unbidden thought.

Maybe she cared enough about *me*.

But I don't have time to process it before Kevin brings one hand to the back of my neck, the other to my face. He kisses my ear, then my collarbone. His mouth, fever-hot on my throat as he presses me into the duvet.

I could do this. It's my chance to get revenge on Sully, on the girl who managed to take what I wanted while convincing me she had given me everything. I could sleep with Kevin. *Game on, Sully. You're not special.*

But I'm the one to put my hands on his chest and push him off me. Because I don't want this anymore. I don't know this man, who tastes like whiskey and desperation. I don't need to know him. Maybe it's different now because Flora isn't here to compete with. Because it was her magnetic softness I wanted the whole time, not her boyfriend.

"I can't do this. I'm married." Adrian, the one constant in my life, who pledged to love me forever. He deserves better.

Kevin nods. He's disappointed. It's nice to be the one letting him down. "I hope you ended up with someone who treats you well. I meant what I said back then. You deserve someone great."

My voice is small. "I did."

Kevin smooths his shirt. "Flora deserved better too. I ruined her life. That's why I really decided to come here. I mean, yeah, I want to clear my name, but mostly I just want whoever did this to get what they deserve."

I stare at the piece of lined paper next to me, imagining Kevin poring over it, trying to solve the mystery. I can't help him piece it together without implicating myself. I sent the messages. Kevin and I went up to the bathroom. Then he was gone, and how long were Sully and I at the party after that?

Long enough for somebody to finish what I started.

"What if—" I hesitate. "What if more than one person worked together?"

Kevin frowns. "I thought of that. But nobody was seen entering the building. And pretty much everyone was at that party."

Nobody was seen entering the building.

But someone was seen running from it. The rumors, the messages on the ACB. *I saw AW running from the Butts that night in a slutty outfit—she did it.*

There were two of me the night of the Double Feature.

She has a pattern, Lauren said. Sully could pressure anyone into doing anything. She put the phone in my grasp, giggled as I typed. She made sure the phone got back to Kevin, wiped it clean to get rid of our prints. Everything looked like it was done on an impulse.

Now I see Sully, hovering over her best friend, Evie, convincing her that the Oxy would be fun to try. I see Sully with her arm around Flora, telling her what Kevin was doing back at the party, pushing her to do something extreme to get back at him.

Sully, I want to scream. *Sully, what have you done?*

I can already hear her answer. *Nothing she wasn't going to do already.*

The phone on Kevin's nightstand rings, making me jump. He picks it up. "Hello?" More impatiently now. "Hello, is anyone there?" He puts the phone back in its cradle. "Wrong number, I guess. That's, like, the fourth call today."

There is no us. I had served my purpose for Sully. I was with Kevin that night, my insides a hideout. Sully made sure that it was the last time we would be together. But I can't tell him any of this.

"I don't know what to think anymore." It feels like the most honest thing I've admitted in a long time.

"Yeah. It's messed up. And all because I didn't have the balls to break up with my girlfriend. Because I wanted to have sex, and she didn't, so I found it somewhere else."

"But you and Flora—" *You and Flora. I heard you in her bed.*

"Flora thought we were waiting until we got married." He pinches the skin between his eyes.

I wait for that to sink in, along with what it means, but it doesn't want to penetrate. Lying in bed, listening to Flora and Kevin, bedsheets rustling. I made an assumption about what they were doing, because it's what everyone was doing. Flora never told me they were waiting. I flash back to Halloween, the pilot and his hands all over Flora, my blind eye to what was happening.

"I have to go." I stand up, sickened with myself. "I guess we both have to live with it." It's all there is left to say. Flora died and we lived, marbled with shared pain.

"Don't go." He reaches for my hand. "Stay. Please. You're safe here."

I memorize his face and see him for what he is, for what I first saw at Dartmouth: a tarnished golden boy with pretty words. I could take him from Sully, but she wouldn't care. Nobody means that much to her anyway. Except maybe me.

"Take care of yourself." I grab my purse, my hands shaking.

"Wait. Aren't we going to figure this out? What are you going to do now?"

"I'm not sure. I just want to move on from all of this." I stop when we're at the door, my last question flickering to life. "You wrote a short story about a girl named Clarissa. Who was she, really?"

"She was you," he says without hesitation. "I wanted to send you the story, but it was too much. I don't know why I sent it to Flora. Maybe I wanted her to realize it wasn't about her. But she was so happy, and I couldn't ruin it."

"I'm sorry I didn't get to read it." Even though I don't believe him,

I'm sorry it existed. Clarissa fed the envy I already had for Flora. Clarissa turned it into an animal, a servant of instinct.

"Me too." He smiles sadly as he closes the door. "Be careful, okay?"

I text Billie when I'm back in the rental car and apply fresh lipstick over Kevin's kiss. I need to feel anchored to something normal, reminded that the world outside of here exists. *I might have done something very bad.*

Her reply is immediate. *I told you he would show up!! What happened?*

Billie, a hopeless romantic, even after she stood up at our wedding, saying she knew from the first time she met Adrian that we'd end up together. I don't know if it's disgusting or impressive that girls can do that for each other. That we can achieve that level of deceit in the name of sisterhood.

32

THEN

It wasn't clear whether the investigation into Kevin's involvement would turn into an actual trial. But his personal trial happened every day. Wesleyan lit up with protests. The Butts C girls—the ones I had once envied for their beauty, their effortless cool—were eternal activists, stopping their regularly scheduled skirmishes against campus authority to take up Flora's cause. They rallied, a riot of hair and teeth. Chalking had been banned the year before, but people stopped caring. We stepped over their messages everywhere we walked. *Justice for Flora. Knives and Guns Aren't the Only Weapons. Words Can Kill.*

My paranoia was a dead weight, making it hard to get out of bed. I skipped classes, holing up in my new room. I didn't want to party anymore. I just wanted to survive the year.

When I did leave my room, I got ambushed by girls expecting me to spearhead a movement against something they had no idea I had caused. Suddenly I was in demand, just when I wanted to be invisible. I avoided them as much as possible, but one day, Lauren caught up with me when I was doing laundry.

"You haven't been to any of the protests." She crossed her arms. "Do you not want this asshole to pay for what he did?"

"Of course I do," I snapped. "But I don't see what some sidewalk chalk will accomplish. It's up to the lawyers, not us."

"You could still show your support," Lauren said. "Don't you think you owe her that?"

Everyone seemed to think I owed Flora something, which pissed me off most of all. She had been a damsel needing rescue in life, and death hadn't stopped her from playing that same role.

"Unless you have another reason for not showing up," Lauren said, turning to leave before I could see her face and figure out what she knew. The Kevin rumor was nothing more than a wisp at that point, but it was about to gain substance.

I'd taken to staring at my *Friend* mug, alternating between stuffing it under the dirty clothes that piled up on my floor and keeping it out where I would see it, a reminder of what happened when I wanted something I wasn't supposed to have. In the end, I left the mug behind when I moved out of the Butts after freshman year but kept the picture of Kevin, the one I had stolen from Flora's wall, flattened inside John Donne, its final resting place.

I barely slept at night, certain that the police weren't satisfied with my answers and would come for me again. I went to MoCon with Sully but only pushed food around my plate. My teeth chattered constantly, my thoughts flipping from mundane to fatalistic.

"You need to relax," Sully kept saying. "It's over. We can go back to normal."

She was wrong.

The day the police found me for real, on my walk back to Butts A from Olin, I should have expected them. I should have known what to say.

"Ambrosia Wellington," the officer said. He was the same one who'd questioned me before. Felty, with the blue eyes and pleasant smile. My legs trembled. I needed Sully to coach me through this, to tell me what to say and how to say it.

"Can I help you?"

"I was just hoping for a few minutes of your time."

We ended up at a window table in Summerfields. I got a black coffee, even though I hated the acidic rot it left in my stomach. Did Officer Felty make a habit of going to campuses, taking girls for coffee, or was he doing this to put me at ease, like being in my own habitat would make me open my mouth and spout out what he wanted to hear?

"Thanks for taking the time," Felty said. He was big on time, I could tell. Probably frustratingly punctual, the kind of person who acted pissy if he had to wait two minutes for his wife to get ready.

"No problem," I said. The coffee burned my gums. "What did you want to talk about? I told you everything I remember about that night." I dropped my voice for the last two words, as if I were suffocating them with a pillow.

"I know." He fished the bag out of his peppermint tea and plunked it on the table. "But I'm hoping you can help fill in the gaps. The timeline just doesn't make sense."

My shoulders instinctively rode up.

"Kevin was with Flora early in the night. You said you saw them around nine thirty. Other witnesses saw them having an argument on the dance floor—an altercation that might have turned physical if a bystander hadn't stepped in."

I nodded. It crossed my mind that maybe I shouldn't talk at all, that I should request that a lawyer be present. But only guilty people needed lawyers. I was just a witness, and that was how I needed to remain.

"You and Sloane spoke with Flora after the altercation. It was then that you told Flora she would be better off without Kevin."

"It was just girl talk." I didn't remember telling him that. How did he know? Suddenly my story, *our* story, was a slippery, wriggling fish, impossible to hold on to.

"Right. Girl talk." A hard edge had entered his voice. He knew something. *He knew.* "What I don't understand are the events that followed."

"We danced. And drank a lot more. It's all kind of hazy."

"And you were never alone in a bathroom with Kevin McArthur."

I shook my head. The coffee was a bad idea. It made me jittery, like if I shook too hard, my brain might become dislodged.

"I've already told you I wasn't." My voice came out gratefully clear, almost snarky, like Sully. "Why did you come here just to go over it again?"

"Did you leave the party at any point to go back to your dorm?"

"No." Even when I told the truth, it sounded like a lie.

He smiled, maybe in an attempt to look casual. "Kevin McArthur is a lazy texter. Smart kid, goes to Dartmouth. But a history of messages sent from his phone would lead you to believe he has no idea how to use proper grammar." His head tilted slightly, as if he were taking me into his confidence. *Kids these days.*

Kevin's emails, scattered with *u* and *ur*, the indolent abbreviations that I came to see as terms of endearment. But the texts we—I—had sent Flora were perfectly constructed, and now I understood, with ear-splitting panic, that we would go up in flames because of them.

"I wouldn't know," I deadpanned. "I didn't know him. We never texted each other. I barely use my cell phone." The photo on it, Flora and the pilot from Halloween. I willed him not to ask me if he could see it. If he did, I would ask for a lawyer.

"What I don't understand," he continued, "is how that night, after Kevin had admittedly been drinking heavily, he managed to perfectly punctuate his sentences."

The silence between us might as well have been a brick wall, something thick and impermeable.

"People act different when they drink," I said.

"You and Sloane spend a lot of time together."

"We're best friends. So yeah, we do." I wrapped my hands around my empty mug and thought of the *Friend* mug and its shattered companion.

"And are you in the habit of making trips to Dartmouth together?"

I tried to hide my shock, but I could tell from his expression that I had let the mask slip. How did he know about Dartmouth? I realized then that somewhere, Sully might have been drinking coffee too, being questioned by an officer like Felty. She wouldn't let anything through the cracks. She would seal them off.

"Dartmouth," I repeated, my tongue too thick for my mouth. "Not in the habit of going there. But I did go once, yes. Sully liked this guy who went there. We went to a party and came home the next day." The actual weekend felt like so long ago that I could almost convince myself the new details added up.

"I see," Felty said. He hadn't touched his peppermint tea. He'd probably only ordered it to be disarming, like somebody's grandpa. "And do you recall seeing Kevin McArthur at this party?"

It was like a video game, some sort of virtual reality. One wrong move and you went over the side of a cliff or ended up in a fiery pit. I chose my words carefully to avoid the land mines.

"It's a big campus, Officer. I'm sure there was more than one party that night."

His eyes were narrowed, but I couldn't tell if it was suspicion or pity I saw in them.

"My sister was fifteen years old when I found her. I was twelve. She was hanging in our garage."

"I'm sorry," I said. So this was personal for him.

"She hid it well. The bullying. The girls at her school—they made her life hell. Our parents had no idea. I was too young to know the signs. Those girls are out in the world now, living their lives, and my sister isn't."

"That's terrible." I pictured those girls, now women, maybe raising girls of their own, perfect little monsters.

"It is," he said. "I think about her every day. Do you have a sister, Miss Wellington?"

I nodded. "I do. But I should really get going. I have a lot of studying to do." That much was true. I couldn't keep up. I wasn't Sully or the other girls, who worked hard and partied harder. I was easily derailed.

Felty slapped his business card down on the table between us. "If you think of anything that could help with the case, I trust you'll let me know." He plucked a pen out of his shirt pocket and jotted something on the back. "This is my personal cell phone."

I took the card, planning to throw it out the second I got back to my dorm room. But it remained with me forever, moving from wallet to wallet, becoming soft and creased. Keep your friends close and your enemies closer.

Later, when I found Sully alone in her room, I told her everything, expecting her to reciprocate with her own horror story about being questioned. She stared at me, eyes wide. "Nobody came for me."

"I wonder why they asked me and not you," I said. "I mean, he knew we were both at Dartmouth that night. Hey, at least this way I can tell you what I told him. So when they question you, we can stick to the same story."

She listened as I combed over the whole exchange with Felty, but I could tell her attention was somewhere else. On her ragged cuticles and the dry ends of her hair. There was a moment when I kept talking but thought, *She doesn't care about any of this.*

By the time I was done, she had crafted her hair into a messy bun, the wisps framing her face. I expected a hug, an *Everything will be okay.* Instead, she said something I really didn't want to hear.

"You're being paranoid, Amb. Nobody's going to arrest you. They can't prove you had Kevin's phone. They're just trying to intimidate you to get you to talk. All you have to do is keep your mouth shut."

I nodded, but my stomach twisted like a tangled bedsheet. All I heard was *you. You you you.* Not *we.* Not *us.* Even though she was the one who'd set the events in motion. If she hadn't taken the phone, I never would have sent those messages. I never would have slept with Kevin and Flora would be alive.

"Let's go out," she said. "We'll find a party somewhere." She had already complained that everyone had become boring in their dogged pursuit of finals, permanent fixtures at Olin, disciples of caffeine and Adderall and candy from Weshop.

"I can't," I said. "I have a bunch of work to do."

"So take a break. I know what we can do." She stood up and grabbed something from the mess of her desk. A silver cell phone. "I took it from a guy who sat next to me at Olin. I think his name's Todd and I'm pretty sure he fucked Lily once. Want to mess with him?"

I gaped at her smirk and the phone, small and innocuous in her hand. "You're kidding me, right?"

She clenched her fingers around the phone. "Why would I be kidding? It would be hilarious to try and hook him up with Lily again or something."

Her expression was almost innocent. It wouldn't be *hilarious*. I wondered how many people's lives we had affected in our quest for entertainment.

"No." I shook my head. "I don't want to do that anymore."

She pursed her lips. "You know, you're getting to be pretty boring. Like everyone else."

"I'm sorry. I promise, I'll be back to normal soon."

"You've promised that before."

I wanted to argue that *before* was a different playing field, one where Flora was alive and it was us against her. I didn't know what normal was anymore. I was scared that Sully and I only worked when we had a common enemy to disarm, and we wouldn't survive without the absence of one.

A few days later, Kevin made a statement to the press. He had been back at his parents' house in Fairfield. Maybe his parents hated him, if it was possible to hate your own children. Or maybe they believed him when he said he didn't send the messages, even though he had no explanation for how they came from his phone.

"I want to apologize to Flora's family," he said, staring into the camera. "I've hurt so many people in ways I'll never fully understand. I'm sorry for my involvement in what happened to Flora. I'm working to find out how those messages were sent from my phone, and I maintain my innocence."

I couldn't sense, through a TV screen, if he was defiant or defeated. His eyes met mine, like I was the only one watching. He could easily tell the police he was with me and that I'd had the best chance of stealing his phone and returning it without his noticing. I didn't sleep for days.

Sully managed to drag me out to a party before winter break, where I had drunken sex with a guy named Jeremy from the lacrosse team. I felt like the sex was necessary to maintain not my own desirability but my friendship with Sully. She hooked up with his friend, and when it was just the two of us walking back to the Butts, she put her head on my shoulder, just like Flora had done on Halloween.

I had never been so grateful to be going back to Pennington.

Over winter break, my mom wanted to talk. She kept cornering me with a cup of tea, asking how I was doing.

"I'm fine," I repeated. "I wasn't the one who found her."

Sometimes, I was. The mental picture was so panoramic that it seemed like I had to have been there. A nightmare, the type that left you wrapped in a cocoon of sweaty sheets. I felt my legs carrying me from Butts C, just like the phantom girl starring in the rumors that had recently started up. I saw Flora on her bed. Head back, eyes staring at the ceiling. Wrists ripped apart, red highway lines down the middle. Red comforter. Red walls. Red ceiling. A girl who was never angry in life was furious in death.

"You don't seem fine," Mom said, her arm warm across my shoulders. "We barely hear from you anymore. And you seem distracted, sweetie. You didn't smile once at the tree lighting, and you usually love Christmas."

"I'm just busy. I promise when school starts again, I'll call more often." I hugged her tight, wondering if she would love me if she knew the truth.

Billie wanted us to get drunk and have a sleepover, like we had in high school. It wasn't the same. Flora's ghost loomed large with Billie's barrage of questions. "What was she actually like? Did you have any idea she was depressed? Was her boyfriend a total prick?" I sidestepped carefully, saying I didn't want to talk about it.

"Okay," she said. "Fair enough. It's kind of morbid. Hey, can you at least tell me what happened with your guy? You were so into him, then nothing. Did he turn into an asshole?"

"Something like that," I said. "I was wrong about him."

She took a sip of Mike's Hard Lemonade. "I'm sorry. That sucks. You know, I always thought it was strange that you never told me his name."

I didn't hesitate. "I did tell you. His name is Buddy."

When I went back to Wesleyan for the spring semester, I made a point of calling home once a week. I understood it was my new role, keeping other people happy. Maybe that was why most of the girls I knew were miserable. We prioritized everyone else's happiness over our own.

I purposely skipped the Theater Department's auditions for the spring season. The last thing I needed was my own personal spotlight. Besides, I was exhausted from performing every day, for an audience that was about to get bigger and a lot less sympathetic.

I could have handled the misery if Sully had been there too. We were a unit, two batteries recharging each other. But the Sully who had sucked me into her star-dazzled orbit never came back to Wesleyan. The girl who came back in her place was an entirely different person.

33

NOW

Dear Ambrosia Wellington,

We hope you've worked up an appetite, because a lot of preparation has gone into tonight's special dinner. Stick around after the plates have been cleared, because there just might be some surprises in store!

Sincerely,
Your Alumni Committee

Adrian doesn't get angry very often. It's one of the qualities that attracted me to him—the even temper, the fuse as long as a garden hose. But right now he's mad. He wants to know where I've been, why I was gone for so long, why he's already in his suit and I'm standing here sweating in a sundress.

"So you disappear for almost two hours and don't answer your phone. What the hell am I supposed to think? I'm asking everyone if they've seen my wife and they're all giving me these strange looks, like they feel sorry for me."

Wife is a missile in his mouth. It means something entirely different than it did in our wedding vows.

"I'm sorry," I repeat. "I didn't realize I was gone that long. I didn't think it would be so hard—hearing people talk about her. I had to get out. It was taking me back to a dark place."

"I thought you weren't even friends," he says.

"I lived with a girl who killed herself. It's complicated. I'm sure you can understand."

He exhales slowly. "I get that you wanted to be alone, but can't you see why I would be extremely worried about you?"

"I know." I grip his fingers and cast a glance at the closed inner door, wondering if Sully is in the other room. "I'm sorry. Being back here is weird for me."

Adrian shrugs me off and sits down on our bed. His dress pants ride up, revealing purple and yellow striped socks, which I'm pretty sure have holes in the bottom. "Yeah. It must be weird. But why have you never once mentioned Flora in all the time we've known each other? Or Sully? You made it sound like Hads and Heather were your only real friends from here, but it's pretty obvious they weren't. I told you about Chad on, what, our third date?"

Chad was Adrian's best friend in high school. In senior year he was having a hard time dealing with college applications and the pressure his parents put on him to be a football superstar. Chad started drinking a lot, and one night when he and Adrian were at a party, he said goodbye and drove himself home. Chad died instantly when his car crashed into a telephone pole. Nobody ever knew if it was an accident or a suicide, but Adrian was racked with guilt. He told me it was the darkest phase in his life.

"I felt like a monster," he said. It was the first time I saw him cry. "I could have prevented it. Chad had beers and drove at, like, every party. I never thought anything different would happen that night."

I cradled his head on my lap and told him he wasn't a monster, just a regular teenage boy. It would have been a good time to reveal that my roommate had died because of me. But there was never a good time for that kind of truth.

I wait for Adrian to soften, but he doesn't. "I asked the girls from Butterfields about you and Flora. They seemed to think that something had happened with you guys. Ella said she saw Flora crying in the bathroom the day before she died and mentioned something cryptic about Halloween."

Ella told me the same thing, once, and I didn't listen. Flora's secret, folded in on itself like origami. The pilot from Halloween. He was her first, when she was waiting for it to be Kevin. And she hadn't even wanted it.

"I have no idea what Ella meant by that. Sully and I took Flora out once, because she was upset about her boyfriend. But nothing strange happened. It was Halloween. All of us got pretty drunk."

"Huh." Adrian props his chin in his hands. "Yeah, the boyfriend. Is it true you had something going on with him?"

The panic in my chest is tight like a balloon. I was an idiot to think that the past wouldn't find not only me but Adrian this weekend.

"Of course not. It's just like Ella to rehash some stupid rumor. I didn't even know Flora's boyfriend. I met the guy once."

He doesn't say anything else, but he's starting to put everything together, like I am, only he's constructing a different puzzle. He's working on Who My Wife Is, and I'm working on What Happened to Flora Banning. If Adrian ever pieces together his puzzle, he'll leave me. How could he not?

"You should get dressed for dinner," he finally says. "Everyone else is already there. We missed Ella's pre-drink thing. I thought it would be wrong to go without you."

My dress is laid out over the back of the desk chair. I don't know who draped it there, like a body, complete with my stilettos at the bottom. It must have been Sully. She liked to control what I wore.

"This dinner is going to be boring," I say. "A bunch of dumb speeches and bad food. We could skip it. You're always saying you wish we were more spontaneous."

When I glance behind me, Adrian is focused on his phone, not even paying attention. Or maybe he heard me and is pretending not to. Maybe he's sick of my excuses.

I slip out of my sundress and shimmy into my black Missoni. The clutch I brought to go with it is beaded, something I borrowed from Billie. I open it to put my phone and lipstick inside and that's when my hand brushes the paper, a little scroll. I unravel it. A promise in crimson ink. *Tonight, you'll find out everything.*

The West Wing is at its red-and-black best, festooned like a proud cardinal. Banquet tables with floor-length tablecloths sweeping the ground, red cushions tied onto silver chairs, bows plump at the back. A band plays low jazz. It's like a wedding, without the happy couple. I'm wilting in a sea of updos and Spanx, men with white shirts stuck to their backs, my own hair lank, armpits slick.

"There's Heather," I say, spying her springy dark curls in the crowd.

But when I get closer, I see that there's no empty spots at her table. "Sorry," Hadley says, sinking into a seat with a jacket on the back. "We texted you and asked when you were coming. We thought maybe you bailed."

"We tried to save room." Heather shrugs apologetically. "But we couldn't keep waiting. There are only so many seats."

"It's okay. We'll just meet up after." Except I can't ignore their darting eyes, the unspoken language between Hads and Heather. They're pissed that I blew them off, that we never got a photo in front of our old house. I try to smile, but I'm sure it looks like a grimace.

"There's Ella." Adrian gestures to the center of the room. "Looks like there's space at her table." *Of course.* Ella stands up and waves us over, cleavage spilling out of a shiny black dress. They're all there, glittering under the lights. Clara's blood-red lips; Gemma and her black sequined dress, long stem legs stretched out; Lily's hair in a tight ballerina bun; the rubies gripping Sienna's collarbones. They're beautiful and terrible, predatory and unapproachable, just like they were then.

I complete the real reunion, the Butts C one. The only girl missing is Sully.

"You look great," Ella says when we get to the table. "Oh, you can't sit there. Lauren and Jonah are there. But you can sit in the ones beside it. Right next to me. You drink white wine, right?"

I drank white wine, until now. The First Response, discarded in the bathroom garbage. It's hard to believe that it happened today, that a handful of hours can change so much. But I guess I should know that already.

"I'm not really in the mood," I say. "I have a massive headache." She pours me a glass anyway.

Adrian's already sipping from his glass. He'll have too much to drink. He'll talk to everyone, dance to the band, and draw people to him like a magnet. A surge of warmth floods me. I like that he's fun, that he's predictable. Kevin never was. Kevin might be gone by now. Sully might be with him, arm hanging out his truck window, laughter cleaving the night.

I eyeball my full wineglass. Ella glances at it too, then back to me. *She knows.*

"I need to ask you something," I say.

"Something about what?" She's louder than she needs to be.

"About the night Flora died. What you remember from before it happened."

"You're kidding, right?" She pushes her hair behind her ears. "Why do you suddenly want to talk about her now? You should have asked me back then. When I really could have used a friend."

"I was your friend."

"I thought you were, at first. But you didn't care about me. I'm giving you the benefit of the doubt this weekend, but I'm not going to make you feel better about anything." She turns away and takes a drink. I'm left wondering if Ella has been the real actress this whole time.

They're already starting to bring the first course around, some kind of tomato tower. Lauren and Jonah join us and sit down, flanked by a couple of the other girls' husbands, all holding drinks. "Look who decided to show up," Lauren says, followed by a hiccup. I try to drum up a good excuse for being late besides attempting to wring the truth out of Kevin McArthur. But they're staring past me, at somebody else.

She's in a floor-length gown with a beaded top, the palest blush rose, almost like a wedding dress. Of course Sully didn't follow the dress code, didn't put on her *red-and-black best*. She's not wearing a bra, but she doesn't need to—she used to hate her small breasts, flicking at her nipples, and I told her she was lucky because they wouldn't sag. She's smiling, waving at people, like she owns the room, like it's her own personal red carpet. Maybe it is, because nobody else is stepping up to claim the throne.

She folds herself into the empty seat beside Adrian, like she knew it was being saved for her. Sully has a place at every table. I suddenly don't want her that close to what's mine, so of course she gets even closer, kissing his cheek like he's her husband.

"Sorry I'm so late," she says. "It took me forever to get ready."

I don't think she's talking about getting ready for dinner. My dress slumped on the chair back, ready for me; the scroll in my purse. She stares at me pointedly, like I'm supposed to have a response, like I ever did anything but agree with her. She picked our outfits for the Double Feature. *We'll wear these,* she said. Nothing was ever a question.

Now I see her striding back to the Butts, wiping Flora's tears. Telling her what I was doing with Kevin. Eyeing the *Best* mug. *Here's how you can really ruin her life, if you're up to it.*

My phone goes off. It's a text from Billie, plastered on my screen. Adrian sees it before I can yank the phone away.

Any updates?? Are you still with him?

His bottom lip finds its way into his mouth. When we first started dating, Adrian was very open about his past. "I've been cheated on," he said. "I still followed her around like a puppy dog. I'm a pretty forgiving guy, but cheating is nonnegotiable." I cuddled into him, gave him the reassurances that he needed. My body tucked around his, my kisses on his bare shoulders. *I'd never do that to you.* I meant it, at the time.

"Billie wanted to know if you were having fun," I explain, my mouth working around the words like they're giant marbles. "I was telling her about the tree dedication. How I had to get away, and that I felt bad about leaving you."

Adrian takes another drink of his wine. "You could have texted me if you felt so bad. Or answered any of mine."

I pick at my salad. The cheese is gummy and tasteless. I didn't bother looking at the menu to see what the next course would be. I doubt I'll be able to eat it.

Adrian refills Sully's glass, which, like his, is already empty. She puts her hand on his arm, pointedly. She hasn't talked to me yet. We're playing some kind of game. She knows I know something, but not how much.

"So what's on the agenda for the rest of the night?" I say. "I forget what the last alumni email said."

"It's the All-Campus Party at Andrus," Lauren says, as if I should already know. "But what email do you even mean? They gave out programs when we checked in, but I haven't gotten any emails."

I blink at Sully, at the tight rosebud her lips make before she trains them into a smile. She got the emails too—she called them *annoying*, but they're more than that. Menacing, their own road map.

I quickly open my email on my phone, ignoring the way Adrian hovers over my shoulder. The last one is still there, read but not deleted. I click on it and scan it for clues, but I don't find any. Until my eyes settle on the address itself. It's a Gmail account.

The emails didn't come from Wesleyan at all.

"Are you okay?" Adrian says. He sounds more irritated than concerned. "You're shivering."

"We're going to need more wine," Sully says. Her tone is girlish and artificial. I stare at the table setup, at the red sash bisecting the middle, at the black candelabra centerpiece. Somebody put a lot of effort into this party. I notice a menu across from Lauren and pick it up, to have somewhere to look besides anyone's face.

A noise comes out of my throat, small and strangled, prey caught in a trap. The lettering. It's the same as what was on the notes. The crimson ink, the tilted letters. The same script that told me *we need to talk* is now telling me that a beef tenderloin medallion is the next item on the menu.

I reach behind Adrian and pass the menu to Sully. Tiny creases appear on her forehead as the realization sinks in. Is she just acting, or is she really as surprised as I am?

She pushes her untouched plate away. "As if Wesleyan shelled out to have somebody make the menus by hand. I mean, I remember when what they served in MoCon was barely above dog food."

The girls laugh politely, probably considering their own relationships with the MoCon food. Sully liked to pretend she could eat anything she wanted, but the reality was, she took everything but picked at it, unable or unwilling to commit. When people commented on her razor-sharp collarbones or visible ribs, she'd chalk it up to a fast metabolism, because skinny with work wasn't as jealousy inducing as skinny without.

I watch Ella. She's slicing her tomatoes into precise quarters and doesn't offer any kind of reaction.

"I wonder how anyone can write this neatly." Sully pretends to inspect the menu. "I can barely write my own name anymore."

Nobody takes her bait except Adrian, who starts talking about how he tried handwriting his novel but couldn't decipher his own chicken scratch. "I could have written the first chapter of the next American classic, but nobody would ever know it."

Adrian keeps talking, and the girls laugh, maybe with him but probably at him, and their husbands remain mostly mute, some of them on their phones. Jonah briefly makes eye contact and he must remember what I look like naked, unless I blend into every other Wesleyan girl.

A cold finger dips into the back of my dress. I didn't see Sully get up, but now she's standing behind me, her voice in my ear. "You need to come with me."

I get up obediently without allowing myself a glance at Adrian. We head into the lobby, which is gratefully empty, minus some red and black balloons crowding the ceiling. Sully spins around. "You went to see Kevin."

I don't acknowledge that or ask how she knows. I have more important questions that need answering. "What really happened? When Kevin and I were together the night Flora died. Where did you go? Did you see that ACB post about a blond girl running from Butts C?"

She runs a finger over her eyebrows, but I catch the shock she's trying to conceal. "I don't even remember. I was with some guy."

I try another entry point. "What happened when we went to Dartmouth? I woke up and you weren't there."

She tilts her head. "Why ask? You already know."

My mouth tastes like metal. "Why?"

"It used to be *us*. Then you were so obsessed with Kevin and Flora. I knew he wasn't that great. Not worth ruining everything for."

I sink into a leather armchair, let its width envelop me in a cold hug. "I wasn't obsessed."

She fans out her hands. "Come on. You practically begged me to go to Dartmouth with you. He kissed me, we fucked. He was just a horny frat boy."

I keep going, before she manipulates her way out of this. "Lauren told me about Evie. You talked about her like she was alive. Did you have something to do with her death?" As I say it, I'm not even sure which *her* I'm talking about, Evie, Flora, or both.

Her head snaps up, but she doesn't answer me.

"Tell me the truth." I lean away from her. "Tell me if you convinced Flora to hurt herself."

"Of course not. But you did. I mean, bravo. Your messages were truly horrific."

I try again, because I know she's holding back. "Did you go back to the Butts and tell her to kill herself while I was with Kevin?"

"Amb," she says, putting her hands on my knees and hovering over me. "You can't make someone do something they weren't going to do already. If you can, then you're the one who killed Flora."

"Sloane," I practically shout. Maybe it's her actual name that gets me her attention.

She sinks into the chair beside mine. "You saw the messages on Kevin's phone. He was texting so many girls. You weren't special to him. But you were to me." She cracks her knuckles. "Why do you even care how it happened? You hated Flora."

"I didn't hate her," I say. "I was just—"

"You did," Sully says. "At least I can admit it. *I* hated her. She was weak. Girls like Flora can't deal if they're not wanted by someone."

It's a dig at Flora but also at me. Flora was wanted by someone. Sully was craved by everyone. I was eaten alive, cannibalized by my own comparisons.

I focus on Sully's face, her big eyes and long hair, the girl I worshipped. It was never about Kevin for either of us. It was about a girl we couldn't become. Sully's jealousy led her to the same place mine did. Maybe it took her further.

This is what it comes down to. Three girls, each with something another wanted. I was the snake that swallowed Flora, and Sully unhinged her jaw to swallow me. Maybe everything would have ended very differently if we had talked, but we didn't exist in a world where our envy was allowed to have a voice.

"You heard what Kevin thinks," I say. "That someone actually killed her."

"Maybe he did it." She drums her fingers. "He's the one who found her. He went looking for her after he was with you. He saw those texts on his phone and wanted her out of the picture, then made it happen."

"He didn't do it." As involved as Kevin was, I'm sure of that.

She feathers a piece of hair between her fingers. "Then he needs to accept that Flora killed herself."

"But what if she didn't?"

"She wanted to die. She said so herself. Why are you surprised that she followed through?"

Her mouth darts into a smile, and *I know.* I know that Flora only would have followed through if somebody got into her head, and only Sully could have done that.

She crosses her legs, her pale skin exposed through the slit in her dress. "You cared more about Flora than you ever did about me."

"You know that's not true. I would have done anything to get your attention." It's pathetic to admit, even after all this time. Especially after all this time.

She laughs gently. "You always had it. You were the *best.*"

We're at an impasse, the truth heavy between us. Maybe we have said all there is to say. Maybe it took the years arching between then and now for me to see that Sully was more like me than I knew. A lonely girl who wanted control. Except I let my emotions muddy everything, and her lack of them allowed her hands to stay clean.

But we still have a shared threat. The ghost of what we did, making sure we're permanently webbed together.

"Somebody wants to hurt us," I say. "I came back to find out who it is."

Sully places an icy hand on my arm and leans closer. "Is that it?" she says, voice soft against my neck. "Is that really why you came back?"

I nod, but I'm not sure at all anymore.

"Let's get out of here." Her tone is urgent. "We can take off. Nobody will be able to find us."

"I can't," I say quickly. I can't leave Adrian. I don't want to go anywhere with Sully. It would only be a matter of time before she got bored and turned on me.

But for just a second, before prying my arm from Sully's insistent grip, I consider it.

34

THEN

The media obsession with Flora Banning was stifling. The world loves a pretty dead girl. Wesleyan, a place where people were always protesting something, became an angry mob gunning for Kevin, faces hidden behind JUSTICE FOR FLORA signs. The Butts C girls kept up a vigil in front of our old room, flowers and teddy bears and candles that were perpetually unlit.

The argument: Kevin was guilty. He hadn't physically done it, but he had emotionally manipulated a girl into doing something completely out of character. Without the text messages he'd sent, Flora would still have been alive.

But Kevin's family hired a defense lawyer who had a different argument. Jon Diamond had a cocky smile and a square jaw and hair that must have left grease stains on his pillow. Jon Diamond, whose services apparently came at a hefty cost, argued that Flora was mentally unbalanced and had obviously been dealing with undiagnosed depression. He twisted what her parents, sister, and friends had said, along with the anonymous testimonies of "classmates" who didn't want to be named. Flora was a young woman who was sick on the inside, according to Jon Diamond, and invisible illnesses are among the most deadly.

"Think about this," he told the press after Kevin's hearing. "Think of all the times you've said the wrong thing to your girlfriend or boy-friend or husband or wife. All the times when you maybe weren't think-ing clearly because you were upset yourself. Are you responsible if that person does something to themselves? Most of you are going to say no, you're not, the blame lies with them, because we can't make anyone do anything they weren't going to do already."

Online, groups of Kevin supporters sprouted up, mostly girls who thought he deserved better. They believed it was Flora's fault. Some-times I agreed with them. Flora had never felt like she needed any armor. The world had rolled her on its tongue, so careful not to bite into her delicate flesh.

We weren't careful. She was chewy when our teeth went in.

I obsessed over every news update, every nasty comment under the articles. I knew my escalating paranoia had become boring to Sully, but I couldn't stop fixating on Flora. On the part I'd played. "Somebody's going to find out," I repeated, ignoring her eye rolls. "They're not done with us yet."

I wasn't wrong. Because eventually, they searched Kevin's com-puter and found our emails, and Felty was able to prove that I'd lied to him about Dartmouth.

"Miss Wellington," he said when I found myself at the Middletown Police Department again. "Or do you go by Amb? That's what Kevin called you, right? In your emails."

I was going to pass out—I couldn't remember the last time I had eaten. Some people, the ones who hadn't been paying attention to the growing rumors, might have assumed I was dealing with grief over my roommate's suicide. In reality, my fear took up too much space. The fear that I would end up exactly where I was that day, with Felty across from me, smug in his uniform.

"It sounds like you and Kevin had a very friendly relationship. A real love story for our time. Is that what you believed? You had such a *connection*."

I was incapable of speaking. I would never make it as an actress if I couldn't deliver even a basic line.

"It seemed like you both wanted the same thing: Flora out of the way. How far did you go to make that happen?"

I squeaked out seven words, a sequence I had heard in the movies, on TV, happening to people who weren't real. "I want to speak to a lawyer."

In the end, I didn't need one. The emails didn't prove anything. They were Felty's attempt to break me. All the emails showed was that Kevin McArthur was an asshole who lied to his girlfriend, and I was the bitch who went along with it. His inbox and text history were a treasure trove to the prosecutors, who smeared him in the media as a serial cheater who didn't care about Flora's well-being.

Felty's last words to me were permanently stamped inside my head. *The truth has a way of catching up, eventually.*

Which meant I had to run fast.

After Felty reluctantly let me go, I knocked on Sully's door. I needed her. I needed everything to go back to how it was. We ended up at a WestCo party, where a bump of cocaine and one drink sent me into a fevered tailspin. My demons weren't gone. They were still attached to me, hanging by thorny tails. The pair of guys Sully wanted us to hook up with found an excuse to disappear when I vomited into a plastic cup.

"It was the scariest moment of my life," I slurred on our walk back to the Butts, grabbing Sully's arm, which she quickly pulled away. "You have no idea what went through my head. Felty isn't giving up. He *knows*. Did I tell you about his sister?"

"You told me," she said. Her hair was tucked up under a slouchy knit beanie and I couldn't read her face.

"Kevin wasn't that drunk," I said. "He's going to put it together. What would you do? I mean, he must know we were the only people who could have taken his phone. It's not like he believes he sent her the messages."

"How do you know?" Sully shoved her hands in her jacket pockets—it wasn't even her jacket, but one she had stolen from some guy—and didn't look at me. "A guilty conscience makes people believe all sorts of things. When you don't want to deal with what you actually did, your brain can convince you that you're somebody you're not."

We weren't talking about Kevin anymore. It was the distance hovering there, the breadth of a hair multiplying into inches.

"What if he's protecting us?" I had never said it out loud before.

Sully sucked in a breath, swallowed part of the 2 a.m. sky. "There is no us."

She said it so quietly that I wasn't sure I'd heard her. "What?"

She stopped and crossed her arms. "There is no us, Amb. You were the one who sent those texts. Yeah, I took the phone. But only as a joke. You're the one who did the rest."

You're the one. There it was, yawning between us. She was cutting her losses. I was her losses.

I had no argument, because what she said was true. I was the one who'd typed those messages and hit send. She hadn't been whispering in my ear, telling me what to say, and the truth of that was like a block of ice lodged somewhere between my throat and my stomach that would never melt. I had to believe somebody else was the bad influence so I could live with myself.

But it was me all along.

35

NOW

Dear Ambrosia Wellington,

Don't forget to sign the guest book at dinner. Write an inside joke, a favorite anecdote, a sentimental memory. We're sure you learned during your years at Wesleyan that words truly are the most important currency.

At least, most of you did.

Sincerely,
Your Alumni Committee

When we get back into the ballroom, Sully trailing behind me for once, we're pinned by dozens of suspicious eyeballs—all of the girls at the table, clearly using our absence to fuel their dinner conversation. Adrian barely even looks up. This time, he doesn't ask me where I've been. After sitting down, I push a medallion of beef around before depositing it on Adrian's plate, a gesture he usually thinks is cute.

"No, thanks," he says. He's still mad. The drive home will be tense and I'll probably get a *We should talk*, except we never will. I'll apologize for leaving him alone for most of the afternoon but never tell him the real reason, and in a few days he'll be back to normal again and so will I.

The emcee for the evening—Braden Elliot, who lived with two other guys in a wood-frame near the one I shared with Hadley and Heather—gives a speech while dessert is served, something chocolate in haphazard squares. A grim thought flits bannerlike through my head: *This is my last meal*. Whoever wrote those notes won't let us get away so easily.

Braden calls out the winners for a ceremony I didn't know was happening, a throwback to awards we gave at graduation—apparently, the idea is to see which predictions we voted on back then align with our guesses now and whether they came true. Most Likely to Appear on a Reality TV Show. Most Likely to Win an Oscar. It should be my name being called for that one. In another world, one where I wasn't Flora's roommate, where I didn't meet Kevin or Sully, maybe it would be me. Most Likely to Get Arrested Protesting. Most Likely to Be Found Naked in Olin. Everyone laughs appreciatively, while I want to disappear.

"Most Likely to Get Away with Murder," Braden says now, followed by a stilted laugh. "Wow, this one's morbid. Ambrosia Wellington?"

My name being called, the drumbeat of blood in my ears. All eyes in the room on me, like sets of daggers. Nobody is laughing this time, nobody is clapping.

"You should go get your award," Ella says. She probably voted for me. Adrian is focused on his plate, his jaw hard. As much as I want to run away, I stand up and walk toward the stage, sucking in my stomach, rolling my eyes like a few of the other winners did. Except when I get to the front, Braden doesn't give me a cheap plastic trophy and shake my hand like he did with everybody else. He opens the box where the votes were placed, several little flags of paper, with confusion furrowing his face.

"This is so weird, but it's like this category didn't really exist," he says, away from the microphone. "There's a box and all these votes, but no record of the category, and no trophy. I'm really sorry. I don't understand."

I gape at him, unable to laugh it off. "Let's just pretend," he says with an apologetic smile. I accept his hand when he stretches it toward me, but instead of going right back to my seat, I open the box and pull out a handful of the votes.

They all have my name on them. Dozens of *Ambrosia Wellington*, written in neat calligraphy. One of them sticks to my sweaty palm, flutters onto the floor as I walk back to the table. I don't look at Sully or Adrian, at Hads or Heather, at the Butts C girls. Onstage, Braden clears his throat and moves on to the next category. Most Likely to Invent the Next Facebook.

I didn't get away with murder, I want to scream. I didn't kill anyone. I did something unforgivable, but I didn't go that far. I don't have the stomach for it. I didn't even have my room key, and Flora would have locked the door—

I didn't have my room key, because Sully did.

There was something on her top—suddenly it slices through my memories from that night. Something on the mesh, a dark strip, almost black. And her choker was missing. I see it like I did earlier today—Sully showing up, playing nice, offering to make Flora a hot chocolate.

Sully, taking the *Best* mug and smashing it against the bathroom floor.

Go ahead and do it. You want to.

But Flora didn't want to.

What did Sully say to me tonight? *You can't make someone do something they weren't going to do already.*

She didn't convince Flora to cut her wrists.

She did it herself.

I don't know how Sully didn't end up with blood all over her. She must have been very careful. She must have known exactly what she was doing. How deep to cut. How to make it look like the shard was held in each hand. How to keep a girl from screaming.

The realization, the absolute certainty, hollows me. Kevin was right. Somebody did kill Flora.

"It was her," I say in a tiny voice.

When I look up, Sully and Adrian are gone.

36

THEN

Kevin McArthur's investigation never went to trial. There was insufficient evidence to pursue the case further or define the extent of his involvement. Too many factors made Flora's suicide solely her own doing. There was her history of so-called depression, the text messages sent from her phone showing a crescendo of paranoia, her browser search about how to tell if you've been raped—a rape nobody had any information about, if it even happened. Kevin disappeared as the media frenzy finally died down. The girls from Butts C sent nasty emails to his lawyer and letters to news stations in an attempt to keep the case alive, but none of their pleas made a difference.

It was over, and I could breathe again. Except the air was different where I lived now. Wesleyan had become hostile, not just the people but the campus itself, an animal wanting to buck me off its back. Sometimes on my walk back to the Butts from the CFA, music would leak from the chapel, bells not chiming church music but contorting into songs Flora used to listen to in our room. I later learned that students were allowed to play the chapel's bells, but I never knew who decided on those songs. Or if they only existed in my head.

I had avoided going to hell, but the rest of freshman year was my own personal purgatory. I had what I had always wanted—attention. But it was the wrong kind. At best, girls were cordial, smiling politely when I sat next to them in lectures or perched on the end of a table in MoCon. At worst, they were downright brutal.

I saw Sully around campus and even in classes occasionally—Wesleyan made it hard to hide, and sometimes it felt like the campus was trying to shove us together, chess pieces on a board. I didn't get close or let myself know if she was watching. The only thing worse than being under Sully's constant gaze was being cast out of it. She was perpetually flanked by girls like her but lesser. Baby Sullies, my replacements. There was no shortage of people to worship at her golden altar. The same rumors that became my yoke were shiny jewelry around her neck.

I still couldn't let go, so I replayed on my laptop the same clip of Flora's mom leaving court after the hearing, shielding her face from the cameras with a trenchcoated arm, Flora's sister, Poppy, trailing behind her, half a foot taller than she had been last year. Not a little girl anymore. Poppy's face had already hardened into a scowl. Pissed off at the world. Poppy had a reason to be pissed off. Her sister had been taken away from her.

And the boy who took her was free. In the eyes of the law, Flora was disturbed, a mentally ill young woman who couldn't handle the pressures of being away at school, and after an argument with her boyfriend, she made the tragic choice to take her own life. That was what it was—a choice.

I ignored an email from Poppy that came two weeks before the end of freshman year. A plea to talk about her sister and Kevin. I couldn't bring myself to answer it and lie, so I deleted it instead but never forgot what it said. *Did something happen to Flora before that night? Did Kevin do something? Please, I need to know, and you knew her better than anyone at school. She said she trusted you.*

I didn't sleep for days, and I bombed my final exams. *She trusted you.*

That was the last mistake she ever made.

NOW

Dear Ambrosia Wellington,

You never ended the night early back then—why start now? Make your way to Andrus to dance under the stars at our annual All-Campus Party. We hear the dance floor will be killer, and we expect to see (almost) everyone there!

Sincerely,
Your Alumni Committee

"Where are they?" I ask Ella. "Where did they go?"

She raises a glass of wine to her lips, clearly savoring my stress. "How should I know? Sloane said something about not feeling well. Adrian said he'd make sure she got back to your room. She had, like, five glasses of wine and didn't eat a thing. Just like back then. Of course she feels sick."

Adrian's suit jacket is gone. If he took his jacket, it means he doesn't plan on coming back. "I need to go."

"You should stay." She drops her voice. "Sorry if I was harsh earlier. I didn't want to go into this weekend with any grudges."

"You did this." I pick up the vote curled in my hand. "You wrote my name."

"I didn't do anything," Ella says, laughing. "I voted for you for that reality TV one. Since drama seems to follow you everywhere you go."

"Did you send this?" I unclasp my clutch, rummage around inside for the note, but it isn't there. It's in my cross-body bag, back at the Nics. I have no evidence. And now I notice that something else is missing, too. My phone.

"Send what?" She arches her eyebrow.

"The notes. You know what I'm talking about. You stayed home sick that night—" *You figured it out.* I know I sound crazy.

"I didn't send you any notes." Her raised voice elicits a giggle from Lauren. "The only person I send mail to is my grandma. She's ninety-four. Seriously, what's up with you?"

"I'm fine," I say. *Sully killed Flora and now she's with my husband.*

"I had a feeling this weekend would end in some kind of drama," she says. "You and Sloane rooming together. Whose idea was that, anyway?"

I get up, then sit back down in a dizzying rush. I should have figured it out earlier, when she showed up at our door. *She knows where to find us.*

"How did you know we were rooming together?"

Ella shrugs. "I don't know. Someone must have mentioned it to me. Oh. It was Poppy. She wanted to meet you guys, then you both bailed at the dedication."

I cup my hand over my mouth. My palm comes back smeared with red.

Poppy Banning, the closest thing the world has left to Flora. She wanted to meet us. *Poppy wants to come for a visit,* Flora told me, the two of us sipping from our mugs. *I told her all about you.*

"What?" Ella says, annoyed with my *drama.* But I don't answer her—I can't—so I get up and weave my way through the tables. I need to find Adrian and get us out of here. Flora couldn't come back to haunt us, since ghosts don't exist. But sisters do.

I come face-to-face with Flora in the lobby. For once, I read the fine print on her poster. If I'd paid attention two days ago, I would have been home by now. Because the fine print is in calligraphy— Poppy's neat hand. The Flora Banning Memorial Foundation. Created by Poppy's Pretty Pen.

Flora's pride, when we were trading details about our sisters. *She's super artistic.* I saw Poppy, a gangly kid whose artwork covered a hulking stainless steel fridge. Not this. The notes. The lipstick. The scroll. The ballot box, stuffed with my name. How long has she been waiting to strike? Flora died almost fourteen years ago. Poppy shares at least one of her qualities. Patience.

Chairs scrape and people brush past me. Dinner is over and everyone will be heading to Andrus for the All-Campus Party. Maybe I should follow them and lose myself in the crowd, where I'll be safe. But I'm not safe anywhere. And Adrian isn't safe as long as he's with Sully. I'm not sure what's worse: that I know what Sully is capable of, or that I don't know the same about Poppy.

I take off my heels and start to run, up Wyllys, past the white tents set up on Andrus, past laughter and music. I run until I'm at the entrance to the Nics, where I notice the plume of smoke. The shadowy figure it leads to.

"Looks like you're trying to find someone," Felty says.

I rattle the door, then remember that my key card is missing. *I'm not afraid of Felty.* He's just a man with a theory that nobody could prove. I almost want to tell him about Sully, about the blackened truth I finally unmasked tonight. But he has no reason to believe me, and I would just end up implicating myself.

"I haven't given up," he says to my back. "One day I'll get a confession out of one of you."

"Amb." I whip my head around and see a figure sprinting across the grass, long dress hitched up. Sully slams to a halt beside me, hair wild and face white. "I think somebody was just following me. Let's get inside."

"Where's Adrian?" I'm both glad she isn't with him and afraid of where he could be. When her bare shoulder brushes mine, I recoil.

"I have no idea. I haven't seen him. But I think something happened to Kevin."

"Don't—" I say as dread thunders in my ears. She hasn't seen Felty yet, glowering in the darkness. I can't get the rest of the words out. *Don't say anything else.*

"I keep calling him. He's not picking up, and he wouldn't have just left."

Felty steps forward. Sully must see his shoes, not the body attached to them. She looks up and I can tell she wants to fall apart, the same way my limbs push to deconstruct. *This is it,* I realize, a static shock. *This is our reckoning.*

Sully doesn't try to think up an excuse. Instead, she rises to her full height, puts her hand on Felty's arm. "We're being threatened. We got these notes—me and Amb. And things have been happening."

Felty clears his throat and pulls his arm away. He has us where he wants us, cornered and scared. "Where is Kevin McArthur?"

Sully narrows her eyes, obviously realizing that Felty is immune to her charm. "Did you not hear what I said? Amb and I are being threatened. Kevin's missing. We all got these notes."

Felty rolls an unlit cigarette between his fingers. "Unless he has been off the grid for twenty-four hours, he can't be considered a missing person. And a note doesn't exactly sound like a murder weapon. Although I suppose people do get creative with words." He glares pointedly at me.

"She's telling the truth," I say. "Somebody wants to hurt us." It's ridiculous that I'm saying *us.* I shouldn't care what happens to Sully. She's a murderer. But I can't shake the thought that I'm just as bad. That I suspected what she did the entire time and absorbed the knowledge into my skin. That I chose to live with it, because what Sully did meant somebody cared enough about me to eliminate the person I saw as my enemy.

"Are you ready to tell me what really happened that night?" Felty says. "If you're ready to tell me, I'll go check on Kevin myself. I'll even bring you with me. How does that sound?"

Sully sets her jaw. "We already told you everything we know."

We're *we* again, now that she needs my help.

Felty's expression is somewhere between amused and annoyed. "If you girls let me protect you, we can sit down and have a conversation and talk about what happened."

"No," I say. Sully may be more dangerous than Felty, but she's not as dangerous to me. If she wanted to hurt me, she would have done it by now. "Sully, let's go. Where's your key card?"

She hands me her purse, wordlessly, and I rummage through it, grabbing the card and swiping it against the door. Felty watches us walk in.

"Goodbye, girls," he says. It almost sounds like a threat.

38

NOW

To: "Ambrosia Wellington" *a.wellington@wesleyan.edu*
From: "Wesleyan Alumni Committee" *reunion.classof2007@gmail.com*
Subject: Class of 2007 Reunion

Dear Ambrosia Wellington,

If you're still around at midnight, there will be celebratory fireworks! Don't miss what is bound to be a dazzling finale to an unforgettable weekend.

It will be the spectacle we've been waiting for—the one we deserve.

Sincerely,
Your Alumni Committee

"It's Poppy," I blurt out when we're inside, doors separating us from Felty. I keep my voice down, certain he's lurking outside. "She wrote the notes. I'm sure of it."

Sully's eyes widen and she brings a shaking hand to her cheekbone. I haven't seen her scared many times, but I think this is as close to terrified as she'll get. "Poppy. She—how would she have found out?"

"I don't know. She lost the person who meant the most to her, so she must have found a way." I watch Sully's face for a reaction—for the confession she'll never say out loud.

Instead, she turns and blazes down the hall toward our room. "Maybe Poppy was the one who was following me outside. Either way, I'm not sticking around to find out what she wants." I jog after her, my shoes dangling from my fingers.

"I know what you did," I yell. "Poppy knows too. She wrote the notes to get us here, and now she's not going to let us leave."

Sully stops. Her shoulders are hiked up around her ears. "She must be on her way here. She knows where we are. I'm leaving. If you're smart, you'll do the same."

"You can't just leave. We have to talk to her."

Sully spins around, wiping greasy eyeliner from under her eyes. "Yeah. I'm sure she really wants to hear anything we have to say."

I put my arm out, even though I'm not sure if I want to reach for her or push her away. "We need to confront her, or else she'll just find us again. This won't stop."

Maybe I'm daring her to repeat her famous line. *There is no us.* She turns and keeps walking instead. "You do what you want, but I'm going home."

I stare at her back, at the beads of her spine, her shoulder blades sharp wings. At the door to our room, she gestures impatiently for her key card. But it doesn't matter, because the door is ajar.

I stop abruptly, my grip tightening on my shoes. "Someone's here."

"Fuck this." Sully pushes the door open.

I don't know what I expected. Poppy lying in wait, crouched in the dark. But it's Adrian, sitting on the desk chair, hunched over, duffel bag at his feet. His pants have ridden up enough to show those ridiculous socks, which I gave him last year for his birthday. Now I'm afraid we'll never celebrate another birthday together.

"Adrian." Even his name sounds guilty coming from me.

"Were you expecting someone else?" He's pissed off, but he doesn't want to make a scene in front of Sully, because that's not who he is. The only spotlight he ever wanted was the one I haven't been giving him. My full attention.

Sully kicks off her heels and steps into her ankle boots. "I need to go." She retreats to her room, where I watch her stuff clothes into her suitcase.

"You're actually leaving."

She looks up. "Come with me. I'm serious."

She grabs my wrists, just hard enough to hurt, but I pull away like I've been stung. She blinks, almost childlike, hinting at a vulnerability I still don't believe is in her arsenal.

Her sad smile makes me think part of her may feel after all, but not a big enough part. Our goodbye is wordless, anticlimactic. I guess we've already had too many highs and lows together. I don't watch her walk away. I've seen her back enough times.

"I'm sorry," I say to Adrian when she's gone. "I didn't know where you went, and I wanted to text you, but I can't find my phone."

"It's right here." Adrian has it in his hand, rose-gold cover against his palm. "I think it's time you explained exactly what the fuck is going on."

I lean against the door. Normally when Adrian and I argue, I bridge the gap between us. My arm around his shoulders, my hands in his hair. But I can tell he doesn't want to be touched right now. "This whole weekend has been a mess. I wasn't ready to come back here."

"I'd ask you why Sully's leaving in such a rush, but I know you'd lie. So who's the other guy?" Adrian says. "I know you've been with him this weekend."

"There is no other guy. I'm telling the truth. Nothing happened."

"Billie says otherwise." He tosses my phone onto the bed and crosses his ankles. "I'm guessing she's a few glasses of wine in. I got a lot out of her."

I walk over and grab the phone, even though I should be fighting for the lie, trying to say something that will make Adrian give up whatever mission he's on. But I need to know what he has already uncovered.

I read the message he sent Billie as me. *I feel bad about this. What about Adrian?*

Seeing his own name on my phone, and knowing he typed it,

is what makes me want to cry. Adrian, loyal and trustworthy, never duplicitous. I've turned him into someone else.

Billie's response is typical post-Riesling Billie, blubbery and incisive at once. I can picture her typing it, cheeks pink, slippered feet on Ryan's lap as he watches hockey or football. *Maybe he isn't your one true love. Figure things out with your college boy. You'll spend another 10 years regretting it otherwise right?*

Adrian didn't respond to that. Billie sent another one. *You told me you looked for him in every guy you ever dated . . .*

Did I say that? I romanticized him, the same way an average vacation blooms in hindsight into the best time of your life.

Billie again, ten minutes later: *I want details!*

I put my phone facedown on the pillow. Adrian stares at the ground. He doesn't want to see me. Doesn't want to, or can't anymore.

"I can explain," I say. "There was someone I thought I loved. But it was a long time ago. He was here this weekend, and yes, I saw him. But nothing happened, I swear."

It's the silence that's the most unnerving. Adrian always has something to say, a joke to clear the air, but he lets me keep talking, keep grasping to defend myself.

"He was—he wasn't the one for me. You have to understand, being here has been so hard—"

Adrian stands up so fast that the desk chair falls over behind him, legs sticking out, an angry beetle on its back. "You're such a goddamn liar. But you always have been, haven't you? I've learned more about you in a day than I have since we met. It took this weekend for me to know you've been lying the whole time."

I open my mouth, but he continues. "You know how I feel about cheating, right? And the vows we made at our wedding? About never betraying each other? That was all a big fucking lie."

"It's not true. I meant it then. Nothing happened. I just needed to see him for closure. And I got it." I scratch my cuticles and my thumb starts to bleed.

"You mean Kevin." Adrian spits out his name. "Flora's boyfriend, who you apparently met once. I know he was the guy in your photo at home. Let's just say I've found out a lot of things I never knew about my own wife this weekend." He paces back and forth, making the room even tinier.

"When I found his picture, you had the nerve to tell me he was dead. Something was off, but I didn't question it. Because I should be able to trust my goddamn wife. You know, Google showed me a lot tonight about Kevin McArthur."

"There are things you don't know about me." I sink onto the bed. "But it's in the past. You know who I am now. I'm the person you think I am. You have to believe that."

His hands go into his hair, making the curls a messy thicket. "I don't have to believe anything you say, Amb."

I flash back to our first Christmas morning in our apartment, when he got up early to put presents under the tiny fake tree we had set up beside our TV. We didn't get snow that year and he knew I was disappointed, so when I came out of our bedroom, bleary eyed, and shuffled my feet into something dry and white, I was confused. Adrian was in our kitchen, the one I despise because there's no space, smiling as he made French toast. We were genuinely happy.

Later, I bitched about the mess, hated how the flecks got stuck to the bottom of my bare feet, hated how we kept finding them in our couch for months. *Sometimes I feel like you don't appreciate me,* Adrian once said, except I don't remember when. Maybe he said it often.

"I'm leaving," he says. "I really can't do this anymore. You know, after we first met, I texted my friends and said I found the girl I was going to marry. They all said I was high on good sex. I have no idea who I fell in love with, but it's not you."

"It is me. We can leave together." Pressure builds behind my temples and my eyes burn. I can't remember the last time I felt this much. Sully desensitized me, her apathy a powerful drug.

"No. I'm going by myself. Now I see why you wanted to get out of here so many times this weekend. You wanted to get me away before I found out too much."

I can't even tell him he's wrong.

"You're never going to be happy," he says. "At least, not with me.

Sometimes I think you like being miserable. So go be with Kevin. Find what you're looking for."

I hold in a breath, knowing that what I say next could define the rest of our lives. I need to make him see that it's just us. That we can be different now.

"I'm pregnant," I say quietly. "I found out today. I was waiting for the right time to tell you." He wants kids so badly. This will change his mind. Maybe this is changing my mind. "We're going to have a baby." It's the first time I've said the words aloud. We don't have room in our apartment for a baby but we can move to the suburbs, out of New York altogether, even back to wholesome Pennington, which Toni says is the perfect place to raise a family. We'll buy a crib and Adrian will put it together and afterward he'll rest his hand on the dome of my belly, feeling the kicks. We won't talk about this weekend ever again.

He turns away from me and bends down, reaching into my cross-body bag, which is slumped against the desk like somebody punched it in the stomach. His hand emerges with my birth control pills, the ones I swap from purse to purse.

"Sure," he says. "You're pregnant. Just like you stopped taking these six months ago. And texted Billie, *No babies for me*. You're such a fucking liar. I can't even look at you." The pack of pills rattles onto the floor.

"No, you don't understand. I took a test earlier today. I had a feeling—"

"Sure you did," he says. "You think I'm so dumb, just because I didn't graduate from college. But you're the one who stole your roommate's boyfriend. The guy who told her to kill herself. And now you're faking a pregnancy because you think a baby will get me to stay. I don't want a baby with you, Amb. I don't want anything with you."

My jaw is slack. It's all careening away. Adrian, our love story, the life with him that I took for granted. I remember when he bought a pack of pregnancy tests, so confident we would be staring at two pink lines. He rubbed my back when they were negative and told me our time was coming. Now it's here, but he doesn't want it.

He slings his duffel bag over his shoulder. His mouth is a straight line, eyebrows pulled down. No dimples, no crinkles around his eyes. I didn't let him know the real me, the girl who never wanted the right amount.

"I love you," I say to his back. "I really do love you."

That makes him pause in the doorway, but it isn't enough to make him turn around. "You don't know what love is. I don't think you ever did."

He leaves the door ajar, even though he has every reason to slam it in anger. I should run after him and fight for him, for us. But he deserves honesty, and if I sat him down and told him everything, he would leave me.

Maybe it's better that he leaves thinking I'm a cheater and a liar, not a killer.

Maybe he's better off without me.

I'm on the floor now, my dress ridden up around my thighs. I lean back and stare at the ceiling. This must have been Flora's last view, boring beige, before her eyes stopped seeing anything. Or maybe Sully hovered over her, watching the life seep out, and the last thing she saw was that knowing smirk. I hope not.

There's a gentle knock at the door. I wipe my face. *Adrian.* He's back and he wants to make us work. We'll go to couples' counseling. Billie and Ryan did it a few years ago, when, she told me, they "legitimately hated each other." We can get through this.

"I fucked up," I say. "Let's talk about it."

The door slowly opens and I see the shoes first. They're not even shoes—they're slippers, bunny ones. Their eyes face the walls, goggling at the room. Flora's slippers, her perennially shuffling feet. Pink bunnies, bobbing on her bed as she watched movies on her laptop, as she talked on the phone with Kevin, as she wrote long emails to her sister.

Her sister, who always wrote back. Who, jaw trembling, told the media that the person who hurt Flora would pay for it, eventually. The world assumed she meant Kevin.

"At least you're finally willing to admit it," she says sweetly, face so much like Flora's, except so much more severe.

It's eventually.

39

NOW

Dear Ambrosia Wellington,

Have you enjoyed all of our planned activities, and maybe taken a few spontaneous detours? Hopefully being back here has taught you something about yourself. Maybe you've atoned for a wrong you haven't stopped thinking about.

Or maybe you're about to.

Sincerely,
Your Alumni Committee

"Ambrosia Francesca Wellington. There you are." She shuts the door quietly behind her. Then she locks it, a click that turns my skin into a tight rubber band.

"Poppy." I push limp hair behind my ears, trying to force down a fresh wave of terror. "I wanted to talk to you at the dedication, but things got really weird today. I had this big fight with my husband." I don't know why I tell her. She didn't come to hear anything I have to say.

"That's too bad." Her red lips twist, a licorice smile. "He's cute, your husband. Such a nice guy, too. I talked to him this afternoon, did he tell you that? I told him I've heard so much about you. But you never even mentioned my sister to him. I guess it would have put a damper on the honeymoon period to mention the girl you killed." She sits cross-legged on the bed.

"I didn't kill her." My nails dig into my palms.

She cocks her head at an almost unnatural angle. "That's what we're here to find out, isn't it? The mystery of who killed Flora Banning. Because my sister didn't kill herself."

I bring my legs underneath me. I try to calculate how fast I could be out the door.

"I wouldn't, if I were you," she says. "You wouldn't get far. Besides, I think your cute husband took your car. Adrian will be so beat up over this. It'll be hard for him to trust anyone ever again, right?"

Over this. *Over what?*

"You're still thinking about it." She gets up, shrugging out of her jacket and setting her purse beside it on the bed. She's wearing one of Flora's dresses, or something exactly like Flora used to wear. Flowery and cute, with a Peter Pan collar. I hid when the family came to collect her things.

"I can explain—"

"Don't." She cuts me off. "Flora told me she did something unforgivable. The boy she had sex with on Halloween. She was disgusted with herself. She said she never would have done that if she hadn't been drunk. I asked her if she ever said yes. She didn't answer, but that meant no."

"I didn't see what happened." She can't possibly know that I did.

Poppy clears her throat. "Maybe. But she said you were there. You knew she was drunk, and you let her go off with some guy she didn't know. You knew she had a boyfriend. She was terrified to tell Kevin what happened. Flora always thought everything was her fault. I guess you wouldn't know anything about that. Nothing is ever your fault."

"I was drunk too. I don't remember what happened."

"How convenient." Poppy rolls her eyes. "I told her to report it, of course. Then she snapped and said it was none of my business. She told me he didn't use a condom. The guy who raped her."

I never allowed myself to think that word. *Rape.* To feel what it really meant, because then I would have had to admit that I could have prevented it.

I open my mouth, but Poppy interjects. "I told her to get tested. She made me promise to never tell. We have a fucked-up family dynamic as is. We had to be perfect, to keep things from collapsing. So I kept my mouth shut. I shouldn't have." She touches her lips. "I hate myself every day for that."

"She never told me any of this. I would have helped her." I never even learned how to help myself.

Poppy laughs. "I told her to talk to you. I figured if you were a decent human being, and an actual friend, you'd go with her to a clinic or something. But you blew her off, didn't you?"

"I wasn't perfect." My fingers edge toward my purse. "I had my own stuff going on. I should have been a better friend. I feel bad about that."

She shakes her head. Wispy hair flies everywhere. "You don't feel bad about a single goddamn thing. Except that Kevin didn't end up with you. You honestly think I don't know about that?"

"I wasn't—"

"I never trusted Kevin. He was the only thing Flora and I argued about. She thought he was this great guy. He had a way of making girls feel special. I bet he made you feel special, too. You probably had this love story in your head, right?"

My phone is on the bed, but I can't reach for it. Poppy will notice. She hasn't gone this far, done all this, without noticing everything.

"I wasn't in love with Kevin. I wasn't in love with anyone. My high school boyfriend cheated on me, and I went a bit crazy when I got here. Hooked up with a lot of guys. I was lost."

If she heard me, she isn't letting on. "Here's the thing. Before I even started at Wesleyan, I knew about the ACB. There's a lot of information on there. Lots of people say they saw AW go into a bathroom with KM. Some of them said AW was running from the Butts. I'm here to figure out which girl you were."

"It wasn't me. I was with another guy that night."

She stands up. "Wrong answer. Because if you weren't with him— if I put the night together correctly—that means you were the girl running away. The one who killed my sister."

"Flora killed herself. The police would have found out if she hadn't. She was drunk and upset. It's horrible. But it wasn't me."

I could end this now and tell her it was Sully. Maybe she would believe me. But she'd ask me how I know, and then I'd have to admit my own role.

"At first I was sure you and Sloane did it together," Poppy says. "And that's why you stopped talking. Because you couldn't handle the guilt. But I changed my mind. One of you was outsmarted and left out of the loop by the other. So here's my theory. You got Kevin's phone and sent the texts. Sloane did the dirty work."

"Kevin sent the texts," I say.

"Come on," Poppy says. "Let's face it. They weren't Kevin's style. They were too perfect. And they were too mean. Yes, he was a cheating asshole who broke my sister's heart. But he wasn't capable of *that*."

I fixate on *was*. Kevin *was*.

"My sister was wrong about you," Poppy continues. "You aren't that good of an actress. Ironic, because your whole life is a lie. Your husband wants kids, and you're trying to lead him on to make him think you do too. Flora wanted kids." Poppy chews one of her thumbnails. Her nails are baby blue with sunflowers on them.

"I do want them." The baby will soften her. She won't hurt me if she knows. "Actually, I'm pregnant. I found out today."

Poppy crouches down on the floor. Her expression slackens and she reaches out, like she wants to touch me. Then she pulls back, balling up her hands and letting out a long exhale. When she speaks, her voice is soft. "Flora was too."

Something bubbles in my throat. Nausea. Or a scream. I bite my knuckles to get rid of it. What she's saying—it isn't true. Flora wasn't. There's no way.

"I'm the only person she told. She made me swear to never tell our parents. Our mom had Flora when she was nineteen. She gave us so many lectures about not becoming teen moms. Maybe that's why Flora was so big on keeping her virginity. I kept my promise and didn't say a word, but our parents found out anyway during the autopsy." She glares at my shell-shocked face. "They kept it quiet. We'd already been through enough."

"I had no idea," I practically whisper.

Poppy closes her eyes, like the memory is too painful to confront. "Maybe she wouldn't have known either. But when I told her to get tested? She went and bought a pregnancy test instead. She called me after she took it. She couldn't stop crying."

The times I came back to our room to see Flora asleep in the middle of the day, facing the wall, sleep mask pulled over her eyes. Her tears in the bathroom, witnessed by Ella. The pregnancy test, hot in her sweaty hands. *I was actually hoping I could talk to you about something.*

"I said she had to get an abortion. She was raped—she didn't do anything wrong. I told her to tell you about it. Her new best friend would be able to talk some sense into her. She said she would talk to you—she was glad to have you."

"I would've helped—"

"I'm sure people thought she was just another cautionary tale. Don't trust the wrong guy." She studies her nails. Flora taught her how to paint them with that precision. "Kevin was the wrong guy. And now he's paid for his role in this. But it was trusting the wrong girls that killed my sister."

I debate what would happen if I screamed. If anyone would hear me, or if anyone would care.

"What did you do to Kevin?"

"Don't worry about it," Poppy says. I hear the shake in her voice. "You won't be around to figure it out anyway."

There's a click in the door, and we both turn to look as Sully spills into the room. I should have screamed. It might have made a difference.

Sully covers her mouth when she sees Poppy. "You," she says, somewhere between scared and defiant. "You did it, didn't you?"

Poppy stands up and tucks her hands into balls, but not before I notice they're trembling. "Welcome to the real party, Sloane. I guess I shouldn't have expected you to be on time."

She's here. She came back. She came back for me.

"You killed him," Sully says, slow and measured.

"Can you prove it? He had so much to drink. And all those pills on his nightstand. I'm sure the two of you made him suffer a lot more."

"Kevin's dead?" I choke out. Sully nods. She isn't upset as much as calculated. She's planning a way out of this, so that we don't meet his same fate.

Now I understand that Sully was never going home. She headed for the hotel, and when she saw whatever Poppy did to Kevin, she could have kept driving. But she wasn't leaving me behind. The loyalty that rises up is sudden and potent. I want to protect her too, no matter what she did to Flora.

When I look at Poppy again her hands aren't balled up, and they're not trembling. She's sliding a knife out of her purse, long and white handled, just like the Wüsthof kitchen knives Adrian and I registered for at Williams Sonoma and never properly used. I start to shiver uncontrollably as I realize exactly how she wants tonight to end.

Sully sways in the middle of the room. "You won't get away with it."

The knife blade darts up and down when Poppy moves her hand. "I have you to thank for letting me know where he was staying. Your drive last night—what was it, a booty call?"

Sully inches toward her. "What the hell do you want?"

"What do you think? I want the truth." She points the knife at me. "You're the one who has a way with words." Now the knife is aimed at Sully. "You have a way with violence. But whoever killed my sister made a huge oversight. Flora would have left a note. That's how I knew she didn't do it."

Turns out Poppy and Kevin agree on one thing. *Agreed* on one thing.

My teeth chatter. That knife—I recognize the handle, can visualize where it's missing from its wooden block in my kitchen. Poppy has been in our building, inside our apartment. She studied me, the same way I used to study the cool girls like a science. Sully once called me paranoid, but I was right all along. I knew someone was watching. The validation would be a relief if the terror behind it weren't numbing my entire body.

All the times I convinced myself I was seeing a ghost. All the times I saw a blond girl turning away. The sensation of being followed. It's because I was.

"What are you going to do to us?"

"I'm not going to do anything." She drums one of her bunny feet. "I'm done. Now the two of you can turn on each other. The one thing you both think you never did all those years ago."

Sully and I remain still. Now is the moment when we're expected to become two caged animals and rip each other apart. But I'm not ready to deal the first blow.

"You're insane," Sully says. "Neither of us had anything to do with it. Just go. If you leave, we'll pretend none of this ever happened. We won't tell."

"Of course you won't." Poppy traces the tip of the knife over her own collarbones. "You're good at keeping secrets, aren't you? Well, not good enough."

My phone dings from its location on the bed. Poppy reaches for it, her eyes scanning the screen. "Oh, Billie wants to know what's going on with the guy you cheated on your husband with. You don't mind, do you?" She puts down the knife as she clacks out a message. "Someone else took him from me, Billie. You don't know the whole story. I'm about to do something very bad." She winks at me. "Whoops! I hit send. I was going to ask you to check it for spelling and grammar first. You're always so diligent with that."

My phone is in her hands. The knife isn't. I try to make eye contact with Sully, to tell her to grab the knife. But Sully isn't looking at me.

"I took Kevin's phone." Sully's voice rumbles in her throat like thunder. "I took it. Flora was so upset that night. I told her to check his phone for evidence he'd been fucking around. She wouldn't do it, so I did. She didn't believe me when I showed her the other girls' names."

"Sully—" I plead, but she ignores me.

"Please, elaborate." Poppy clutches my phone. Wherever Billie is, I beg her to call the police, to send them here. She'll be at home, maybe opening a second bottle of wine, Netflix and baby monitor on, scrolling through Instagram. She has to see my message. *She has to.*

"Then Amb grabbed the phone and ran off with it."

"No," I say. *No.* This isn't happening.

"I was pretty wasted, but I saw her run upstairs, so I followed her. I didn't see her anywhere. And eventually, I stopped looking. I guess I figured, what was she really going to do with Kevin's phone? Probably snoop through it, maybe enter her phone number in there."

"That's not what happened. She's the one who took the phone. And she told me what to say."

"So you were her puppet." Poppy looks from me to Sully, from Sully to me. "Well, I can't say either of you inspire much confidence at this point. But go on."

Sully does. "When I saw her again, she put the phone in my hand. I asked her what she did with it, and she said it was nothing. So I put it back in Kevin's jacket pocket. I figured since I was the one who took it, I'd put it back. Then she started being all over Kevin. I said to her, 'That's your roommate's boyfriend.' Then I asked her where Flora was. She said she didn't care."

Poppy's gaze falls on me, heavy and stifling. I can't breathe. I'm supposed to defend myself, to think of a better lie than Sully's. But she can still one-up me at anything.

"They went somewhere together. Then I saw some friends, and did some shots, and lost track of time. I messed around with this guy. When Amb came back, she told me she fucked Kevin. I didn't say anything. I was so drunk. I just wanted to go back to the dorm. And when we got there, that was when we saw all the sirens."

"Interesting," Poppy says. My phone bleats, but she doesn't look at it, just rubs it against the fabric of her dress. "Amb, is that an accurate retelling of history? You sent the messages, then fucked my sister's boyfriend at the party?"

My life might depend on my ability to lie but I can't think of a lie that fits, one slippery enough to fill the cracks in Sully's story.

"Yes," I say, hoarse. "But it was her idea to send the messages. I followed along. And yes, I was the girl in the bathroom with Kevin. But I didn't kill her."

Poppy drops my phone and claps so loudly that I almost jump. "Finally, some goddamned honesty! You must feel better now. Unburdened. Good for you."

My view of the knife is half-obscured by her full skirt. She fixates on Sully. "That means you were somewhere else."

"Yeah," Sully says. "I was with that other guy. I don't even remember his name."

"What I find interesting," Poppy says, "is that there weren't any fingerprints on Kevin's phone besides his own, even though you both just admitted to handling it. So whoever put the phone back"—she looks pointedly at Sully—"had the foresight to wipe it clean. You wouldn't think most people would do that, right? Unless they knew something a lot worse than some text messages was about to happen."

I wait for Sully to do what she does best. To talk her way out of this.

"Amb sent the messages," she says, almost a whisper. "Amb told your sister to kill herself."

"I know." Poppy picks up the knife. "She did. But you're the one who actually killed her."

She's across the room so quickly that I can't react. Sully doesn't make a sound when the knife goes in, but I do, even before it has entered her skin. Sully's face goes slack, her eyes dazed. Then there's the blood. It slithers down the beads on her dress, an elaborate labyrinthine maze. She stares at the red mark. Wesleyan red.

"If you ask me, you're both terrible actresses," Poppy says quietly. "You wouldn't have made it anyway."

The knife quakes in her hand. Now she's coming to give me the same wound. But Poppy wipes the handle on her dress and hands me the knife instead. I take it.

Then she screams.

It's the loudest sound I've ever heard, the kind of sound I'll be hearing for the rest of my life. I stare at the knife as Sully falls to her knees. I crawl over to her, letting go of the knife to put my hands over the bloody patch on her dress.

"We can stop the bleeding," I mumble, or at least that's what I try to say, but it comes out as incoherent babble.

Sully's skin looks almost gray. When she opens her mouth, there's no sound. Then she leans toward me.

"She deserved it." Sully laughs, a sick gurgle. "We're the same, you know."

Me and her, or her and Flora? "We're not," I whisper. I finally stand up to her and she can't hear it. One of my tears falls onto her cheek.

I pick up the knife and stagger toward Poppy on quivering legs, but I know I won't be able to use it. What I said was true: Sully and I never were the same.

Poppy isn't alone anymore. She's still screaming, her face bright red, and two guys in formalwear have rushed in and are gaping at our carnage, pulling out their phones to call the police. Poppy clings to one of them, using his body as a shield.

From me. From the girl with the bloody knife. I try to drop it but it remains stuck in my hand.

"It's her," Poppy wails. "She did it."

I wait for Sully to yell out the truth. *Poppy's a crazy bitch. She stabbed me.* But Sully isn't saying anything ever again.

40

ONE YEAR LATER

He looks strange in the kitchen of my new Chelsea apartment. He's timid, standing with a glass of red wine, wearing a soft gray T-shirt. At least, it looks soft. I haven't found out yet. I'm draining pasta in the sink. One of the linguini noodles curls into a snake by the drain. I flush it down, put it out of its misery.

"Thanks for agreeing to meet," he says. "It's just—it's messed up. I've been channeling all my energy into writing. I almost have a first draft of my novel done now, but it's nowhere close to how I imagined it would turn out."

"It never is." My hair is down, around my shoulders, like my sister wore hers. "Nothing creative ever turns out quite how you expected."

He moves toward one of the barstools at the kitchen island, eases himself onto it, splays his hands on the granite. His left ring finger is bare now.

"I don't want to unload on you," he says. "That's not why I wanted to meet. And that's what I pay a therapist for." He laughs, so I do too, obligingly. "I thought I wouldn't miss her at all. But I do. I miss who she was before I found out who she really was, if that makes any sense."

I leave the strainer in the sink. The noodles are soggy—I let them boil too long. It doesn't matter. I walk around the kitchen island and put my hand on his back. He doesn't stiffen under my touch, but he doesn't relax, either.

"I completely understand. You went through a huge trauma."

"So did you." He pinches the skin between his eyes. "She could have—I mean, she would have, maybe."

"Maybe." The slightest hint of steel enters my voice. I'll have to get rid of that. "But she can't hurt me now."

We won't have to find out what she would have done, because Ambrosia Wellington—she went back to her maiden name—is serving life in prison for one count of first-degree murder and one count of attempted murder. I'm not sure what people at Wesleyan are calling this bloodbath, since there's already one Dorm Doom. I had no idea Sloane Sullivan's wretched heart could pump that much blood.

"I'm surprised you even agreed to see me," Adrian says. "I almost talked myself out of asking. It's just, our emails have kind of been my lifeline. You've been so easy to talk to."

I keep my hand on his back, on the hot skin underneath his T-shirt. "I ran from my demons for a long time. I know what it's like."

One of his hands finds mine and squeezes. I squeeze it back. God, he's a good guy. He leans in—he's going to kiss me. Except then his phone interrupts us. "Sorry. Just one sec. It's my mom. Probably about Jane."

Jane. She's the one complication in this whole situation. As it turns out, Ambrosia wasn't lying when she told me she was pregnant, and as much as I'm sure Adrian didn't expect to be the father, he is. Now he's a single dad, raising the baby on his own.

After everything, Adrian told me that Amb wanted to name the baby Jane. The plainest, simplest name. Maybe it was the one nice thing she ever did, not bestowing on her daughter a multisyllable monstrosity like the one she was given.

My sister would have been a good mother. When we were girls, she fed Goldfish crackers to her baby dolls, turned them over and burped them, rocked them lovingly. I wasn't sure I wanted to be a mother, but I can learn. I'll protect this little girl, innocent Jane. Flora would have wanted it this way.

I heard that barely anyone went to Sloane Sullivan's funeral. Just a few former classmates, a couple of family members, stragglers from a community theater troupe she was too embarrassed to tell people she'd joined. She'd made a lot of enemies over the years. Devotion and fear aren't the same thing.

I listen to Adrian on the phone. He's singing a lullaby to Jane. She must be three months old by now. Amb was visibly pregnant at her sentencing, touching her stomach, pretending to care. She told the jury that I was the liar, that I was the one who killed Sloane Sullivan. It was easy for me to explain why I was there. My sister's former roommate invited me over to talk. Why would I suspect anything but a little reminiscing?

Only three of us were in that dorm room, but there were other witnesses that weekend. People who saw her acting strange and erratic. The former Butterfield girls, who thought being back had done something to her brain. The clerk at the Super 8, who saw her leave in a hurry. Poor Kevin. His death was ruled a suicide, because they couldn't prove otherwise. And if that isn't justice, I don't know what is.

Most people thought Amb went crazy with jealousy when she found out her former best friend had slept with the boy she was still obsessed with. So she did something about it.

Felty gave the best testimony. He said he'd never fully closed the door on Flora Banning's death. He said he'd always believed Ambrosia Wellington had something to do with it.

Nobody believed Amb, not even the man she married. The knife was hers—it came from a wooden block in her cute little kitchen. Maybe she had already known about Sully and Kevin and had gone to the reunion with a plan.

Amb brought up my notes, but the thing is, nobody found a note like the ones she described in any of her belongings, or Sloane's belongings, or Kevin's. The judge said it best. *You're trying to concoct a fantasy to lessen your guilt.*

And the emails—they weren't traceable. It's not that hard, if you buy a separate laptop and send your messages from public Wi-Fi connections. They could have come from anyone.

Adrian sits down on my couch, still singing to Jane over the phone. Amb didn't know she had one of the decent guys. Flora always counted her blessings, certain that everyone in her life was there for a reason. Kevin. Amb. *The girls are all so nice here,* she gushed over the phone. *Especially my roommate.*

I'm not sure Flora would like what I did. Still, a sliver of her, the same sliver that exists in every wronged one of us, would be lit up, finally justified. Mostly, I like to think I made her proud. I started the memorial foundation in her name and I donate 10 percent of every sale from Poppy's Pretty Pen to charities that help teen girls in need. I fight for good in the world, even if some of my methods are unorthodox.

My parents were surprised when I still wanted to go to Wesleyan. Of course, Ambrosia and Sloane had already graduated by the time I started. I grew close with my roommate, Molly, a friendship I thought was real until I learned she was using me to help do her coursework while spreading rumors behind my back. It was my time at Wesleyan that made me really dig into what happened to my sister. Because the girls weren't nice at all.

There was the ACB, a treasure trove of theories for anyone to read. I learned so much about AW and SS. They left such a messy trail.

So I became part of the Alumni Committee after I graduated. I started Poppy's Pretty Pen—I have the cutest Etsy shop. All I had to do was wait and draw them back. It didn't take much. They're both narcissists. Maybe above everything else, they needed to size each other up.

"Sorry about that." Adrian pockets his phone and stands up. "She's pretty attached to Daddy. This is one of my first times out of the house without her."

I push his glass of wine across the counter. "Don't be sorry. She's precious. And she's lucky to have you." And me. If Adrian and I get closer, she'll have me to help her grow the armor she'll need. I'll make damn sure she wears it.

He takes a drink. "I think she's down for a bit now. She's still getting used to her crib at my parents' place. I'm just grateful they moved out here to be closer to me."

I read between the lines. He left her at his parents' house, probably told them he didn't know when he'd be by to pick her up, and he doesn't want to disrupt the angel's sleep, so maybe he should just come in the morning? I smile. I'm not wearing a bra.

He wasn't part of my plan. My plan was to have them turn on each other, the two girls responsible for ending my sister's life. Sloane did it physically, so I gave her the easy way out—death. Amb picked my sister apart in far more brutal ways. For that, she gets a harsher sentence.

She gets to live, but from behind bars. She gets to see her family and friends slowly forget her. She gets to watch Adrian move on. She gets to watch me, a permanent reminder of my sister and the life she took away.

The wine is making Adrian's lips red, but I won't kiss him yet. I'll feed him first. The pasta sauce simmering on the stove came from a jar, but he doesn't need to know that. There's a lot he doesn't need to know.

"I'm glad you're here," I tell him. I'll help him finish his novel. I'll help him get it published. I'll make his ex-wife see how good she had it. How stupid she was for thinking the world owed her something more.

"Me too." He eases onto a barstool. "I mean, all of this is weird for me. But maybe not in a bad way."

Flora and I were different. She thought good things happened to good people. I know that girls are exempt from that logic. Good alone gets us nowhere.

I lean across the counter. Adrian's eyes flit to the dip in my shirt.

No, good things don't come to those who wait, and they don't come to the Ambrosias and Sloanes of the world, who take without fear of consequences in an endless quest to shock each other. I could have let what they did to Flora ruin my life. But instead, I discovered my own version of sisterhood. It doesn't have to be merciless, feeding on the chunks it tears from its own flesh. It can be softer, more forgiving. Because there are girls like me, fighting to make the society we're fenced into a more hospitable place for all of us.

Somewhere, Jane slumbers, milk-fed and peaceful.

"We should toast to something," Adrian says, holding up his wine. "To new beginnings. That feels right."

I raise my glass and clink it gently against his. He thinks something has ended, something we can close the door on. He's not wrong. But he's wrong about me. I don't see beginnings, only opportunities. Flora isn't here, so I have to do enough good for both of us. The world needs so much work.

In a way, I'm just getting started.

ACKNOWLEDGMENTS

The girls in this story might not be very nice, but the women who worked tirelessly on it with me are not only extremely kind but also brilliant and inspiring. Firstly, thanks to my agent, Hillary Jacobson, whose passion for this book has taken it farther than I ever thought possible. There's nobody I trust more with my stories, and nobody who works harder on my behalf. Thank you for being the best and fiercest advocate I could imagine and the absolute most fun to work with. I know we will continue to do great things together.

To my powerhouse trifecta of editors—Carina Guiterman at Simon and Schuster, Nita Pronovost at Simon and Schuster Canada, and Emily Kitchin at HQ—you're truly a star-studded dream team, and I'm grateful to be aligned with people who so deeply understand my writing and what I want to convey. Working alongside you has been a joy, and I could not be prouder of what we've achieved. I love seeing your names in my inbox and feel lucky every day to call you my editors. I'm a stronger, more capable writer because of you.

Thank you to my incredible film agents, Josie Freedman and Randie Adler, and to my brilliant UK agent, Sophie Lambert. To my stellar foreign rights team of Sophie Baker and Jodi Fabbri at Curtis Brown UK, for helping my not nice girls find homes around the world.

I've felt so welcomed by the team at Simon and Schuster, and am honored to have their support of my work. Thank you to everyone who has worked on this book's development, including Maggie Southard,

Elizabeth Breeden, Lashanda Anakwah, Marysue Rucci, Richard Rhorer, Jonathan Karp, Jonathan Evans, Aja Pollock, Erika R. Genova, Kimberly Goldstein, and Rafael Taveras. Thank you to Zoe Norvell and Jackie Seow for going above and beyond to design the cover and book jacket of my dark and twisty heart.

It has been amazing to work with the talented, hardworking team at Simon and Schuster Canada, including Rita Silva, Alexandra Boelsterli, Adria Iwasutiak, Felicia Quon, Karen Silva, and Kevin Hanson. Thank you for everything you've done to get this book in the hands of so many Canadian readers.

To the creative, dynamic people at HQ in the UK, including Katie Seaman, Claire Brett, Lucy Richardson, and Melanie Hayes—thank you for your hard work and insanely cool ideas, and the magic you're doing overseas. Special thanks to Kate Oakley for designing a striking cover that so perfectly encapsulates the spirit of the book.

So many people were instrumental to the creation of this story, and supported me from the first (very, very long) draft. I'm grateful that *Girls* had such passionate early readers. Emily Martin—thank you for your constant support and friendship since before either of us were agented or published. Erika David, for being one of the most genuinely nice girls I know (and for introducing my kids to so many good books). Nicole Lesperance, for providing a wealth of information about Wesleyan and letting me ask countless random questions. Samantha Joyce, for never failing to celebrate (even though weird things happen when we do...) or commiserate (always with the best GIFs).

To Darcy Woods, my kindred spirit in bubbles, for the most revitalizing long phone calls, sage advice, and fierce loyalty. To Marci Lyn Curtis, for DMs that are both heartfelt and hilarious (and occasionally dirty).

A huge thank you to Caroline Eisenmann for sharing so many incredibly helpful details about Wesleyan. Your generosity is so appreciated!

To the authors who took the time to read early and provide blurbs, including Andrea Bartz, Chandler Baker, Karen Hamilton, Megan Miranda, Robyn Harding, Samantha M. Bailey, and Samantha Downing.

I admire your work so greatly, and having you read mine is truly an honor.

To my writer friends, of whom there are many, you are my people. Thank you for your role in my journey, and for letting me be part of yours.

To my parents, Denis and Lucy Burns, for too many things to ever list, but above all: a lifetime of believing this was what I was meant to do, and not letting me doubt it. You were right, of course.

To my sister and best wine drinking friend Erin Shakes, brother-in-law Jermaine Shakes, and Fiona, Malachi, and Naomi—thank you for being the cutest cheering squad.

To my in-laws Jim and Doreen Flynn for being so supportive of my work. To all of the Flynn clan—especially my sisters-in-law Suzanne Flynn and Kelly Bryan for being super cool book aunties.

To my extended family, near and far, especially Aunt Linda, Uncle Tom, and Aunt Pat. And to my grandmas, Honeybee and Betty, who aren't here to see this but whose presence I feel regardless.

I've been extremely lucky to have befriended so many smart, funny, generous women. To all of my girlfriends, those near and far, ones I'm close with now and ones I don't see as often—thank you for being part of my life. You know who you are. Thank you to Lauren Badalato, whose friendship and inside jokes go back decades. Special thanks to Tory Overend for many nights out that I won't speak of here, and for being the other half of the real-life "we're together, and we're worse."

To my husband Steve and the wonderful little people we've made together, Astrid, Cullen, and Delilah: you are my home. Thank you for putting up with me even before I've had my coffee, for allowing me the time and space I need to create these stories, and for thinking Mom has a cool job. My babies, I'll always be your greatest fans in whatever you do.

Thank you to all of the booksellers, teachers, librarians, bloggers, and Bookstagrammers for reading, reviewing, and recommending my books, and taking such beautiful pictures of them. Your passion and enthusiasm makes this community such a lovely place to be.

Reader, I've saved you for last. Thank you for picking up this book. This story has always felt much bigger than me, and it is my hope that you might feel seen while reading it. For the girls who are nice and the ones who aren't, I wrote this for you. Sometimes our true nature lies somewhere in the middle.

ABOUT THE AUTHOR

Laurie Elizabeth Flynn is the author of three young adult novels: *Firsts*, *Last Girl Lied To*, and *All Eyes On Her*, written under the name L.E. Flynn. She lives in London, Ontario, with her husband and children.